Praise for *Last Bus to Coffeeville*

'exceptionally good... the characters and plot are fantastic
and I really couldn't praise it enough'
– *Bookseller*

'I found myself laughing out loud with the characters.
I really enjoyed this story'
– Jane Brown, *Book Depository*

'A wonderful cast of eccentric people in the best tradition
of old-time American writers like Capote and Keillor.
I was enthralled throughout and recommend it to
anyone who wants a feel-good read'
– *New Books Magazine*

'There is heartbreak... black humour... and the charm
of *The Unlikely Pilgrimage of Harold Fry*'
– *Daily Mail*

'A fascinating and poignant novel'
– *Woman's World*

'... the shimmering humour and life values Henderson explores
are certainly something you wouldn't want to miss'
– *The Star Online*

'A funny road trip story... but this brave debut novel also tackles
sensitive issues and does so in a confident manner'
– *We Love This Book*

'Deftly handled with an offbeat humour and a
of worldly compassion'
– *Sunday Sport*

'J. Paul Henderson is someone to watch out f
– *The Bookbag*

Praise for *The Last of the Bowmans*

'An amiably weird take on family life'
– *Daily Mail*

'There were some bittersweet moments, some strange moments
and some outright funny moments… a lovely, surprising read'
– *Novel Kicks*

'laugh-out-loud funny'
– *Reviewed The Book*

'The black comedy mixed with a bittersweet and
compassionate drama frequently reminded me of the late,
great David Nobbs in style'
– *Shiny New Books*

'There's a rich vein of surreal black comedy throughout
The Last of the Bowmans'
– *The Book Bag*

'A quirky story using black humour to help us feel
connected to and to understand events that we could all
at some time have to face'
– Helen Appleby, *Library Thing*

'This was a gorgeous little story… you will not want
to stop reading'
– Sarah, *Goodreads*

'This is an enthralling tale full of eccentric characters
whose stories are cleverly woven together'
– Anna Elliot, *Waterstones*

Titles by J. Paul Henderson

LARRY AND THE DOG PEOPLE

J. Paul Henderson

NO EXIT PRESS

First published in 2017 by No Exit Press,
an imprint of Oldcastle Books Ltd,
PO Box 394, Harpenden,
AL5 1XJ, UK

noexit.co.uk
@noexitpress
© J. Paul Henderson 2017

ISBN
978-1-84344-854-9 (Print)
978-1-84344-855-6 (Epub)
978-1-84344-868-6 (Kindle)
978-1-84344-869-3 (Pdf)

2 4 6 8 10 9 7 5 3 1

Typeset by Avocet Typeset, Somerton, Somerset, TA11 6RT
in 11.5pt Minion Pro

Printed in Denmark by Nørhaven

For the Bassets: Hope, Mic, Bert, Rachel and Martine
(1983 to the present)

ACKNOWLEDGEMENTS

A big thanks to John and Pat Henry for guiding me through the environs of Georgetown and chauffeuring me, without complaint, to locations in West Virginia they'd have probably preferred not to visit. I also owe a debt of gratitude to Trevor Armstrong, Richard Farrar, Val Henderson, Steven Mair, Hazel Orme and Mike Solberg, and an especial one to the heroes of No Exit Press who make everything happen: Claire, Clare, Frances and Ion.

Contents

Oct 5, 2015. Explosions Rock Georgetown Church

Three people were killed and seventeen injured when a dog and pipe organ exploded in the Church of Latter-Day Lutherans yesterday, the Feast Day of St Francis of Assisi. Congregants were gathered for the annual Blessing of the Animals and a large number of pets also died in the blast.

Oct 8, 2015. Body Found in East Village

Police investigating the St Francis Day Massacre raided a house in the East Village of Georgetown yesterday and recovered the body of a man in his late sixties. Another man, thought to be in his early thirties and severely injured, was taken to Georgetown University Hospital where he remains in a critical condition. The FBI is anxious to talk to Laurence MacCabe, the owner of the property.

Oct 21, 2015. Georgetown Man Arrested

Laurence MacCabe, an emeritus professor of Georgetown University, was arrested yesterday and taken to Metropolitan Police Headquarters. He is being held in connection with the bombing of the Church of Latter-Day Lutherans and the deaths of two men found in the East Village. He is also being questioned in relation to the July shooting of Lydia Flores.

1

The Lonely Professor

Larry MacCabe was a man who needed people more than most. The problem for Larry was that most people had little need for him. It was an equation without solution.

Larry wasn't a bad man. On the contrary, he was an innately nice person. He liked people, enjoyed their company and could find something of interest in anyone he met. People such as Larry, however, who tend toward friendship with the multitude rather than the few, often fall into the category of being a friend of everyone and a friend of no one. Niceness, too, is often accompanied by dullness, and this was certainly true of Larry who had amassed the quality in spades. He created no controversy, avoided argument at all costs and never spoke badly of anyone, living or dead. On first meeting, or in short bursts, Larry's company was easy enough to bear but never willingly sought, and that he and his wife had been invited to functions rather than more intimate gatherings when she'd been alive, told a story.

In many ways Larry's presence in a room was no more disturbing than the magnolia paint that coated its walls, and in all likelihood he would have remained a part of life's invisible filler but for one thing: he got on people's nerves. It wasn't his physical appearance that agitated them – his jug ears and large forehead, for instance, or the unfortunate tic that caused him to blink every thirty seconds – but the fact that he talked too much, and invariably about subjects that were of little interest to anyone but himself.

Larry assimilated information as easily as blotting paper absorbs ink, and nothing, absolutely nothing, escaped his interest. His mother had been overwhelmed by the facts and figures he'd trotted out as a child and wondered, largely on account of his large forehead, if her son was a genius. Larry's father, who for a time had worried that Larry's forehead was a manifestation of hydrocephalus, was happy to agree with this prognosis but suggested that it might be better for them – and certainly for him – if Larry took his burgeoning knowledge outside the house and shared it instead with the neighbourhood kids. 'I don't know about you,' he'd said, 'but that boy's chatter is about to drive me up the wall. I don't need to know how a kettle works, and I sure as hell don't want to hear another word on tic-borne diseases! I mean, I love the kid and all, but, well… you know what I mean.' His wife did, but maternal instincts dictated that she sprang to Larry's defence. 'I think he's interesting,' she'd said. 'God in Heaven, woman!' her husband had exclaimed. 'Jesus Christ Himself wouldn't find Larry interesting. You've got to stop kidding yourself!'

A compromise of sorts was worked out. While Larry's mother was allowed to encourage her son's pursuit of knowledge and affirm the interesting nature of his conversation, she was also to stipulate that it would be better if he shared it with his friends rather than his father. It was important, she told him, that his father's mind remained blank: 'We don't want him coming home from the production line with any missing fingers, do we?' Effectively, Larry's parents washed their hands of their son's peccadillo, and in doing so unwittingly unleashed it on an unsuspecting world, in much the same way as Larry had described the letting loose of rabbits and camels in Australia.

Larry's contemporaries proved as unreceptive to his enthusiasms as did his parents. Until this time they'd considered him a regular kid – one of them. Sure, he was a geek kid, all that blinking and everything, but a geek kid whose forehead came in handy for noughts and crosses when no one had paper. Once Larry started to hold forth, however, their opinion of him quickly changed. They didn't want to hear about the workings of a washing machine or the theory of continental drift. They weren't in school, for God's sake! And who in God's name cared if the state capital of North Dakota was Bismarck or the capital of Niue, Alofi? His conversation, they also noted, was structured rather than spontaneous and always accompanied by bullet points: one, two, three; firstly, secondly, thirdly. They started to avoid him, leave him to his own devices rather than encourage him to share in theirs and, if cornered, would simply drift away and leave Larry mid-sentence.

If someone in Larry's younger years had actually mentioned to him that he talked too much or told him once in a while to shut the fuck up, then Larry might have learned to moderate his discourse and embrace the accepted to-and-fro of conversation. But surprisingly, considering the innate cruelty of children, no one ever did, and Larry's stunted personal skills were such that he never even realised there was a problem. The clues, however, were always there: he stopped being invited to parties, never got a second date with a girl and eventually no dates at all. He went to the Senior Prom with his mother and, for a person who supposedly liked the company of others, found himself spending an inordinate amount of time alone in his room, reading books or playing solitaire.

Larry's attributes, however, if not fitting him well for society at large were eminently suitable for a career in academia, where one-sided discourse was the rule and audiences captive. No one, therefore, was in the least surprised when he took a position in the history department of a well-known university after completing his doctorate. There he taught the same course – The Emergence of Modern America – for thirty-seven years, and during that time became the country's – and therefore the world's – leading authority on the Desert Land Act of 1877, probably the dullest piece of legislation to have ever rolled over Capitol Hill.

The intention of the act was to help settlers acquire and reclaim land in the western desert areas of the United States. On the understanding that the land was to be irrigated and brought to cultivation within three years, the government sold single tracts of 640 acres to prospective small farmers at a special price of eight hundred dollars. Although well intentioned the legislation was ill-conceived and idealistic, for there was little economic opportunity for the common man in these areas. Cattle companies, irrigation companies and speculators moved into the void, and when it became apparent that the act was benefitting special interests rather than the intended small family man there were calls for the law to be repealed. The Desert Land Act, however, remained on the statute book, a silent acknowledgement that practical men in the land of the free had every right to utilise poorly drawn laws.

While most historians shared the opinion that the act deserved no more than a footnote in American history, Larry viewed it as a representation of the American story in microcosm, and to his way of thinking – and his alone – Bill Clinton was as much a product of its passage as he was of Hope, Arkansas. There was, however, another reason for Larry's interest in the Desert Land Act, and one he wisely kept to himself. In the same way that squirrels are lured by nuts, he was drawn to sand!

The aberrational spell was cast in California when Larry was sixteen months old. He and his parents had gone to Santa Monica for a vacation and it was here, on the beach, that Larry took his first mouthful of sand. Until the gritty nature of his bowel movements and the developing diaper rash had been recognised for what they were, Larry had been eating this new-found source of food by the handful. It gave him goose bumps, soothed his gums, and he relished its textured and salty taste. Larry's parents naturally tried to discourage this practice, and on subsequent visits to the beach encouraged him to take an interest in sand as a building material or hiding place rather than a three-course meal. Larry's father dug holes with him, built castles with defensive moats that filled with water when the tide came in, buried small coins and pieces of inexpensive jewellery his wife wore to the beach and then sat back while Larry went in search of lost treasure. At the time these diversions appeared to work, but Larry's pica-esque behaviour never fully abated and in later life, when backs were turned or no one present, he continued to take the occasional pinch of sand whenever he visited a beach or made research trips to western desert areas.

Longevity of service in the department and a stream of published articles in scholarly journals secured Larry the title of professor but no real friendships, and on the occasion of his retirement only two people showed up for his send-off: the head of department who *had* to be there and who spent most of his time detailing the reasons why others couldn't, and a janitor named Clive, whose job it was to clean the room after the party ended.

Though disappointed by the turnout Larry was pleased to see Clive there. He had fond memories of their conversations over the years – especially their discussions of cleaning products and Clive's mop technique – and he'd always found the janitor a ready and interested listener. But like most people Larry talked to, that was all Clive ever was – a listener. He'd never encouraged these conversations and on occasion had locked himself in the storage room and pretended not to hear Larry's knocks on the door: 'Clive? Clive? You in there? Walmart's got a new floor polish in stock and I think it's better than the one you're using. Clive? Clive?' If by any chance Larry was still in the corridor when he exited the closet, Clive would simply tell Larry that he had an ear infection and couldn't hear a damn thing. 'No point trying to talk to me now, Professor MacCabe: I'm as deaf as a post.'

When the head of department made his own excuses and left the room – a CT scan, he explained to Larry a little too cheerfully – a shiver ran down Clive's spine. It was now just the two of them, and it would only be a matter of time before Professor MacCabe started banging on about the Desert Land Act again. He looked at his watch.

'The Head's a good man, Clive. We got a good one when we got him – even though he is a mediaevalist. I don't know whether you know this, Clive, but the mediaeval period dates from the collapse of the Western Roman Empire in the fifth century and runs through to the fifteenth. Of course it's subdivided into other ages – early, high and late, for instance – but not one of them has a Desert Land Act! That's my real interest, you know, even though most people do think it's a *dry* old subject.' He waited for Clive to register the joke, which Clive had probably done a thousand times before, and when no smile was forthcoming he continued. 'Get it, Clive? Desert? Dry? It's an old joke but it still cracks me up. My students loved it. Humour's always the best way to connect with people, don't you think?'

Clive thought that he'd connect better with Professor MacCabe if the man was dead, but said nothing and instead gave a weak smile. Then a thought struck him. 'Tell me, Professor MacCabe. Once you retire,' which by his watch was in about three minutes, 'will you still hold any sway in the department?'

'None whatsoever, Clive. By tomorrow morning I'll be a yesterday's man. You'll probably see me on campus from time to time, because I still have work on the Desert Land Act to do, but it's a labour of love now – a lot like you polishing floors…'

Clive glanced at his watch and walked out of the room: the three minutes were up and tomorrow morning he'd use his mop any damn way he pleased!

Larry returned home that evening with a small box of personal belongings and set it down on the kitchen counter. 'It was a lovely send-off, Helen,' he told his wife, 'and there'll be more than one person in the department sorry to have missed it. You know how it is though – dental appointments, family emergencies, research trips – it's like herding cats trying to get everyone in the same room these days. Clive was there though, the janitor I've told you about: the one who can't stop talking and just about chews my ear off every time he sees me.' He paused for a moment when he remembered Clive's abrupt departure from the room, but quickly gathered himself. 'Did I ever tell you how I got the job in the first place? How they'd been let down by their first choice of candidate and didn't have time for another round of interviews...'

Helen, whose eyes were increasingly glassy these days, smiled at her husband and occasionally nodded, but otherwise appeared to be in another room as he described his last day at the office. 'How does macaroni and cheese sound?' she asked out of nowhere.

'It sounds wonderful, dear, but just let me finish the story and then I'll start dinner.'

Unlike her husband Helen MacCabe was as quiet as the proverbial church mouse, in many ways the complementary *yin* to Larry's *yang*. As she attached little importance to most things in life, she consequently thought there was little point in talking about them or holding opinions of any kind for that matter, and while more than happy for Larry to talk, at no time felt it necessary to actually listen to him. Although in her own way she loved Larry, like all things in life she attached little importance to him and sometimes wondered if she'd married him simply to escape her parents. Having never expected much from life, however, Helen's marriage to Larry had been no more disappointing than a birthday card with no money inside, but while quite happy to be with him herself she could easily understand why others went out of their way to avoid him.

Helen wasn't academically inclined and had gone to college only to please her parents. There she'd graduated unspectacularly with a degree in Liberal Arts and then gone to work as a cashier in the bank where Larry deposited his cheques on a Friday lunchtime. A plain and unworldly soul, she'd mistaken his winks and incessant chatter about abaci, sand tables and slipsticks as acts of romantic interest and come to the conclusion that Larry was about to ask her out. When he didn't she determined to take matters into her own hands and ask him out. By nature, however, Helen was timid, and was only able to contemplate such an act after taking two of her mother's anti-anxiety pills, which one Friday morning she did – about an hour before Larry walked into the bank. By the time he was standing in front of her Helen was completely relaxed though yawning heavily. Straightaway she asked him to the bank's annual picnic and Larry readily accepted. With the aid of another cashier he then escorted her to the staff lounge where she spent the rest of the afternoon asleep on the floor.

It turned out that Larry and Helen had a lot in common: he'd never had a girlfriend and she'd never had a boyfriend. To make up for lost time they decided to marry in what most people would have considered haste, and two years later – and a year after they'd mastered the act of sex – Helen gave birth to twins: Rutherford and Grover – the Christian names of Larry's two favourite presidents. As Helen thought names were unimportant she was happy for Larry to decide them, and only smiled when he told her they now had a balanced ticket. (Rutherford Hayes was a Republican and Grover Cleveland a Democrat, he would have explained to her if she'd thought it important enough to ask.)

Although fully intending to be present at the birth of his children, Larry had inadvertently embroiled himself in a conversation with one of the hospital's elevator attendants and missed the actual delivery. It appeared to Larry that the attendant had been more than interested to learn that the first elevator had been built by Archimedes in 236BC, and encouraged by the man's reaction he'd gone on to explain the differences between various types of hoist mechanisms. 'You see there's a traction elevator with its worm gears, Gary – it is okay if I call you Gary, isn't it – okay then, so where were we? Worm gears, that's right...' It was only after he'd got to describing the self-ascending climbing elevator with its own propulsion system that he remembered his actual reason for being in the hospital: his wife was doing a bit of propelling herself!

Two years after Larry retired Helen died. She rose from bed one morning and immediately felt strange: light-headed and slightly nauseous. She returned to bed and stayed there for three days, refusing to see a doctor. Her malaise, she told Larry, was too vague to be of any importance and she fully expected to be back on her feet by the end of the week. On the fourth morning Larry brought her coffee and two slices of toast and placed the tray on the bedside table. He then ran errands for the next three hours, errands that would have taken another person only thirty minutes. Larry's problem, however, was that he never stopped talk... (His talking was endless.)

Larry returned to the house just before midday and sat down at the end of his wife's bed. He talked to Helen for two hours, telling her about the operation of the Desert Land Act in California and Nevada and how, when the act had been drawn up, it had addressed surface water and agricultural uses only and never given a second thought to ground water or the fact that water might be used for recreational purposes. He then looked at his watch and told her he'd leave her to get some rest. He kissed her gently on the forehead and only then did it dawn on him that something was wrong: his wife was cold as a block of ice. He then noticed the untouched coffee and toast.

The subsequent autopsy revealed nothing untoward, and the coroner ruled that Helen's death had been natural. He noted, however, that her liver had been at a more advanced stage of deterioration than would normally have been expected of a woman her age, and also expressed dismay that a well-educated man like Professor MacCabe had conducted a conversation with a corpse for two hours. Those who knew Larry, however, showed no such surprise and at least one thought he should have been charged with manslaughter for having talked his wife to death.

Larry and Helen had been married for thirty-one years when she died and her departure hit him hard. He'd loved Helen and instinctively known that she too had loved him. He could never remember a time when she'd actually told him this, but he'd known. Larry had always known. For how could a wife of thirty-one years not love her husband? And how could a mother of estranged children not love their estranged father? And, come to think of it, where the hell were Rutherford and Grover these days? Larry had no idea if they were alive or dead.

The twins were in fact alive, but it was debatable if they were well. Rutherford and Grover had grown up in a house full of their father's words and eventually been overpowered by them.

When they were small and the words in the house only ankle deep, the boys had paddled and splashed in them untroubled, but as they'd grown older and the words from their father's mouth continued to fall, they became anxious. By the time they were seven the level of words in the house had reached their knees, by twelve their waists and by fifteen their chests. Increasingly the boys struggled to wade through their father's outflows and by their eighteenth birthdays, fearing they would drown, left home for college and decided never to return. There they became reclusive and some would say strange. They avoided people, made no friends and rarely spoke to each other. They graduated at the top of their respective classes, shook hands at the campus gates and parted company forever, each determined to pursue a life as free from words as possible. Rutherford became a Trappist monk in rural Oregon, and Grover went to live among the Kodiak bears in Alaska.

'Not even a postcard,' Larry ruminated as he stared at a photograph of Helen and the two boys. And then he started to cry, big blobs of tears that splashed on the protective glass. 'Who am I going to talk to now, Helen?' he groaned. 'There'll never be another person like you.'

Despite the fact that Helen had remained mute most evenings, Larry had always considered his wife the perfect conversationalist. She'd sit quietly in her chair as he recounted his day – out of interest for what he was saying, he'd always supposed – sipping from, and occasionally refilling, a tumbler of what Larry had assumed was iced water. (That Helen had been largely comatose and living on another planet during these conversations only dawned on Larry after he discovered a slew of empty vodka bottles in the back garden, buried close to the rhododendrons.)

For the first time in his life Larry felt completely alone. The silence of the house deafened him, his own company threatened him and he feared he would never adapt to life as a single person. He needed someone to talk to, someone to listen to him and affirm his existence. And as his sex drive had crashed years ago this companion would in all likelihood be a man; the last thing he wanted was to get involved with a woman still revved up and ready to go.

This thought led him to his next-door neighbour, a retired plastic surgeon called Dr Young and one of the few people Larry actually disliked. In his opinion Dr Young had a poor set of ethics for a doctor and an even worse set of morals for a man, trawling as he did through the divorce and death notices in the town's newspaper for the names of recent widows and divorcees he'd previously encountered in a professional capacity. 'I built these women,' he'd once bragged to Larry. 'And I know exactly what I'm going to find once I get their damned clothes off and into their pants. It's payback time, MacCabe. Know what I mean?' A lascivious grin had then crossed his face and a small piece of tongue poked through his teeth. His manner had made Larry squirm, and on the occasions he'd later seen Dr Young with a woman on his arm, he was unable to escape the thought that the women looked more like the victims of a fire than the beneficiaries of a doctor's scalpel.

'Larry, Larry, old son,' he said to himself in the shaving mirror one morning. 'You've got to get a grip on yourself. There's a world out there and it's waiting for you. You've another twenty years left in you yet, and there are people out there wanting to meet you. Now get your tail in gear and get on out there!'

But where? The university might have been the obvious choice, but Larry tended not to go there these days. It wasn't just the fact that its sidewalks and corridors parted like the Red Sea whenever he visited the campus, but the uncomfortable truth that he was, at least for the time being, as estranged from the Desert Land Act as he was from Rutherford and Grover. The coroner's words still rang in his ears: *how could a well-educated man like you, Professor MacCabe, have conducted a conversation with a corpse for two hours*? Why, he wondered, had he been telling his wife about the Desert Land Act when he could have been saving her life? He'd watched her die and found it hard to forgive himself, and even harder to forgive the Desert Land Act which, ultimately, he held more responsible for her death than he did himself. (Larry was being too hard on both himself and the act: Helen had died during the night. Not only had Larry talked to a dead corpse, he'd also slept with one – and for more than any two hours.)

It was then Larry remembered a man living further down the street, a widower by the name of Cotton who was close to his age and educated to a similar level. He recalled bumping into Mr Cotton shortly after the man's bereavement and was pleased to think that in a small way his detailing of the concept of reincarnation had alleviated his neighbour's grief. 'Who knows, Mr Cotton,' he'd said. 'That pigeon on the roof over there might well be your wife.' He remembered the man pointing to the pigeon droppings on his car and Helen tugging at his sleeve. 'Not now, Larry,' she'd whispered.

He decided to pay Mr Cotton a visit and one day knocked on his door. He introduced himself, reminded the man that they'd met shortly after his wife died and suggested, now that his own wife was dead, that they start meeting for coffee on a regular basis. Mr Cotton had no intention of becoming Larry's best friend simply because they enjoyed widowhood. He well remembered their conversation on reincarnation and Larry's effrontery to suggest that his wife had returned to earth as a pigeon, and as far as he was concerned that conversation had been one too many. (If such a notion did have validity, his wife would have returned to earth as a princess or a Mother Teresa figure with conjugal rights, and not some damn scavenger.) He also recalled that it had taken him fifteen minutes to extricate himself from Larry's gibbering and that the man's incessant blinking had brought on one of his optical migraines – and one that had lasted far longer than its usual twenty minutes. 'I don't mean to be rude, Mr MacCabe, but I think I have more in common with a parrot than I do you.' He then – rather rudely, Larry thought – shut the door in his face.

In the weeks that followed Larry struggled with lonesomeness. He switched on the television, turned on the radio and filled the house with disembodied voices. He cleaned the house, pottered in the garden, spoke to spiders and talked to birds, counted the number of stairs in the house (27), the number of windows (14) and the pairs of socks in his drawer (28). Occasionally, he called talk radio stations but rarely got through, and if he did get through was invariably cut off before he could finish saying what he'd intended. He took aimless taxi rides for the sake of conversing with cabdrivers, phoned companies whose stickered vehicles asked for feedback on their drivers only to find that the people answering his calls weren't in the least bit curious as to what he thought, and certainly not interested in pursuing any other conversations. He visited garden centres and asked about plants, asked if there was any horticultural reason for empty vodka bottles to be placed close to rhododendron shrubs. He made unnecessary appointments with doctors and dentists, had tradesmen call at the house to discuss renovations that would never take place and ate out in cafes and restaurants and attempted to draw waiters and other customers into idle conversation.

It was only after colliding with an eighty-three-year-old woman in a supermarket he frequented on an unnecessarily daily basis that he hit upon the idea of becoming a voluntary worker in a retirement home. It was without doubt a win-win situation, and he kicked himself for not having thought of this before. Starved of company, and more often than not unable to walk, old people represented the perfect captive audience and one that would be glad of his or any company. Immediately he contacted the nearest residential centre and arranged to visit the home for three hours daily. He told the care administrators that he expected no recompense for his services and that brightening the lives of senior citizens was compensation in itself. The administrators thought Larry a saint and were overjoyed to accept his offer. Three weeks later, however, they changed their minds and banned him from the premises.

It was mid-way through the third week of Larry's visits that the managers started to become alarmed. They noticed that those residents who weren't deaf became agitated whenever Larry walked into the room, and on a closer examination of the people he talked to on a regular basis discerned an actual deterioration. These old-timers described Larry either as a man sent by the Devil to torment them or as a crazy person meaning them harm. Either way, Larry didn't come out of these discussions looking too good, and on the Friday morning the head of the residential care centre called him to her office.

Although a tough administrator Ms Parker was a kindly person, and having spent a lifetime caring for sorrowful souls recognised in Larry many of their traits. She didn't tell him that the old people there thought he was an emissary of the Devil or a lunatic on the prowl – descriptions she thought more suited to some of them than Larry – but did make it clear that his services would no longer be required at the centre. Larry was dumbfounded by the news. 'I know most of the old folk here are challenged, Ms Parker – that's what we say these days, isn't it: *challenged* – but I know for a fact that Frank's always glad to see me. He nods away at everything I say.' Ms Parker tactfully explained that Frank had Parkinson's disease and nodded at everyone.

For once in his life Larry decided to save his breath. Ms Parker, he realised, wasn't about to change her mind. Dejectedly he stood up, and Ms Parker walked with him to the door. They shook hands and she watched as Larry walked to his car with his shoulders slumped. It was then a thought struck her and she called after him. 'I know it's none of my business, Professor MacCabe, but have you ever thought about getting a dog?'

Larry thought about what Ms Parker had said. It was true that dogs had a reputation for being man's best friend, but having been bitten six times by six different dogs he was unsure if a dog was ever likely to be *his* best friend. The first occasion had been on a lake shore in Maryland. He'd been skimming stones at the time, and for no apparent reason a Bluetick Coonhound had jumped up and bitten him on the arm. He remembered the incident less for the discomfort of the bite and more for his father sucking the wound and spitting his blood on the ground. 'That's snakes, Dad,' he'd said. 'You only do that if a snake's bitten you.' His father had ignored the comment – just as he had his son's succeeding recitation of the twenty species of venomous snakes living in the United States – and, after a few more sucks, taken Larry for what would be the first of many tetanus shots. He was subsequently bitten by a German Shepherd (butt), a West Highland White Terrier (ankle), a Rough Collie (thigh), a McNab (calf) and a Plott Hound (hand).

The only bite Larry could ever understand from a dog's point of view was the one delivered by the Rough Collie. Then he'd been in a Greek restaurant looking for the restroom and misinterpreted a server's sideways nod of the head to indicate that he should climb a nearby flight of stairs. Though wondering why no sign pointed to the restrooms being this way, he'd followed the waiter's advice and eventually found himself standing at the open door of the owners' living quarters. By then he'd been desperate and called to anyone who might have been inside. When no answer was forthcoming, and rationalising that the proprietors of the establishment would have no issue with him using their private facilities after he'd already paid for two of their early-bird specials, he'd ventured through the door and into the apartment. It was then, seemingly out of nowhere, that a Collie had appeared and sunk its teeth deep into his thigh. Larry had stumbled back down the stairs but mentioned nothing of the incident to the owners. Instead he'd returned to the table where Helen was sitting and asked if it was okay if they stopped by the hospital for a tetanus shot on the way home. 'Not again, Larry!' Helen had sighed.

This was the downside of Larry's experiences with dogs. On the upside he had no lasting fear of dogs and had been assured by a doctor that he had enough anti-tetanus serum in his system to last a lifetime. He also remembered the many times he'd stroked and patted dogs without consequence, and after careful consideration decided that the bark of a dog in the house was preferable to unremitting silence. It was, in other words, a gamble worth taking.

Larry's first dog was a mutt, a mongrel borne of other mongrels, its lineage as crooked as a barrel of fish hooks. It was, however, the only dog in the pound to have shown any interest in Larry: it had wagged its tail, licked his fingers and rolled on its back. Unbeknownst to Larry, the dog was a veteran of pounds, a recidivist; it knew all the ropes, all the tricks, and recognised a ticket out of there when it saw one. The dog's name was Loop and its fur, Larry noted, was the colour of desert sand. (Had Loop been human he would have hung out on street corners, whistled at passing girls and rolled dice; he would have smoked stogies, pared his nails with a flick-knife and drunk neat bourbon.)

'I'll take him!' Larry said to the young girl who'd accompanied him on his tour of the pound. 'You're sure, Professor MacCabe? Loop can be a bit of a handful,' she replied. Larry's mind, however, was made up. He left the pound with Loop, and as the gates closed behind them the dog turned its head and appeared to give the girl a wink.

As Larry had never owned a dog before he had no idea how to control one, and the pound assistant's warning that Loop could be *a bit of a handful* turned out to be an understatement – *has deep-seated behavioural problems* might have been a more accurate description. The dog barked incessantly, ran from room to room knocking over lamps and small tables and drank from the toilet bowl. It chased its tail for long periods, dug up the garden and chewed cushions, made Larry's favourite armchair its own and slept uninvited on his bed. And when Larry and Loop went for walks through the neighbourhood it was the dog that decided the pace and direction, one minute idling at a bush and the next straining at the leash and dragging Larry helter-skelter down the street. (Loop, however, preferred to wander the streets alone, and when opportunity presented itself – which invariably it did, considering that Larry's yard was far from escape-proof – it ran riot through the neighbourhood, terrorising cats and small children, dumping its faeces on lawns and urinating on the wheels of parked cars.)

Even though Larry was in thrall to the dog, he loved its company. Loop brought life to the house, made the bricks and mortar a home again and provided him with an audience. He talked to Loop as enthusiastically as he'd talked to Helen: 'Blah, blah, blah,' he would say; 'Ruff, ruff, ruff,' the dog would reply. They were oblivious to each other's meaning, often talked at the same time and at cross purposes, but it mattered little. Each in their own way had suffered abandonment, and a bond of mutuality grew between them.

Whenever Larry returned from an errand Loop would be there to greet him, wagging his tail and licking him on the face. Larry, after all, was the man who'd sprung him from jail, put a roof over his head and supplied him with food. He recognised Larry as a meal ticket and became protective of him. If anyone came too close when they were out on their walks – especially Dr Young who Loop sensed to be a particular threat – he would growl, bare his teeth and demand a wide berth. (Ironically, this was the one thing Larry hadn't wanted. He'd hoped that having a dog would lead to conversations with other dog owners or people drawn to the innocence of animals.)

Only once did Loop bite Larry and that, Larry was convinced, had been an accident. It happened early in their relationship when they were still learning each other's ways and misunderstandings were inevitable. That day Larry had returned to the house with a stick of shortbread in his mouth – put there while he unlocked the door – and Loop, mistaking it for a dog biscuit, had jumped to retrieve it and accidentally bitten Larry on the chin. The wound wasn't sufficiently serious for stitches but it did make shaving difficult, and for the first time in his life Larry let the whiskers there grow.

Although the presence of Loop enriched Larry's life it had the opposite effect on the neighbourhood. The neighbours quickly tired of his barking and chaotic wanderings, but fearing a simple complaint to Professor MacCabe would entail an hour's lecture on the history of dogs, mentioned nothing of the matter to him and only muttered amongst themselves. Things came to a head, however, after Loop, on one of his unofficial walks, bit Dr Young on the rump.

The retired plastic surgeon waited for Larry to return to the house and then banged on his door.

'That dog of yours is a menace, MacCabe! He's a danger to the neighbourhood!'

'You mean Loop?' Larry said somewhat incredulously. 'Loop's not dangerous, Dr Young, he's just playful.'

'You call these teeth marks playful?' Dr Young shouted, lowering his trousers and showing Larry a perfect imprint of Loop's teeth.

'You're sure it was Loop that bit you?' Larry asked, slightly off-put by the wide expanse of dimpled flesh in front of him. 'He's never bitten anyone before.'

'Of course it was Loop! My eyes aren't as good as they were but they sure as hell know Loop when they see him. And what kind of damn fool logic says that just because he hasn't bitten anyone before he hasn't bitten me now? There's a first time for everything, MacCabe. Check it out with the people of Hiroshima or Nagasaki if you don't believe me. Ask them if they ever doubted it was us who dropped atomic bombs on them just because we'd never dropped atomic bombs on them before. Use your goddamn common sense, man: who else is it going to be? You got the dog from the pound, for fuck's sake. Did it never cross your mind that there was probably a good reason why someone dumped him there in the first place?'

Larry could hear Loop barking in the backyard and was perplexed. 'I don't understand it, Dr Young. What were you doing in my garden?'

'I wasn't in your damned garden! Your dog was out on the street, shitting and pissing like it always is.'

Larry was aware that Loop had escaped from the backyard on a couple of occasions, but had no idea it was a regular occurrence. (It had certainly never cropped up in any of their evening conversations.)

'Well if that is the case, Dr Young, I'm very sorry. But a dog bite is nothing like an atomic bomb. I've had six of them myself – seven if you count the one on my chin – and it's a lot less painful than being stung by a wasp. Anyway, I'll make sure it won't happen again.'

'Damn right it won't happen again. I'm having your dog put down! And just because you've got hair growing round your mouth these days doesn't mean you can talk to me like a…!'

A passing laundry truck backfired and Larry misheard the last of the sentence.

'I'm sorry, Dr Young, I didn't realise I was,' he apologised. 'I've never even read Kant. Look, can't we settle this in a more civilised manner – man to man? After all, we *are* both doctors.'

'No!' Dr Young said. 'And as far as I'm concerned there's only one doctor in this conversation and that's me. In my book a PhD counts for nothing! I'm off for a tetanus shot now and I'll be sending you the bill. Make sure you pay it!'

That night Loop was put down, and the next day a hastily scribbled note pushed through Dr Young's letter box. *Dear Dr Young: One day, I hope someone puts you down. Yours sincerely, Larry K MacCabe (Professor).'*

Dr Young thought it was a hoot and had the letter framed.

It was Ms Parker who once again rode to Larry's rescue. He was walking across the parking lot of a supermarket when she saw him, struggling with three large sacks of dog food and apparently in the process of making a delivery. One of the sacks fell from his grip and she called out to him. 'Professor MacCabe! Professor MacCabe! Wait there and I'll give you a hand.' Larry turned and smiled, and then rested on his haunches while Ms Parker finished loading groceries into the trunk of her car.

'I'm afraid this old beanpole body of mine isn't as strong as it once was,' Larry smiled. 'By rights it should be me helping you.'

Ms Parker took hold of one of the bags, and while they

walked, Larry told her of Loop and how he was hoping to get a credit for the unopened sacks of dog food he'd bought. 'I don't suppose you have time for a cup of coffee, do you?' he asked, once the matter had been resolved. 'It would be nice to talk to someone.'

Ms Parker looked at her watch and then searched her conscience. 'Sure, Professor MacCabe,' she said after a moment's hesitation. 'I'll be glad to have coffee with you.'

They walked to a small coffee house close to the supermarket and Larry told her the full story.

'That's simply awful,' Ms Parker said. 'What kind of a man has a dog put down!'

'A plastic surgeon,' Larry explained. 'I don't know if all plastic surgeons are like Dr Young, though.'

'I'm sure they're not,' Ms Parker replied for want of anything more interesting to say. 'Incidentally, I think the beard suits you. It makes you look distinguished. Like Trotsky.'

'Trotsky!' Larry exclaimed. 'No wonder people have been avoiding me. They'll have been thinking I'm a communist!'

Resolving to shave his beard when he returned home, an uncomfortable thought struck him – had Ms Parker been flirting with him when she'd mentioned his beard, trying to hitch a ride on his broken-down old wagon? He enjoyed her company but, for reasons mentioned, didn't want to risk the possibility of any sexual shenanigans. He sought to clarify the situation. 'Your husband won't mind you being here, will he?'

'I don't have a husband, Professor MacCabe. Alice is my life partner.'

Larry was relieved. 'That's a strange name for a man, Ms Parker. Then again, there was that boy named Sue, wasn't there? You know, the song recorded by Johnny Cash in Folsom Prison. Funny thing that. Because he had an outlaw image, most people thought he'd been in prison himself, but he never had. He had a few scrapes that landed him in jail overnight, but nothing serious. One time he got arrested for trespassing in someone's garden and picking their flowers. Now where was that? Starkville, that's where it was, Starkville, Mississippi. I guess the moral of that story is that you don't mess with the people of...'

'Alice is a girl's name, Professor MacCabe. I'm attracted to women.'

'Well, there's nothing to be ashamed of there, Ms Parker.'

'I'm not ashamed,' Ms Parker said. 'There hasn't been a day in my life when I have been ashamed of my sexuality.'

'Quite right too, and good for you. Well done. It's a pity there aren't more lesbians in the world.'

There was a lull in the conversation and Larry took advantage of the pause to blow his nose. 'I don't suppose Frank's been asking about me, has he?' he asked.

'No, but I wouldn't take it too personally. He doesn't ask about anyone these days. He has trouble talking.'

'I'm very sorry to hear that,' Larry replied. 'I think Frank and I would have become good friends if we'd met earlier in life. By the way, now that we're not meeting in an official capacity, is it all right if I call you by your first name? My name's Larry.'

'Feel free. It's Laura – Laura Parker.'

'Well, I'll be! That was the name of the girl killed in *Twin Peaks*, wasn't it? I tell you, that was just about the strangest piece of television I ever watched. That dwarf who danced and all those cherry pies. I've never been a fan of cherry pie myself. I much prefer a pie that's made from apples, or apples and pears. Helen used to…'

'Her name was *Palmer*,' Laura interrupted, a slight tone of impatience creeping into her voice. 'Laura *Palmer*.' How, she wondered, could a man meander from one aimless topic to another, dredge up everything he knew on a subject and pump it willy-nilly into a conversation.

'Larry,' she said. 'Focus for a moment. Forget about *Twin Peaks* and Johnny Cash and think dogs. Why don't you get another dog?'

'Oh, I don't know about that, Laura. I still feel responsible for Loop's death.'

'Don't be silly, Larry. Your next-door neighbour shoulders that responsibility. You took good care of Loop. It seems to me, though, that he did have a few behavioural problems.'

'You mean he was challenged, like the old folk in your home?'

'If you like. A lot of dogs in the pound are like that. People take them there for a reason and in that respect Dr Young had a point. What you need is a purebred, a dog with a good lineage and I know just the one. A friend of mine's mother has just died and she's trying to find a home for her dog. What do you think, Larry? Are you interested?'

Larry stroked his beard for a moment, remembered it was a communist beard and quickly changed tack and rubbed his bald head instead. 'What kind of dog is it?' he asked finally.

'It's a Basset Hound, Larry. And he has ears just like yours!'

2

The Care Administrator

'Well, we might both have long ears, Moses, but at least mine don't trail in my food when I eat. Now keep still, will you, and let me give them a wipe.'

Moses stopped fidgeting and allowed Larry to clean his long velvety ears with a damp cloth. The dog looked sad, as if about to burst into tears, but the sadness was congenital rather than of the moment. There was no other way a Basset Hound could look.

Moses was a purebred, a hound descended from the hounds owned by St Hubert of Belgium in the sixth century, and had the papers to prove it. He was three-and-a-half feet long, twelve inches high and weighed around forty-five pounds. His legs were short and crooked, his head big and his nose large. He had long dangling ears, pendent brown eyes and a coat that was black and tan, soft and short-haired. Folds of loose skin concertinaed round his neck and a wide white stripe ran down the middle of his wrinkled face. Indeed, the only part of Moses' body that didn't droop was his white-tipped tail which curved upward like a cavalryman's sabre and waggled from side to side like a metronome, its movement the only indication the dog wasn't about to commit suicide.

'Now let's take a look at those eyes of yours. We don't want Miss Laura thinking I'm not taking good care of you.'

In Larry's opinion mongrelism had a lot to offer the world. Loop had been a mongrel par excellence and had needed no special care. He'd stayed healthy on his own account and had been untroubled by problems peculiar to a *lack* of breed. Moses, however, was a different kettle of fish altogether. The structure of his ears, for instance, inhibited the free circulation of air inside them and they were prone to infections and ear mites, just as the folds of his mouth were also susceptible to yeast infections. The configuration of his eyes, which allowed dirt to collect under the eyeballs, was another design fault, and unless Larry wiped them with a damp cloth every day they would clog with mucous.

'There you are, old son. Good as new!' Larry said. 'Stick with me and you'll live to be a hundred.'

The chances of this were remote. Moses was already a year old, and in all probability would live for no more than another eleven. In human terms, and if he was lucky, he would die at the age of seventy-four and leave Larry heartbroken – if, indeed, Larry's heart was still ticking at this future date.

Although Larry sang the praises of mongrelism, he would have plumped for Moses' company over Loop's any day of the week. While Loop had been independent, Moses was happily dependent and hated to be left alone. He was more sociable, friendlier, hardly ever barked and was naturally well behaved. He was also too sluggish to rampage the house as Loop had done, and spent most of the day asleep on the floor and usually in the same room as Larry. Despite this indoor inactivity Moses was the polar opposite outdoors. He was after all a scent hound, bred for hunting rabbits and hare and would have run for hours if given the chance. Larry remembered Laura warning him to keep Moses on a firm leash whenever they went for their long daily walks, which she'd insisted they take. 'Basset Hounds might appear lazy, Larry, but they need exercise – and plenty of it!'

And these walks had become the highpoint of Larry's day. Despite the dog's name being Moses, the sidewalks no longer parted like the Red Sea when Larry traversed them. People smiled at them, bid them a cheery hello and often stopped to fondle Moses and chat with Larry. Larry was happy to answer their questions on Basset Hounds and, against Laura's encouragement, often in more detail than was strictly necessary. Though wary of Larry's gasbag tendency, people now stayed on the same side of the street when they saw him and greeted him by name, even though they were more interested in his dog. Moses, Larry realised, was providing him with an entrée to the world he'd never had before, and he mentioned this to Laura. 'Good! Make sure you don't blow it!' she'd replied.

Although young enough to have been his daughter, in the weeks following Larry's adoption of Moses, Laura in many ways became his surrogate mother. She thought of him as a gentleman loser, a well-meaning person who unwittingly drove people nuts, and couldn't help but feel sorry for him. Larry was a lost soul, she decided, walking along life's hard shoulder with an empty gas can in his hand and unlikely to reach a service station without the help of another person. She was under no illusion she could change his essence – it was far too late in his life for this to happen – but at least she could seek to moderate his more annoying traits. And she had the patience and temperament to do this.

It was Laura who'd facilitated the transition of ownership, assured her friend that Larry would provide Moses with a good home once he got his backyard fence fixed, and had then bought her protégé a book on Basset Hounds. She'd visited his house and observed the two of them together and given Larry her critique. 'You can't be a milquetoast with Moses, Larry. You have to show him that *you're* the boss. If you want him to obey you then you have to be firm with him – and for God's sake try and look a bit more confident. Prove to him that your balls are bigger than his... No, of course I don't mean this literally!'

Larry responded well to her instruction and the correct relationship of master and dog was established. If only training Larry had been as easy!

Laura despaired of his garrulousness. She'd ask him the time and he'd give her a lecture on clocks; mention how pleasant the day was and be treated to a spiel on weather; and a casual pleasantry on one of Larry's rugs would lead to a travelogue on the Orient. Occasionally there was a nugget of interest in something he said – the addition of tanks to Afghan rugs after the Russians invaded the country, for instance – but these were rare, and the time came when Laura could take no more of his detours.

'Larry! Has anyone ever told you that you talk too much?'

Larry looked at her surprised. 'No, I don't think anyone ever has,' he replied carefully. 'I've always found that people enjoy my conversation. Everybody likes to learn something new, especially if it's an interesting fact.'

'Well, believe me, Larry, they don't! I'm as bright as the next person and there are *lots* of things I don't want to know about. Everyone is different. What interests you might well not interest another person – *any* other person. You can't bulldoze things into a conversation that don't belong there just because *you* happen to find them interesting. It's not polite and people don't have the time or patience for it. You're a nice man, Larry – and I'm telling you this as someone who cares about you – but your conversation puts people off!'

Larry's blinking intensified and he tugged at one of his long ears. He was genuinely shocked by what Laura told him. Surely she was confusing him with another person? She had to be! 'I... I think you're wrong there, Laura,' he stammered.

'Okay then, name me three friends!'

'Friends of yours?'

'No! Your friends! Tell me the names of your three best friends.'

'Well, there's...' He paused for a moment and stroked his beardless chin. 'There's Clive,' he continued, 'and the Head of Department... and I think I've already told you that I hit it off with Frank.'

'Forget Frank, Larry: you only knew him for two weeks! When was the last time you saw Clive or the Head of Department? And the mere fact that you refer to him by his title rather than his name indicates that the two of you aren't particularly close. And who's Clive?'

Larry swallowed hard and decided to answer the easier question first. 'Clive's a janitor at the university... and the Head of Department, well, he has to keep his distance for professional reasons. I think he looks upon me as a friend, though.'

'And the last time you saw them?' Laura pressed, unwilling to give up on the issue having come this far.

'About two years ago,' Larry confessed. 'But they both came to my leaving do.'

Laura showed no sign of triumphalism and was careful to ensure that Larry's crest didn't fall too sharply. 'Okay then, Larry. Today we start afresh. Today is the first day...' She stopped mid-sentence. She hated that cliché, couldn't believe she'd been about to repeat it. 'Today you start a new life,' she started again. 'When the time's right I'll take you and Moses to a dog park I go to and introduce you to some people there. But you have to take what I've said seriously. You have to watch what you say and for how long you say it, and if I think you're talking too much I'm going to tell you. And believe me, the people in the park won't be shy of telling you this either. Tell them about yourself and spare them the facts and figures, and ask about them and listen to their answers.'

That particular conversation had taken place three weeks ago, and although Larry had taken it to heart its message sometimes had difficulty getting through to his head. He did, however, now start to notice the expressions and body language of the people he talked to – as much in the hope of disproving Laura's theory as to confirm it – and on the occasions he did discern any discomfort in his audience immediately pulled the plug on himself. It was growth of a sort, even though the shoot was small and its colour a pallid green.

'Now where's Miss Laura got to?' he asked Moses. 'She should have been here half an hour ago. She's showing me how to trim your toenails tonight – have I told you this already? That's something else we have to do regularly. At this rate I'm not going to have any time to look after myself!' He laughed at his joke and Moses gave a short bark. 'You think I should call her, Moses? Make sure she hasn't forgotten? You do?'

When the intercom buzzed Laura was deep in thought, chewing the end of a ballpoint and staring into space. 'It's Larry MacCabe on line one, Ms Parker. Do you want me to put him through?' Laura glanced at her watch. Shit! Six-thirty! She'd forgotten all about Larry. 'Tell him there's been an emergency at the home and I'll be there Friday, will you?'

To the receptionist's request for a fall-back date should Larry be busy that evening, Laura replied tersely that the chances of that were non-existent. She then replaced the phone in its cradle and continued to stare into space. There was indeed an emergency at the home, and one that struck at the very heart of her care philosophy: command of the television controls.

Laura Parker had come to care administration by way of a degree in anthropology – which was no suitable avenue for earning a living – and a Master's in Business Administration, which was. She'd grown up on a small dairy farm in Windham County, Vermont, and life there had been uncomplicated. People milked cows and that was about it. She came from a large family, three brothers and one sister, and until their deaths her grandparents had also lived close by. When she was fifteen, the family was informed that a distant relative had been taken into care in Brattleboro and asked to visit. 'Who the heck's Elizabeth Longtoe?' her father had wondered out loud. 'I don't think she's from my side of the family.'

It emerged that Elizabeth Longtoe was the first cousin of his wife's mother. Grandma had never mentioned her by name when she'd been alive or even alluded to her existence, and so it was with more than a hint of curiosity that the family descended on Brattleboro one Saturday afternoon.

'My oh my,' Laura's mother said on the return journey.

'Who'd have thought the family had a skeleton in its closet? That poor old soul!'

'Well, she's a skeleton in a care home, now,' Laura's father replied. 'She must have more years to her age than she does pounds to her body. She has Grandma's hair, though, doesn't she? Looks like someone stuck a big ball of cotton wool on a knitting needle.'

'Can't she come live with us, Mom?' Laura asked. 'It seems, like, well, you know, just cruel, leaving her there like that. And she is family, isn't she? And that place stinks, I mean, *really* stinks. I can still smell the pong, can't you? God! I think I'm going to gag. Dad, roll down the window, will you?'

'It's true she's related to us, Laura,' her mother replied, 'but we don't know Aunt Elizabeth from Adam, and I'm not sure your grandma would have approved of her living with us. Besides we have enough on our plates and I don't want the added responsibility of having to look after her. No, she's better off where she is. We'll make a point of visiting her when we can, but the idea of Aunt Elizabeth moving in with us is out of the question.'

The family did visit occasionally, more out of duty than love, but never spent more than an hour with her at any one time. To all but Laura, Elizabeth Longtoe remained a distant, and therefore unimportant, relative. Laura, however, was intrigued by her great-aunt. For Vermont, Elizabeth Longtoe was an exotic.

'Me and your grandma fell out over a boy,' Elizabeth laughed. 'Your grandpa, believe it or not! I dated the man once and I think he always had a soft spot for me, but it was no skin off my nose when the two of them got engaged. Your grandma was jealous of me, though. Stopped talking to me and didn't even invite me to the wedding. I was the only one in the family *not* to be invited. Pure silliness! What did she think I was going to do? Drag the man from the altar and run off with him? I ask you, who in their right mind would have done a thing like that? Besides, by then I was already seeing Steve.

'I hadn't told anyone about this because most people in those days used to frown on white girls dating Indians, and my Mom and Dad would have had a fit if they'd known. But the time came when me and Steve thought we should get married, and the day I told my parents was the day they showed me the door and told me I wasn't a daughter of theirs anymore. And Steve's parents were no better. I learned then that prejudice runs both ways.

'Steve was an Abenaki, and the whole tribe had to agree to our marriage before we could go ahead with it. He went home and told his dad to stick a pole in the ground – that was their way of deciding things in those days: if no one knocked it down then it was okay for us to get married. But his father said no, said there'd be no point because he'd knock the damn pole down himself. He told Steve he didn't want any son of his marrying into white trash. That was hurtful to hear.

'Anyway, our minds weren't for changing and so we went ahead and got married, and when his people heard about it they came to our door and told Steve he was no longer an Indian – that was the worst thing an Abenaki could say to another member of their tribe. So it was just me and Steve against the world after that, but there's never been a day in my life I regretted marrying him. He was the handsomest man I'd ever met, big as an ox and just as strong, and he had long black hair that he tied back in a ponytail. He was good-hearted, too.

If you got paid money for being kind, that darling man would have been a millionaire!

'We were comfortable for a time. Steve got a job in the slate quarries over in Rutland County and we didn't want for anything. But then he went and did something to his back and that was that. It was hard for him to earn a living after that. I got work when I could; minimum wage jobs mainly, most of them in laundries. I think that's where my arthritis started. Have you seen my fingers? Crooked as a Virginia fence, aren't they? I pay them no mind, though.

'The important thing is that me and Steve grew old together and stayed happy. The saddest day of my life was the day he got killed. He was out hunting in the woods and got struck by lightning. Can you believe that? An Indian struck by lightning!

'I was in the kitchen, washing up, when I got the news. A flock of crows had just flown over the house and two minutes later there was a knock on the door and a sheriff standing there. I don't know if the crows were a sign or not... Steve would have been able to tell you.

'Children? No, we weren't blessed that way, dear. It wasn't meant to be. And maybe that was a good thing, because there were times when we couldn't even afford to put food in our own mouths. I know what you're thinking, though. You're thinking that if we'd had children I wouldn't be living here now, aren't you? You're thinking that I'd be living with them. No, I wouldn't have wanted that, dear. You don't give life to a person just so you can suck it out of them when you get old. They'd have had lives of their own to live, children of their own to look after and there's no way I'd have wanted to burden them. I'm an invalid, Laura. It wouldn't have been fair.

'This place? It's not all that bad, and it's better than living on the street. I have company here and you come visit me. Sometimes it does get a bit strange, the screams in the night and strange people coming up to you and shouting at you as if you've done something wrong to them. But we're all God's creatures and I try to remember that. I count my blessings that I'm not like them, at least not yet. Oh well, there's no point dwelling on these things...

'Why don't you tell me something about yourself, Laura? How are you doing in school? Have you got a boyfriend?

'No, of course I won't mention this to your parents. If that's the way you feel then you have to follow your heart. That's what I did. People frowned on me, but I didn't care. It was my life, not theirs. Nowadays people don't blink an eye when they see a white girl with a Native American and nor should they. And the time will come when they won't raise an eyebrow when they see two girls together, or even two boys for that matter. You have to be true to yourself and be proud of who you are. *I'm* proud of you, Laura, and if Steve were alive today he'd be proud of you, too. The only advice I'd give you is not to let your girlfriend work in a slate quarry.'

Three years after entering the nursing home, Elizabeth Longtoe died. She bequeathed her entire estate to Laura, and Laura spent the forty dollars on books about Abenaki Indians. A year later, and inspired by her reading, Laura enrolled in college and took a major in anthropology. She read about primitive societies and extended families, and started to wonder why the ties that bound them had become so unfastened in her own world. Surely a society that dumped elderly and inconvenient family members on the doorstep of others had questions to answer. Laura had crossed one such doorstep and been appalled by what she'd seen. There had to be a better way, and she decided that it was up to her to find it. She owed it to Aunt Elizabeth – and to all the other Aunt Elizabeths in the world.

On graduating from college Laura studied for an MBA and then registered for a postgraduate diploma in healthcare administration. Over the next fifteen years she climbed ladders, worked in three different states and four different care homes. Eventually, and in her opinion not before time, she was appointed manager of a struggling care facility in the historic neighbourhood of Washington DC's Georgetown. It was privately owned and enjoyed a poor reputation; a home of last resort. Laura's brief was to turn it around, give it competitive edge. She asked for, and was given, the resources to engineer such an outcome and was then left to her own devices. It was the opportunity she'd been striving for: the chance to put her own ideas into practice!

She started by dismissing those employees she deemed unsuitable, there for the sake of employment – often on minimum wage and with no real command of the English language – and replacing them with fully-qualified care assistants, professionals who were motivated by kindness and consideration. Next she got rid of the smell, an unpleasant potpourri of harsh disinfectant, overly-boiled vegetables and body wastes, and replaced the worn carpets and chairs that the odour had permeated. She contracted a local florist to deliver and maintain large plants and vases of flowers, and paid an electrician to take out and replace the harsh strip lighting.

The home was reborn, and the task now was to bring the residents back to life.

Laura encouraged her team to spend time with the residents and not restrict themselves to simply taking care of their physical needs. And she led by example. Rather than shutting herself in an office, she spent two hours of every day chatting to the people she now described as clients. It was their home away from home, she told them, and it was for them to help make the rules. Even though they were now living in a community, they were still individuals and their opinions mattered. The administration, she said, would listen to them, take on board their concerns and try to implement any suggestions they might make. Together, she told them, they would *make a difference*! (It was a slogan she'd unashamedly plagiarised from a garage forecourt.)

The fortunes of the care home turned: it filled to capacity, there was a waiting list, and its standing in the local community zoomed. It also attracted the interest of a journalist and Laura's interview appeared in the local paper.

'We focus on the dignity of souls rather than the physical and mental indignities that encase them. We treat every person as an individual, allow them choice and encourage independence. We are also conscious that the vast majority of our residents are here not by choice, but by courtesy of infirmity, despairing families or legal rulings. This is their last stop in life, and it is therefore our duty to make this stop as comfortable and enjoyable as is humanly possible.'

It was a mission statement that had read well on paper five years ago, but Laura was now increasingly aware of its gloss. She had, in fact, written the declaration fifteen years prior to coming to Georgetown and solely with Aunt Elizabeth in mind; more importantly, she had also written it well before the white horses of dementia had started to ride into town and trample the increasingly ageing nation underfoot. (Growing *too* old was now a problem in itself.)

It was idealistic, she now realised, fit more for a retirement centre than a care home. Independence? Choice? Who had she been kidding? For the practical running of the home and the residents' own safety there were too many turnings in the road where the administration *had* to roadblock choice. The residents had to get up at a certain time, eat their meals at given times and retire to await the next day at an appointed time. They weren't allowed to leave the building and wander the neighbourhood, and neither could they choose not to take their medicines.

And how could a resident be expected to live an independent life on the inside, having already failed to do so on the outside? And did the residents really want to make their own decisions? The experience of the last five years told her no: choice only confused them, made them anxious. The sad truth was that the only vestige of choice and independence left to them was ownership of the television remote control, and because it was such a sad truth and her idealism reduced to such an absurdity, it became a point of principle for Laura to uphold at all costs: a line in the sand she was unprepared to cross. But then came violence – and then death.

Despite the daily activities organised by the carers, and the entertainers they brought to the home, the focal point for the residents remained the television. It had a soothing and distracting influence on them and they would sit transfixed and becalmed by the changing and colourful images that appeared on its giant screen. They watched films they didn't understand and programmes they couldn't follow. It mattered little if the channel was changed before an item finished; the residents would simply adjust to whatever new programme replaced it and return to their own jumbled thoughts without so much as a skip of a beat. But because television was so central to their lives it became of paramount importance to Laura that they should have the right to control it.

There had always been the occasional squabble between residents over who should have charge of the remote control, but these were rare and always surmountable. More annoying and time consuming for the staff were the occasions when the controls went missing, whether simply misplaced or taken back to a room by one of the residents. But again, such difficulties were rare and surmountable. What hadn't been foreseen was that the remote control could be used as a weapon. Made from metal and ten inches in length, the control weighed approximately ten ounces and in the wrong hands made for an effective baton. This discovery was made by a newly-arrived resident who then hit an eighty-two-year-old woman over the head with it. 'Teach you!' he'd said to her.

Just what he'd been intending to teach the old lady wasn't clear – or ever understood for that matter. Mrs Beauchamp had never before met the man and had been sitting nowhere near the television at the time of the assault. Although the incident had been brought up at the weekly manager's meeting, apart from monitoring the possession of the remote control more closely, it was decided not to take any immediate action. But then death visited the community and stole the life of Mrs Lorna Green from under their very noses.

Mrs Green had been one of the community's more glamorous and popular guests, and it had been fully expected that she would live for at least another ten years. It was therefore a surprise when she keeled over dead in the lounge one evening. It unfolded that Lorna had suffered a heart attack after heroically battling with the ever-lengthening television listings for two hours, and the rights – but mainly the wrongs – of choice again elbowed their way to the fore and this time the owners of the care home became involved. Unnecessary death, they argued, could never be construed as a positive advertisement for a care home.

Laura pondered the problem, wrestled with her conscience, chewed the ballpoint pen some more and stared into space. She missed her appointment with Larry, and Moses' toenails continued to grow. She stared into space again and then stopped. She took the pen from her mouth, tore a sheet of paper from a memo pad and started to write. The good times were about to end.

True to her word, Laura arrived at Larry's house on the Friday evening. She declined his offer of a glass of iced tea and without delay handed him a pair of nail clippers. 'Okay, Larry, let's get started. It's Friday night and I have plans.'

Under her tutelage Larry turned the dog on its back, straddled him and then, holding a paw in one hand, used the guillotine clipper with the other. Moses didn't like his feet being touched and made this clear. 'Be firm with him, Larry – and mind the quick!' Laura said.

'I'm being as fast as I can, Laura. I don't think I can go any faster.'

Laura sighed. 'I'm not asking you to be quick, Larry, I'm telling you to *mind* the quick – the live bit that runs down the centre of the nail, remember? You have to leave at least two millimetres between its end and the end of the nail. That's it... Careful now... You've got it... Okay then, try again.'

It took Larry an hour to complete the task, and once he'd finished Laura told him to make a fuss of Moses. 'Reward him with a treat, Larry. Once he gets used to you handling his feet it will get easier.'

Noticing the large beads of sweat on Larry's brow, Laura figured that he too was probably in need of a treat, and on the spur of the moment invited him to join her and Alice for a bite to eat. Larry had been happy to accept. He couldn't, in fact, remember the last time he'd been invited out to dinner. 'You're sure Alice won't mind?'

'I'm sure she won't. But remember what I said about conversation. Don't just talk about things that interest *you*. Ask Alice about herself.'

By the time they arrived at the restaurant Alice was already sitting at an outside table, flicking through the screen of her smartphone and occasionally smiling. She was younger than Laura by about ten years and dressed in an expensive business suit. Laura introduced them, and a surprised Alice told Larry she was pleased to meet him. Larry said that he too was pleased to meet her and promptly asked how tall she was.

'Five feet five,' she replied, looking at Laura quizzically.

'Larry's trying out as a conversationalist,' Laura explained. 'You're his audition.'

Taking Laura's comment as a sign of encouragement, Larry proceeded to share his own stature (six feet one inch) with Alice, pointing out that both of them, for the United States, were of above average height, her by a half inch and him by three.

'Hah! I always told you I was above average, Laura, and now Larry's confirmed it!'

'I've never once doubted that you were, darling. Now where's the waiter? I need a drink!'

'So do I,' Larry said. 'A long stiff one, too! Trimming Moses' nails has completely drained me.'

The waiter arrived and Larry ordered a large strawberry milkshake, settling for a diet coke after Laura informed him that the restaurant was for grown-ups. She then ordered a carafe of house red for her and Alice to share.

'Cheers!' Laura said, after the glasses were poured. 'Cheers!' Alice and Larry replied in unison. Again remembering Laura's advice, Larry then asked Alice what she'd had for breakfast that morning.

Once the food was on the table Laura started to talk about the crisis at the nursing home. 'I was trying to give the residents a semblance of their old lives back,' she said, 'allow them a say in matters that affect them. Control of the television was all they had left and now they don't even have that. The owners won't allow it. They say it's too dangerous and they use Mrs Green's death to prove their point. I was in the middle of telling them that Lorna's death was an aberration when Mrs Beauchamp wandered into the office with the stitches fresh in her forehead and told them a strange man had tried to kill her with the remote control. Any chance I had of changing their minds went up in a puff of smoke after that. Talk about bad timing!'

Laura waved to one of the waiters and gestured for another carafe of wine.

'So what's happening now? Aren't they allowed to watch television?' Alice asked.

'Not in any real sense. The television listings and remote control have been removed from the lounge and the set's been programmed to receive Christian channels only, so it's Jesus or nothing these days. I just hope to God they don't start sending money to those charlatans. I'm seriously tempted to put a brick through the screen and be done with it!'

'Maybe you've been trying to give them something they don't want,' Alice said. 'Did any of the residents actually suggest any changes they'd like to see in the home?'

Laura thought for a moment. 'Not really,' she said. 'Two old-timers once came to my office and asked if they could watch pornography, but I had to say no. I didn't think it was appropriate. You always have to think of the majority.'

'Is it all right if I say something?' Larry asked.

'Of course it is, but bear in mind we only have an hour of daylight left.'

'Why don't you play them DVDs of television shows they grew up with, programmes from their younger years they can identify with? You could even operate the DVD player from your office, and if you play consecutive episodes you'd only have to change the disc every few hours. I've got box sets of quite a few of them and I'd be happy to lend them to you.'

Laura put down her glass and considered Larry's suggestion. 'You know, Larry,' she said, 'I think you might have hit upon something there.'

She took a pen and small notebook from her handbag and opened the pad at a fresh page. 'Okay,' she said. 'Let's give this some thought. As a rule of thumb I'd say the residents were most active in the decades of the fifties through the eighties, so let's start by choosing one programme from each of those four decades.'

'Well, let me know when you get to the eighties, because I wasn't even born until then,' Alice said.

As Laura herself hadn't been born until 1970 it was left to Larry to decide the first two programmes. From the fifties he chose *I Love Lucy* and from the sixties *The Dick Van Dyke Show*. 'Those should cheer them up,' he said.

Both had been comedies and Laura suggested they choose a family drama from the seventies. Having grown up on a farm she'd always had a fondness for *Little House on the Prairie* and Larry had no objections to this. 'One of Helen's favourites,' he'd commented.

With Alice now participating the three of them spent more time discussing which programme from the eighties they should choose, a decade they could all remember with greater clarity than the preceding three and consequently a decade that presented them with a wider range of choice. After much debate, some of it heated, Laura decided to go with Larry's choice of *Murder She Wrote* rather than *Hill Street Blues*, which had been Alice's. Larry, after all, was nearer in age to the demographic they were trying to cater for and so his views counted for more.

Murder She Wrote revolved around a character called Jessica Fletcher, a widow who wore sensible shoes and had hair that didn't move. She wrote mystery books under the name of JB Fletcher and in her spare time solved murders, which seemingly happened every time she stepped out of her front door. She had friends – whose hair also didn't move – coming out of her ears and made new ones every episode. She didn't drive a car but always travelled first class and stayed in the best hotels. Everyone she met was an admirer of her work, claiming to have read all her books and be her biggest fan. She didn't let all this praise go to her head though, and kept her feet firmly on the ground. And as Larry pointed out, the actress playing the role of Jessica Fletcher, although slightly bug-eyed, had the most winning of smiles and was the epitome of decency and optimism.

'I want it on record that this isn't my choice!' Alice said. 'There are too many people wearing wigs in that show, and the central character's more like a warm-up act for the Second Coming than she is a real person. But if you two think that the residents will be happy to watch an affirmative action programme for washed-up actors then go ahead and suit yourselves. I still think you'd be better off choosing *Hill Street Blues*.'

'If I was choosing something for my own viewing then I'd agree with you. But I'm not. This isn't what we're doing, Alice. The residents would find *Hill Street Blues* too gritty and violent, and not at all life-affirming.'

'For God's sake, Laura, there's an act of murder in every episode of *Murder She Wrote*! How can you suppose that this programme's life-affirming and *Hill Street Blues* isn't?'

Larry quickly pointed out that the murders in *Murder She Wrote* were always bloodless and tastefully executed, and more than compensated for by the cheerful theme music. He also thought that the show's distinctly middle class ambience would lift the spirits of any resident who might have been adversely affected by watching a poor family eke out a living in rural Minnesota for 211 consecutive episodes. 'My late wife used to love the show,' he added.

It was difficult for Alice to argue with the views of a dead woman so she gave up trying. She thought, however, that she too would prefer to be dead than have to watch *Murder She Wrote* for the rest of her life.

At that moment her phone rang. She looked at the screen and excused herself from the table. 'I'm sorry, this is a call I have to take,' she said.

Alice had been distracted by her phone all evening, constantly checking it for messages and postings, and occasionally sending texts. 'That damned phone!' Laura muttered. 'I love the girl to bits but that phone of hers drives me crazy. It's the one thing we fall out over. I keep telling her it's rude to leave your phone on when you're talking to someone, but does she listen? I despair of technology, Larry, I really do. In my experience it fragments society rather than holding it together.'

'A bit like central heating, really,' Larry mused.

Having no idea what Larry meant by that statement, but for once interested in something he might have to say on a subject, Laura asked him to explain.

'Well, in times before central heating there was only one warm room in a house and that was where the family used to congregate; they'd sit around an open fire talking to each other or playing games, parents and children together. Central heating changed all that because the system warmed *all* the rooms in a house. Most people don't realise this, but it was the Romans who pioneered central heating. They built...'

'Larry!' Laura said. 'I don't want a history lesson. Stick to the point! Which is what?'

'That once people installed central heating systems in their homes there wasn't any practical need for the family to stay together in the same room any more. Sons and daughters started to spend more time in their own rooms and away from their parents. Of course, you could argue the same thing about television.'

Laura gave him a warning glance.

'No, this is relevant, Laura, because for a time televisions were the equivalent of open fires – another reason for the whole family to gather in the same room. Once televisions became cheap, though, and people more affluent, children were given televisions for their own rooms. I wish now that we'd never given Rutherford and Grover their own sets because once we did, the only times we saw them were at mealtimes or on their way to the bathroom. I think that's when we started to drift apart, and I'm sure it was the same for other families. And when families drift apart, so too does society. It goes back to what you were saying about technology, Laura, how it fragments rather than holds it together.'

Laura nodded and quietly murmured her agreement.

'And what with the number of television channels there are today and those gadgets that allow people to watch what they want when they want, it's not surprising there's little common experience left. I remember the days when people at the university used to gather around the water cooler and discuss what they'd seen on television the previous night, but that doesn't happen much anymore. And as most people carry a bottle of water with them today I suppose it's only a matter of time before even the water cooler becomes obsolete. Did you know that they sold bottled water in Boston as early as 1767?'

'No, I didn't, but the rest of what you say interests me. I grew up with central heating and a television in my room so I've always taken those things for granted. But you're right: they have impacted society – and in much the same way as the digital revolution's affecting people today. I'm no Luddite, Larry – and I'd be the last person to give up my computer and mobile phone – but it does concern me how today's technology has taken over the lives of so many people. Rather than them controlling technology, it's the technology that controls them. It really depresses me when I see young people walking with their heads down, reading screens and oblivious to their surroundings – the people they pass and the beauty of the buildings and monuments. They may as well be living in a windowless cubicle.'

Larry nodded in agreement. 'It wouldn't surprise me in years to come if the residents in your home don't arrive with tablets and smartphones. They'll probably stop talking to each other and just sit around checking their pages on Facebook or reading tweets. What a sad old world that would be.'

'I doubt very much if they'd still have the know-how, but if they did then you're right: it would be a sad old world. A sad old world for sad old people. Do you have a Facebook account?'

'I did once, but I could never get anyone to befriend me. After a whole year I still had only one friend and that was Helen. There seemed little point in having an account when I could talk to Helen at home.'

'Alice has 430 friends,' Laura said. 'Can you believe that?'

'Boy! She *must* be popular. What does she do for a living?'

'Maybe that's a question you could ask her when she gets back to the table. You already know how tall she is and what she had for breakfast this morning, so this might well be your next best query.'

While Laura and Larry worried about the fragmentation of society at large, Alice agonised on the phone over fragmentation of a more personal nature: Repo's brain.

Alice and Laura had been together for four years. They met after Laura contacted a local recruitment agency specialising in healthcare, and it was Alice who'd supplied the nursing home with many of its new appointments. Their professional relationship became casual, and within a year they were living together in civil partnership with a nine-year-old Golden Retriever called Repo. The dog was Laura's, but became an integral part of Alice's life, too. They doted on Repo, revolved their lives around him; took him to the best vet and spent a small fortune on premium dog foods. The care and love they lavished on Repo secured his physical advance into old age, but did little to affect the physiological changes taking place in his brain.

At first, Repo's increasingly long daytime sleeps were seen by Alice and Laura as no more than a symptom of age: the dog was old, the dog was slowing down. Similarly, they interpreted his decreased activity as a sign of advancing arthritis rather than anything more complicated, and his lack of response to the calling of his name simply an indication of hearing loss. The possibility that something more sinister might be at play only struck Alice after she found Repo wandering aimlessly around the lounge in the early hours of one morning, strangely always taking the same route. She mentioned this to Laura, but Laura was unconcerned. 'He's always been crazy,' she'd laughed.

Alice's concern, however, grew. Working from home two days of the week and returning other days at lunchtime to feed Repo, she saw more of him than Laura, who was tied up at the nursing home and often stayed late. She'd look up from what she was doing and find Repo staring blankly into space or gawping at a wall; she'd return to the house some days and find him stuck in a corner or helplessly wedged in the legs of a dining room chair; and other days come home to a wet patch on the carpet.

'He's probably got a urinary infection,' Laura said. 'That

would explain his confusion, too. It should be a simple enough matter to treat.'

Alice, however, was unconvinced, and took advantage of her visit to the vet to discuss Repo's changing behaviour. 'It's not just a matter of him pissing on the carpet, Jim. He genuinely looks lost.'

Jim listened, nodded his head and made grunting noises. 'I don't think there's anything to worry about, Alice, but just to be on the safe side I think we should give Repo a complete overhaul.'

While Alice waited in the reception room, Jim filled small phials with Repo's blood, did ultrasounds and took X-rays. By the time he rejoined Alice he had his suspicions but remained tight-lipped. 'I should have the results by Friday. As soon as I get them I'll give you a call.'

On the evening of the designated day, Alice's phone rang. She excused herself from the table and moved away from the restaurant's al fresco dining area.

'Sorry for the hour, Alice, but it's been a hectic day. You okay to talk?'

Alice said she was; asked him to give her the news straight.

'We found brain lesions. I'm afraid Repo's suffering from Canine Cognitive Dysfunction.'

'Not that straight, Jim. I don't even know what that is!'

'In layman's terms it's known as doggie dementia or old dog syndrome. It's the canine equivalent of Alzheimer's.'

'Jesus, Jim! How am I going to tell Laura that? Repo's her child!'

'It's not the end of the world, Alice. Repo's world might be changing but he's not going to keel over dead anytime soon. One out of three dogs his age has CCD, and there's a drug on the market now that's proved successful in treating some cases. If that doesn't work we'll try behavioural interventions. But like I say, it's not the end of the world. Apart from the dementia Repo's in perfect shape. Why don't you and Laura stop by the office next week and I'll explain things in more detail?'

After the conversation ended Alice stood for a while, wondering whether to mention the news to Laura now or wait until they returned home. She decided it would be better to tell her while Larry was with them. He was a strange old bird, but might well have something to say on the subject. He certainly had plenty to say on every other subject.

Alice rejoined them at the table and topped up her wine glass. She carefully rehearsed the words in her head, took a deep breath and parted her lips…

'What do you do for a living, Alice?' Larry asked.

3

The Dog Park

'Well I never, Moses,' Larry said. 'It says here that you're descended from a wolf!'

The book Larry was reading was a basic primer and tended toward reduction: Moses' genes were more likely a mixture of wolf, jackal and coyote. But Larry was right in supposing that Moses' appearance and behaviour bore little resemblance to those of his wild ancestors.

According to the primer the relationship between man and dog had started some 14–17,000 years ago when the first wolves were domesticated. Although by nature hunters, wolves were quite happy to scavenge: easy pickings in their book being just as tasty as the more dangerous ones they had to run to ground, and which could be found in abundance close to where humans made their camps. Consequently they started to locate their dens nearer these encampments and a symbiotic relationship developed. By eating their discarded leftovers wolves provided humans with a daily garbage collection, and the commotion they made whenever a wild animal or group of strangers approached the camp also made the lives of their two-legged neighbours safer.

Not all wolves, however, were capable of adapting to this new world order of co-existence and the more aggressive and threatening ones were killed. Only the docile and friendly were ever interbred, and it was humans who determined which of their characteristics were passed from one generation to the next. Over time, and through a process of selection, distinct breeds of dog came into being: some useful for guarding, some for herding or hauling and others for hunting (dogs were always expected to work for a living).

It was only after the Second World War that dogs became household pets in the modern sense; brought indoors, commoditised and made a member of the family. They were now fed premium foods and taken to vets, given their own beds to sleep in and toys to play with, and all that was expected of them in return was their companionship. In the conventional sense, a dog's life was no more *a dog's life*.

'I don't like the sound of this at all, Moses,' Larry said. He'd just read a short section on sexuality and learned that dogs were a lot more promiscuous than wolves – a fact that probably explained why there were now 400 million of them in the world.

Larry bent down and took Moses' head in his hands and looked him square in the eyes. 'Now then, young man: I'm counting on you to be on your best behaviour when we go to the park tomorrow. It's our first visit and we have to make a good impression. Miss Laura's a respectable woman and she's not going to take kindly to either of us if she sees you fooling around with another dog. Now do we have an understanding?' (It was doubtful they did. Moses might one day understand 165 of Larry's words, but at this time in his life his vocabulary was limited and certainly didn't include the phrase *fooling*

around. All Moses could surmise from Larry's tone was that
he was the most wonderful dog in the world.)

Larry and Moses had been set to go to the park the previous
Saturday but Laura postponed the visit. News that Repo was
suffering from dementia had thrown her into a spin; more of
a spin, in fact, than if she'd been told that one of her elderly
relatives had been diagnosed with the condition. Although
she coped with dementia at the nursing home on a daily
basis – it was par for the course, something she took in her
stride – the revelation that it had crossed her own doorstep
came as a shock, especially when the sufferer was her own
surrogate child. (Despite Repo's advancing years, Laura still
looked upon him as an innocent.) Immediately, she'd insisted
on returning to the vet with Alice as soon as possible, and
the only available appointment all three could make was the
morning of the following Saturday, the day they usually went
to the park.

For a time, Laura wondered if she'd been in denial these
past few months, purposely turning a blind eye to patterns
of behaviour she would have readily identified had Repo
been an aged man. After some consideration she decided she
hadn't: after all, she'd never even heard of CCD or known
that a dog could actually sustain dementia. The diagnosis was
so out of left field that she wondered if Alice had somehow
misunderstood Jim or, in her own mind, overly dramatised
the situation – which Alice often did.

Although Laura envied Alice her zest for life she was forever
puzzled by her partner's need to enliven it unnecessarily: life,
it seemed, always had to be more eventful than it actually
was. A straightforward disagreement between spouses, for
instance, would be construed by Alice as a couple teetering

on the brink of divorce, while a neighbour's downsizing of car would just as quickly – and mistakenly – be interpreted as a sign of impending bankruptcy. And to Alice's way of thinking a person never simply fell ill, but went straight to the door of death and hovered there uncertainly until – and against all odds – they miraculously recovered.

Laura could still remember the day she'd bumped into Travis Laidley on the street, a man in his mid-forties who'd once worked as a volunteer at the organic food store they frequented and whose bones, according to Alice, were now so fused that he even had trouble moving his littlest finger. Yet there Travis had been, dressed in shorts and T-shirt, jogging towards her at a lick and glancing at his wristwatch. 'You okay, Travis?' she'd asked cautiously. 'Never better, Laura,' he'd replied cheerily. 'I'm on track for a personal best!' When she'd mentioned the encounter to Alice, Alice had riposted that if Travis hadn't been kidding her then he was certainly kidding himself. 'By the end of the year he'll be in a wheelchair, Laura. You mark my words.' Three years later and Travis was still jogging through the neighbourhood.

And Alice brought the same melodrama to her own life. Other people's deaths became *her* close encounters with death. Someone falling off a platform and being hit by a train at Dupont Circle was, but for the grace of God, her death: 'Jesus, Laura! I was standing on that platform only last week. That could have been me!' And another time, after a tornado had swept through Oklahoma not five miles from where she'd been driving just three years previously, Alice had again claimed the disaster as yet another of her narrow escapes from death. 'This is getting scary, Laura. I'm either a marked person or a cat with nine lives. How weird is this?'

'How weird are you?' Laura had smiled at the time. Now, however, she took comfort from her partner's weirdness and, until the visit to the vet proved opposite, dared to believe that Alice had got it wrong.

Repo was put on a course of Anipryl: one 1.0mg tablet per day for two months; if after this time there was no noticeable improvement in his behaviour the dosage would be doubled. 'It's early days yet, Laura, but Repo's in good hands,' the vet said. 'All being well he'll be as right as rain in no time.' He then handed her the bill.

Laura glanced at the invoice. 'I don't think you've charged for the clichés, Jim.'

The vet smiled, took back the statement and added two cents.

The day of Larry's visit to the park dawned. He woke early and turned the radio to an easy listening station. Percy Faith and his Orchestra were playing *Theme from a Summer Place*, one of his favourites. He stared at the ceiling and pictured the day ahead: Laura and Alice calling for him at eleven, the three of them driving to the park and there being introduced to new people. He'd take an interest in them, listen to what *they* had to say and not talk over or at them: 'Speak only when spoken to, Larry, and keep your answers short,' he reminded himself. Who knew, with Moses as his wingman, there was every chance he might make new friends. The day, in fact, could well turn out to be the start of that new life Laura had talked about.

Strangers in the Night started to play and Larry decided it was time to switch off the radio and climb into the shower. He liked Sinatra's voice but was as unsure of the singer as J

Edgar Hoover had been. He could imagine Dr Young palling around with Ol' Blue Eyes though, sharing dirty stories and drinking too much, dropping cigarette butts in the street and then shouting rude words through his letter box at four in the morning. No wonder Helen hadn't liked him.

Larry ran the water and climbed into the shower. He used a bar of soap rather than the gel that Helen had favoured, and then applied a small amount of conditioning shampoo to what was left of his hair. 'What's the condition?' he asked the bottle, as he did every morning. 'You'll wash my hair in return for what? What do you *want* from me?' It wasn't the funniest of jokes, but it was his joke and it always made him laugh. It was good to start the day with a chuckle.

He dried himself on a clean towel, shaved and dressed and then went downstairs to prepare breakfast. Moses was awake but still in his basket, unmindful of the day's promise; he raised himself slowly, stretched and then padded to his feeding bowl in the kitchen.

Larry couldn't decide whether to have cereal or toast that morning. He usually alternated: cereal one morning and toast the next. The previous day he'd eaten toast so today, and by rights, he should have eaten cereal, but for some reason the prospect didn't appeal. He hummed and hawed for a while and then looked at his wristwatch. 'Pancakes!' he suddenly announced, 'Gosh darn it, Moses, I'm going to have pancakes for breakfast!'

Laura and Alice arrived ten minutes late. Laura, who was driving, honked the horn while Alice climbed out of the station wagon and opened the tailgate. 'Come on, Larry, we're running late,' she said. 'Move that skinny butt of yours and let's get this show on the road!'

Larry was well aware they were running late: he'd been sitting on the front step with Moses for the past fifteen minutes! He'd even started to wonder if they'd forgotten about him or that he'd got the day wrong. 'Be right there, Alice,' he said.

He walked briskly to the open tailgate and Alice gave him a hand lifting Moses into the wagon. The dogs sniffed each other, wagged their tails, and once the vehicle started to move settled into a companionable silence verging on sleep.

'Sorry we're late, Larry,' Laura said. 'Repo got himself stuck in some chair legs just as we were leaving.'

'Oh dear,' Larry said, 'I'm sorry to hear that, Laura. I suppose it's going to be some time before you know if the pills are working?'

'Mmmm,' Laura murmured, and reached for Alice's hand.

Larry was sure the ensuing silence was companionable, but it appeared to be verging on tears. It was up to him, he decided, to lighten the mood and introduce a new topic of conversation. 'Guess what I had for breakfast this morning?' he asked.

Alice turned to look at him and after only a moment's pause said: 'Pancakes.'

'How on earth did you know that?'

'You've got syrup on your shirt.'

'Oh shoot!' Larry said. 'It's one of my best shirts, too.'

Alice stared at him. 'Your best? How long have you had it?'

'Not long,' Larry said. 'No more than ten years. Helen bought it for me at Walmart one Saturday.' He searched in his trouser pocket for a handkerchief and came up empty. 'I don't suppose either of you has a spare tissue, do you?'

'You can have this one,' Alice said, handing him a crumpled

tissue she found in the glove compartment. 'I doubt it will do much good, though: the fibres will just stick to the syrup.'

Alice was proved right and Larry gave up. 'I don't suppose we have time to go back to my house, do we? I feel a bit uncomfortable being introduced to new people with a stain on my shirt.'

'You suppose right,' Laura said. 'And besides, we're almost there now.'

They'd been in the car less than ten minutes, and much of that time had been spent idling at stop signs or stationary at traffic lights. It dawned on Larry that the park must be only walking distance from his house and he wondered why he'd never known this. Well, for one, he reasoned, he'd never had a dog before – excepting for Loop, of course, who'd always taken *him* for walks – and secondly, because they were now on the other side of Wisconsin in a neighbourhood he seldom visited, especially after the incident with the shopping trolley.

The car started to slow and an open area came into view on the left. 'There's a space there, Laura – behind the Humvee!' Alice pointed. Laura braked, carefully reversed into the opening and turned off the ignition.

'How much gas do you suppose one of those things guzzles?' Alice asked.

'I have absolutely no idea,' Laura sighed.

'About nine miles to the gallon,' Larry said.

'Nine? Jesus! Who can afford to run a monster like that?'

'Well, rich people, I suppose,' Larry said, wondering if he was falling into a trap by answering so simple a question. 'And as DC has the highest median per capita income of anywhere in the country there's a good chance that a lot of them live here. There's a guy on my street who could afford to fill the tank of a Humvee every day of his life if he wanted to.'

'I don't think it's a question of whether a person can afford the gas, Larry,' Laura replied. 'It's more a matter of whether the planet can spare it. Now, come on, let's get the dogs out and go to the park. Who knows, from what you say we might even meet some rich people there, but the chances are they won't be my friends!'

Volta Park occupied a block of prime real estate in the West Village of Georgetown. It had started life as a place for dead people – fallen soldiers and members of a local Presbyterian Church – but towards the end of the nineteenth century the bodies were exhumed and the cemetery transformed into a park for the living. Alger Hiss, the accused Soviet spy, had walked there, John F Kennedy, a future president of the United States, had played touch football there, and Herbert 'Flight Time' Lang, a Harlem Globetrotter, had shot hoops there.

The park was divided into two spaces. The stretch backing on to 33rd St was split into tennis and basketball courts, a children's play area and an outdoor swimming pool, while the larger space, fronting 34th, was open and grassy, intended for little league games and the exercise of dogs. Most grounds in the area enforced leash laws, but here dogs were allowed to run free and consequently the park had become a popular destination for owners. There were occasions, in fact, when a visitor might count as many as two dozen dogs. This Saturday, however, the day of Larry's inaugural visit, there were only six.

The three of them entered the park through an opening in the ornamental iron fence and walked down a grassy slope towards a picnic table backing on to the tennis courts.

Two large people were sitting there: a man in his early fifties sporting a severe crew cut and appearing to have been hewn from a slab of granite, and a woman in her late thirties with Shirley Temple curls and a red ribbon in her hair who, less gloriously, looked to have been moulded from a tub of beef dripping. Two dogs were playing close by: a sable long-coated Chihuahua weighing no more than five pounds and a giant mahogany-coloured Dogue de Bordeaux twenty times heavier.

Repo started to bark and Laura unleashed him. Immediately he bounded in the direction of the picnic table but then stopped, seemingly unsure of where he was or what his intention had been.

'Hi girls,' the woman called out. 'And who's this cute little boy you've brought with you?'

'It's Larry,' Larry called back. 'Larry MacCabe. I'm an emeritus professor of history at Georgetown University.'

'She means Moses,' Alice explained. 'I don't think you qualify as a boy these days.'

Larry blushed and started to blink. This wasn't the start he'd been hoping for.

The woman approached them and bent down to fondle Moses. She then stood and held out her hand to Larry. 'I'm Delores – Delores Bobo,' she said, breathing heavily. 'And if I'm not mistaken you've brought Israel to see us.'

'Israel?' Larry replied, perplexed by the question. 'No, his name's Moses, Delores. I think Israel must be someone else's dog.'

Here Laura stepped into the conversation. 'Originally Moses *was* called Israel,' she explained. 'And you can blame that clown over there for the name change,' indicating the man with the crew cut. 'When Moses first came to the park he was a puppy and forever wandering off and Mrs Eisler – the woman whose dog he was – used to call for him. She'd shout: "Israel! Where's Israel? Does anyone know where Israel is?" And Tank would reply that it was in the Eastern Mediterranean, bordered by Lebanon, Syria and Jordan and then laugh his stupid head off. That type of joke is as old as the hills and once it's been told it's been told; after that it's just annoying. But did Tank see it this way? No! He went on and on with the same stupid comment and then, to cap it all, the kids in the park started to shout the same thing. The poor woman was in her nineties by then, confused enough as it was, and all this malarkey just confused her more. It was her daughter – the woman I got Moses from – who persuaded her to change the name.'

'I'm sorry, Larry,' Delores said. 'I must be getting as confused as Mrs Eisler. I'd forgotten all about the name change. Anyway, it's good to see him again and know that he's found a new home.'

The man, who Laura had referred to as Tank, disentangled his legs from the picnic table and came to join them. 'Did I hear my name being taken in vain?' he asked.

'I was telling Larry about the stupid things you say. And don't you dare start calling Moses Israel again. You've done enough damage as it is. I still find it surprising that the State Department gave you a job. I thought they recruited people with discretion.'

'Don't you worry on that score, darling. I'm a reformed character these days. So tell me, how's Retro doing?'

'If you call Repo by that name again I'll slap that stupid face of yours, Tank Newbold. You should pray to God that

Sherman never gets CCD. You wouldn't be making fun of the situation if that happened.'

'Sherman's not going to fall victim to any disease,' Tank laughed. 'He can't afford to. The day he starts costing me money is the day I have him put down, and he knows this. We have an understanding. Ha!'

Tank then turned to Larry, who had been a bystander through these exchanges, occasionally holding out his hand to shake Tank's and then withdrawing it when Tank had failed to notice. But Tank had. 'You some kind of slot machine, Larry? One of those one-armed bandits?'

'Compared to you he's the jackpot,' Alice said, who had also taken affront at Tank calling Repo Retro.

Tank again laughed but this time shook Larry's hand. 'You wouldn't know it, but we're all good friends here, Larry. A word of warning though: don't try any guy humour on these broads – it's a waste of breath.'

Larry, who had no idea what guy humour was, said he wouldn't, but asked Tank if he'd like to hear a joke he'd made up about hair shampoo. He then told the joke which aroused in his audience no more than a unified blank expression.

'Tell me, Larry,' Tank asked. 'Has anyone ever laughed when you've told them that joke?'

Larry had to admit that no one had, but here Delores chipped in and said that although she hadn't understood the joke she had a feeling that it *was* funny, and that if only she'd followed her parents' advice and gone to college as they'd wanted her to, she might very well have laughed out loud. And then, fortunately, she changed the subject entirely.

'I lost two pounds this week, girls. I think this new diet's really working.'

'Good for you, Delores. Keep that up and you'll be a new person in no time.'

'But still fat,' Tank interjected. 'What you need, Delores, is a five-year plan, like the Soviets and Chinese used to have; either that, or go and live in India for a year. And it's no use you rolling your eyes like that, Alice. You women are all the same. You never say boo to a goose. Instead of telling Delores the truth – that she's a cascade of fat and likely to die of a heart attack or lose a foot to diabetes if she doesn't do something about it – you give her a bunch of life-affirming compliments that will end up killing her. You ever hear the expression "cruel to be kind"? As her friends, that's how we have to be. You should be encouraging her to do some exercise – and you could start by walking to work, Delores. The museum's not two miles from where you live. What do you think, Larry?'

Larry was hoping that Tank was referring to the Soviet and Chinese five-year plans. He could talk all day on those subjects if wanted to – even India, come to think of it. But surprisingly, he understood that he was being asked to comment on a woman's weight, something he was reluctant to do, especially after Delores had been kind enough to almost laugh at his joke.

'That's a difficult one, Tank. My own wife, Helen, never had a weight problem and so I have no experience in these matters. I think she might have had a drinking problem, though – if that's of any help.'

Laura looked at Larry with what could only be described as a look of puzzled pride. She too had been expecting him to launch into a detailed account of Soviet five-year plans and when he hadn't, but instead revealed information of a personal nature, she felt inordinately proud of her new protégé.

'It does help, Larry,' Delores said, 'and thank you for sharing this.' She then went on to explain that addiction wasn't a life choice but a disease; that some people became addicted to food in the same way others became addicted to drink, drugs, gambling or even shopping. And none of it was their fault. It was a condition they were born with. Daily life for them was a struggle and not always successful. (As if to prove this point Delores took a half-eaten bar of chocolate from her pocket and appeared to swallow it.)

'I've tried one diet after another, Larry, but even when I do watch the calories I still end up putting weight on. It just doesn't seem fair.'

'You've probably got a slow metabolism,' Alice said. 'Or a thyroid condition,' Laura added. 'Or maybe you're a cormorant,' Tank said. 'Maybe you should go to the zoo and get yourself checked out.'

'What on earth do you mean by that, Tank? That's just silly! Larry, you're an intelligent man, do you know what he's talking about?' Delores asked.

Larry, who for once in his life had been happy not to be part of a conversation, answered reluctantly. 'Well, because a cormorant's a seabird with a big appetite, some people use the word as, well, as a euphemism for a glutton.'

'Look, Dolores, all I'm saying is that you're as likely to be a bird as suffering from some disease! That's just psychobabble. Every person has to take responsibility for their own life. You got yourself on this hook and only you can get yourself off it. You're the size you are because you eat too much – and probably the wrong foods – and you don't do enough exercise. Any doctor will tell you that. You have to stop making excuses and do something about it. I'm telling you this as your friend.

And Laura and Alice should be telling you the same thing. Isn't that right, Larry?'

Larry hadn't felt less like talking than at any other time in his life. Argument and discord always discomfited him. The worst thing about academic life had been the monthly departmental meetings when members of one faction would squabble with those of another over seemingly trivial matters. Larry had joined no faction – hadn't, in fact, been asked to – and would, in most votes, abstain rather than take one side and risk offending another – a practice that had endeared him to no one. How, he wondered, could he answer such a question without antagonising either Tank or Delores? He'd come to the park to make friends not enemies 'Well...' he started to say.

'Leave Larry out of this, Tank – and you too, Delores,' Laura said. 'This is his first day at the park so let's try and make it an enjoyable one. And Larry, you can let Moses off his leash now. He can have an enjoyable day, too.'

Larry did as he was told, relieved not to be answering the question, and Moses ran to the far end of the grassy park where Repo, Sherman and Button, the Chihuahua, were playing. The dogs sniffed each other, jumped up at each other, play fought and took turns chasing one another. How easily dogs made friends, Larry thought. If only friendship for him had been this easy.

The four of them moved to the picnic table and sat down on the attached benches. 'I don't know whether you know this,' Larry said, 'but if dogs were humans they'd vary in height from between two and thirty-one feet.'

'Wow!' Delores said. 'I didn't know that! I'm going to tell that to Petey. I know – why don't we play a game and take it in turns to say something interesting about dogs that the rest of us might not know?'

'Dogs see things in slow motion,' Tank said. 'That's why they're good at catching Frisbees and balls.'

'Dogs hear things four times further away than a human and twice the pitch,' Laura said.

'Dogs have a sense of smell forty times stronger than a human's,' Alice said. 'They can smell events months after they've happened – that's why they're good at finding missing people.'

'Dogs are colour-blind but they can see blues and yellows,' Delores said. 'Your turn again, Larry.'

Larry thought hard but drew a blank.

'A dog has four legs,' Tank said, who was losing interest in the game as fast as Larry's knowledge was running out. 'And Repo's got three of his stuck in that picnic table over there.'

It was Alice who went to Repo's rescue, and in the lull that followed Tank took a cigar from a leather case and proceeded to light it. A cloud of thick pungent smoke filled the air and Delores started to cough in theatrical disapproval.

'Don't give me any shit over this, Delores. If you felt so strongly about tobacco then you wouldn't work where you do. It's your guys that set the ball rolling.'

'Delores works at the National Museum of the American Indian,' Laura told Larry.

'You know as well as I do, Tank, that the Indians smoked tobacco for religious reasons. It was a sacred plant to them, a gift from God and not something to be used recreationally. And I've never heard of any Indian getting addicted to tobacco like you are.'

'I'm no more addicted to tobacco than you are to broccoli!

I have one cigar a week and that's it – and always at the park. And what's more I'm doing you a service. You ever notice how many mosquitoes there are in this park since people in the neighbourhood started having their yards sprayed? This smoke keeps them at bay, keeps us all safe from their bites. You should be thanking me, Dolores: I'm risking my lungs for your well-being.'

It wasn't the mosquitoes that were worrying Larry at this moment, but the wasp that had been attracted to the syrup stain on his shirt. When he'd told Dr Young that a wasp sting was a lot worse than a dog's bite, he hadn't been joking with the plastic surgeon. As a child his face had once swollen to the size of a small pumpkin after a wasp sting, and though his body was more attuned to the venom than it had been, he still lived in dread of being stung. He whisked at the buzzing insect, tried to swat it and then panicked.

'What's wrong, Larry?' Delores asked. 'Is the smoke bothering you, too?'

Larry had no time to answer. He jumped from the table and ran towards the edge of the park, flailing his arms and zigzagging like a man in the throes of St Vitus' dance. Eventually he came to a halt under the branches of a large Osage orange tree, and once certain the wasp was no longer following him, sat down on the grass and drew breath. He was on the point of returning to his companions when he caught sight of a bucket of fresh sand close to the fence and the temptation proved too great. The unpleasantness of the wasp attack had weakened his resolve, left him exhausted and – on such an important day in his life – in need of a pick-me-up. He looked around to make sure no one was watching and casually walked to the bucket. Once there, he bent down in front of it and pretended to retie a loose shoelace. After glancing behind him one more time he reached into the bucket, took a quick pinch of sand and placed the grit in his mouth. Immediately the euphoria of old returned, but it lasted no more than a moment, blown to smithereens by a voice out of nowhere: 'What you eating sand for, Mister? That's for the Little Leaguers.'

Larry turned but saw no one. The closest person was more than twenty yards away and not even looking in his direction. 'I'm up here,' the voice said, 'just above...' And then there was a crashing sound and a man came hurtling from the tree, landing no more than three feet from where Larry was kneeling.

The man groaned. 'That tree's stupid!' he whined. 'Ain't no reason to its branches. You hear that, tree? Your branches are dumb – D U M M!'

Larry was in a state of shock, unable to speak but at least now on his feet. He looked down on the man who appeared to be about the age of Grover and Rutherford. He wore a short-sleeved shirt buttoned to his neck and a pair of trousers that at one time would have belonged to a suit. The man's complexion was pallid and his arms white. He had short blonde hair, thinning at the crown, and a small snub nose with wide nostrils. His frame was slender and his height no more than five feet eight inches.

'Are, are you all right?' Larry stammered. 'Can I help in any way?'

'I'm fine, Mister. Ain't the first time I've fallen out of a tree and it won't be the last. Happens every dang time I climb one. I know how to land these days, though – haven't broked a bone in six years. Did you see me do that roll like those parachute men do?' His speech was slow, deliberate and hopelessly ungrammatical, and his facial animation was dictated by a desire to conceal two dead teeth in his upper jaw. He talked with his mouth almost closed, his lips contorted in a downward arc. His manner, though, was now mild and Larry's initial disquiet subsided. The man climbed to his feet and held out his hand. 'My name is Wayne,' he said. 'What's yours?'

'It's Larry,' Larry said. 'Larry MacCabe.'

'You're a lot older than me, Mr MacCabe, but if you let me call you Larry then you can call me Wayne and not Mr Trout. That okay with you?'

Larry told him that this would be fine, but that his title – if he was interested – was Professor and not Mister.

'Man! I ain't never met no professor before. Met plenty of doctors in my time, but never no professor. You must be one of them clever people. Tell me something, professor: what's a clever man like you eating sand for? Ain't normal, is it?'

'It isn't, Wayne, it's anything but. I wasn't eating sand, though. It might have looked as if I was, but I wasn't. I'd been sucking a mint and it dropped into the bucket and I was just retrieving it. I hate waste.'

Larry's ad-lib struck a chord with Wayne. If it was one thing Wayne understood, it was mints. They were his favourite candy, and if he'd dropped a mint in a bucket of sand he'd have retrieved it too.

'People say I ain't right in my mind, but I am,' Wayne said. 'And I don't eat sand, neither. Do you have another mint, Larry? One you could give me? I like mints.'

'It was my last one,' Larry lied, relieved that Wayne had bought his story. 'Maybe next time.'

'You with the Dog People?' Wayne asked, pointing to Laura and the others.

'Yes, I suppose I am,' Larry said with pride. 'I came with Laura and Alice. That's my dog over there, the Basset Hound.'

'Miss Laura's nice. She's kind to me. Gives me mints all the time. The big man though, he scares me. He don't smile much and sometimes he says things that hurt people and then laughs his head off. He's never once given me a mint and I've seen him sucking them.'

He looked at his watch. 'Jeepers Creepers, Larry, I got to go. People going to be wondering where I'm at.'

He then went behind a thick bush and retrieved a small battered handcart. 'Next time you come to the park bring some mints with you, will you? I like mints.' He then set off for the gap in the fence, pulling the cart behind him.

'I see you met Wayne,' Laura said once he'd returned to the picnic table. 'What were the two of you talking about?'

'Mints mostly,' Larry said. 'He scared me half to death when he came crashing out of that tree. It seems strange for a person to climb a tree when they don't know how to climb down one. He had a cart with him too. What does he need a cart for?'

'Probably his meds,' Tank said.

'Don't start on Wayne again, Tank,' Laura said. 'He suffers from challenges that you and I luckily don't.'

'What kind of challenges?' Larry asked. 'He's not dangerous, is he?'

'Wayne wouldn't harm a fly,' Laura assured him. 'The best I can figure is that he suffers from a neurological disorder that affects his coordination. But there's more to it than that, something deeper. A stress disorder, maybe. He's in his thirties now, but talking to him is like talking to a small boy who just happens to shave.'

J. PAUL HENDERSON

'You're a saint, Laura. You know that?' Delores said. 'A beacon for lost souls. There's a place in your heart for all the waifs and strays of the world.'

'And talking of waifs and strays, where's Mike?' Tank asked. 'I thought he'd have been here by now.'

'He said he'd be late today,' Alice said. 'He's standing in for the organist at the Latter-Day Lutheran Church and he has to practise the hymns for tomorrow's service.' She then turned to Larry. 'That's the church where Laura and I are hoping to get married next year.'

'Well, many congratulations to you both,' Larry said. 'Helen and I got married in an Episcopal church. I'm not much of a believer myself, but Helen was. She liked going to church.' He paused for a moment. 'Come to think of it, it might have been the communion wine that started her drinking.'

'You wouldn't catch me drinking wine from a communion cup,' Tank said. 'I can't think of anything less sanitary.'

'Maybe *you* can't, Tank, but have you ever in your life heard of anyone being rushed to hospital after taking communion?' Alice asked.

'No, but it takes time for a germ to incubate. Any fool knows that. You tell me that you've never heard of a person being rushed to hospital *two to three weeks* after a church service and maybe I'll change my mind. I doubt you can, though.'

'You're impossible, just impossible. You'll be lucky if we invite you to the wedding.'

'You'll be lucky if you find a minister prepared to marry two broads,' Tank laughed.

'Here he is! Here's Mike,' Delores said. 'Mikey!' she shouted. 'Mikey, we're over here!'

A man who looked to have been airlifted from the 1960s

sauntered towards them, wearing an orange T-shirt and blue bib overalls made from hemp. He was tall and slim, appeared to be in his forties and his long thick hair was tied back in a ponytail. The dog with him was a medium-sized black Chinese Shar-Pei, weighing about 50 pounds.

'Larry, I'd like you to meet Mike Ergle,' Delores said. 'Mike, this is Larry MacCabe. He's the one that got Mrs Eisler's Basset Hound.'

Larry held out his hand and Mike clasped it soul style. 'Hey, Larry, what's happening, man?'

'Well, I made pancakes this morning,' Larry replied, mistaking Mike's greeting for a question, 'and then I came to the park with Laura and Alice. Then I got chased by a wasp and a man fell out of a tree. I've only just got back to the table.'

'That's cosmic, man,' Mike replied and then turned to the others. 'Wayne fell out of a tree again?'

'Yes, but he's fine,' Laura said.

'Yeah, but how's the tree? Is the tree fine? Those Osage oranges have been there for over 150 years. They're not climbing frames and I've told him this. I told him that if he wanted to commune with trees then he should sit in their shade. That's all The Buddha did, and no one loved trees more than that dude.'

'Especially the rose apple and fig trees,' Larry commented.

Mike nodded and looked at Larry admiringly.

'And what did old Wayne say to you when you told him that?' Tank asked.

'Nothing,' Mike said. 'He just asked me if I had any mints.'

'He asked me the same question,' Larry said.

'I'd have thought as a Buddhist you'd be more concerned with his welfare than that of a damned tree,' Tank said.

'How many times do I have to tell you, Tank? I'm not a Buddhist, I'm a Buddhist Christian. How do you think I got the gig at the Lutheran church?'

'I think trees are important to Wayne,' Alice said. 'I heard somewhere that he spent five years living in one when he was growing up.'

'I told you that,' Laura said, 'and, if you remember – which you obviously don't – I told you not to tell anyone! It was a confidence Wayne shared with *me*.'

'Oh, sorry, Laura, I didn't realise. But if it was a confidence then you shouldn't have told me. You know how hopeless I am at keeping secrets.'

'Oh, I do. Until you announced to Larry that we were getting married next year, I thought we were keeping that a secret, too.'

'Don't worry about us, Laura, we won't tell a soul,' Delores said. 'And I certainly won't tell Petey: it would probably end up in one of his books. Which reminds me, I'm supposed to pick him up at Union Station in an hour.'

She called to Button. 'Come on, sweetie, come to Mama. Let's go meet Daddy.'

Even though Mike had just arrived, he said he had to split too, and that he'd just been making a pit stop. He was having problems with one of the hymns and needed to get it nailed. He gave Larry a hug, told him it had been a blast meeting him and then embraced Laura and Alice and put his arms as far round Delores as he could. He then bent down and kissed Tank on the top of his head.

'Stop doing that!' Tank shouted.

'What am I supposed to do? You won't hug me, man.'

'I don't hug anyone, you damned fool. Why can't you just

shake hands like men are supposed to? Larry's going to go home thinking you're a fruit.'

Delores put Button into her large handbag and she and Mike left the park together. It was now just the four of them. Larry asked if Delores was married to Petey, but Tank said no, that Petey was a stick insect from New York who claimed to write books but made his living fixing other people's computers. Laura asked Alice if they should invite Wayne for a meal one night and Alice said no, that she'd once seen him showering in the waterfront fountain and didn't fancy the idea of him sitting on their cushions. Alice asked Tank why he'd been so hard on Delores that morning and Tank said it was because she and Laura hadn't. Tank then wondered out loud – as it appeared he did every Saturday – why a man like Mike, who'd been born in the seventies, dressed and talked like a man who'd come into his own during the sixties.

Alice left the table and threw a tennis ball for Repo, but came back three minutes later after it was clear that Repo no longer understood the game and it was her who had to retrieve the ball. Sherman followed her back to the table and sat by Tank's feet. Moses, however, continued to run around the park, sniffing butts and wagging his tail. Larry was proud of him.

At one o'clock two men started to divide the open area with a heavy net – something that always happened before a Little League game – and Repo found himself on the wrong side of the park and started to bark. Alice went to get him, attached his leash and then told Laura it was time for them to make tracks, and that she'd told Janet they'd call round that afternoon to view her new house and wanted to get it over and done with so they could spend the rest of the day together.

'Do you want us to drop you off at your house, Larry?' Laura asked.

'Thanks for asking, Laura, but I don't think there's any need. I know where I am now and I'll be able to find my own way back. It's closer to where I live than I thought.'

'Where do you live?' Tank asked.

'The other side of Wisconsin. On Dent Street NW.'

'Dent St? That's not far from where I live. If you don't mind taking a short detour while I run some errands, we can walk back together.'

Larry readily agreed, and Laura told him that he and Moses were welcome to join them in the park any Saturday.

When Tank rose to his feet and stretched – the signal they should be on their way – Larry went to Moses and slipped the leash over his head. The two men left the park and headed south on 34th. They crossed Volta Place and P St, and then, after crossing O St, Larry told Tank that he wasn't allowed to walk on 34th between O and N Streets. When an incredulous Tank asked him what kind of guff that was, Larry had no option but to tell him the story of the shopping trolley incident. Until today, it had been the last time he'd ventured into the West Village on foot.

The date was 17 January 1998, a Saturday, and Larry and Helen had been returning from a lunchtime trumpet and organ recital at the Holy Trinity Church on 36th St. It had been Helen's idea they go, but Larry's that they walk there; the exercise would do them both good, he'd reasoned. The temperature that day was two below, but no precipitation was forecast and the sun was shining brightly. They'd donned thick overcoats, scarves and hats, and at Larry's insistence worn woollen balaclavas and dark sunglasses.

Just as they'd turned on to N St Larry noticed an abandoned shopping trolley, too close to The Tombs not to be the result of a student prank. (The Tombs was a popular drinking place for Georgetown students.) 'Those students!' he'd said to Helen. 'I'd better sort this out before the university gets wind of it.' There was a name on the trolley – *Albright's* – and to Larry's way of thinking it didn't take a genius to figure out who it belonged to. 'This is Madeleine Albright's personal shopping trolley,' he'd told Helen. 'She used to be a professor at the university and I know where she lives. If we return it in person, I'll be able to discuss the Balkan crisis with her. I wrote a seminar paper on the region when I was in graduate school and my reading of the situation is that Kosovo's about to blow. I think she should know this.'

Helen doubted that any person owned a shopping trolley and suggested that it probably belonged to a local grocery store. 'There is no local grocery store,' Larry replied, 'and besides, Madeleine Albright is Secretary of State. A shopping trolley probably comes with the job.' Helen gave way to her husband's lack of common sense. As she thought most things in life were unimportant she wasn't about to make an exception for a shopping trolley.

Larry pushed the trolley along N St and turned left into 34th. Madeleine Albright's house was a short way up on the left; a large red brick property with black shutters. The sidewalk outside the house was monitored, but the agent patrolling it was walking north at the time Larry and Helen entered the street and had his back turned to them. By the time he changed direction Helen was already standing at the front of the house and Larry in the process of manoeuvring the trolley up the path. Their heavily-disguised appearances immediately alarmed the agent: at worst these people were Serbian malcontents, and at best a couple of homeless derelicts up to no good.

He spoke into his sleeve and then shouted for Larry and Helen to stop. The doors of an SUV parked on the opposite side of the street were flung open and two men jumped out pointing guns at Larry and Helen and telling them to hit the deck. Helen did, but Larry, unable to hear much of anything with his ears covered by the balaclava, continued his journey and was about to knock on the door when he was grabbed from behind, pinned to the ground and handcuffed.

Larry's explanation that he was returning Dr Albright's shopping trolley and hoping to discuss the Balkan situation with her, was interpreted by the three agents as the ramblings of an escaped mental patient, and it was only after a delay of some thirty minutes that Larry's credentials and identity were verified and he and Helen allowed to leave. (The encounter had, in fact, so weakened Helen that Larry had to push her home in the trolley, which was returned a month later, at his expense, to its rightful owners – a grocery store in the small town of Corunna, Indiana.) Their names, however, had been taken, security logs updated and warnings issued: if either of them ventured within two hundred yards of the property again, they would be arrested. The following week a restraining order dropped through Larry and Helen's letterbox.

'Albright left government years ago,' Tank said. 'She's not protected by the secret service now. Besides, I work for the State Department. No one will hassle you if you're with me.'

They walked down N St and passed the Albright residence without incident. Larry's blinking calmed and his voice returned. 'What do you do at the State Department, Tank?'

'I'm a janitor,' Tank replied.

'A janitor? You won't believe this, but one of my best friends at the university is a janitor. Tell me, what kind of floor polish do you use? I always thought that Clive was using the wrong one.'

Tank looked at him as though Larry were a piece of gum stuck to the sole of his shoe. 'I'm not that kind of janitor, you dimwit! I clean up other people's messes, not their damned floors. I'm a trouble-shooter.'

They turned on to P St and headed for Wisconsin. Tank made stops at a dry cleaner's and a pharmacy and left Sherman outside with Larry and Moses. They then walked up the busy thoroughfare and turned right when they got to R St. A short distance from Dumbarton Oaks – the location for the 1944 diplomatic talks that resulted in the UN Charter – Tank stopped at the entrance to a large detached house with a big sculpted tree in its yard.

'I'd invite you in for coffee, Larry, but I've had enough of you for one day,' Tank said.

Larry looked at him alarmed. 'I haven't been talking too much, have I? Laura says I tend to do that.'

Tank looked at him. 'For a man of intellect you're not the most perceptive of fellows, are you? You'd be a perfect fit for the State Department! No, you haven't been talking too much. I was joking when I said that. But tell me, Larry, how are you with heights? Can you climb a ladder without falling off?'

Larry said he could, that heights had never been a problem for him.

'In that case I might have a job for you in the near future. Give me a number I can reach you on, will you?'

Larry did, and then told Tank that ladders had been around since Mesolithic times and that one was depicted in a 10,000-year-old rock painting in Valencia, Spain: two people trying to reach a wild honeybee nest.

'Okay, Larry, *now* you're talking too much!' Tank said.

4

The Waterfall Tuner

Laura and Alice lived in an apartment building overlooking
the Potomac. It was close to Washington Harbor, a complex
of restaurants and more apartments, and within easy reach
of Watergate and the Kennedy Centre for Performing Arts.
Across the street, and siding the river, was a landscaped area
of lawn and plantings and a footpath that linked Georgetown
to the central district of Washington. Their apartment was on
the sixth of the building's seven levels. It had two bedrooms,
a large kitchen dining area and a lounge that opened on to a
planted terrace. (It was from this terrace that Alice had seen
Wayne showering in the waterfront fountain.)

It was now Saturday evening. Laura and Alice had returned
from their friend's house an hour ago and were sitting in the
lounge drinking cocktails. It was Laura who answered the
phone.

'It's me, Laura – Delores. You know how I said I was getting
as forgetful as Mrs Eisler? Well I must be, because the one
thing I meant to tell you this morning was that the museum's
planning an exhibition on the Wabanaki Confederacy next
month and there'll be some Abenaki artefacts included... I

thought you would be… Okay I'll put you down for two. I'm going to check with Mike and Tank and see if they want tickets, but what about Larry? Do you think he'd be interested…? Okay, give me his number and I'll call him… Petey? Yes, he's here now. I've just prepared a salad for us… I know, nothing healthier. We're just waiting for the pizza to arrive…'

'That was Delores,' Laura said. 'We've been invited to an exhibition at the museum and she's going to invite Larry. It was nice of her to think of him, wasn't it?'

'I guess so,' Alice replied.

'Look, why don't you go and relax on the terrace while I make dinner? I know Janet can be a bit wearing.'

Alice took Repo with her and lay down on one of the rattan recliners. She checked her phone for messages, updated her Facebook page and tweeted that she was sitting on a terrace overlooking the Potomac drinking a gin and tonic. It was then that something Delores had said in the park that morning started to turn in her mind, something about Laura being big-hearted and a beacon for lost souls. She knew very well that Laura had a big heart – she took that fact for granted. But why, she wondered, did her partner find it necessary to share it with others – the lost and the neglected – and not keep it for her alone? It always seemed that Laura had a project on the go – if not rescuing bag ladies from the street then volunteering at soup kitchens – and now she'd brought Larry into their lives and had even suggested they invite Wayne for a meal. Were their lives always to be encumbered by the needy?

Alice knew she was being selfish, but accepted that it was within her nature to be this way. She expected to be the nucleus of Laura's life – of any life she shared – and not just one of several orbiting planets. For her it had always been this way. Alice had always been the centre of attention.

She was born in the guest room of her grandparents' house in Lebanon, Kansas; her birth premature and the location unintended. It was, however, an accident that forever coloured her life. If she'd been born at the Community Hospital in Junction City where the birth had been planned, then Alice would have been spared the knowledge that she'd been born at the centre of the United States. But her parents would never let her forget this. They told her over and again that she'd been born at the very centre of the nation, and therefore the world, and that minus the guiding star, the three wise men and the shepherds, her birth had been no less special than Jesus'.

And to her parents, Alice was special. She was their only child, the heart of their universe and they turned every day of her life into a birthday. They showered her with clothes and presents, gave her a generous allowance and bought her a small Cadillac when she turned sixteen. Alice took these things for granted: this is what happened when you were born at the centre of the world. She never once longed for a brother or sister, feared in fact that the arrival of a sibling might take the limelight from her, and was happy to be an only child at the centre of every family photograph.

Alice grew up in Junction City, a small town in Kansas located at the confluence of two rivers. It wasn't long before she became the centre of its attention, too. The town was a social organism that lived and breathed high school football, its weekly moods defined by the outcome of the Friday night game. Monday morning quarterbacks would pore over the runs and passes, the tackles and the touchdowns. They would discuss the plays that went right and those that went wrong; dissect the coach's tactics and hypothesise what they'd have done differently had they been in his place. But if at times they were critical of the coach and the players, not once did they speak ill of the team's cheerleaders; and for the head cheerleader – Alice Manzoni – they had only praise.

Alice was the epitome of girl-next-door goodness. She had long blonde hair, a pretty face and a smile that lit up the neighbourhood. She was also naturally athletic and no one could do jumps, motions and tumbles better than her or stand more assured at the top of a pyramid. The pompoms came alive in her hands and the chants she led brought the crowd to its feet: *Hey, Junction City, Get Down, Get Mean, Help the Jaguars Kill the Other Team.* 'That girl's got it all,' one man in the crowd once said to another. 'Hell, if I was twenty years younger I'd be taking her to a parking area…' The other man interrupted him. 'That's my daughter you're talking about, buddy!'

But at high school Alice did have it all. She was the girl other girls wanted to be. She wore the coolest clothes, got invited to all the parties and had the hottest dates. Accolades were sprinkled on her like confetti – *the girl most likely to succeed, the girl with the most school spirit, the girl with the most winning smile* – and it was no surprise when, at the end of her senior year, she was elected Prom Queen. It was also no surprise that Chip Nelson, the Jaguars' star quarterback and Alice's boyfriend, was chosen Prom King. It was the natural union.

Chip Nelson was the quintessential American male. He was rugged in looks, square in the jaw and had broad shoulders; he ate turnips and the eyes of fish and could throw a ball eighty yards. He expected to marry Alice and Alice expected to marry him. But no expectations were higher than those of Junction City. The town rooted for their relationship, held its breath when Chip left for Wichita State on a football scholarship and only exhaled after he broke his arm in two places and returned to work at his father's car dealership.

Alice meanwhile had remained in Junction City. She liked doing rather than theorising, and had no interest in going to college. Her strength, she believed, was people pleasing and her weakness money. By the time Chip returned she'd been selling real estate for a year and been voted employee of the month three times. Their relationship, strained by absence and a two-hour commute, revived, and two years later Chip phoned her at the office and told her to look into the sky. Alice did and saw a small plane trailing a banner: *Alice, will you marry me?* Rightly, she presumed it was Chip doing the asking.

Alice hadn't been the only one to see the banner: the whole of Junction City had seen it and they expected her to say yes. And so she did. Alice, after all, was a people pleaser. They married shortly after her twenty-first birthday and moved into an apartment she'd been unable to sell. It was only a matter of weeks, however, before she realised that she'd fallen in love with the idea of marriage rather than Chip himself and been deceived by the small town's expectations. What she also hadn't expected to realise quite so quickly was that she preferred the company of women to men, and this was something that only dawned on her after the sink got blocked.

'And before then you had no idea?' Laura once asked her. 'I had a suspicion,' Alice replied, 'but I thought I was just going through a phase all girls went through. And it wasn't as if it was something you could talk about in Junction City.

Remember, this was small-town Middle America. People who grew up there were supposed to get married and have kids.'

The sink in question was the kitchen sink. Chip had tried to unblock the clog with first a plunger and then a chemical drain cleaner, but when the obstruction remained he left Alice to find a plumber. She checked the listings and called a company that prided itself on technical excellence and competitive price. She arranged to meet the plumber at the apartment the following lunchtime and was surprised when a young woman knocked on the door dressed in overalls and carrying a toolbox.

The girl's name was Charlie, short for Charlotte. She had short peroxide hair, hands like bricks and was about six years older than Alice. She gave the sink a cursory examination and then pulled a flexible augur from her toolbox. 'It's what we call a plumber's snake,' she told Alice, who was hovering over her shoulder and taking more interest in a sink than she ever had done before. Once the blockage was cleared and the water again draining, Alice insisted on making Charlie a sandwich. There was something about the plumber that mesmerised her. After the topics of indoor plumbing and sandwiches were exhausted, the conversation turned to more intimate matters. Charlie told Alice she was gay, Alice speculated to Charlie that she *might* be gay and then, to settle matters, they continued the conversation in the bedroom. What happened there is uncertain, but when the door opened and Alice walked out she was a new woman – or a dyke, as Chip was wont to phrase the metamorphosis.

Alice moved out of the apartment the following week and moved in with Charlie, who lived in a perfectly-plumbed house in Fort Myers. The rest was history. Alice and Charlie stayed together for no more than three months. It was a relationship of transition, but one that confirmed Alice's sexuality. Her parents, as ever, were accepting of their daughter's choice, but for the sake of Chip's injured masculinity and future car sales, Alice moved to the more open and forgiving city of Minneapolis. There, on the strength of her personality and business background, she was hired as a recruitment consultant.

Life for Alice was never the same after she left Junction City. There she'd been a big fish in a small pond, the Queen Bee of a pocket-sized colony where the name Alice Manzoni had counted for something. In the wider world she was just another person, a smaller cog in a more faceless machine. But Alice never forgot that she'd been born at the centre of the world or had, for a time, been at the centre of Junction City's small world, and the conviction that her rightful place in life was at its centre stayed.

Several relationships and two agencies later Alice moved to Washington and met Laura. They fell in love and bought an apartment with a terrace overlooking the Potomac River and there, one evening, Alice remembered something Delores had said in the park that morning, something about… 'Dinner's about ten minutes away,' Laura said, joining her on the terrace. And then, noticing the forlorn look on Alice's face, took hold of her hand. 'What's wrong, hon?'

The question Larry was asking Moses at that moment was less tendentious, more a wondering out loud why dogs behaved the way they did. 'If I went around sniffing people's butts I'd get punched in the face or taken to jail. I'm not suggesting you shake paws with your friends, but have you ever considered rubbing noses? That's what Eskimos do and it works for them. I wonder if...'

The phone on the kitchen wall started to ring and interrupted Larry's train of thought, if indeed there had been one. The telephone rang so rarely these days that his first thought was that the oven timer was malfunctioning. It was Delores inviting him to a future exhibition at the museum. 'The whole gang's going to be there, Larry... Now? Just finishing dinner... Apple pie and ice cream... I know. You can't expect to keep healthy if you don't eat fruit...'

'Well, I'll be,' Larry said to Moses when he returned to the lounge. 'It looks like we were a hit at the park. I'm in a gang, now. Wait till I tell Helen this!'

Until that moment Larry hadn't been certain how their visit to the park had gone. He knew Moses had made a good impression – Moses always did – but was less decided if he had. He thought he'd acquitted himself well enough, but in light of Laura's previous comments wasn't sure if he was the right person to judge the situation. On the downside he'd arrived with a syrup stain on his shirt, been attacked by a wasp and been caught eating sand, but on the upside hadn't talked too much – and that was the important thing! In truth, he'd never had the opportunity or even the desire. Larry was a person who enjoyed meat-and-two-vegetable conversations. He liked talking about things and imparting knowledge and was troubled by discussions involving controversy and demanding opinion. The free-for-all arguments of the morning had alarmed him, especially when Tank and Delores had tried to drag him to their sides, but he'd resisted – or Laura had resisted for him – and he'd managed to offend no one.

Now that Delores had called and invited him to an exhibition, he revisited the day and left it feeling more optimistic. Laura had told him he could join them at the park any Saturday of the week, Tank had told him he could climb his ladders and Mike had described their meeting as a blast. And then, of course, there was Wayne. After the initial surprise had worn off, Larry had enjoyed the young man's conversation, and Wayne had certainly been impressed that he'd been talking to a professor. Next time he went to the park he'd take a bag of mints with him. That would please Wayne. But first he needed to bring Helen up to speed.

Oak Hill Cemetery was a large, historic burial ground dotted with sarcophagi, obelisks and statues. It was the resting place for the Jim Morrisons of yesteryear – politicians, military men, diplomats and philanthropists – and covered an area of some twenty acres. It was only a short distance from Dent St and Larry and Helen had walked there often, wandering its paths and hilly terraces, reading the gravestone plaques and sitting on its benches.

Helen had visited Oak Hill purely for its landscape and had never once expressed a desire to be buried there – or anywhere, for that matter. Indeed she'd told Larry on more than one occasion that if she died before him, he could wrap her body in a blanket and dump it in the recycling bin. (If Helen had taken little interest in life, she'd registered even less concern for death.) That her remains would be interred in the wall of Willow Columbarium – a granite structure just beyond the cemetery's arched bridge – had never once crossed her mind and neither had it crossed Larry's, who was unaware at the time of her death that the Columbarium even existed.

Fortunately the funeral director knew of its construction – it was his business to know these things – and, with tact, he'd broached the subject of cremation with Larry. The burial plots, he explained, had been taken and filled years ago and the only ticket into Oak Hill these days was incineration. 'And there's no better resting place for the wife of an esteemed Georgetown academic, Professor MacCabe. This is where Helen deserves to be. And think of the convenience: you could be there in fifteen minutes and see her any day of the week.'

And in the months that followed his wife's death Larry went there often. He was under no illusion that Helen could hear his words or that anything remained of her save a few pounds of ashes, but he still took solace from his visits. He'd stand in front of her twenty-four-inch allocation and talk to the stone wall for hours on end. He saw nothing unusual in this behaviour and neither, for that matter, did those who knew him: the *brick walls* he'd talked to over the years. Moreover, if talking to a collection of limestone blocks was good enough for the Jews, then who was to say that talking to an assortment of small granite boulders was any less befitting. (In all likelihood, the Jews would have been chanting devotions at the Wailing Wall rather than recounting the day's trolley shop and, instead of squeezing crumpled supermarket receipts into its crevices, would have wedged small prayer slips.)

When Larry set off for Oak Hill with Moses the following Wednesday it had been more than two months since he'd visited the Columbarium. On that visit he'd told Helen how Dr Young had arranged to have Loop put down and left him with three bags of unopened pet food that the supermarket might not allow him to return. In death, as in life, Helen had said nothing, but at least the visit allowed Larry to get things off his chest. He now felt guilty for not visiting her since and telling her the good news in his life. And, today, there was so much good news to tell!

Larry had barely walked through the cemetery gates before a member of the grounds staff stopped him and pointed to a notice: *No Dogs and Bicycles*. Larry had been completely unaware of the rule. He apologised to the man and suggested to Moses they go for a walk in Montrose Park, the open area adjacent to the cemetery. Both dogs and bicycles were welcomed in the park, but for a variety of reasons explained by a prominently placed notice, all dogs had to be kept on a leash: loose dogs bit people, got lost and scared and injured wildlife. (It had always baffled Larry why grey squirrels populated Oak Hill and only black squirrels inhabited Montrose; it was as if an invisible fence separated the two species.)

Moses had no reason to believe that this park was any different from the park he'd been in on Saturday (not that he'd have known the day) and strained at the leash. There was a world of adventure here, dogs to sniff and black squirrels to chase; why, he wondered, was he being kept on a rein today of all days? Larry sensed Moses' frustration and decided to cut the walk short and head to Volta.

It was towards lunchtime when they arrived at the park and no other dogs were present. Two nannies were sitting at one of the picnic tables eating bagged lunches and occasionally glancing at the toddlers in their strollers. Larry let Moses off the leash and the dog ran to the table. One of the young girls, a Filipino, patted Moses and gave him a piece of meat from her sandwich. The other girl, however, moved slightly away and pulled one of the strollers closer to her. Larry was about to join them when he heard a voice call his name: 'Larry! Professor Larry!'

Larry turned and saw Wayne standing on a table close to the hedge dividing the park from the outdoor swimming pool and flapping his arms like an aircraft ground handler. Larry checked his pocket to make sure the mints were there and started towards him. Wayne stopped waving, took a step backwards and toppled from the table as gracelessly as he'd fallen from the tree. By the time Larry reached him he was back on his feet brushing the grass from his arm.

'Dagnabbit, Larry: I tumbled again! Did you see me? There ain't no telling when I'm going to be right way up or wrong way down. It's one of them mysteries no one can solve, like the Bermuda Triangle. You heard of that, Lar... I'm sorry, but I don't think I can call you Larry no more. You're too old for me to call you by your first name and people will be thinking I'm disrespectful. I'll call you Professor. No one can say that ain't respectful.'

Larry was always happy to be called Professor and used the title whenever possible: on official documents, billing accounts and in all correspondence. 'I'll be happy to answer to Professor, Wayne, and if you like I could address you as Mr Trout.'

'Ain't no need for that, Professor. Only people calling me that is doctors, and I don't like doctors much. Ask too many nosey questions for my liking. Do you go to doctors?'

'Now and again. Usually when my throat gets sore. I don't know why, but it dries up more than most people's.'

'Mints is good for that, Professor. Mints is good for everything.'

Larry was reminded of the packet of mints in his pocket and offered one to Wayne.

'That's kind of you, Professor. Mind if I take two? Wednesday's my big day.'

When Larry asked him what he meant by that, Wayne told him that this was the day the *Current* came out – the free newspaper that served the communities of Georgetown, Burleith and Glover Park. It was his job to deliver the paper; throw the plastic-wrapped tubes into yards or push them through the letter boxes of houses that didn't have yards.

'This is why I've got the cart,' Wayne said. 'It's easier if I put the papers in a cart. Most people put them in a bag but I lose balance when I do that and so I don't. What you doing today, Professor?'

'Well, I was intending to visit Helen,' Larry answered, 'but it seems I'm not allowed to visit her with Moses. I'm not allowed to cycle there either.'

'Who's Helen? Is Helen your girlfriend? Is she afraid of dogs and bikes?'

'No, Helen's my wife, Wayne. A man my age doesn't have girlfriends,' he laughed.

'Well if she's your wife why do you have to go visit her? Don't she live with you? I thought husbands and wives lived together.'

Larry explained the situation: how Helen was dead and now interred in the wall of Oak Hill's Willow Columbarium.

'You ever talk to Helen?' Wayne asked.

'I do!' Larry replied. 'I talk to her all the time.'

'I talk to dead people, too,' Wayne said. 'Not so many as I used to since Kevin started scaring them off. Doctors tell me it's wrong but I don't see nothing wrong with it. I think dead people like being talked to. Dead people get lonely.'

'My feelings exactly,' Larry replied, pleased at last to be talking to someone who understood.

'You waiting for the Dog People?'

'I think they'll be at work today, Wayne. Apart from me they all have jobs. I think they just come here on a Saturday.'

'Some of them come by themselves in the week, but it's usually late in the afternoon and right before dinner. If I didn't had papers to deliver I'd stay and talk with you, but I have and so I cain't. I get paid good money for delivering papers, Professor. I'll think of you though. When I'm sucking that mint you give me, I'll think of you. Might be you'll hear me thinking. I make a lot of noise when I think.'

Wayne retrieved his cart from behind the hedge and headed for Wisconsin, the drop-off point for the newspapers. Larry sat there for a while pondering. Surprisingly, considering the nature of their conversation, the only thing that troubled him was Wayne's use of the past tense – *didn't had*. Many of the students he'd taught at the university had been from overseas countries where English was, if anything, a second language and he couldn't help but wonder why Wayne's command of the language was so much poorer than theirs. It appeared that Wayne had been failed by the same educational system that had allowed him to triumph, and in the moment, and on its behalf, he was moved to make atonement. As Mentor had guided Telemachus and Henry Higgins Eliza Doolittle, he, Larry MacCabe, would take Wayne Trout under his wing and school him in the ways of the English language.

Larry was jolted from his thoughts by the sound of Moses barking. He looked up and saw Mike walking towards him with Uji, his Shar-Pei. The dog had small triangular ears and a block-shaped head and from a distance looked like a small hippopotamus, an animal as Larry recalled with more human deaths on its conscience than any other. Uji growled at him and Larry became uneasy.

'Hey, cool it, Uji,' Mike said. 'Larry's good people.'

Uji quietened, but Larry still feared the worst. 'He's not going to bite me, is he?'

'Nah, not old Uji,' Mike laughed. 'Shar-Peis were bred for guarding so it's in their nature to be suspicious of people. You two never formally met Saturday, so to him you're still a stranger. Once he gets used to you he'll be fine. Go ahead, stroke him, Larry. Get close and personal.'

Larry did, and was surprised by how prickly Uji's short coat was. He noticed the deep wrinkles in the dog's face, its blue-black tongue and the furrows that ran along its shoulders and at the base of its tail. He gently and carefully placed his hands at either side of Uji's face and looked into the dog's deep-set eyes: 'Hello, Uji. I'm Larry MacCabe.'

Mike bent down and patted Uji on the back. 'Good boy, Uji. *Good* boy.' He then let Uji off the leash and the dog ran to Moses. 'He's accepted you, dude. You're on his Christmas card list! Now if you'd told him your name was Mao Tse-tung it would be a different matter. Mao's on his genetic shit list and for good reason. That sonofabitch damn near wiped his ancestors out. Can you believe that?'

'As a matter of fact I can,' Larry said. 'A visiting professor from Hong Kong told me that more than fifty million dogs died during the Cultural Revolution. At the time I thought it was an odd thing to say because until then we'd been discussing the Desert Land Act and I hadn't mentioned anything about dogs.'

'Wheeeeew,' Mike whistled. 'Fifty million! Wow, that's genocide, man!'

Larry thought canicide would have been a better choice of word but didn't mention this. 'I know what you mean, Mike. I can understand the communists wanting to kill Pekingese dogs...' Mike flinched when Larry said this and he rushed to explain. 'I'm not excusing their behaviour, Mike, but you have to bear in mind that the Pekingese was the breed of dog favoured by the Imperial Court. It became symbolic of everything the communists hated about the old regime. What I don't understand, though, is why they decided to exterminate all dogs. I can only suppose they thought dog ownership was decadent, and I think the government is still uneasy with the concept. I read in *The Washington News* only last week that there are all kinds of restrictions in place. In Beijing, for instance, they won't allow any owner to have a dog taller than fourteen inches.'

'Man, that rules out Shar-Peis, then. I doubt they'd look too favourably on waterfall tuners, either.'

Larry looked at him, in all probability the same way he'd looked at the visiting professor from Hong Kong when he'd interjected the fact that fifty million dogs had been killed during the Cultural Revolution into a conversation on the Desert Land Act. Mike noticed Larry's confusion. 'That's what I do for a living, man. I tune waterfalls.'

Mike Ergle had found his true vocation late in life, around the time he realised he wasn't simply a Christian but a Buddhist Christian.

Mike was a native of New Haven, Connecticut, an engineering graduate of Columbia University and a casualty of the subprime mortgage crisis. Without giving much thought to the matter, he'd followed his brother into investment banking. It was something to do, something other than civil engineering, and an opportunity to wear the suspenders and floral tie he'd been bought for Christmas that year. He proved adept and until 2007 the dice fell in his favour, first at Goldman Sachs and later at Lehman Brothers, the small grocer made good. But then the recession hit and house prices slumped, mortgage delinquencies and foreclosures rocketed and the value of securities dependent on the housing market tumbled. Overnight billions of dollars were wiped from the investment bank's balance sheet, and in 2008 Lehman Brothers went bust.

Mike had been uneasy about life at Lehman's even before the collapse. The company had lowered its standards and increased risks by selling mortgages to people with weak credit histories and without knowledge of their employment or earnings. But no one else seemed to care. Profits were big and investment banks invincible. It was a macho culture of excess fuelled by the testosterone of its leader, a man who took a private elevator to his office, pumped weights in the basement gym and who, even as the shit hit the fan, took home $22 million that year.

Like most Lehman employees, Mike had left the Midtown office with only a cardboard box of personal belongings. His bank and savings accounts, however, were overflowing with what he now considered to be ill-gotten gains. He was thirty-seven, unmarried and without responsibility, but still troubled. The system he'd helped maintain for sixteen years, and for most of that time believed in, was crumbling and the world being rocked by its aftershocks: ordinary people and nation states both. Whatever else the future held for him he was determined that his next occupation would be one that benefitted others and harmed no one.

New Haven, Mike's home town, had been founded by English Puritans in the late seventeenth century. It was now overwhelmingly Catholic and also the international headquarters of a Catholic men's fraternal benefit society called the Knights of Columbus. Mike had grown up in the Catholic Church but had long since parted company with its teachings on birth control and abortion. He remained, however, a believing Christian, and after leaving Lehman Brothers enrolled at the Union Theological Seminary, an independent and ecumenical theological college in New York. It was something to do, something other than investment banking, and an opportunity to throw away the suspenders and floral ties that had dominated his life for sixteen years. He also anticipated that the experience would lead to a life of service, to an occasion when he could compensate society for the ills that he and others like him had inadvertently bestowed upon it. After four months at the seminary, however, and in the hope of salvaging his Christian faith, he jumped ship and headed for the Shambhala Meditation Centre on West 22nd Street.

Mike's beef wasn't with Jesus and His teachings, but with the way churches *presented* Jesus and His teachings. At one end of the spectrum were the Catholic and High Episcopal Churches: hierarchical, distant, overly ritualised and coldly intellectual; while at the other end, and growing in popularity, were the Evangelical Churches: unduly emotional, shallow and purely of the moment. No church provided Christians with any method or technique that would allow them to advance their spiritual experience in their own time, and for this reason Mike turned to Buddhism – not to become a Buddhist, but to learn from them and apply the tools of their wisdom to his life and beliefs. For two years he practised meditation and yoga, learned how to breathe and how to relax. He found inner peace and, at last, connected with God. God was no longer an outside entity, but a part of his very being. Om Mani Padme Hum! Hallelujah!

Being schooled by Buddhists it was inevitable that Mike would learn about Buddhism, and what he learned convinced him that Christianity and Buddhism had much in common – almost too much in common. On the subjects of murder, adultery, theft, bearing false witness and coveting, for instance, the moral pronouncements of Jesus and Buddha were almost identical; and both urged people to be kind and peaceful, to give to the poor and love both their neighbours and their enemies. In fact, Jesus' Sermon on the Mount was little more than a restatement of Buddha's Turning the Wheel of the Dharma. It appeared to Mike that Christianity was the Buddhism of the West, and as Buddha had lived 500 years before Jesus was born, it was likely that He had been influenced by Buddhist teachings rather than vice versa. And then it dawned on him…

'Don't you think it odd that there's no account in the Bible of what Jesus was doing from the age of fourteen to twenty-nine? What do *you* think He was doing, Larry?'

Larry had been listening patiently, more interested in learning about waterfall tuning – something he didn't know about – than Buddhism, a religion he was already familiar with, and was keeping his fingers crossed that Mike wasn't about to detail the Four Noble Truths and the Eightfold Path.

'I'd always supposed He was working in His dad's carpentry shop in Nazareth. And considering the socio-economic make-up of Galilee at that time, I think He'd have been making affordable furniture – a bit like IKEA does today.'

'Suppose for the sake of argument that He wasn't living in Nazareth, Larry. Where do you figure He was? Go on, take a guess.'

'I'm afraid you'll have to tell me, Mike. I've never been very good at guessing.'

'India, man! The Cat was in India!'

Jesus, Mike explained, had travelled there with merchants and spent sixteen years studying Buddhist teachings in Kashmir, and ancient Chinese, Muslim and Persian texts affirmed this. They referred to Jesus as Yesu, Issa or the Son of God.

'Judea and Palestine had been awash with Buddhist ideas for two hundred years by the time Jesus was born, Larry. Emperor Ashoka of India sent missionaries there, traders talked the talk and it's pretty obvious that the Essenes and Gnostics were influenced by Buddhist ideas. Jesus tapped into them, man, decided to travel to the source and learn about Buddhism first hand. The Dude needed to chill, get prepared, and he figured the best place to get Himself sorted was India.'

Larry had listened intently, but having failed to understand why Jesus would go to a hot climate to chill, was now lost. 'Sorry, Mike, but why did Jesus need to chill? I didn't realise He was suffering from anything as a teenager, and there's certainly no mention of Him having acne.'

'Larry,' Mike said somewhat despairingly, 'Jesus' problem was that He was an asshole! He suffered from assholism. That's why He had to go live in India.'

Larry's eyes grew to the size of saucers and Mike wondered if he'd overstepped the mark. 'Look, man, I'm not being blasphemous describing Jesus this way. I'm telling it like it is, the same way Jesus would be telling it if He was standing here today. He'd be the first to admit He was a badass in his youth. He'd tell it to you straight, man. He'd say: "Larry, I might be a Democrat now, but back then I was a Republican!"'

'And don't you ever wonder why we never get to read about Jesus as a child in the Bible; that He just shows up in the temple at twelve and then goes missing again until He's thirty? It's because the people who compiled the Bible didn't want us to read about Him – and for good reason, too. But if you read the apocryphal books – the ones they decided to leave out – there's more than one account of what Jesus was like as a child; and there's no two ways about it, the guy was a one percenter, a real downer, as capricious and destructive a person as any you're likely to meet. Anyone who crossed Him got it in the neck and the neighbours hated Him. He shrivelled up one kid for messing with a pool He'd built, killed another for accidentally bumping into His shoulder when he was out on the street and blinded anyone who complained to His parents about His bad behaviour. It got to the point where His dad had to tell Mary not to let Him out of the house anymore, because every time He went out people died. There was no less Christian a person living in Judea than Jesus, man. The guy was a bringdown, a total buzzkill! And you don't get from being the Country's Number One Bringdown to the Saviour of the World in a hop, skip and a jump. Something big in His life had to happen, man, and that was His trip to India and learning the ways of Buddhism. That trip changed Him!'

'So, let me see if I've got this right, Mike. Are you saying that Jesus is just an enlightened person, a Bodhisattva of some kind, and that there's no real difference between Buddhism and Christianity?'

'No, Larry, I'm not saying that! There are big differences between Jesus and Buddha and between Christianity and Buddhism. Buddha might have shown the way but he never claimed to *be* the way. He was a great teacher but that's all he was; he was mortal and he died the death of all men. The big difference is that Jesus rose from the dead and is alive today, not buried somewhere in the foothills of the Himalayas.

'And Buddhism and Christianity part ways on some major-league issues, man. For one thing, Buddhists don't believe in God. The only accountability they have is to the cosmic law of cause and effect, and because they have no concept of sin, they don't have any need for a Saviour. There's no Heaven for them, just an absence of consciousness. But that's not to say that Jesus didn't see things in Buddhism that He liked and wanted to incorporate into His own teachings. In that respect He *was* a Buddhist and, to a degree, so am I. But I'm a Buddhist *Christian* and not a Christian *Buddhist*. It's all in the noun and the adjective and where you place the emphasis.'

Larry was agnostic, happy to let the unknowable remain unknowable, but always pleased to discuss religion. He'd read the Bible cover to cover and had more than a passing knowledge of the world's other religions. Nothing he'd read, however, had convinced him of any truth other than that the world was a cauldron of superstition that occasionally boiled over and scalded mankind. He kept these thoughts to himself though, stored them away in a dry attic and allowed people of belief to believe that he too was a person of belief who probably believed the same things that they did. 'I don't mean to pry, Mike – and you don't have to answer if you don't want – but were you influenced at all by the Fifth Step of the Eightfold Path when you decided to become a waterfall tuner? And what is a waterfall tuner? I never even knew there was such a profession.'

'Man, Larry, you're a dude on the ball! I suspected you knew a thing or two about Buddhism when you connected Buddha to the rose apple and fig trees on Saturday but, man, that question blows my mind! Apart from Buddhists there aren't many people who know about the Eightfold Path – you're not a Buddhist, are you, Larry? Well, no sweat either way. It's a pleasure rapping with you, man.

'The truth though is that it didn't. I'd already committed myself to pursuing a Right Occupation and reading the Fifth Step only confirmed that I *had* made the right decision. But Buddhism did give me an appreciation of nature that I'd never had before; made me realise that humans are a part of it and not distinct – which is more a Christian belief. I never thought I'd earn a living working with nature, though. That was kind of serendipitous, but serendipitous in a good way.'

It turned out that Mike, if not appreciative of nature, had always been fascinated by water, especially its flow. Growing up on Long Island Sound and within spitting distance of the Atlantic Ocean, it was unsurprising that his attention had first been drawn by the sea, its vastness and changing moods. But it was an article in a magazine written by a sailor who'd navigated the world's oceans single-handedly that had captivated him. Until then he'd always assumed that the sea, apart from the occasional swell, was flat; but the article suggested that if an ocean was magically frozen on even the calmest of days, an explorer negotiating its changed landscape would encounter plateaux and valleys differing in height by sixty feet.

If Mike had been able to sit in a boat and keep his lunch down he might well have become an oceanographer, but motion sickness kept him and his feet on dry land and his interest turned to hydrology and later hydraulic engineering. Until he started attending classes at the Shambhala Centre his interest in water had been purely technical; he was concerned by its flow and turbulence, its conveyance and power and had never stopped to consider its spiritual nature. (He learned that in Buddhism water symbolised calmness, clarity and purity; and in Christianity deliverance from sin, God's blessing and the gift of eternal life.)

It was a teacher at the centre who first encouraged Mike to meditate close to water. Mike had taken the advice and driven upstate and found a stream, sat on its bank and lost himself in the sound of its motion. He found that he'd never meditated better and returned there often. But then, one visit, he ventured further upstream and found a small waterfall, sat cross-legged next to it and the results were better still. Thereafter he returned to the waterfall to meditate until the day he realised that another waterfall had taken its place. The new cascade was out of synch, the plops irregular and the gurgles jarring. The whole sound had changed and meditation impossible.

When Mike climbed the bank to investigate the problem he found a large branch wedged in one of the channels, and behind it a small wall of rocks. The unwanted debris had been washed downstream by a heavy rainfall. He removed the rubble, pulled out the tree branch and returned to the spot below the waterfall where he customarily meditated. The sound had improved but it still wasn't the same. He climbed back to the top and made an adjustment; climbed back down, climbed back to the top again and made further modifications until the sound was as he remembered – in fact, better than he remembered. It was the most meaningful thing he'd ever done. If only he could do this for a living!

At the Shambhala Centre the next day Mike met with the teacher who'd first encouraged him to meditate outdoors. He told him about the waterfall, its deformation and asked if he'd been right to reconfigure the force to his liking. Was it wrong for a person to interfere with nature and arrogance to believe that nature could be improved? As man and nature were one, the teacher replied, the waterfall was Mike and Mike was the waterfall; by changing the waterfall Mike had changed himself. He took a soiled business card from a fold in his robe and handed it to Mike: *Bill Pringle: Roofer*. When Mike questioned why he thought he needed a roofer, the teacher apologised and pulled another card from his robe: *Summer Gale: Waterfall Tuner*. This card made more sense.

'I think you should talk to Summer,' the teacher said. 'She doesn't have a phone.'

It also appeared that Summer didn't have a pen, because it was more than two months before Mike heard back from her. The answer when it came though was positive: she'd be happy to share her knowledge with him.

While all skin is exterior, Summer Gale's was more outdoors than most. She was in her mid-fifties but appeared older; her tanned face wrinkled and blotched by the sun's rays. She lived in Phoenicia, a small hamlet in the Catskills, and owned three dogs with no corresponding abilities. She floated places in long billowing dresses and danced to the music of Joni

Mitchell, dined on fruit and vegetables and sipped camomile tea. People went to her house for conversation rather than a good time, to pour out their troubles and sometimes borrow money. It hadn't always been this way.

Although Summer's body was now a temple for the mind, it had at one time been a blind pig for substance abuse. She'd smoked enough dope in her younger years to fuel an expedition to Mars, drunk more whiskey than Ulysses S Grant in his lifetime and taken more acid trips than a Greyhound Bus makes stops. She was the ultimate wild child, the party girl voted most likely to crash and burn. It therefore came as a relief to her parents – though a disappointment to her friends – when Kateri Tekakwitha, the patron saint of the environment and ecology, appeared to her in a dream one night and told her to get her ass in gear and do something about the damn waterfalls. Her father, a landscape architect, was appreciative of the hallucination's visit, but found it difficult to believe that the Blessed Kateri had been referring to *his* ornamental waterfalls when she'd made that comment – as his daughter insisted she had. Ruffled pride, however, was but a small price to pay for his daughter's redemption and, albeit reluctantly, he agreed to put her in charge of all new water features. It was reluctance ill-founded. By the time of her third divorce, Summer was a waterfall tuner of renown.

'And you're completely self-taught?' Mike asked.

'Yeah,' Summer replied.

'And you'll teach me?'

'Sure.'

'And in more than two words?'

For the next six weeks Mike shadowed Summer, spending the weekdays with her and returning home to New York on weekends. She'd just started work on a commission in Saugerties and was building a waterfall from scratch and tuning it to the key of C. He watched, listened and assisted; became her apprentice and learned the rudiments of building and tuning. This is what he learned:

The sound of a waterfall depended on the volume of water falling and the height from which the water fell; the greater the volume and the greater the height, the greater the sound. The sound of water falling directly into deep water was different from that of water hitting a rock either above or just below the surface of the pool, and also different from water whose descent was broken by rocks. All sounds could be altered by building a hollow area behind the falling water, and the construction of this cave – its height, width, depth and the nature of its walls – would further determine the sound of the falling water. Tuning a waterfall wasn't a science but a process of experimentation, and the tuner needed to be patient and prepared to spend time tweaking the variables until the desired sound – crisp, muted, melodious or torrential – was achieved. It was also an advantage, though not an absolute necessity, if the waterfall tuner had perfect pitch, or at least an ear for music.

'Well, I didn't have perfect pitch, Larry, but I had better relative pitch than most and certainly an ear for music. I'd grown up playing the piano, and the organist at church gave me lessons on the organ as soon as my legs grew long enough. I knew what sounded good and what didn't and Summer said I was a natural. She also thought it would be a good idea if I plied my skill in the Washington area. She'd heard that the tuner there had retired and made it clear there wasn't room for two waterfall tuners in New York. That's the only downside to tuning waterfalls: there's not much demand for it. But when you do get a gig, it pays well.'

Larry asked Mike if business was good and Mike told him he got by. That's all he wanted to do. The big bucks no longer interested him and he could supplement his tuning income by playing church gigs or dipping into savings. His needs were simple. He rented cheap rooms and house-sat for others; his belongings were few and fitted into a large duffel bag; he ate two meals a day and drove a ten-year-old pickup with *Ergle for Gurgles* emblazoned on its sides. He was, however, in the process of branching out and recording the sounds of water with the intention of selling them online or through health food shops. 'No better White Noise, man! It's a VIP ticket to the Land of Nod.' To this end he'd been retuning and recording the higher reaches of Rock Creek, a small river that rose in Maryland and emptied into the Potomac by the Swedish Embassy, and was also planning to record two waterfalls in Virginia: Stubblefield Falls and The Great Falls.

'Of course, I'll need a wingman when I record those beauts, Larry… Hey, man. I've had a thought. Why don't you ride out with me one day and give me a hand? It'd be a blast, man, and we could take the dogs with us.'

'I'd be glad to, Mike. Believe it or not I've never been to either of those falls. Helen wasn't much for the outdoors. She liked walking in the cemetery but that was about as far as her love for nature went. She never felt comfortable driving with me and so a long trip was out of the question. She said that she never worried about us having an accident – because I drove too slowly for that to happen – but worried that I'd cause other people to have accidents. But that was Helen for you: always thinking of others.'

'She sounds quite a woman. I'm sorry for your loss, man.'

'Thanks,' Larry said. 'I'll never be able to replace her but at least I have Moses in my life now. And I'm meeting new people all the time. Tank's asked me to climb his ladders, Delores has invited me to an exhibition at the museum and now you've asked me to help you record the sound of waterfalls. Everything's starting to fall into place.'

'Sounds to me like you're a man on a mission, Larry!'

Larry was a man on a mission, but missions for other people. His own mission arrived the next day when the Head of the History Department phoned.

5

The Tank Commander

Laura walked into the lounge just as another episode of *The Dick Van Dyke Show* was about to start. All eyes were on the television and her appearance went unnoticed. Rob, the character played by Dick Van Dyke, had just left the house in a huff and the camera turned to an aquarium. 'What are the tropical fish talking about?' Laura asked the elderly resident closest to her. 'Beats the hell out of me, Miss Parker, but Rob's just had a hissy fit.' 'Hey! Either keep it down back there or turn up the volume,' someone called out. 'How are we supposed to hear anything with you two jibber-jabbering?' Laura smiled and excused herself.

'I don't know who that friend of yours is, Laura, but the man's a genius. Who'd have thought a DVD player would have made such a difference?'

'And the residents are happy with our choices?'

'More than happy – just look at their faces.'

All faces were turned to the television and Laura could only see the backs of their heads. There was laughter though, a commodity scarce and precious in any residential home, and her heart warmed to Larry. Who'd have thought that the man responsible for this transformation was the same man who'd caused so much consternation when he'd first visited the home? She decided then and there to invite Larry for a celebratory meal, but in light of Alice's comments, it was unlikely to be at their apartment.

Laura had supposed that Alice liked Larry and had been surprised when her partner told her differently. 'It was supposed to have been just us at the restaurant,' Alice had said. 'The *two* of us! But then you turned up with Larry, a man I'd never even met before, and then there were *three* of us. And it was *me*, Laura, *me* who ended up feeling like the odd one out. And he's strange, too, Laura, he's not normal. Who in their right mind asks you how tall you are when they first meet you or what you had for breakfast that morning? You might as well have brought Wayne! And it's not the first time you've done this to me! Can't you understand that it's you I want to spend time with when we go out and that if I wanted to spend time with the likes of Larry and Wayne I'd go to the zoo?'

It wasn't the first time Alice had expressed such thoughts, and Laura had to wonder if it was her own lack of consideration that caused these outbursts. On the surface Alice was a picture of calm and self-possession, a successful businesswoman with more friends than a person could count. It was easy to forget – and, in truth, difficult to believe – that a person with such outward blessings could have such internal insecurities, especially when they appeared to be of her own making.

Laura had always known that Alice was self-centred, but found this more an amusing delinquency than a cause for concern. Theirs, she reminded herself, was a match made on earth and not in Heaven. She didn't expect her partner to change and neither did she wish her to. Alice was a part of the imperfect world she inhabited, the broken world that had always attracted her. Her partner would always come first – and it was obvious she needed to make this clearer to Alice – but she had no intention of throwing Larry and Wayne to the kerb. No, she would learn to juggle the world and keep its imperfections separate; and she'd start by taking Larry out for a meal the next time Alice went out of town.

With this thought in mind she returned to her office and checked the calendar. She then picked up the phone and dialled Larry's number. The line was engaged. 'That's odd,' she thought. 'Who in the world would be calling Larry?'

'It's Bob Parish, Larry, the Head of the History Department... It's good to talk to you, too... Yes, far too long... Anyway, the reason I'm... The Desert Land Act? I don't think anyone's teaching it... Well the new guy doesn't see the point... It's not up to me, Larry... The Dean? It wouldn't matter to him if we were teaching back-to-back courses on nineteenth-century dolls' houses... Look, Larry, I've a meeting in five minutes so we'll have to keep this short. A letter arrived for you yesterday from the Hebrew University of Jerusalem and... I've no idea... Yes, very mysterious. I'd have forwarded it but we've been told to cut down on postage... By the Dean... Yes, I suppose it must sound odd that he takes more interest in postage stamps than he does the Desert Land Act but if you could... Yes, this afternoon would be fine. I'll leave it with the secretary... I'm not sure I'll be available... Okay, good talking to you, too, Larry... I will, and you take care, too. Give my regards to your wife.'

'Well that's a turn-up for the books, Moses. The Head of Department thinks that Helen's alive and someone from Israel's sent me a letter.'

A memory flickered in Moses' brain when Larry mentioned the word Israel and the dog climbed to its feet. 'My thoughts exactly, Moses. Once we've had lunch we'll go to the History Department and find out who it's from.'

Shortly after two o'clock Larry put a leash over Moses' head and set off for the university. There'd been a downpour earlier in the day and though the rain had now stopped the cobbled pavements were wet and puddly. They walked down 30th and took a right on Q St, headed south on Wisconsin for two blocks and then turned west on O St, the road that led to the gates of the university.

Georgetown University was a hilltop agglomeration of grey stone and red brick buildings overlooking the Potomac. It had been founded in 1789 by John Carroll, the country's first Catholic bishop, and was the oldest Jesuit college in the United States. There was a statue of Carroll in the middle of the turning circle – a kindly man sitting in an armchair and dressed in a long flowing robe – and close by was Healy Hall, the neo-mediaeval centrepiece of the campus and the backdrop for a movie called *The Exorcist*. There were cannons set at either side of the building's doorway and a tall clock tower rose 200 feet into the sky. Larry strained to see if the clock hands were in place and was pleased to find they were. He'd never understood the student prank of stealing them and mailing them to the Vatican.

There was a game of Frisbee being played on Copley Lawn and Larry decided to stick to the path. Passers-by smiled at him, stopped to stroke Moses and one asked his name. 'It's

Larry,' Larry replied. 'Good name,' the girl commented. 'How old is Larry?' 'Sixty-seven,' Larry replied.

The History Department was on the sixth floor of the Intercultural Centre, one of the university's red brick buildings. It was almost three years since he'd retired and his heart fluttered when the centre came into view. He walked through the doors and into the long foyer, past the bust of Dr Sun Yat-sen (the Father of Modern China) and pressed the button for the elevator. He climbed out at the sixth floor and headed for the office.

The department was unusually quiet, but then he remembered it was Summer School, a time of year when afternoons were always quiet. Larry knocked on the door and walked in. The secretary was new: she didn't recognise him and he didn't recognise her. 'It's Professor MacCabe,' he said almost apologetically. 'I believe you have a letter for me.' The secretary handed him the letter and returned to her work. 'I see they're keeping you busy,' Larry smiled. The secretary nodded. 'I don't suppose Professor Parish is available, is he? We used to be good friends when I worked here.' The secretary explained that Professor Parish was in a meeting and had left instructions not to be disturbed. 'Well, just on the off-chance you see him in the next half hour, would you mind telling him that Larry MacCabe is in the faculty lounge and that his wife is dead.' The secretary told him she would, but doubted she would see him. Larry was about to head for the lounge when a thought struck him. 'Who's teaching The Emergence of Modern America these days?' he asked.

He then went to the lounge and put four quarters in the machine, waited for the plastic cup to drop and then watched as it filled with the fair-trade coffee favoured by the department.

The room was deserted and Larry sat alone. 'I had some of the best conversations in this room,' he reminisced to Moses. 'We might have taught different subjects, but we all had enquiring minds. There's nothing better for good conversation than an enquiring mind.' (Several of these enquiring minds walked into the lounge while Larry was there, but made abrupt about-turns when they saw their former colleague talking to a dog.)

He remembered the letter in his pocket and decided to open it rather than wait until he returned home. It was an invitation (all expenses paid) to be a guest speaker at a symposium on Desert Reclamation organised by the Advanced School of Environmental Studies and to be held at the Hebrew University of Jerusalem in early October. As an authority on the Desert Land Act of 1877, the writer of the letter suggested, his contribution would be of great interest to the delegates. 'Jiminy Cricket, Moses, I've been invited to give a talk in Israel!'

Moses barked and Larry rebuked himself for mentioning Moses and Israel in the same sentence. He then looked at his watch. Forty minutes had passed since he'd entered the lounge and it appeared that Professor Parish wouldn't be joining him after all. Buoyed by the contents of the letter he decided to pay a call on Professor Clayton.

Professor Clayton's office was his old office. It seemed odd knocking on a door that had once been his own and then waiting for someone else to open it. A voice from within boomed out: 'Enter!'

Scott Clayton was a large man in his fifties, powerfully built but also squat, as if his body had been compressed by a large weight he'd tried but failed to lift. His head was shaven, his clothes casual and he wore a pair of green rubber high tops.

His feet were propped on the desk and he was reading the previous day's edition of *The Hoya*, the student newspaper. He looked at Larry for a moment and then rose to his feet.

'I'm sorry to bother you, Professor Clayton, but I thought you might like to meet me. I'm Larry MacCabe and you're my replacement.'

Clayton held out his hand. 'I don't think of myself as your replacement, Professor MacCabe. From everything I've heard you're irreplaceable.'

Larry blushed. 'It's kind of you to say so, Professor Clayton, but with time I'm sure people will think the same of you.'

'I hope not,' Clayton mumbled, and then noticed Moses. 'Is the dog house-trained?'

'There's no need to worry about Moses,' Larry laughed. 'He did his business this morning and watered a tree less than an hour ago.'

'Well, now that we have met, is there anything in particular you'd like to say or can I get back to my newspaper? I'm not one for conversation for its own sake.'

Larry had been hoping that Clayton would ask him to sit down and was surprised by the man's brusqueness. 'Well, there is one small matter, Professor Clayton. I was talking to Professor Parish this morning – he's one of my oldest friends in the department – and he happened to mention that you'd dropped the Desert Land Act from the syllabus. I don't think he was trying to get you into trouble or anything – I think it just slipped out – but I was wondering why you decided to do that, and if it's a matter of your own confidence in the subject whether you'd like me to give guest lectures from time to time.'

Clayton snorted. 'I *do* mention the Desert Land Act but

only in passing, Professor MacCabe. That's all anyone in their right mind *would* do. There are far more important fish to fry in The Gilded Age than the Desert Land Act of 1877! Now, if you'll excuse me...'

'I don't mean to contradict you, Professor Clayton, but I think you're wrong – and the people of Israel agree with me. In fact, they've just invited me to speak on the very subject at the Hebrew University of Jerusalem, and there's no more prestigious a university.'

'I can think of several,' Clayton replied, 'and Georgetown is one of them! And I can also tell you with certainty that the Desert Land Act will remain a footnote in any course I teach unless, after meeting you, I decide to delete it altogether.'

There the conversation ended and Professor Clayton ushered Larry from the room. If he were a betting man, Larry would have wagered dollars to donuts that Professor Clayton was a good friend of Dr Young's!

Larry walked back to the elevator wondering what had become of the world – especially the world as it had been in the late nineteenth century – and was about to push the button when a familiar voice rang through the corridors: 'Who in the name of Hell brought a dog into the department? There's paw marks everywhere!'

Larry didn't return home directly but instead headed for Volta Park.

The indignant sound of Clive's voice had panicked him, and rather than wait for the elevator to arrive and run the risk of bumping into the irate janitor, he'd hurried to the stairwell and coaxed an unwilling Moses down twelve flights of stairs. The visit to the park was the dog's reward for its endeavours and a chance for its short, stubby legs to regain their composure. It was also a chance for Larry to regain his composure, too.

The park was empty when they arrived and the grass still damp. Mosquitoes were in the air and a buzz-saw sounded in the distance. Larry let Moses off the leash and wiped the remaining drops of rain from a bench with his handkerchief. He sat down and retied a loose shoelace, looked at his watch and then stared into the distance and sighed. 'Well, that was unexpected,' he said.

The visit to the Intercultural Centre had been an unsettling one, not at all as he'd imagined. The department had marched on without him and his position usurped by a man who bore more resemblance to a wrestler than an academic. What had once been familiar was now strange, and it slowly dawned on him that he no longer belonged there. Neither, it seemed, was he wanted.

Another man might have been more troubled by such thoughts but Larry, who was an optimist at heart, consoled himself with the belief that at least his reputation remained intact – and for an academic, this was the important thing. He'd left his mark on the department and would forever be a part of its history. And what was it that Professor Clayton had said about him? What was the word he'd used? That was it: *irreplaceable*. He was considered irreplaceable. Larry could think of no better accolade. And it appeared that it wasn't just the History Department of Georgetown University that held this view: it was also the Advanced School of Environmental Studies at the Hebrew University of Jerusalem. Just wait till he told the gang on Saturday.

The thought of meeting up with his new friends cheered

him. Maybe his old world had disappeared but a new one was taking its place. The dog park was his campus now and the Dog People – as Wayne referred to them – his new circle. And then, of course, there was Wayne himself, another new friend and potential protégé. He wondered where Wayne was at this moment, what he did with his time when he wasn't delivering the *Current* or climbing trees, and smiled at the thought of how pleased he'd be when he told him of his decision to make him his charge.

Moses by now had tired of exploring the park and was sitting on the grass by Larry's feet. 'Sorry about the stairs, old pal,' Larry said, rubbing the dog's scruff. 'You're not built for them and I'm getting too old for them. How about we both stick to flat surfaces in future?' Moses said nothing but appeared to agree, and made no fuss when Larry put the leash over his head and prepared to leave the park.

It was after they'd crossed Wisconsin and were walking down R St that a black Smart car drew up alongside them and slowed to a halt. The passenger window slid down and a voice called out: 'Hey, MacCabe! You up for some ladder climbing?'

'Now?' Larry asked, surprised to see Tank behind the wheel of such a small car.

'No, next December! I like to plan ahead.'

The window slid shut and Tank eased the car into a driveway two houses down. Larry followed on foot, unsure if he was expected to climb the ladders now or in December until he saw Tank manhandling a set of aluminium triple extension ladders out of his garage.

'You're sure you're okay with this, Larry?'

Apart from climbing the ladders Larry had no idea what *this* was. 'I'm quite happy to climb a ladder, Tank, but what do you want me to do when I get to the top of it?'

'I want you to take a look at the guttering. There's a blockage somewhere and the run-off's not draining into the downpipe. I'm guessing it's leaves from that tree over there,' he said, pointing to the large sculpted tree in the yard.

Larry looked at the tree admiringly. 'What kind of tree is that?' he asked. 'It's not one I'm familiar with.'

Tank glanced at the tree and appeared to give the matter some thought. 'It's a wooden one,' he said eventually. 'Now let's get the dogs settled.'

Larry followed Tank down a narrow path at the side of the house and through a high gate into the back garden. By Georgetown standards the yard was large, but compared with the garden at the front sadly neglected. The lawn was in need of a mow, the borders were overgrown and the water in the ornamental pond had turned green. It appeared to Larry that the gutters were the least of Tank's problems.

There was the sound of barking and Tank's Dogue de Bordeaux came running towards them. Sherman's build was powerful, his body thick-set and muscular, and from floor to ceiling he measured two-and-a-half feet. The dog's most notable feature, though, was its massive, trapezoid-shaped head which, by Larry's estimate, accounted for half its 140 pounds. The head was broad and wrinkled, and a thick upper lip draped over the lower jaw. The dog's eyes were set wide apart, its ears were small and pendent and there was a mask of red under its large nose.

Larry hung back while Tank quieted the large mastiff and then stepped forward and held out his hand. Sherman accepted it, licked it for all it was worth and then turned his attention to Moses. At Tank's bidding Larry took the leash off

Moses and the two dogs ran to the far corner of the garden. Larry looked at the slobber on his hand and turned to Tank. 'Just wipe it on the grass,' Tank said.

They returned to the front yard and Tank propped the ladders against the wall of the house. He extended them without effort until the rungs were resting just below the guttering and close to the downpipe. He then tested their rigidity. Once satisfied, he handed Larry a small trowel and told him to shovel any debris he found on to the ground.

'Just out of interest, Tank, why am I climbing the ladders and not you?'

'I don't like heights, Larry, and I'm not prepared to employ someone to do something I could do if I wasn't afraid of heights. This job's worth a cup of coffee, but no more than that.'

'You must suffer from acrophobia, then,' Larry said as he started to climb the ladder. 'You don't have anything to be ashamed of though: a lot of people are afraid of heights. Some other phobias are a bit more niche. Take apiphobes, for instance, they're afraid of bees. And then there are people who are afraid of the number thirteen and they're called triskaidekaphobes. And people who don't like needles are called belonephobes. With every rung climbed, Larry told Tank of other phobias: ailurophobia (cats), astraphobia (lightning), achluophobia (darkness) and so on until he reached the top of the ladder. In the hope of seeing Dent St he turned to look over the roofs of houses opposite, but was soon distracted by the smell of cigar smoke rising from below.

'I thought you told Delores you only smoked one cigar a week,' Larry called down to Tank.

'What can I tell you, Larry? I lied. Now what are you seeing up there?'

Larry looked into the guttering. There were a few leaves here and there and a weed growing further along, but nothing that would explain the water pooling at the mouth of the downpipe. He reasoned that the blockage was in the pipe and started to prod the inside with the trowel. Sure enough, something was wedged there. 'You don't have any rubber gloves, do you, Tank?' he shouted.

'Probably, but I don't know where they are. Just use your hand, Larry. Use the one that Sherman slobbered over.'

Reluctantly Larry did and got hold of something sodden and bristly. He pulled gingerly at first and then, as the object moved, with more force. What looked like a tail came into view and then claws, and then Larry gave a short scream and launched whatever it was he was holding into the air. The water in the gutter drained and as Tank looked upward a dead squirrel landed on his face and broke his cigar in two. 'Goddamn sonofabitch! What in the name of God, Larry!'

Larry quickly descended the ladders and started to wipe Tank's face and head with his damp handkerchief. 'Sorry, Tank. I didn't mean for that to happen. It just slipped out of my hand.' He looked down at the dead squirrel. 'You're not sciurophobic, are you?'

Tank glared at Larry, grabbed the handkerchief from his hand and placed it over the squirrel. 'Goddamn sonofabitch!' he said.

It was unclear to Larry if Tank was addressing him or the rodent and so he remained silent. Tank spat on the ground a couple of times and then opened the front door of the house and led Larry through an empty lounge into a kitchen without table and chairs. They washed in the sink – Tank his head and Larry his hands – and wiped themselves dry on an old tea towel. Tank then took a bottle of bourbon from a cupboard and poured two glasses: one for him, and the other also for him after Larry declined the whiskey in favour of lemonade. 'It's a bit early in the day for me, Tank, and Thursday night's Moses' bath night. Laura would never forgive me if I drowned him.'

Glasses in hand they left the kitchen and walked to a small den off the lounge crammed with furniture and a bed. 'This is where I do most of my living,' Tank said. 'One thing I don't suffer from is claustrophobia.'

Theodore 'Tank' Newbold was fifty-four years of age and worked at the State Department. He was a Foreign Service Specialist attached to the Bureau of Near Eastern Affairs and had spent more nights in hotels than his ex-wife had cooked him hot dinners. His love of the confined, however, though confirmed by these stays, dated to his time as a tank commander in the 1st Armoured Division, as did his byname.

Tank was born and grew up in San Antonio, Texas. His father worked in construction and his mother at the city's Visitor Information Centre across the street from the Alamo. He had two older brothers and one younger sister. The Newbolds like all parents wanted the best for their children, but had never been sure what Tank's best was. Unlike his brothers who were now in college, one studying petroleum engineering and the other business administration, Tank had never excelled in the classroom and had barely made it through High School without having to repeat a year. While both school and parents acknowledged that Tank wasn't stupid, they were baffled by his inability to see further than the end of his nose and recognise that there was more to life than tinkering with old cars and watching endless repeats of *Star Trek*. It appeared to the Newbolds that their youngest son was without ambition. But then, one morning, Tank surprised them. He sat down at the breakfast table and announced that he was going to become a tank commander. 'Like Humphrey Bogart in *Sahara*,' he said by way of explanation.

The previous night's late movie had inspired him, and by morning his mind was made up. 'I think it's something I could do for a living and enjoy,' he said. And it was something his parents thought he could do for a living, too. Whether or not he'd enjoy it they had no idea, but it would at least get him out of the house. 'You get the forms and I'll sign them,' his father said, crunching his way through a piece of toast.

Tank's application was accepted and he was despatched to Fort Knox, Kentucky, where the 70th Armor Regiment was stationed. He was eighteen at the time and, until introduced to the M1 Abrams tank, had never before been in love. It was a relationship that lasted longer than any of his four marriages.

A commander rose through the ranks, and for the next six years Tank familiarised himself with the tank and its operations. He learned how to maintain the mechanical and electrical systems, how to load the munitions and target the guns, how to communicate with other tanks and the commanding officer and eventually how to drive the juggernaut. And a juggernaut it was. The Abrams was 32 feet long, 12 feet wide and 8 feet high. It was heavily armoured, weighed 68 tons and could reach speeds of 45 mph. It was armed with machine guns, grenade launchers and flame throwers and its cannon could deliver rounds of 120 mm armour-piercing or high explosive ammunition. (A battalion of such tanks – forty-eight in number – had the firepower to level a major city in less than three minutes.)

Tank was promoted to Staff Sergeant, became a tank commander in the style of Humphrey Bogart, and in March, 2003, when American forces invaded Iraq, rolled into his very own *Sahara*. By then he was a Lieutenant, a platoon leader commanding four tanks. He and his crews were at the vanguard of the assaulting forces and the first to secure a bridgehead over the Euphrates. They cleared routes, secured areas and destroyed enemy forces at Al Hillah, Al Kifl and closer to Baghdad, and, once the fighting was over, helped control and stabilise the situation.

Tank's ambition was modest. All he'd ever aspired to be was a tank commander. He had, however, qualities of leadership and split-second decision-making that were recognised by his commanding officers and it was they, rather than him, who put his name forward for promotions. As long as Tank could sit for hours in the bowels of a tank it mattered little to him if he was a Staff Sergeant, a Lieutenant or a member of the Klingon High Council. During the time of pacification, however, it was noted that Tank was as effective outside the tank defusing situations as he'd been inside it creating them, and his services were co-opted by the Coalition Provisional Authority.

Tank's mediating style was matter of fact and to the point. He believed that all parties in Iraq had an obligation to make the lives of its people as comfortable as the situation allowed, and the only way to do this was by compromise. It would be to no one's advantage if one party left the table on foot and the other drove home in a top-of-the-range SUV. Both should leave the meeting behind the wheels of mid-range cars.

It helped in these discussions that Tank had a fundamental grasp of the native language. Although no conventional linguist, as a teenager infatuated with *Star Trek* he'd taught himself Klingon, and while serving in Kuwait (another *Sahara*) during the Gulf War had recognised its similarities to Arabic. To the ear, both languages sounded as if the speaker was trying to cough up a ball of trapped phlegm, and there was nothing to suggest that a person who could pronounce one would be incapable of pronouncing the other. Tank decided to give it a try and found Arabic far less complicated to learn than Klingon. His vocabulary was limited but sufficient to make a difference.

The outcome of these meetings was not always favourable or even as expected, but Tank acquitted himself well. His reputation as a skilled negotiator spread, and in the spring of 2004, his time in the military drawing to a close, he was approached by the State Department and offered a position in the Bureau of Near Eastern Affairs. The job sounded interesting, and with no other irons in the fire Tank accepted their offer. The only part of the deal that didn't appeal was moving to Washington DC. His fourth wife, Missy, however, loved the idea.

Tank Newbold was the marrying kind, but probably shouldn't have been. He was a romantic and fell in love easily, but for most of his married life was out of love. He first married when he was twenty-eight, again when he was thirty-four and for the third time at the age of forty-one. None of these marriages lasted more than four years, and one (his second) only six months. He'd met all three wives while on leave, married in haste and then, once back in his tank, repented at leisure. By the time he met and married Missy he had two daughters and one son, each living with a different mother and stand-in fathers with children of their own. Tank acknowledged that the situation was messy, but rationalised his behaviour on the grounds that it was more important for the nation to have a full arsenal of nuclear weapons than it was to be populated by nuclear families. He saw his children occasionally, but his support was more financial than emotional and he looked forward to the day his youngest child graduated from college.

Missy was supposed to have been the keeper, and at the outset of their relationship the augurs were good. She was from Texas, her father and brothers were in the military and she herself had been divorced twice. It appeared they had lots to talk about and for seven years the marriage worked. But then, as always happened, Tank found himself in a bar wondering what it would be like to return home to an empty house.

He made a list of things he liked about Missy and things he didn't. On the plus side was her looks, but that was as far as the plus side got. Against Missy was a full page. She talked too much and her conversation was inconsequential. Her laugh was too loud and the things she found funny he found stupid. She was tone deaf and whistled out of tune. She had too many teeth in her mouth and prepared too many salads. She spent money on clothes she never wore and bags she never carried. She was allergic to cats and didn't like dogs and was talking about getting a budgerigar. She collected miniature armadillos. She dragged him to plays that bored him and concerts that made him want to kill the conductor. She was too social climbing and her friends and their husbands were all phonies. She'd furnished the house with too many rugs and too many cushions, and the antique chairs she'd bought were all uncomfortable and not one of the settees long enough to stretch out on. She'd bought his and hers towels and matching dressing gowns. She… and the list went on.

Of all her faults it was the whistling that irritated him most. Her damned, tuneless whistling! What person in their right mind whistled these days, let alone a woman? Yet his wife would whistle along to every shit song that came on the radio and to every bird-brained tune that played in her head, and on occasion she'd even accompanied the kettle while it boiled. The last thing they needed in the house was a budgerigar! And once, after they'd finished making love and he'd moved to his side of the bed, she'd lain on her back and whistled the jingle to an old antacid commercial: *Plop, plop, fizz, fizz, oh what a relief it is* and left him wondering if she'd been glad they'd made love or was simply relieved that they'd finished.

Tank was aware that he wasn't the easiest person to live with, and he wasn't. Out of necessity for the lives and well-being of the crews he'd been responsible for, and for the thousands of others depending on the crews' performance, his manner had grown gruff and no-nonsense. He spoke his mind, didn't pussyfoot around a subject to spare another's feelings and despised pleasantries and small talk. He was unsociable and suspicious of likeable people, and completely distrustful of anyone who joined anything too easily. To his way of thinking there was little difference between those people who joined conga lines and the Germans who'd joined the Nazi Party. They were all jerks.

In courtship and early marriage Tank would be accommodating, solicitous and in his own way loving. But once the bloom fell from the rose he became impossible to live with. He stopped making an effort, went out of his way to be disagreeable and if his wife didn't like it, too bad: she knew where the door was. He'd come home on an evening and strip down to his vest and shorts, take a beer from the refrigerator and sit down in front of the television. He'd make no attempt at conversation and only grunt replies. Eventually the wife of the time would grow weary of his behaviour – as Tank had hoped she would – decide he was a slob and start divorce proceedings. Five years after moving to Washington Missy decided the same.

If no longer in love with Tank at the time of their move, Missy was still enamoured by his standing and was acutely aware that, socially, life was always easier when part of a couple. Society embraced young single people but not older ones, who were often viewed by their peers with suspicion. People of their generation arranged dinner parties rather than mixers, and numbers were expected to be even and comprise only couples. For such occasions the marriage was convenient: Missy attended Tank's functions and he accompanied her to hers. But as Tank became less willing to oblige his wife Missy started to make alternative arrangements and the relationship became one of formality: husband and wife in name only. By the time Larry made Tank's acquaintance the relationship had taken on a different formality.

'So when you say your wife's gone, do you mean she's dead?' Larry asked his host.

'I wish to God she was, Larry, because the damn alimony payments are *killing* me.'

'The two of you are divorced then?'

'Well, we're not married and she's not dead so I reckon we must be. Who'd have thought, eh?'

'I suppose Helen and I were lucky,' Larry said. 'We never even had ups and downs.'

Tank looked at him. 'You're telling me that there was *no* time in your marriage when one of you got an itch? And I'm talking here about one of those itches that just about drives you crazy and one you can't scratch.'

Larry thought about this. 'There were times when Helen got yeast infections… and I once had athlete's foot… but we just bought over-the-counter creams at the pharmacy and they cleared up in no time. Generally speaking it's best not to scratch an itch. My experience is that scratching only makes it worse.'

Tank shook his head and poured himself another whiskey. 'You want another lemonade, Larry?'

'I'd best not, Tank, but thanks. I try not to drink too much after the late afternoon or I end up having to get up in the middle of the night and go to the bathroom. The doctor says it's nothing to worry about, but I don't like my sleep to be disturbed. Once my head hits the pillow I like it to stay there for at least seven hours.'

'You ought to drink whiskey, then. Dehydrates the hell out of you, and if you drink enough of it you won't have to piss till lunchtime.'

There was a pause in the conversation and Larry was spurred to ask Tank another question. 'Did your wife take the furniture with her when she left? I couldn't help noticing that this is the only downstairs room that's furnished.'

'She did, and if she hadn't I'd have burned it. It was God-awful stuff: far too fancy for my liking. The things I brought into the marriage I dragged in here and this is the only room I use. Everything's to hand and it's cheaper on the air-conditioning. I eat, sleep and live in this room and shit in the can. It's enough for any man.'

'But what happens if you have visitors?' Larry asked.

'I don't have visitors. If any family comes to town they stay with my mother over in Arlington and I visit with them there and take Sherman with me.'

'Does your wife miss Sherman?'

'Hah! Sherman's the reason she left me,' Tank said. 'She told me I had a choice to make: him or her, so I chose him. And there's not a day gone by that I've regretted the decision.'

The point came in Tank and Missy's marriage when a straw would have broken its back, let alone a dog Sherman's weight. To Missy's way of thinking a marriage of convenience was one thing but dog hair in the house another matter entirely, and the night she and Tank watched *Turner & Hooch* on the television and Tank said that he wouldn't mind having a dog like Hooch was the night she gave him the ultimatum. Two weeks later Tank returned home with a small Sherman (named after the World War II Medium Tank) on a leash. It was Tank's way of asking her to leave, and the next day she packed a suitcase and left the house on R St for good. In her absence the gutters filled with leaves, the downpipe got blocked by a dead squirrel and the grass in the backyard grew tall. This reminded Tank…

'How do you feel about gardening, Larry? I take care of the front lawn to keep the neighbours happy, but the backyard's got a bit overgrown. The guy Missy hired stood around for too much of the time he was here and so I fired him and figured I'd get another gardener who charged less. Turns out that gardeners are hard to come by in Georgetown.'

'Oh… um… I don't think I have time for that, Tank. My days are pretty full as it is, and I've just been invited to give a paper at the Hebrew University of Jerusalem in October and I'll have to spend any free time I have preparing my speech.'

'Don't sweat it, Larry, it was only a thought. I'll get some illegal to do it and keep him off the books. Where are you staying when you go to Jerusalem?'

'I think they're arranging accommodation on campus for the duration of the conference, probably in a hall of residence, but I'm hoping to go a few days early and explore the Old City and maybe visit Masada. I'll need a hotel for those days. Is there any particular one you'd recommend?'

'Yes, the King David. If you're only going to Jerusalem the one time then the King David is where you have to stay. I've got a brochure somewhere…' He riffled through a stack of papers piled close to his chair but came up empty-handed. 'It's somewhere, Larry, but I don't know where. Tell you what I'll do. I'll dig it out when I have time and make a present of it to you. In my book one good deed deserves another and I owe you one for clearing the gutters. But after that we're quits, right?'

'Right,' Larry said. 'I must admit I'm excited about the trip. I've never been to Israel before but it's a country I've been familiar with since I attended Sunday school as a boy. What are the people like?'

'Plain rude if you ask me, but don't quote me on that. I'm supposed to get on with everyone out there and if it gets back to the Israelis that I've been badmouthing them they might launch a strike on R St.'

'I won't say a word, Tank. You have my word. And I think

I have a solution to your gardening problem. Why don't you ask Wayne to take care of the backyard?'

'Wayne? You mean the kid who hangs round the park?'

Larry nodded.

'You must be out of your mind, Larry. I don't want that kid anywhere near my house! I'd take my chances with a Sandinista rather than hire him. The guy's not wrapped tight.'

'I know he comes across as a little strange, but my feeling is that his heart's in the right place. I don't know his full story, but it strikes me that he's had a few hard knocks in life and his grammar's suffered. Once he learns to speak English properly...'

'He's in his damn thirties, Larry! He's not going to change the way he speaks now and even if he did he'd still talk the same weird shit. Tell me, you ever heard the joke about the man who goes to the meat counter to buy kidleys?' Larry admitted he hadn't. 'Okay, I'll tell it to you then: a man goes to the meat counter and asks for a pound of kidleys. The butcher looks at him and says: kidleys? You mean kidneys, don't you? And the guy replies: I said kidleys, *diddle* I? And that's as far as you'll get with Wayne! If you want my advice you'll steer clear of the kid.'

'But Laura thinks he's nice.'

'Laura collects driftwood. She's got no quality control when it comes to people.'

Larry was about to say something when a car pulled into the drive and Tank got up to see who it was. 'What the hell's she doing here?' he said.

Larry looked at his watch. 'It's time I was going, Tank. I'll go and get Moses and leave you to your guest. It's not your ex-wife, is it?'

'No, it's worse than that. It's my mother.'

It took Larry a while to separate the two dogs and get Moses back on his leash, and by the time he got to the front garden Tank was in a heated discussion with his mother, a fragile but stern-looking woman in her eighties. 'Mom, how many times have I told you *not* to walk on the grass? That's what the path's for. I use the path, Larry here used the path and if I catch you walking on the grass again I'll turn the damn sprinklers on you!'

Larry gave a small cough to let Tank know he was there.

'Larry, this is my mother. Mother this is Larry.'

Larry held out his hand and the old lady accepted it hesitantly. 'Your face looks familiar, young man,' she said. 'Are you the gardener?'

'No, I'm a friend of your son's, Mrs Newbold. I've just been cleaning his gutters.'

'Larry's an *acquaintance*,' Tank corrected. 'And he's the one that threw the dead squirrel on my head. It was deliberate, Mom.'

The old lady let go of Larry's hand and scowled at him. 'Well, *really*, young man!' she said. 'You ought to be ashamed of yourself!'

She then turned to her smiling son. 'Did he hurt you, Theodore?'

Larry gathered the tools for Moses' bath and laid them on the bathroom floor: a pH balanced coconut oil-based shampoo, cotton balls, a washcloth, a blow-dryer and some towels. First he brushed and combed Moses, placed a cotton ball in each ear and then lifted him into the bathtub. Once the dog settled he ran the water through the shower attachment until it was lukewarm and then started to wet Moses, careful to keep the water away from his head and especially his eyes and ears. Larry rubbed shampoo into the coat, made sure to rinse all the soap out of the fur and then wiped the dog's face with a wet washcloth. He then lifted Moses out of the tub, gently rubbed him dry with a towel and finished the job by blow-drying the fur on a no heat setting.

Throughout the bath, Larry talked to Moses.

'You see, the way I see it Moses, Tank and I have a lot in common. He lives by himself and I live by myself and we both have dogs. He hasn't got a wife and I don't have a wife, but I don't have a wife because Helen died and he doesn't have a wife because Missy left him. I'd have hated it if Helen was alive and dating other men. I think that would have hurt more than her dying did. It doesn't seem to bother Tank, but it would bother me. I think I must have loved Helen more then he loved Missy. And I'm not going to listen to him about Wayne, either. I think Wayne's a nice young man. He's polite and he calls me professor. I miss being called that. I don't think I miss the department, though. I didn't enjoy visiting it today. I thought I would but I didn't, and I don't like the man who's teaching my course now. It's not because he's dropped the Desert Land Act from the syllabus, though. It's because he's not a nice man and he reminds me of the plastic surgeon who had Loop put down. I told you about Loop, didn't I? He was my first dog, the one I got from the pound. It was after he died that I became friends with Laura. And that reminds me: there was a message on the answering machine from Laura when we got home today and she wants to take me out for dinner as a thank you for suggesting they play DVDs at the nursing home. We're going to decide where to eat when we meet at the park on Saturday, but I'm thinking Mexican. I like Mexican food. It's going to be just the two of us this time because Alice is going out of town on business and won't be here to join us. That's a pity, because I like Alice and I think she likes me, too. And that's another thing: I've been invited to give a talk in Is...' (Here Larry caught himself and remembered the confusion the word Israel caused Moses) '... a foreign country and I'll be gone for a few days myself. But there's no need for you to worry, Moses. I'll make sure you're well looked after while I'm gone.'

In bed that night, his bladder emptied, Larry thought of who might take care of Moses while he was away. Laura and Alice would have been his first choice, but they had their hands full with Repo these days and it was unlikely Tank would agree to take Moses. There was Mike, of course, and Delores, but they lived in rented rooms and barely had space for their own dogs. He could take Moses to a kennel he supposed, but didn't like the idea of doing that. There might be dogs there that didn't like Basset Hounds and there was also a good chance that he'd get fleas or catch some other kind of dog disease that couldn't be cured.

And then the answer came to him. Why on earth hadn't he thought of this before?

6

The Weird Kid

By the time Tank arrived at the park that Saturday morning, Laura, Alice, Mike, Delores and Larry were already sitting at their preferred table. He unclipped Sherman's leash and walked up to them.

'Tell me something,' he said. 'How the hell can a person who works in an ice-cream parlour *not* smile?'

'It's good to see you, too, Tank,' Alice replied. 'Are we well?' She looked around the table. 'I think we are, but it's always nice to be asked.'

'If you're so concerned about people's manners, Alice, then you should go to the ice-cream parlour on Wisconsin and lecture them on the subject. Have you ever been there?' Alice indicated that she hadn't and Tank continued. 'They've got this photograph on the wall of the owner shaking hands with Obama and he's got a smile on his face the size of a Mac truck. If the guy can smile at the President when he's handing him a *free* ice-cream, the least he can do is tell his employees to smile at customers who are actually *paying* for ice-creams. I told the guy serving me that and he just shrugged! Told me to have a nice day and to come back soon. Fat fucking chance of that happening!

'You know the curse on this town? It's full employment! Used to be that stores only employed people who could put a smile on their face and act interested, but now, well now they take anyone they can get.'

'A bit like the State Department, then,' Alice said.

Tank ignored the comment and turned his attention to the seating arrangement. Mike, Laura and Alice were sitting on one of the benches attached to the table, and Delores and Larry on the other. 'Delores, why don't you change places with Mike?'

'Why do I have to move?' Delores asked. 'I was here first.'

'Because you take up too much room and we need to balance the skin with the meat. The only way we can make this work is if you sit with Laura and Alice and I sit with Mike and Larry.'

'You stay where you are Delores,' Laura said. 'It will be easier if Alice and I move to your side of the table and Larry sits here.'

'That means I'll have to move,' Alice said, 'and we were here *second*.'

'I don't mind standing,' Larry said. 'I could sit on the grass, if you like.'

'You'll do no such thing,' Laura said. 'Now come on, Alice. Show some of those good manners you've been lecturing Tank about.'

As Mike had to stand to allow Alice room to swing her legs over the bench, the rearrangement of the seating positions resulted in the displacement of four people rather than the two that Tank's plan would have required, and the complicated manoeuvre took three minutes.

'Happy now?' Delores asked Tank, once everyone was seated again.

'Tank doesn't do happy, do you, Tank?' Alice said.

'No, but I do satisfied, Alice, and this arrangement satisfies my ass. It's been in need of a seat ever since it left home this morning.'

Delores now took Tank to task. 'I don't think there was any call for that comment of yours about meat and skin. We all have meat on our bones – you as much as anyone.'

'That's very true, Delores,' Tank said. 'But there's a difference between having meat on your bones and a herd of cattle.'

Before Delores could respond Tank slapped a brochure on the table and slid it to the far end of the table where Larry was sitting. 'That's the information on the King David I promised you.'

Conversation then turned to Larry's forthcoming trip to Israel, which Larry was happy to talk about – especially the part that related to the Desert Land Act of 1877. It was Delores who interrupted him.

'You're going to miss the Blessing of the Animals, Larry. St Francis of Assisi Day falls on October 4th and you'll be in Israel. What a pity. It would have been Moses' first blessing too, because Mrs Eisler's synagogue didn't bless animals. I suppose it must be a Christian practice.'

'There's some cool rabbis out west who bless animals, Delores,' Mike said, 'but they're few on the ground and they anoint them on the same day they commemorate the New Year for trees. Tu something or other.'

'Tu B'Shevat,' Larry said. 'It's the 15th of Shevat on the Jewish calendar and usually falls in January.'

'Isn't it wonderful to be surrounded by such clever people?' Delores said, seemingly to the less clever people at the table. 'I could never have had these conversations if I'd stayed in Portland.'

'If I'd stayed home in bed this morning I wouldn't have had to *listen* to these conversations,' Alice sighed. 'And why do you suppose that Mike and Larry are more intelligent than the rest of us just because they know shit that we don't? Sometimes shit is just that, Delores: shit! You don't need to know it, and do you really think any one of us is likely to be in a future social situation where Tubshit is the topic of conversation?'

'Tu B'Shevat,' Larry corrected.

'Okay, Larry, we get it. You know the word and I don't.'

'Oh I'm sorry, Alice,' Delores said. 'I didn't mean to imply that you and Laura were any less clever than Mike and Larry. I know for a fact that you're not.'

'Hey, how come my name's missing from this equation?' Tank asked.

'That's because you don't *fit* into any equation,' Laura smiled. 'You're a cat among pigeons, Tank, and don't say you don't know it.'

Laura had been largely detached from the preceding conversation, watching Repo and searching for signs of improvement. It appeared the pills were having little effect on his behaviour and the mention of St Francis of Assisi Day sparked her interest. It was a long shot she knew, but both time and hope were running out for Repo. The dog was slowly drowning in its own body, and for his sake Laura was prepared to clutch at any straw.

She'd been aware that St Francis was the patron saint of animals since childhood but now, for the first time in years, remembered the thick ceramic plate that had hung from her parents' lounge wall. The relief had depicted the saint in a monk's habit surrounded by rabbits, squirrels and a small fawn; birds perched on his shoulder and some feeding from his open hand. But other than this memory, she had no real knowledge of the man or his powers.

'What do you know about St Francis, Mike?' she asked, fully expecting – and for once hoping – that Larry would contribute to the conversation.

'He's one of the most super-chilled cats that ever lived, Laura: a saint in the true sense of the word. And it's really neat how his life parallels that of The Buddha's. Both of them were born into wealthy families and both of them took vows of poverty and chastity after witnessing suffering in the wider world. St Francis and The Buddha could have been brothers. But that's Christianity and Buddhism for you: two peas in the same beautiful pod.'

Larry filled in the historical details and told the stories of St Francis preaching to the birds, talking to a wolf and founding the religious order that still bore his name.

'Man, the dude would have dug waterfalls!' Mike concluded.

Tank bristled at the drivel spilling from Mike's mouth, bit the end off a cigar and lit it. As usually happened in these circumstances Delores started to cough and waft at the smoke but no one else appeared troubled, especially Laura who was keen to know if a patron saint was able to plead the cause of those he purportedly patronised.

'I'm assuming so,' Mike said. 'The Catholic Church has always believed in the power of intermediaries. That's why they hold the Virgin Mary in such high regard.'

Laura thought for a moment. She and Alice had always made a point of not taking Repo to the annual Blessing of the Animals service. She'd looked upon it as an unnecessary novelty act to swell the ranks of the dwindling congregation, and Alice as an occasion for overly proud owners to show off their pets. Besides, before now Repo had never been in need of any supernatural help; any complaints he might have suffered from had been taken care of by the vet. Now, however, it appeared that Jim's treatments weren't working.

'Alice, can I have a quick word with you?' she asked.

The two of them left the table and walked out of earshot. When they returned Laura announced to Delores that she and Alice would like not only to attend the service this year but also help her and the Pastor organise it.

'Oh, that's wonderful news, Laura. And I know the Pastor will be pleased to hear this. She's always telling me she can use more help. I'll let Patricia know, too.'

'I don't think Patricia will be playing the organ this St Francis' Feast Day,' Mike said. 'It's looking like I'll be the organist.'

Patricia, he explained, was currently under arrest in the Netherlands. She'd been there on holiday, touring the canals and art galleries, and been detained by police after purchasing three grams of cocaine from an undercover narcotics officer.

Patricia – never Pat – had been the organist at the Church of Latter-Day Lutherans for nine years. She was in her late thirties and worked as a barista in one of Georgetown's coffee houses. Until her arrest Patricia had been unaware that she had a drug problem. After all she was middle class and had never before had any dealings with the police, though, as she was now ready to admit, had probably had many dealings with those known to the police.

And neither had anyone at church ever suspected that Patricia might have a narcotics problem. The writing had always been on the wall they now supposed, but at the time it had been too illegible to read and open to misinterpretation. It had always been assumed, for instance, that Patricia's slim form and nervous energy were the products of a healthy diet and the number of coffees she drank during the day, and that her sinus problems were the consequence of allergies. Similarly, they had dismissed her mood swings and occasional touchiness as the hallmarks of a gifted musician. What had been noted at the time, however, and never fully explained, was the rapid tempo she'd played the hymns which, on occasion, had shortened services by as much as five minutes and left some of the older members of the congregation quite breathless.

The arrest, however, had now clarified the situation for all, especially Patricia who had resolved to check into rehab once the unpleasantness of Amsterdam was behind her and she was allowed to return to the United States. The Pastor had already made it clear to her that the church was there to forgive and not judge her: this, after all, was what Christianity was all about. There was, however, an element of practicality to this decision as, since the unfortunate epidemic of the eighties when many male organists had stopped playing the organ forever, the Pastor was more than aware that church organists were thin on the ground. In other words the Church of Latter-Day Lutherans would not only forgive Patricia, they would also hold open her position until she was well enough to return. In the meantime, Mike Ergle, the neighbourhood's popular waterfall tuner, would keep her organ seat warm.

'Oh that poor, dear girl,' Delores said. 'What a dreadful time of it she must be having.'

Alice gulped. 'I suffered a trauma of my own last week, Delores. I don't know if Laura's mentioned this, but I bought a replacement address book for my miniature Filofax and it didn't fit! I only realised it once I got home, but two of the holes were in the wrong place. I thought I'd bought the wrong size or the assistant had made a mistake, but when I went back to the store I was told that the format of the inserts had changed and that my style of personal organiser was now obsolete. I wouldn't have minded so much but I'd only had it fifteen years and it was a present from my grandma. I can't begin to describe how much sentimental value it has. But it's only when something like this happens to you that you can identify with the bad things that happen to other people. I can really empathise with Patricia. It's like I'm sitting right there in the prison cell with her.'

'Jesus H Christ!' Tank spluttered, choking on his cigar. 'You people ought to listen to yourselves: animal blessings in a church! Changed inserts for personal organisers! Empathy for some druggie in lock-up! You need to get your priorities sorted, and if you want something worthwhile to do with your time then complain about the goddamn sidewalks in this town. They're a disgrace!'

The cobbled pavements of Georgetown had long been Tank's bugbear. For one thing they weren't cobbled but bricked, and most of these flat, red paving blocks were loose and uneven, following contours dictated by tree roots and interrupted by small protuberant gas and water valve shut-offs. The whole neighbourhood was an accident waiting to happen, but for the sake of old-world humbug and tourism the residents' concerns were being ignored. 'If I was a goddamn lawyer,' Tank said, 'I'd get me the biggest shingle ever made and hang it outside an office on M St. I'd have clients queuing round the block and I'd become the richest man in Georgetown. But, you know what? I sure as hell wouldn't stay in Georgetown. I'd move to a neighbourhood with proper sidewalks, ones you could roller-skate on.'

The other thing about the sidewalks that ticked Tank off was the ornamental gardens planted at the base of the maple and oak trees that lined the streets. There was no need for them, no room for them, and the planted groundcover was less than remarkable. And to make matters worse the authorities had surrounded the miniature plots of blue lilyturf with black iron railings that came to the kerb and made exiting a car on that side impossible. 'If you don't believe me count the door dents!' he said.

'Man, you gotta give up on the sidewalks, Tank. Georgetown wouldn't be the same without them.'

'I know it wouldn't. That's my damn point! And Georgetown wouldn't be the same without you either, Mike. On both counts the place would be better off.'

Mike laughed and Delores told Tank not to be so mean. 'Sometimes I wonder how a dog as nice as Sherman can live with a man like you,' she said. 'I don't suppose you'll be bringing Sherman to the blessing, will you?'

'Damn right I won't, but you'll be glad to know I'll be joining you at the museum exhibition next month. I've checked my schedule and I'm in town that week.'

'Well that's something, at least. It's looking like we'll all be there, and Petey's coming down from New York for it. You don't know of any other people who might be interested, do you?'

Tank shook his head.

'What about your mother?' Larry suggested.

Tank glared at him.

'You have a mother?' Laura asked surprised.

'Of course I have a mother! How the hell do you think I got here; some passing stranger blew me up with a football pump?'

'Stop being silly, Tank,' Laura laughed. 'You've never mentioned your mother before so I just presumed she was dead.'

'Oh no, Laura, she's not dead,' Larry said. 'She lives in Arlington, isn't that right, Tank?'

Once again Tank glared at Larry.

'Why don't you bring her along?' Delores said. 'It would be nice to meet her.'

'Believe me, Delores, it's not nice for *anyone* to meet my mother. No one benefits from her company and I try and avoid it as much as possible. The hell I'm bringing her to the museum with me! I still don't know why she moved to Washington in the first place. It's not as if I'm her favourite child. Anyway, the good thing is that she's old, so there's a good chance she'll die soon.'

'That's a horrible thing to say!' Alice said. 'You should be ashamed of yourself.'

Tank smiled to himself, pulled on his cigar and waited for the conversation to move on.

'Did I tell you I've arranged to be buried in a pet cemetery when I die?' Delores said.

For a woman who adhered to dog blessings, belonged to a K-9 rescue organisation called Operation Paws for Homes and helped organise the annual Howl-o-Ween adoption event, the news shouldn't have come as a surprise, but as much for its morbidity as Delores' choice of location the announcement did.

Delores had been thinking about this for some time, but had only made the arrangement after she and Petey had toured the Furry Angel Pet Cemetery the previous Sunday. The cemetery, located in Maryland, was an adjunct of a human cemetery, and the area designated for pets was adjacent to an area reserved for people of the Jewish faith.

Delores had always had more faith in dogs than people: their love was unconditional, their loyalty assured and not one of them, as far as she knew, had ever suggested that she was fat. She also believed that it would be a lot more peaceful resting in the ground next to the likes of Magnum, Ling-ling, Rusty and Fluffy than it would be Tank Newbold.

She and Petey had toured every square foot of the burial ground, reading the inscriptions on plaques decorated with hearts, small photographs and dog bones and occasionally shedding a tear. *Sleep Little Lady until We Are Together Again; You Have Left My Life but You Will Never Leave My Heart; A Tiny Angel Dressed In Fur; Wait For Me On Your Side Of The Rainbow, Sweet Girl.* There was so much more love to be found in a pet cemetery than a regular cemetery, where tombstone inscriptions were limited to dates and genealogies. It was reading the following inscription that clinched it for Delores: *She Asked for Nothing but Gave Us Her All.* 'That's me, Petey!' she'd said excitedly. 'That describes me perfectly. This is where I belong and this is where Button and I will stay together forever. It's decided!' (On closer examination of the plaque it turned out that the inscription had been written for a ferret called Snickers.)

'Well, no, my body won't actually be buried in the cemetery but my ashes will be interred there,' Delores said in reply to Alice's question.

'And is the cemetery for all pets or just dogs?'

'It's for all pets, Mike. We saw plaques for birds, cats, rabbits and goldfish and I'm sure there were other pets there that we didn't notice. It was like a Noah's Ark.'

'How about whales, Delores? Did you see any plaques for whales?'

'Of course we didn't see any plaques for whales. Who's ever heard of anyone having a whale as a pet?'

Tank thought of Button but said nothing, just pulled on his cigar and smiled. Laura thought of the Middle East and wondered why the government had employed a person who brought so much discord to his own world to bring peace to that region.

An hour passed in such fashion. Occasionally one of them would rise from the table to throw a ball or fuss with their dog and then, close to one o'clock, Delores' stomach rumbled. She looked at her watch. 'It's time I was going,' she announced. 'I only had four croissants for breakfast and I'm starting to feel peckish. Button! Button!' she called. 'Come to Mama, baby. It's time for Mama to eat.'

Button ran to the table and jumped on Delores' wide lap. Relative to its body the dog's head was large, its round eyes protruding and luminous and its large ears pointed. It was the most fragile-looking of all the dogs in the park, but tended, unlike many Chihuahuas, toward the placid. Despite their difference in size Button and Delores made for ideal living companions: each was devoted to the other, neither liked exercise and both appreciated warmth. And Button was also perfectly sized for the small basement apartment that Delores rented on Prospect St. Its owners, who lived on the ground and first floors of the house, were an old married couple who read and then gave their daily newspaper to Delores, who would use the pages to line Button's indoor litter box.

Delores plopped Button into her shoulder bag and de-wedged herself from the picnic table. Laura and Alice, who had to stand to let Delores out anyway, decided they too may as well be on their way and then Mike, whose gig at the church was now open-ended, decided that he'd better leave and start practising some new hymns. For a few minutes it was just Larry and Tank sitting at the table, but once Tank caught sight of a young man dragging a cart towards them he made his excuses. 'You can deal with the weird kid, Larry. I'm leaving!'

It was the weird kid Larry had been hoping to meet.

Wayne Trout's day hadn't got off to the best of starts, but then again neither had his life.

Wayne had grown up in Charles Town, West Virginia, a town founded by Charles Washington, the youngest brother of the more famous George. It was a small community, little more than 5,000 in number and had only one claim to fame: it was here, in 1859, that John Brown, the abolitionist and madman, had been tried and publicly hanged for raiding the federal armoury at Harper's Ferry and killing seven men. His body was given no resting place in Charles Town but taken by train to New York. It now *lies a-mouldering* on the outskirts of Lake Placid.

Wayne was the youngest of three children, the product of carelessness rather than family planning, and his welcome to the Trout household was muted. Mr & Mrs Trout hadn't bargained for another mouth to feed at this stage in their lives, and neither had their two daughters, Millie and Etta aged twelve and ten respectively, expected to share a bedroom. With time, however, the Trouts mellowed, and though never fully accepting Wayne as one of them at least got used to having him around the house.

Wayne's birth had been premature, but there was nothing at the time of his delivery to suggest that he might be odd in any way. That he might be, only struck his parents once they realised he was taking a longer time than usual to reach his milestones. He was late sitting up, for instance, late standing and walking, and an entire age passed before he started to talk. And then, when he had mastered these accomplishments, it turned out he wasn't very good at any of them. His gait was awkward and his balance poor. He tripped and fell easily, bumped into things and had trouble catching and hitting balls. He fell off bicycles, struggled with cutlery and could never fasten his buttons or tie his own shoelaces. The time came when Mrs Trout had to wonder if she'd been wrong to smoke during his pregnancy and she mentioned this to Mr Trout.

'There's nothing to worry about, Ma,' Mr Trout told his fussing wife. 'The kid's just clumsy, is all. No law in the land says a kid can't be clumsy.'

Mrs Trout thought Mr Trout's attitude a touch *laissez faire* even for West Virginia, but was hesitant to take Wayne to the doctor without his say-so. Besides, her concern for Wayne was more for the neighbours' sakes than his, worrying as she did that the impression he made on them would in some way reflect badly on her. Once Wayne was in school, however, the matter was taken out of their hands and placed in those of a professional.

It was at the start of Wayne's second year that the

headmaster called the Trouts to his office and shared his concerns. Their son, he said, was falling behind: his reading and math skills were substandard and his pencil grip was poor; he struggled to draw pictures and write words and was always the last to hand in work. He didn't concentrate and was easily distracted, was floundering in Phys Ed and had problems banging a drum; he...

'I'm not saying Wayne's simple, Mr & Mrs Trout, but it does appear that your son has some unusual difficulties. I think it's important we get to the root of these as soon as possible and so, with your permission, I'd like to send him to an educational psychologist.'

Although reluctant to put their son in the hands of a shrink the Trouts agreed to the headmaster's suggestion and after several meetings with Wayne and a barrage of tests, the educational psychologist made his diagnosis. Wayne Trout, he decided, was suffering from dyspraxia.

He met with the Trouts the following week and chose his words carefully, words he believed the odd-looking couple sitting opposite him would understand.

'He's got clumsy kid syndrome,' he said, coming straight to the point.

Mr Trout was about to ask for his money back when the psychologist continued. 'There's a part of the brain called the cerebellum, and this is the brain's skill centre. If the cerebellum malfunctions it transmits inaccurate messages to the body. While the brain is expecting the body to do one thing the body thinks the brain is asking it to do something different. It's a classic case of miscommunication – a bit like a Chinese whisper.'

'So it's a foreign disease, then?' Mr Trout ventured.

'Of course it's not a foreign disease!' the psychologist unintentionally snapped. 'It's neither foreign nor a disease. It's an *innate* disorder.'

Mr Trout tried again: 'So what you're saying is that Wayne's ate something and not digested it properly.'

'No, no, no, Mr Trout! What Wayne has is a *condition*, a condition peculiar to him and one he was *born* with. It has nothing to do with food!'

'It's nothing we've done, then?' Mrs Trout asked, relieved that the psychologist had made no mention of tobacco.

The psychologist shook his head and Mrs Trout rasped a sigh of relief.

'Is it something the boy will grow out of?' Mr Trout asked.

'No, I'm afraid Wayne's stuck with the condition, Mr Trout, and it's a condition he'll have to get used to. It's not the end of the world but his world will have limitations. He won't be able to drive a car, for example, or play a musical instrument, and I think it's probably best if you keep him away from firearms for as long as possible.'

'But he could work at the racetrack if he wanted to?' Mr Trout suggested.

'If he wanted to I'm sure he could,' the psychologist replied, wondering why anyone with a modicum of ambition would want to work there. 'Your son isn't stupid, you know.'

And so Wayne's life went on as abnormal and became more peculiar still when his father died and his mother remarried.

Wayne's father, whose ambition *was* less than a modicum, worked at the Charles Town racetrack, though no one, including Mrs Trout – who had more reason to know than most – had any real idea of what he did there. Mr Trout was a taciturn man and kept himself and his affairs to himself, and even if St Peter had asked his reasons for crossing the track during a race, he too would have been told by Mr Trout that it was his business to know and no one else's – Saint or no Saint. The half-empty bottle of Jim Beam that fell from his pocket at the time of impact, however, was explanation enough for the coroner.

After the death of her husband Mrs Trout went to work at one of the town's diners whose clientele on any given day of the week was unlikely to have a full set of teeth between them. She served plates of fried chicken, pork chops and catfish during working hours and, once her shift was over, the occasional plate of herself. She met these paramours for the first time in the bar area of the diner and usually for the second time when she woke up beside them the next morning. Most of these encounters were no more than one night stands, but they allowed Mrs Trout to feel wanted and good about herself. It was a form of self-medication, an under-the-counter antidote to the loneliness of single parenthood in a one-horse town. What she really hoped for from these encounters, though, was a husband, and six years after the death of Mr Trout she found one.

Unusually for Mrs Trout she met her second husband in a tattoo parlour. She'd gone there to deliver an order of fried chicken and mashed potato to its owner and found him in the middle of a heated conversation with a man complaining about the image of Marilyn Monroe the tattooist had recently inked on his arm. 'It looks nothing like her!' he kept telling him. 'It looks more like Hillary Clinton!'

The tattooist turned to Mrs Trout for an unbiased opinion. She brushed the hair from her forehead and looked at the image. 'It's Mrs Clinton,' she said. 'And it looks like she's having a bad day, too.'

She then held out her hand to the good-looking man she'd never seen before and introduced herself. 'Hi, I'm Merlene Trout,' she said. 'I work at the diner across the street.' The man took her hand and smiled. 'I'm very pleased to meet you, Merlene,' he said. 'My name's Howie Pillsbury and I make bird tables.' It was love at first sight and an infatuation that cost the tattooist a refund of seventy-five dollars.

Howie was a widower, the father of four girls and a recent incomer to Charles Town. His wife had committed suicide and he'd moved the family from Keyser to spare both him and his daughters the gossip and innuendo surrounding her death. He lived on the outskirts of town in a large sprawling house bequeathed to him by his grandmother, and it was here that the Trout and Pillsbury families planned to live after he and Merlene tied the knot. But then the uninsured house burnt down and both families were forced to repair to the Trout family home.

Even though both Trout daughters had by now left home – Millie to Washington and Etta to rehab – the three-bedroom house still proved too small for the combined family, and it was then that Howie hit upon the idea of building a tree house in the backyard. 'It's no different from building a bird table,' he told Merlene. 'It'll just take more wood, is all.'

Wayne watched as the tree house took shape, wondering what kinds of big birds Howie was hoping to attract to the garden. He didn't like his stepfather, didn't appreciate his shouting or the cuffs to the head he gave him if he spilled milk or made a mess at the table. And he called him stupid, too, kept telling him he was a clumsy ox. He didn't talk that way to his own daughters: he never called them idiots. What hurt Wayne most, though, was that his mother never stuck up for him but always took Howie's side; told him how Howie was her last chance at happiness and warned him against ruining things for her. And on top of everything else he didn't even have his own room anymore but had to sleep on the couch in the lounge and be up in the morning before anyone else in the house made it out of bed.

The day came when the tree house was finished. Merlene filled a suitcase with Wayne's clothes, gathered his bedding and took them to the base of the tree. Howie then hauled them up the ladder and dumped them on the floor of the tree house. Husband and wife then returned to the house, poured themselves a large celebratory drink and waited for Wayne to return from school.

'From now on you're living up there,' Howie Pillsbury told Wayne. 'You can shower in the house and eat meals with us but that's the sum of it. You got me, kid? Man descended from the trees and now you're going back up one. It's what's called evolution.'

Wayne was flabbergasted by both the news and the apostasy. 'But... but Mama,' he stammered, 'I thought you said we was Creationists?'

'Not anymore we're not,' Mrs Trout snapped. 'Now get up that damned tree!'

And so for the next five years, and from the age of twelve, Wayne lived in a tree, reading and doing his homework by flashlight and sleeping in the house only on the coldest of winter nights. Fortunately for Wayne he grew to like his new home, especially after Howie built a slide to make his return to the ground less hazardous, and the tree house became his sanctum. No one bothered him here and the arguments in the house went on without him. Occasionally, and against the rules, Kevin, his oldest and probably only friend, would also spend the night in the tree.

Kevin was one of only two constants in Wayne's early life. From the day they were first seated together in a classroom arranged by alphabetical order, the two friends became inseparable and Wayne, Kevin Trull's shadow. It was an unlikely friendship, but one that worked.

Kevin was big for his age and strong, but had no interest in sport and even less for learning. He yearned to be dumb and envied Wayne his natural inabilities. He liked the way his friend bumped into people and tripped over things, admired the messy schoolwork he handed in and his capacity to ruin team games. And in return for these distractions he rewarded Wayne with his protection, happy to beat the crap out of any classmate who taunted him in his presence.

The teachers despaired of Kevin as much as they tried to understand Wayne. He came from a good family – his father was a dentist and his mother a motel receptionist – yet seemed intent on living life at the fringe, aiming for the dirt and arriving there face down. And they worried that he might lead Wayne astray and take him down with him – which, in effect, was what he eventually did.

The other and more stable of the two constants in Wayne's life was the Baptist Church which, unlike Kevin, tended to be against glue sniffing.

It was Mrs Trout who'd insisted the family attend services every Sunday, but after her marriage to Howie and the drinking started, it was only Wayne who attended. Wayne liked the time he spent with God and looked on Him as a pal. He liked it that He was cut and dried about things and didn't expect people to think too much. Life for Wayne was always easier when he didn't have to think about things.

Wayne took his relationship with God seriously and didn't confine it to Sunday services. He prayed to God in his tree house, on the bus to school and occasionally during lessons. Mostly he prayed for others. He prayed that his mother would stop drinking and divorce Howie, that Kevin would stop sniffing glue and do his homework and that his younger sister, Etta, would kick her addiction to the prescription drugs she bought at the Charles Town Casino. Sometimes, though, he would pray for himself: pray that someday he'd be able to drive a car. And then, most everything he prayed for – apart from him driving a car – did come to pass. His mother was pulled over for drunk driving, Howie was sent to prison and Kevin was born again.

His mother and Howie had been driving home from a bar when a tree – as Merlene described the incident – stepped into the road without looking. When the officer doubted her story Howie, who'd been throwing up on the grass verge at the time, wiped the back of his hand across his mouth and said that if his wife said it happened that way then it fucking happened that way. He then slugged the policeman on the chin.

Howie was sentenced to a year in prison and Merlene to a stretch in rehab, where she met and reacquainted herself with her youngest daughter, back there by popular demand. Howie's four daughters were sent to live with their aunt, the sister of their deceased mother, while Wayne, once the police had located his whereabouts in the backyard, was taken from the tree and into care, eventually being fostered by a family known to him from church.

It appeared that things for Wayne were on the up, but then

Kevin stopped sniffing glue and events were set in motion that made it impossible for either of them to remain in Charles Town. Kevin, who against all odds graduated from High School, joined the Marines while Wayne, denied this avenue of escape by virtue of his dyspraxia, went to live with his oldest sister, Millie, in the Glover Park neighbourhood of Washington.

Of the two friends it was Wayne who'd been most traumatised by the incident, and it was during the time he lived with Millie that the voices started – about nine of them so far as he could make out. He visited a doctor who prescribed medications that kept him on an even keel, but a part of his mind had gone AWOL and there was no telling when, or if, it would return. And then Millie was knocked down and killed by an emergency ambulance on its way back to the depot and once again the Social Services stepped into what passed for Wayne's life.

Although Wayne was old enough to live by himself, the Social Services judged him incapable of doing so. Neither, though, did they consider him a person requiring full-time institutionalisation. His surviving family in Charles Town, usually the first port of call in such circumstances, proved eminently unsuitable: his mother was an alcoholic, his sister a drug addict and his stepfather a man who'd made him live in a tree for five years. In the hope of salvaging as much of Wayne's independence as possible they referred him to a halfway house in the neighbourhood already familiar to him. With a little help from others, they reasoned, and the occasional push in the right direction, he had every chance of making it on the outside.

The neighbourhood was Glover Park, an area of small

businesses and restaurants about half a mile north of Georgetown, and home to the Washington National Cathedral and the Russian Embassy. The housing was a mixture of apartment buildings and row houses, and the halfway house, run by a non-profit organisation, was located midway along 37th St.

During the day the house was staffed by carers who supervised the daily drug regimens of the guests and provided them with hot meals. Wayne shared the 1930s row house with four other men, each as battered by life as he was. Occasionally he sat in the lounge with them, but mostly he preferred to spend time alone, watching television in his room or eaves-dropping on the conversations in his head.

Most of Wayne's weekly social security cheque went towards his board and lodging and he liked to supplement his meagre spending money by doing odd jobs in the surrounding neighbourhoods. His best paying job, and the one he enjoyed most, was delivering the *Current*, but he also earned money delivering mail shots advertising restaurants and other local services. Occasionally, and usually on a Saturday, he collected aluminium cans from the streets, and the Saturday he chanced upon Larry in Volta Park was one such day. By then he'd been rooting through trash cans and street dumpsters for almost two hours and still only managed to gather eleven cans.

Wayne Trout's day hadn't got off to the best of starts.

'Hey, Professor, how you doing?'

'I'm doing fine, thank you, Wayne. I was hoping I'd bump into you,' Larry said.

'What were you and the big man conversating about?'

Although Larry had hoped to ease into the question of

Wayne's English a little further down the line, he decided that this was as good a time as any.

'Well, we weren't actually conversating about anything, Wayne. We were *conversing*. There's no such word as conversating.'

'I think you're wrong there, Professor. I've been using that word my whole life and not once has someone argumented with me about it. People in Charles Town use it all the time.'

Larry thought it best not to *argument* with Wayne over this particular word, and instead decided to broaden the subject. 'They might well have done, Wayne, but you're not living in Charles Town now. You're living in Washington and people here speak differently. If you spoke more like them you'd fit in better and, who knows, maybe someone might give you a full-time job. And I could help you, Wayne: I could teach you how to speak grammatically.'

Wayne scratched his head. 'I cain't believe I don't speak right, Professor. I've got a High School diploma and they don't just hand them things out. Besides, I think God wants me to talk this way. I think it's part of His plan.'

'I'm sure God wouldn't mind if you spoke grammatically, Wayne. He lets other people talk that way,' Larry replied.

'But I ain't other people, Professor. I'm damaged. God's made me special and He wants me to be this way. If I go changing He might not like me no more.'

Larry found it hard to argue with Wayne's illogic. 'Well, maybe you could pray to Him about it and see what He says. Tell Him that Larry MacCabe has your best interests at heart and that he's an emeritus professor of Georgetown University.'

'I guess I could do that,' Wayne said. 'And I could talk to

Kevin, too, and see what he says on the matter. I cain't see Kevin liking it, though.'

'That's that friend of yours, isn't it?'

'Yes, he's my best friend, Professor. Knowed him since I was five. He don't like Washington much. And he don't like the big man you were conversating with either. Blames him for his troubles.'

'You mean Tank?' Larry asked. 'What's Tank done to him?'

'It's not my place to tell, Professor. Kevin don't like it if I talk about him behind his back.'

'Well, Tank's always been very nice to me, Wayne. In fact, he's just given me this pamphlet on the King David Hotel. It's supposed to be the grandest hotel in Jerusalem. I'm going there in October.'

'Gee, you're going all the way to the Holy Land? That's where I want to go. What you going to pray about when you get there?'

'I'm not going there to pray, Wayne. I've been asked to deliver a paper.'

'I don't know nothing about airfares, Professor, but wouldn't it be cheaper if you just mailed it? It makes sense for me to deliver the *Current* because I live locally, but I cain't see them ever asking me to go all the way to another country to push it through someone's letter box.'

'It's not a newspaper I'm going to deliver, Wayne, it's an academic treatise. They want me to tell people about the Desert Land Act. But this is an example of the things I could teach you about the English language: a word can have several different meanings. You can deliver a parcel or a newspaper, for instance, but that's a lot different from delivering a baby; and you can also deliver on a promise you've made someone as well as delivering a speech. It's a simple word, but it has four different meanings. Shall I reiterate them for you?'

Wayne looked at Larry puzzled. 'What's reiterate mean?'

'Say again,' Larry explained.

'What's reiterate mean?'

It took a second or two before Wayne's confusion dawned on Larry. 'Reiterate means say again, Wayne. It's another way of saying the same thing and this is something else I could teach you. I could help broaden your vocabulary.'

Wayne looked studious, as if seriously considering the proposition and Larry started to take heart. The breakthrough he'd hoped for, however, never came.

'Will you take an umbrella with you when you go?'

Once again it took Larry a moment to find his feet in the conversation. 'Oh, I doubt I'll have any need for an umbrella, Wayne. Israel's a dry country and the weather will be warm. October's an ideal time to visit.'

'I wish I could go there with you,' Wayne said. 'I've read about Israel in the Bible and I know it better than I do my own country. I'd go visit all the places Jesus visited and see where he was born and crucified. It would be like a pilgrimation.'

No doubt Wayne would conversate about Christianism on this pilgrimation Larry thought, but made no comment. After all, he had a favour to ask Wayne.

'While I'm there, Wayne, I'd like you to do something for me. And it would be a paying job, too.'

The mention of money pricked Wayne's interest. 'As long as it ain't no full-time job and don't interfere with my shows then I'll be glad to, Professor. What is it you had in mind?'

'I'd like you to take care of Moses for me. I can't stand the thought of him being cooped up in a kennel while I'm away.

I know we've only recently met but I have a high opinion of you, Wayne, and I know Laura does, too. And you're a natural with Moses. Look at the way he always comes up to you when he sees you and the way he's curled up on your feet now.'

Wayne smiled and a blush came to his face. 'I'd be glad to do that for you, Professor. We ain't supposed to have pets in the house, but I could hide him someplace and feed him every day when no one was looking.'

'Oh, there's no need for you to go to all that trouble, Wayne. I was thinking you could move into my house while I'm away and live there. How does that sound?'

'I'd have to get permission from the house, but if you came and explained it to them I cain't see it being a problem. You've got a television though, don't you? I don't want to miss my shows.'

'I have, Wayne. It's not the most modern of sets but the picture's clear and it gets all the channels. What shows do you watch?'

'The ones on the Christian channels, Professor, and Saturday afternoons they show films. That's what I'll do after I've finished collecting cans. Go back to the house and watch a Christian film. You any idea why there ain't many cans round today? I usually get more than this.'

Larry said he didn't, but told Wayne about the two sacks of aluminium cans he had stored in his basement, cans he'd kept to remind him of Helen and never got round to throwing out. Wayne said he'd be happy to take them off his hands and so the two companions – Larry leading Moses and Wayne pulling a cart with eleven cans in it – set off for Larry's house on Dent St. It would also be an opportunity for Larry to familiarise Wayne with his house.

'How many windows do you say you got, Professor?'

'Fourteen,' Larry answered.

Wayne whistled. 'I just got one,' he said. 'There's probably another nine in the house, but if you divide the windows by the number of people living there it still comes down to only two windows each. And you've got fourteen all to yourself! If your Ma and Pa were alive I'd be guessing they'd be proud of you.'

Larry showed Wayne the upstairs rooms first and suggested he might want to sleep in either Rutherford's old bedroom or Grover's, both of which had televisions. Next he showed him the lounge, dining room and kitchen areas before leading him down a flight of stairs to the basement.

'Moses sleeps down here,' Larry said, 'and I keep the washing machine and dryer here. I'll go through everything with you before I leave, show you where the switches are and how things work, but what's your first impression? Do you think you'll be happy living here for a week or so?'

Wayne had grown strangely quiet since entering the basement, and it was difficult for Larry to know if it was the dog's basket that had overwhelmed him or the utility appliances. He asked the question again: would he be happy living here for a week or so?

'I would,' Wayne replied, almost whispering. 'And if it's okay with you, Professor, I'd like to sleep down here.'

7

The Museum Attendant

'You do realise Kevin's dead, don't you?'

This was news to Larry!

It was a Thursday night, early July, and Larry and Laura were sitting in a Mexican restaurant on M St eating burritos. Larry had been telling Laura of his plans to turn Wayne's life around and had just confided a stumbling block: Kevin didn't want Wayne to change.

Larry put down his fork and cautiously sipped the margarita Laura had insisted he try.

'But Wayne speaks of him all the time, Laura – and in the present tense, too – and...' He winced and a more disturbing thought came to mind. 'I think the waiter's brought me a dirty glass: there's salt on the rim.'

Laura explained that the salt was there for a reason, and that this was the way a margarita was meant to be served.

'Oh, I didn't know that...' Larry said. 'But are you *sure* Kevin's dead? Wayne led me to believe he'd met Tank – right here in Washington – and that he didn't like him.'

'Kevin was killed in Iraq, Larry, and only a short time after he arrived there. Wayne accepts this but keeps his memory alive by using him as a sounding board for any decisions he has to make. He bounces ideas off him. What Wayne is telling you is that *he* doesn't like Tank and that *he* doesn't want to change. It's the same as another person talking about themselves in the third person: in the third person Wayne becomes Kevin. It's a harmless coping mechanism, but it's probably better if you don't mention this to anyone. I haven't spoken to Alice about it – you might have noticed she's not very good at keeping confidences – and I haven't mentioned it to Delores or Mike, and certainly not to Tank. They'd assume the worst and suppose him dangerous – which he isn't. Wayne's a human being with problems and I wish more people would respect this. I'm pleased that you're making an effort to spend time with him. If more people spent time with him he'd probably have less need for Kevin.'

'So Kevin's like his security blanket, then?'

'Yes, that's a good way of looking at things,' Laura replied. 'Kevin provides him with a form of psychological comfort, and that's probably no different from me hoping that St Francis will take pity on poor Repo.' She remained silent for a moment and then asked Larry if he believed in miracles.

Larry chose his words carefully. 'I don't know if I believe in miracles per se, Laura, but I do believe that good things can happen when they're least expected. Take me, for example. After Helen died I didn't know what to do with myself but then I bumped into you and before I knew it I had Moses in my life. And through you I met Alice, Delores, Mike and Tank – and Wayne, too, for that matter. Unexpectedly my world changed for the better and there's no reason to believe that Repo's world will be any different.'

Laura could have kissed Larry for his thoughtfulness. She'd

invited him out without any real expectation of enjoying the evening herself. The meal was his reward for suggesting they play DVDs at the home, but unexpectedly his conversation was proving a bonus for her. And, apart from his overly-detailed rendition of the fall of Masada, the two of them *had* had a conversation. A two-way conversation! Miracles did happen, she decided. There was no other explanation for Larry's change in behaviour. If there was hope for Larry then there was certainly hope for Repo!

'It's a pity Alice couldn't have joined us tonight,' Larry said. 'I think she'd have enjoyed it here.'

'I think she would, Larry, but she had to be in St Louis this week. That's where her head office is.'

'My head office is located on my shoulders,' Larry smiled. 'I used to have an office in the Intercultural Centre but when I retired they gave it to a wrestler.' He then drained his glass and smacked his lips. 'Ugh!'

'You ought to drink more often,' Laura laughed. 'Alcohol doesn't suit everyone, but it does you good. How about we have another?'

Larry agreed and Laura called the waiter.

'I've asked Wayne to look after Moses while I'm in Israel,' Larry said when the drinks had been served. 'He's going to live in my basement.'

'Your basement? Why didn't you offer him a bedroom?'

'I did, but as soon as he saw the basement he fell in love with it. He called it a special room and said that Kevin would want him to live there. I didn't quite understand what he meant at the time, but from everything you've told me this evening I suppose it means that *he* wants to live there.'

'Well, I think it's a laudable idea, but are you sure he'll be able to manage by himself? I'd be happy to look in on him.'

'That's kind of you, Laura, but I'd appreciate it if you didn't. I want Wayne to feel as if he has full responsibility for both Moses and the house, and if he knew people were watching over him he might not get the full benefit of the experience. I'm hoping that independent living will make him more confident and, who knows, even help him find a full-time job. I still have hopes of that happening.'

'Well, if you're happy with the situation then I am,' Laura said. 'But who's going to cook for him? Have you thought about that?'

'He's going to cook for himself, Laura, and he's looking forward to it. He's fed up with all the vegetables they serve at the house and he's going to try something different.'

'And you'll be away for how long?'

'Ten days,' Larry replied.

'Okay, but if Wayne has scurvy by the time you get back don't come running to me. This one's on your head.'

'It would take more than…' Larry turned sheepish. 'That was a joke, wasn't it? I'm afraid I'm a bit slow when it comes to getting jokes.'

Laura smiled. It was a triumph of sorts that Larry had let the subject of scurvy go by so easily. Three months ago he would have been detailing its symptoms, pathology and history and no doubt telling her of its impact on seventeenth-century shipping. Larry, she decided, deserved a reward: another chance to talk.

'So apart from delivering your paper and visiting Masada, what else are you going to do in Israel?'

'Oh, the usual tourist things I suppose, but apart from the trip to Masada I'll probably limit myself to Jerusalem. I'd like to explore the Old City in depth, spend time at the Western Wall and on Temple Mount, wade through Hezekiah's Tunnel and see if there are any tortoises in the Biblical Zoo.'

Laura's instinct warned her against asking the question, but the mention of the Western Wall, Temple Mount and tortoises in the same sentence piqued her interest. 'Why on earth would you want to see if there are any tortoises in the zoo? I didn't even know they had tortoises in Israel.'

'Oh they have them all right, Laura, but I don't think the Israelis have ever appreciated them. They're described in the Bible as unclean, lumped together with weasels and rats, and I've always found that unfair. They've got short legs and that's why they have to crawl everywhere, but it's not as if they asked for them, is it? Given a choice, I'm sure they'd have gone for longer legs.'

'But why do you have a soft spot for tortoises? They're not exactly cuddly and you can't take them for a walk in the park.'

'Because if I had to come back to earth as another living creature I think I'd want to come back as a tortoise. I'm not saying I believe in reincarnation but I do like to prepare myself for all situations and I've decided there are advantages to being a tortoise. First of all, you arrive with a ready-made house on your back; secondly you chew grasses and leaves and don't have to eat insects; and thirdly, no one can ever tell how old you are. It would be like being Andy Warhol.'

'You've lost me there, Larry. How can a tortoise be anything like Andy Warhol?'

'Because Andy Warhol wore silvery-grey wigs from the time he was a young man. When he got older no one really noticed. That was his plan. In that sense he was like a tortoise, because no one could ever tell how old he was.'

It was easy to understand Larry's developing friendship with Wayne, Laura thought. Listening to him was as strange as it was listening to Wayne, and sometimes stranger. It was as if both had embraced the oddness of life but only one from choice. Laura looked at her watch and decided it was time to call it a night. She caught the eye of the waiter and gestured with a tick. When the check arrived she paid with a no-frills credit card and left notes for the service.

Outside the restaurant Larry thanked her for the meal and reminded her of the full sets of *The Mary Tyler Moore Show* and *The Rockford Files* he had at his house. All she had to do was say the word and he'd bring them to the home. He waited while she crossed the road, waved goodbye and then headed home.

It had been a long time since Larry had ventured on M St. He and Helen had always felt out of place here, preferring the more down-to-earth neighbourhoods of Burleith and Friendship Heights. Theirs had been the world of Safeway, but here on M St it was the world of Dean & DeLuca's, boutique shops bordering on the exclusive and of unnecessarily expensive restaurants and coffee houses. It was an area that favoured the young and the hip, people as far from death as the spectrum allowed. It was little wonder that Helen had always looked upon M St as one to cross rather than dally on.

Larry decided he'd mention this to Moses when he got home, but in the meantime kept his head down and passed the journey wondering if life as a Mediterranean spur-thighed tortoise would be preferable to that of a Negev tortoise. By the time he reached Dent St he'd decided: if given the choice he'd return to earth as a Negev tortoise. It would allow him to live in the desert.

The National Museum of the American Indian was located at the intersection of 4th and Independence. It was the youngest of the Smithsonian's eighteen children, but bore little resemblance to its neoclassical siblings: it was curvilinear and domed, coated in rough Kasota limestone and looked like a weathered rock formation. It was built to celebrate the culture and history of the nation's indigenous peoples, to let bygones be bygones and allow mainstream America to move on with its life. In a roundabout way it had also allowed Delores Bobo to move on with hers.

Although now a museum attendant, Delores had at one time been one of the West Coast's premier hand models, earning up to $2,000 a day. She'd stumbled into this world by accident, the one positive outcome of a blind date with an advertising executive. The man had been arrogant and prided himself on speaking the truth. His exact words to her that evening were: 'Your face isn't up to much, Delores, but you do have beautiful hands. I'm not going to ask to see you again, but I think you should try your hand as a hand model. We'll split the bill 50/50.'

Delores' hands had been beautiful, like those of a Victorian doll. Her fingers were long and straight, her thumbs exquisite and she had good nails and neat cuticles. The backs of her hands were narrow and unblemished and, most importantly, she had flat knuckles. She decided to act on the executive's advice and the next day phoned a modelling agency.

For the next four years Delores made a living from holding things. She held yogurt cartons, packets of cheese, varieties of cleaning products, tubes of toothpaste and tubs of cosmetics; and hers were the hands that doubled for those of models whose facial beauty alone had won them leading roles in advertising campaigns. She travelled widely and worked in cities across the United States: Los Angeles, San Francisco, Houston, Chicago and New York. And then, one day, she walked through a plate-glass window and her modelling career came to an end.

Delores had been driving in Los Angeles at the time, nervously looking this way and that for the studio hired to shoot a scouring-pad commercial. Once she realised she was lost, and also late, she'd halted the car outside a small delicatessen and gone to ask for directions. The entrance to the shop comprised three identically-sized glass panes stretching from floor to lintel but only the middle pane was hinged. In a moment of flustered confusion she'd pushed her way through the left pane and found herself standing half-in and half-outside the shop, shards of glass falling on her head and blood dripping from her hands.

She stepped out of the broken pane, walked into the delicatessen through its door and said something to the effect of: 'I think I've just walked through your window.' The owners of the shop were only too aware of this and appeared more shocked than she was. They had the presence of mind, however, to phone for an ambulance, and the luckless Delores was whisked to hospital. There the nurses carefully brushed the powdered glass from her eyelashes; used tweezers to remove the glass still embedded in her hands and stitched her wounds. She'd left the hospital in bandages, taken a taxi to the airport and gone home to Portland.

When the bandages were removed and the stitches unpicked, Delores' hands were left permanently scarred. She looked down on them with a depth of sadness she'd never before experienced, and only then resigned herself to the fact that her career as a hand artist had come to an end.

At moments of crisis in her life Delores would head for the Portland Art Museum, sit on a bench in the quiet of one of its galleries and ponder the problem at hand. This particular visit she noted a leaflet stapled to the notice board advertising for a gallery attendant. She scanned the requirements – high school diploma, polite helpful manner, friendly, enjoys meeting people, likes art – and mentally ticked all the boxes. She completed an application form and two weeks later was standing in a gallery wearing the uniform of the Portland Art Museum. She worked there six years, patrolling rooms, monitoring security systems, talking to visitors and helping with enquiries, but most of the time she just stood or sat there.

As a child Delores had tended toward the chubby, but her weight had been kept in check by balanced home-cooked meals and enforced school exercise. And as a hand model the agency had insisted she *lose* weight: there was little demand in the world of commerce for podgy hands, they told her. Once she stopped modelling though and adopted the stationary life of a gallery attendant and moved into her own apartment, all constraints were lifted. Calories that at one time would have only squatted in her body now took up permanent residence, and word went out to the other homeless calories of the region and to all the illegal calories that had crossed the border from Mexico that Delores' body was a warm and welcoming place that asked no questions.

As the number of mouths to feed mounted so did Delores' appetite. She ate burgers and hot dogs, pizzas with extra toppings, fried chicken and fried fish, portions of fries and more portions of fries. During the day she snacked on

Almond Joys, Big Hunks, Idaho Spuds, Denver Sandwiches, Cow Tales and Butterfinger Crisps and at night drank beer with her friends in a local bar and grazed on potato chips and salted peanuts. She'd never known such comfort.

There was, however, a downside to this contentment. She became larger and changed in shape, grew breathless easily and started to sweat. And she had to remodel her wardrobe and buy loose fitting dresses and elasticised pants that disguised her new size. She joined a gym but went only occasionally, bought magazines and cut out diet plans and experimented with every over-the-counter slimming aid sold at the local drug stores.

Although Delores recognised that she was overweight she was reluctant to accept that fast food had made her the slow person she'd become, and rather than change her diet opted instead for eating smaller portions of the same food and avoiding all-you-can-eat restaurants. The weight, however, remained loyal to Delores, and rather than take responsibility for her own lack of action she started to blame her environment: Portland's slow pace of life was affecting her metabolism, sapping her of willpower. What she needed was a fresh start in a new and more vibrant city: a city that burned fat!

Two weeks after having made this resolution, and as if by fate, a flier appeared on the museum's notice board advertising an opening at the National Museum of the American Indian. Delores filled out an application form and was eventually called to Washington. She did her homework, beefed up on Native Americans and the National Museum and interviewed well. By nature she was friendly and amenable, and her round appearance spoke volumes for her approachability. For purposes of equal opportunity the museum was, at that time, also in need of a non-Native American on staff, and the appointment of a fat non-Native American was difficult to pass on: it was like killing two birds with one arrow.

Delores was offered the position of gallery attendant and shortly moved to Washington. As the museum's newbie she spent her first year floating from floor to floor, filling in for others and familiarising herself with the NMAI's artefacts and permanent exhibitions. She worked at the Welcome Desk, in the Roanoke Museum Store, in the Lelawi Theatre and in the family activity centre. And as her knowledge and confidence grew she was given added responsibilities: conducting tours, and helping organise special exhibitions in the Sealaska Gallery and cultural events staged on the floor of the museum's atrium.

For the first month Delores made a point of climbing the stairs that linked the museum's four levels but soon lost interest, especially after she discovered the Mitsitam Native Foods Cafe on the first floor and started to lunch there. She continued to descend the flights on foot for a time, but eventually gave up even this exercise and took the elevator. Unsurprisingly, in the city that burned fat, Delores' weight remained constant.

What did change, though, was her worldview. Working in the National Museum opened her eyes to the history, philosophies and traditions of American Indians and to their struggles to survive in a world no longer their own but that of foreign invaders: white men who'd arrived with suitcases packed with deadly diseases, alcohol and firearms and who'd gone on to exterminate the buffalo herds – the Indians' main source of food and resources – and seize their homelands. And Delores was even more shocked when she learned that her own family had played a role in the Indians' ignominious downfall, and recoiled when she thought of her long-dead ancestor who had supposedly helped rout a dangerous band of Cheyenne at Sand Creek.

The family had lived in Colorado at the time, and Lucas Bobo, according to the story, had been one of the bravest soldiers to have ever lived. He'd served with Colonel Chivington in the High Plains and fought with honour at the Battle of Sand Creek. She now knew this story to be a lie: Sand Creek hadn't been a battle but a massacre – and Chivington's battle cry no less than an exhortation for ethnic cleansing: *I have come to kill Indians, and I believe it is right and honourable to use any means under God's heaven to kill Indians. Kill and scalp all, big and little; nits make lice.*

One hundred and thirty-three Indians were killed and mutilated that day, and two-thirds of them had been women and children. Not satisfied with their deaths the soldiers had disembowelled the bodies, ripped out foetuses and cut off genitalia. They'd scalped the dead, cut off noses, ears and fingers and paraded their trophies in the downtown theatres of Denver...

Delores shuddered. Could it be that Lucas' tobacco pouch – the family heirloom displayed in her grandparents' cabinet – wasn't made from the testicles of a white antelope after all, but the testicles of White Antelope, the Cheyenne chief who'd fallen in battle that day? Immediately she'd phoned her grandparents and told them to burn the pouch; told them it was no less evil than having a lampshade made from human skin in their house and that if they didn't they could forget about their trip to Washington next spring and she'd change her name to Antelope! The Bobo buck stops here, she'd told them.

But it didn't: the buck remained with her grandfather. He told her not to be so silly and that he had no intention of burning what was left of a dear family ancestor on the strength of a whim and that he and Grandma could go anywhere they damned-well pleased in the country and that she didn't own Washington and that for all he cared she could change her name to Buffalo!

Having already left home it was difficult for Delores to leave home again, but she decided that as long as White Antelope's testicles were on display in her grandparents' cabinet she would never set foot in Portland again. She talked about changing her name to Antelope with a couple of friends at the museum, but as in their opinion she looked nothing like an antelope they advised against it and proposed instead that she go with her grandfather's suggestion. Delores didn't understand their logic. Chief Black Kettle hadn't been called Black Kettle because he'd looked like a black kettle, so why did it matter if she didn't look like an antelope? And she certainly wasn't going to choose the name her grandfather had suggested: Delores Buffalo was unsuitable for any woman trying to lose weight.

So instead of changing her name – which was tokenistic at best she realised – she stuck an eagle's feather in her hair ribbon and embraced the concept of the Noble Savage – wholeheartedly and without proviso – and became more native than the Native Americans. And on their behalf, and often to their bemusement, she decried the crimes of her own civilisation – whose food additives she now blamed for her size – and was happy to go toe-to-toe with anyone prepared to contradict her.

She found her match on the third Friday of July, the opening night of the Wabanaki Confederacy exhibition.

It was the first time in weeks the gang had been together. Tank had missed two Saturdays, Delores one and Laura and Alice another; often it had been just Larry and Mike sitting at the table in Volta Park. Wayne had joined them on one such occasion, but left when Mike started to lecture him about climbing trees and Larry had run out of mints. Unsurprisingly, Wayne hadn't been invited to the exhibition.

By the time Larry arrived at the museum, Mike, Laura and Alice were already sitting on a bench in the huge Potomac Atrium.

'How you doing, man?' Mike smiled. 'Got the use of your legs back?'

'Just about, Mike, but my keyboard skills are still a bit hit-and-miss. The mouse had a life of its own this morning. Did the recordings turn out okay?'

Mike made a circle with his thumb and forefinger and gave Larry the A-okay sign. 'And I couldn't have done it without you, man. You're the dude, Larry!'

Larry had spent most of the previous afternoon suspended by his feet in the Great Falls Park recording the sound of the Potomac River as it rushed over the jagged rocks of Mather Gorge. It was an action that ran counter to the park's rule that visitors should only view the falls from the overlooks provided, but from Mike's point of view it had been necessary. 'I need to hear the force of the water, Larry, feel its speed and get the drama on tape.'

Mike had been happy for Larry to suspend him, but worried that his ageing friend might well drop and kill him –

something that had also crossed Larry's mind when the idea was discussed. 'I've no upper strength, Mike; no muscles. It's probably best if you hold my legs.' And so on and off for the next three hours, and moving from one rock to another, it was Mike who gripped and squeezed Larry's ankles, cutting the circulation to his feet and channelling the blood to his head.

When Mike hauled him up for the final time Larry's shirt was wet through and his face bright red. 'Man, that was a blast,' Mike said. 'How about we drop by Stubblefield Falls on the way back and record Scot's Run falling into the Potomac?' On the grounds that he didn't have any feeling in his legs and wasn't sure where his arms were, Larry politely suggested they do that another day.

'You're becoming quite the gadabout, Larry,' Laura said.

'I am, aren't I?' Larry smiled. 'It's a good job I'm retired these days or I wouldn't have time for all these adventures.'

'What adventures?'

The question had been asked by Tank. He'd come straight from work and was wearing a dark pinstriped suit, suspenders, a maroon tie and black dress shoes.

'I went with Mike to the Great Falls Park yesterday and we recorded the sound of the water,' Larry said.

'How come you can find time to help Mike when you can't find time to help me? When I asked you to do some gardening the other day you said you were too busy. You can't be that busy if you've got time to help a Hippie. I was going to pay you, too. How much did you pay him, Mike?'

Mike ignored the question and Tank drew his own conclusions. 'Just as I figured,' he said. He scanned the room for a bar or a waiter carrying a tray of drinks and came up empty. 'Where the hell's Delores when you need her? I thought she was supposed to be looking after us.'

'She's tied up with the exhibition,' Laura said. 'She'll be joining us after the opening ceremony.'

'I think this is the first time I've ever seen you in a suit,' Alice said. 'If you just stood there and kept your mouth shut you could almost be mistaken for an attractive man.'

'You ought to see me at a funeral, Alice. I cut quite the dash there. That reminds me, I've decided to take Sherman to that animal blessing service you were talking about the other week. I want him to meet the Pastor.'

Mike laughed. 'You old dog, Tank. You're smitten with the Pastor, aren't you?'

'I might be and I might not,' Tank replied. 'All I'll say on the subject is that she conducts a fine funeral service. What's her name, anyway? All it said on the service sheet was Pastor Millsap.'

'It's Donna. Donna Millsap,' Mike said. 'Who died anyway? No one mentioned a funeral to me.'

'Oh, just some guy at the State Department. I didn't know him all that well – never even shook his hand for that matter – but for the sake of internal politics I had to show up at his funeral and look sad. Donna's not gay, is she?'

'Not that I know of,' Mike said. 'All I've heard is that she's divorced.'

'We've got that in common, then. Next time you see her, put in a good word for me, will you? Do that and I won't tell her about this woman I know of who can whistle hymns better than you can play them. Now where's that bar?'

Tank walked off and left the group in a state of shellshock. 'He didn't even ask us how we were,' Alice complained. 'And he hasn't seen us for two weeks! He never asks us how we are.'

'Well, I suppose we're as guilty as he is on that score,' Laura said. 'We didn't ask him how his trip went.'

'He never gave us the chance,' Mike said. 'He just turned up and started haranguing us.'

'He's always like that when he gets back from the Middle East,' Laura said. 'He has to be nice to people out there and it's not in his nature. He'd rather knock heads together than listen to spout, but it's his job to listen and so he has to bite his tongue. And if he's been biting his tongue for two weeks in the Middle East, you know for a fact that he's going to bite us in the ass when he gets home. We're like his safety valve.'

'I think you're just making excuses for him,' Alice said. 'My job's as stressful as his and you don't hear me talking to people like that. It's not easy finding jobs for people, especially when most of them are losers. There are days when I have to have the patience of a saint.'

A microphone was tapped and a voice called for attention. There were short introductions, a longer overview of the five Nations that comprised the Wabanaki Confederacy and then the invitees to the exhibition, close to 150 in number, were asked to make their way to the Sealaska Gallery on the second floor where they could read more about the Confederacy and view the exhibits.

Larry and the others, now rejoined by Tank, climbed the stairs and headed for the Gallery. There was a wigwam made from birch bark at the centre of the room, and a canoe to its left made from the same material. There were mannequins dressed in ponchos, wraparound skirts and leather tunics; breechcloths with leather leggings, cloaks, pointed caps and moccasins decorated with beadwork. Elsewhere in the Gallery, and behind glass, were deer facemasks, horned-owl hoods, headdresses made from ostrich feathers, heavy wooden clubs, pronged spears, bows and arrows and wampum belts.

'You could get a few pointers from the way they dressed, Mike.'

'Do you want my help with Donna or don't you?'

'I do,' Tank said, 'and, if you don't mind me saying so, you're wearing a fine pair of overalls this evening.'

'I don't think I quite understand this,' Alice said. 'Are the Wabanaki American or Canadian Indians?'

'They're both,' Laura replied. 'They lived – and still live – in the states of Maine, Massachusetts, New Hampshire and Vermont and in the Canadian Maritime Provinces of Nova Scotia and New Brunswick. They banded together to defend themselves against the Iroquois.'

'So is this relative of yours American or Canadian?'

'American. He was born in Vermont.'

Delores came to join them. 'Did you see the cradleboard, Laura? That's one of the Abenaki artefacts I promised you, and the cornhusk dolls and black ash baskets are Abenaki, too. It makes you proud to be Indian, doesn't it?'

So far as Laura was aware, neither she nor Delores had the slightest drop of Indian blood in them and just smiled. 'Where's Petey? I thought he was coming tonight.'

'He's over there talking to Larry. As they both write, I thought they'd have something in common.'

It was true that both Larry and Petey wrote, but their styles and reasons for writing had little in common. Larry's writing was practical and no-nonsense, designed to convey facts and analyse data, while Petey's words were more patterned and his subjects less tangible. Notwithstanding these differences the two men appeared to have hit it off and were in deep conversation. Larry had been explaining the Desert Land Act to Petey and now Petey was asking him if he was happy with his agent.

'I've never had an agent,' Larry replied. 'I just sent the articles to a journal.'

'And the journal sent you the cheques?'

'Oh I never got paid for them – not directly anyway. I got promoted on the strength of them and that was the payoff. I suppose it's different when you write commercially.'

'It is,' Petey sighed. 'If you don't have an agent there's little chance of a publisher ever seeing your work – and finding an agent isn't easy. Everything you read tells you to choose your agent carefully, feel from your gut that this is the person for you, but in truth you don't have any real choice. You're thankful to get any agent.'

'And do you have one?'

'I do, but it's not working out. She spends more time at the hairdresser than she does promoting me. Every time I check the agency's website her hair's a different colour. And she strikes me as being a middleperson rather than a decision maker. It was another guy who found my manuscript in the slush pile and recommended it.

'Anyway, it was her who read it and she's the one that invited me to discuss the manuscript over lunch. She brought another guy with her, the Foreign Rights Director. He struck me as indifferent, more interested in what was going on in the room than he was at the table, and when he did speak all he said was that he'd graduated from Harvard and couldn't understand why a mainstream publisher hadn't snapped him up. The agent took more interest in my manuscript though, told me it was brilliant and that I had a distinctive voice and that with a few minor tweaks it would be ready for sending out to publishers. I didn't feel good about either one of them to tell you the truth, but there was no one else knocking on my door and so I agreed terms with them.

'Three weeks later I heard back from her and she told me she'd decided to send the manuscript to a brilliant – she uses that word a lot – a *brilliant* freelance editor the agency used. He gets back to her and tells her the story needs work – lots of work! Says the strong silent character at the heart of the book is so strong and silent that he's verging on the mute and needs to talk more and there should be more action scenes in the story. "And how's that supposed to happen?" I asked the agent. "The guy lives alone in a remote cabin in the Rockies!" And all she says is that she agrees with everything the editor says and to jump to it. It was then I realised she didn't have a mind of her own.

'So I changed the book the way they wanted and hated myself for making the changes. I wasn't happy with the end product and neither were the publishers when they read the manuscript. The next thing I know, this brilliant freelance editor's bringing out his own book and it's filled with big talkers and lots of action scenes and the first person he thanks in the Acknowledgements is her. All he was concerned about was me writing like him and all she was concerned about was me being him. I can't prove anything, but I think there was something going on between the two of them...

'And they made me change the title, too; made me change it from *Hail Marys and Snow Gods* to *The Man who Hid under his Eyebrows*. The book was about Catholicism and Nature and nothing to do with a guy's eyebrows, which were lost anyway after a gas canister blew up in his face halfway through the first chapter.'

By now Petey was grinding his teeth and Larry didn't know what to say for the best. Eventually a suitable phrase came to mind. 'You deserve better, Petey.'

'That's what Delores is always telling me. And wait till you hear this, Larry. The agent's had my second manuscript for five months and hasn't even read the first page! Last time I mentioned it to her she told me to be patient and that she was having personal problems. Who doesn't have personal problems? Anyway, I'm going to give her another month and if I don't hear back I'm going to start looking for another agent. No one makes a fool of Petey Muckleberry, Larry, no one. That's my department!'

'Quite right, too,' Larry said.

'It's none of my business, Larry,' Tank butted in, 'but if I were you I'd walk around the room a bit more. That frame of yours and those big jug ears make you look like a totem pole when you stand still... You doing okay, Petey?'

'I'm doing fine, thanks. I have the love of a good woman.'

'Well, if that's Delores you're talking about then you have the love of *three* good women,' Tank said. 'Amazes me how she's never crushed you.'

Petey did look fragile, almost emaciated, and Tank had often wondered if the man had a tapeworm or suffered from an eating disorder. He was a pint-sized version of Larry, a man-sized version of Button, and it made no sense to Tank that he was dating a woman Delores' size.

Petey and Delores had met at a Redskins game while Petey was in Washington visiting an old college friend. Delores had gone to the stadium with a colleague from the museum and happened to be sitting next to him. When the people in the row in front stood up – which was most of the time – Petey lost sight of the game and Delores took pity on him – the way she'd taken pity on Button when she'd first seen him at the adoption agency. She asked him if he'd like to sit on her shoulders and Petey accepted her offer and found her shoulders more comfortable and padded than the seat he'd been sitting on. They started to date and had now been together two years.

'Tell me, Petey, why is it that some writers feel the need to be so damn pretentious?' Tank asked – again out of left field. 'I read the other day about this woman who thinks she was born with a bunch of literary spirits buzzing round her head and how they keep visiting her and whispering stories into her ear. Do you buy that?'

'No, I don't,' Petey said. 'It was probably something her agent told her to say. Writers should keep their mouths shut and let their words do the talking and stop buying into the idea that they're celebrities. That's my philosophy, anyway. You won't find me on any talk shows.'

'I think you're getting ahead of yourself there, Petey. I can't even find you on any bookshelves!'

Larry came to Petey's defence and explained the problems he was having with his agent, how she spent most of her time at the hairdressers and was having personal problems.

The numbers started to thin and Delores suggested they go to the Mitsitam Native Foods Cafe for a drink. There they found three opened bottles of wine on a table marked 'Reserved'.

'My treat,' Delores said, 'and I'd like to thank you all for coming and making the evening such a success. And Petey and I have an announcement to make, don't we, Petey?' Petey nodded, and the gang, with differing levels of enthusiasm, waited for news of their impending marriage.

Delores continued. 'Petey and I are staging a protest at the FedExField on Sunday and we'd be happy for you to join us.'

Delores' current obsession was the name of the city's football team, the Washington *Redskins*. It was derogatory, prejudicial, and to her way of thinking as injurious to the Native American psyche as the N-word was to blacks. The controversy wasn't new but appeared to be in danger of running out of steam and Delores had decided to boil her own kettle and get things moving again.

'So who's with us?' Delores asked.

It turned out no one was. Laura and Alice were busy that Sunday, Mike tied up at church playing the organ and Larry working on his presentation to the Hebrew University of Jerusalem. Tank was happy to point out that he was free all day Sunday, but couldn't think of anything more pointless to do with his time. 'You're overthinking things, Delores. There's nothing negative about the name. Hell, even the majority of Native Americans don't have a problem with it. How can anyone have a problem with a name that signifies strength and courage?'

'I'm not overthinking anything, Tank. The name belittles Native Americans and it's a form of ethnic stereotyping. If we can get it changed it will be a way of atoning for the white man's crimes.'

She then turned to address the whole group. 'Our forefathers tried to wipe out the Indians' culture and religion. They broke treaties, stole their lands and made them live on Godless reservations with nothing to do but twiddle their thumbs and drink alcohol... Cheers, by the way. Good Health, everyone...! And they robbed them of their freedom and their dignity and reduced them to poverty. The plight of the Indian is our guilt and the least we can do is show them some respect by changing the name of the capital's football team.'

Petey broke into applause. 'Well said, Delores! Well said!'

Delores beamed at him and then looked at Larry. 'And you'll back me up on this, won't you, Larry?' she continued. 'The late nineteenth century was when most of the bad things happened to the Native Americans, and this was your period of study, wasn't it? The bad things happened on your watch.'

Larry, who was in the habit of withdrawing to the perimeter when discussions flared, not only stood his ground on this occasion but climbed to its highest point. The late nineteenth century was his reason for being, the past his professional life had been staked on, and without a moment's hesitation he picked up the gauntlet from the floor of the Mitsitam Native Foods Cafe and stood to face his audience. He was back in the lecture theatre.

'You're right, Delores: bad things did happen during those years. But you're wrong to judge events of the past by modern standards. The demise of the Native American was inevitable. You're not to blame, Tank's not to blame and I'm not to blame. The direction of history is to blame.'

'I didn't understand a word of that,' Alice whispered to Laura.

'It's what happens when a Stone Age culture goes head-to-head with an advanced industrial civilisation,' Larry continued. 'One society is static and wants to live as one with nature, while the other is dynamic and wants to conquer and bend nature for its own purposes. The only common ground they have is the ground they compete for and a clash is inevitable. It's also inevitable that the weaker and less adaptable of the two parties will be the one to suffer...'

Larry's summation was detached – cold, Delores thought. While he appeared to sympathise with the sufferings of the Indians, at no time did he condemn the wickedness of the white man. He argued instead that their forefathers were victims of the cultural values of the time and it was wrong to judge their actions by today's standards. Neither was it helpful to idealise the Native Americans. Indians should be seen as Indians and not as a symbol of humanity's innate goodness brought to its knees by civilisation.

'I still have no idea what he's talking about,' Alice said to Laura. 'He's your friend. Can't you tell him to sit down?'

But Larry had finished what he had to say and was already in the process of sitting down, silently congratulating himself on a lecture well delivered but wondering if he should have said more about the locomotives.

'That's the most common sense we're likely to hear tonight,' Tank said, slapping Larry on the back. 'Pass the wine, will you, Delores? All Larry's talking has made me thirsty.'

'Well, I don't care what Larry thinks,' Delores said after she'd passed the bottle. 'It's a free country and my opinion counts as much as his. And working at the museum gives me an insight into the mind of the Native American that he can't get from reading books. I don't mean to offend you, Larry, but this is something I feel strongly about.'

'Oh don't worry on my account,' Larry said. 'I've enjoyed the evening and our discussion. I wonder though, could I just say a few more words about the impact of the locomotive? The

Indians used to call them bad medicine wagons...'

'Maybe another time, Larry,' Laura said. 'The Cafe's about to close and we're holding things up.' She then turned to Delores. 'It's been a delightful evening, Delores, and I wouldn't have missed the exhibition for the world. It's something my Aunt Elizabeth would have enjoyed, too.'

Delores and Petey stayed to help clear up after the exhibition and the others headed for the museum's exit. Laura and Alice decided to walk home along the waterfront, and Mike and Larry, who had arrived by Metrobus, started to walk towards the bus stop.

'Hey, you guys can ride back with me if you like,' Tank said. 'It won't be comfortable for one of you, but you'll both be home quicker than if you wait for either the Metrobus or the Circulator.'

Mike and Larry took him up on his offer and walked with him to where he'd parked his Smart car. Without being asked, Mike climbed into the trunk. 'I'm younger than you are, Larry, and I'm wearing overalls. Besides, I owe you for yesterday, man.'

Tank made an illegal U-turn and pulled into the traffic.

'You know what's missing in that museum?' Tank said. 'Cowboys! How can you have an Indian Museum without any cowboys in it? It's like having a ham-and-cheese sandwich without any ham in it or going to an Abbott and Costello movie and finding only Abbott in it. It makes no sense to have one without the other. It's like having peaches without cream or a horse without a carriage.'

'You know what doesn't go together?' Mike said. 'A man your size driving a car this size! Why didn't you buy something bigger?'

'Tank likes confined spaces,' Larry explained.

'It's a pity he doesn't like cleaning them, then,' Mike replied. 'All I can smell back here is Sherman, and his hairs are everywhere. Uji's going to be wondering what I've been up to tonight.'

Tank ignored the comments and continued to head for Georgetown. 'I'll drop you at my house and you can walk from there,' he said. 'There's no point wasting gas.'

Ten minutes later Tank drew into his drive. 'How much is the Metrobus these days?' he asked.

'A dollar fifty,' Mike answered.

'Okay, just give me a dollar each, then,' Tank said.

8

The Road to Jerusalem
(Via Charles Town and Arlington)

The Monday following the exhibition Larry started work on his thesis. The conference on Desert Reclamation was scheduled for October, not for another eleven weeks, but the organisers of the symposium had requested a draft of his paper by the end of August. Unsurprisingly, nothing new had been written on the Desert Land Act since Larry's retirement, and he was left to review his own research and publications, slicing and dicing the information as he saw fit.

After five weeks of disciplined routine, and slightly to his alarm, Larry found that he'd reduced his life's work to an address of no more than forty-five minutes. He read the paper aloud to Moses and timed himself with a stopwatch: forty-four-and-a-half minutes. Nothing wrong with that, he thought. For a Basset Hound though, whose internal clock ticked differently to that of a human's, the monologue had lasted closer to four-and-a-half hours and when Larry looked up from his paper Moses was fast asleep on the floor, snoring gently. It wasn't quite the reaction Larry had been hoping for and he decided to read his paper to Wayne that evening.

Larry and Wayne had fallen into the routine of eating Friday dinner at Larry's. It made sense for Wayne to familiarise himself with the house and its appliances before he moved in, and also logical for him rather than Larry to cook their evening meal. Wayne had quickly mastered the workings of the oven, but his manual dexterity and grasp of pan handles had caused Larry some concern, especially after Wayne dropped a saucepan full of hotdogs and boiling water on to the kitchen floor. Pans became off-limits, as did the hob, and it was agreed that Wayne would only prepare meals inside the oven. Aware of Wayne's aversion to vegetables – and Laura's cautionary mention of scurvy – Larry had also encouraged him to eat salads, something that Wayne had been reluctant to do until Larry introduced him to the world of Thousand Island dressing, a cosmos that magically transformed green leaves and tomatoes into something he found palatable.

This Friday Wayne arrived early.

'I ain't due for another twenty minutes, Professor,' he called through the letter box. 'Do you want me to wait outside or can I come in?'

Larry opened the door and invited him inside. 'You're welcome here any time of the day, Wayne. Come on through to the kitchen and I'll pour you a glass of iced tea. Just out of interest, though, why are you so early?'

'One of the men at my house is drinking beer,' Wayne explained, 'and he's not supposed to. None of us is supposed to. It's against the rules. I told him that and he told me... well, I cain't tell you what he told me because we're not supposed to use words like that either and I told him that, too. I told him I'd tell on him for drinking *and* cussing, and he said that if I did he'd break into my room and put a brick through my television.

'I told him that if he did that he'd have God to answer to because the only shows I watch on television are Christian shows. And I told him something else, too, Professor. I told him that if he did put a brick through my screen I'd get Kevin to come and put a brick through his screen and that Kevin wasn't a person he'd want to mess with if he knew what was good for him because Kevin was fearless and smoked cigarettes when he pumped gas into his car. That quietened him, but his dander was up and so I thought I'd better leave the house and make myself scarce for a while. I'm still telling on him, though.'

'And does Kevin do that?' Larry asked.

'Do what?'

'Smoke cigarettes when he fills up his tank.'

'No. Not no more, he don't.'

Larry had never mentioned to Wayne that he knew Kevin to be dead, but took from Wayne's answer – that Kevin had *stopped* smoking – that Wayne was also aware of this, as Laura had intimated, and not living in a state of denial.

'I thought we'd eat pizza for a change tonight,' Larry said. 'I went ahead and took one out of the freezer this morning so all you have to do is read the instructions on the box and put it in the oven. And once we've eaten, I'd like to read you the paper I'm delivering in Jerusalem. It would be good to get your feedback.'

Wayne slowly traced the words on the pizza box with his finger and then grunted – the sign that he'd understood them. He took the pizza out of the box, stripped it of cellophane and placed it on a metal tray. He then joined Larry at the kitchen table and waited for the oven to preheat.

'And this speech of yours, Professor, is it about that desert thing you keep talking about?'

'Yes, I've been asked to give an overview of the Desert Land Act. I have to explain it to the delegates in forty-five minutes.'

'Wheeeeew!' Wayne whistled. 'That's a long time to talk, Professor. You'll need to suck a mint or your mouth's going to go all dry.'

'Oh I'm not worried about that happening, Wayne. I've got more spittle in my mouth than I know what to do with. No, what worries me is that forty-five minutes isn't going to be long enough. I don't want the delegates going home thinking I've short-changed them.'

One of the lights on the cooker went out and Wayne pulled on some thick oven gloves. He opened the door carefully, slid in the tray with the pizza on it and then closed it. 'It'll take thirty minutes, Professor. Is it okay if I go down to the basement and sit for a while?'

'Sure. Fill Moses' bowl while you're down there, will you – you know where the food is. I'll give you a shout when the pizza's ready.'

What Wayne saw in the basement was still a mystery to Larry. It was the least comfortable room in the house, unair-conditioned and lit by a single naked bulb. It was where Moses stayed when he left the house and where Larry did laundry. He could remember tidying it occasionally but never cleaning it, and it was only after Wayne had decided to sleep there that he'd been forced to make it more habitable. There was now a canvas camp bed in the room and a small side table, a portable 12 inch television and a forgotten easy chair that Larry had discovered under a pile of old dust sheets and dragged to the middle of the room.

Wayne spent time in the basement every time he visited the house and usually alone, as on this occasion. Every so often the sound of his voice would drift up the stairs, sometimes in conversation and sometimes in song. Larry didn't consider this odd – after all, *he* spoke to himself – but only a sign that Wayne had spent too much time alone as he, since Helen's death, had also done. He could hear Wayne's voice now, but the words were drowned by the noise of the oven's fan. He poured himself another glass of iced tea and waited for the oven to ping.

'That sure was a good pizza, Professor. And it was me what done the cooking again, weren't it?'

'It were,' Larry replied, quickly correcting himself. He'd given up trying to rectify Wayne's grammar. It was a full time job and one that would have to wait for another day. One thing at a time, he kept telling himself: first responsibility and then diction.

'I've been thinking, Professor. Is it okay if I make some jam while you're away? I made it all the time when I lived in Charles Town.'

'Oh, I don't know about that, Wayne. That would involve a pan, wouldn't it, and you know how you are with pans. Remember what happened when you boiled those hotdogs?'

'It's not that kind of pan, Professor. It's more like a bucket than a saucepan. And I wouldn't have to lift it when it got hot because all I'd do is ladle the jam into jars. And I'd give some of the jars to you and clean up any mess I made.'

'I don't think I have a pan like that or any jars for that matter. Helen never made jam. She always bought it at Safeway.'

'I got all the stuff, Professor. I got it stored in Charles Town. That's where I grew up. All we have to do is drive there and get it. It ain't that far and you've got a car, don't you?'

Larry promised to think it over and started clearing the

dishes. Larry washed and Wayne wiped, and Wayne told Larry about all the blackberries growing wild in the area and how blackberry jam was the best jam there was and better for a person than any vegetable he knew of.

They moved to the lounge and Larry told Wayne to make himself comfortable for the next forty-four-and-a-half minutes. He then clicked the stopwatch and started to read: 'In the history of America's public domain the Desert Land Act of 1877 plays a dual role...'

Wayne made it through the first fifteen minutes and then his eyelids drooped. Ten minutes later he was snoring loudly and Larry stopped reading and put the paper aside. Again, it wasn't quite the reaction he'd been hoping for and wondered if he should take his paper to the park in the morning and read it to the gang. But then an even better idea came to mind.

The next day he rose early and walked to Oak Hill Cemetery. A couple of groundsmen were standing by the gates when he arrived, one smoking a cigarette and tapping the ash into his hand and the other drinking coffee from a Starbucks container. Larry bade them a cheery hello and then made his way down the winding path to the resting place of Helen and the cemetery's other Johnny-come-latelies.

The Columbarium was shaped like an amphitheatre and Larry positioned himself at its centre. He cleared his throat, pressed the stopwatch and started to speak. He spoke undisturbed and with growing confidence to an audience of granite boulders, blue jays and grey squirrels, and for the first time since completing his paper was able to appreciate the flow of its words, the cogency of their argument and, ultimately, the importance of his life's work. He pressed the stopwatch for a second time and glanced at the readout: forty-five minutes on the dot – an allocation as precise as the twenty-four inches dedicated to his wife!

He went to Helen's niche and thanked her for her time, for her stony reassurance and for being there when it mattered. He had lots of news he said, but no time to tell her now as he had to email his paper to Jerusalem and take Moses to the park. He'd return in a few days, though, because there were things he wanted to run by her: was it wise for Wayne to make jam in their kitchen and did she know anything about an old armchair he'd found in the basement. He was about to leave when he noticed a new plaque on the wall: *Lydia Flores, loving wife of Herb and devoted mother of Daphne and Stanley.* Larry quickly did the math. Lydia Flores had died at the age of 49. He decided to do some digging.

An hour later Larry was heading for Volta Park. He and Moses looked forward to their Saturday visits: it was a chance for Moses to sniff butts and run free, and an occasion for him to spend time with his friends and listen to their news. And amazingly Larry had become a listener – or, at least, a better listener. He'd taken Laura's advice to heart and always considered her likely reaction to anything he might say before actually saying it. There were times when his mouth opened and then silently closed, when people would turn to him and ask what he'd been about to say, only for him to reply that it had been nothing, nothing really – certainly nothing of importance.

And if Larry was cowed by Laura's salutary words he was even more unnerved by the nature of her friends' conversations. The exchanges between Tank, Delores, Mike and Alice were often sharp and confrontational and flitted from one topic to another without so much as a pause for breath. He found it difficult to find his feet in such discussions – especially when he could never tell if the repartee was in jest or serious – and if not content to remain silent, he at least preferred speechlessness to the possibility of upsetting one by agreeing with another. These apprehensions were peppercorn, however, when set against his overriding joy at being a part of their group and sharing their company. It gave him a sense of belonging, something – bar his marriage to Helen – he'd never before truly enjoyed.

And just as Larry accepted his new friends, so did they – with the possible exception of Alice – accept him. They were a shifting accumulation of dribs and drabs rather than a select club, a group of dog owners who'd become park friends rather than friends in the wider sense and quite open to others joining them, especially if that person was vouched for by one of their own and arrived with a dog as likeable as Moses.

And because Laura had never mentioned any of Larry's idiosyncrasies to them, he'd arrived in their midst without the word-of-mouth baggage that had dogged him throughout his professional life, when people new to the department had avoided him simply because those who'd been there longer already did and because it was politic and made life easier if common cause was made with the many against the one. As long as Larry was the butt of the department they remained safe.

In this respect life for Larry had improved fourfold since he'd retired. He was now but one of four butts, and the butt being baited when he arrived at the park that morning was Mike, who since the exhibition at the museum had grown a beard.

'You don't think I get my fill of beards in the Middle East?' Tank said. 'I get sick to death of seeing them. Every corner you round there's a guy with a beard waiting to bump into you. And I'm not talking George Clooney beards here. I'm talking shit beards, straggly wisps of hair more suited to a piece of cheese than a man's face. And I'll tell you this for free, Mike: that beard doesn't suit you! It makes you look like Grizzly Adams.'

'I can live with that,' Mike said. 'Donna thinks I look like Jesus.'

'That's Pastor Millsap to you,' Tank said. 'Only her special friends get to call her Donna.'

'And are you her special friend yet?' Alice smiled.

'No, but I'm working on it. It's just a matter of time.'

'I think the beard suits you just fine, Mike,' Delores said. 'And I don't know why you're so surprised by all the beards in the Holy Land, Tank. It's an important part of their religion.'

'Well, if it *is* so important to their religion, then someone explain to me why some men wear them and others don't. They all read the same books, don't they?'

'I can answer that,' Larry said. He looked across to Laura and she smiled back, the go-ahead for him to continue.

'It's because Modern Orthodox Jews believe that the Bible only bans razors and not *electric* razors because electric razors have two blades and are more like scissors. Hasidic Jews disagree with this interpretation and point out that there wasn't any electricity when the Bible was written. They believe the beard is a bridge between the mind and the heart, a point of connection that allows their ideals to influence their everyday living.'

Alice rolled her eyes. 'More useless shit no one needs to know,' she thought.

'Is that why some Muslims have long beards and other Muslims don't?' Delores asked.

'In a way,' Larry said. 'It's a matter of how things are interpreted. The Koran doesn't proscribe beards but the Hadith – that's the collected sayings of the Prophet – says that Muslims have to grow their beards and trim their moustaches. There was a similar controversy in the early Christian church when...'

'Now do you understand the crap I have to put up with,' Tank interrupted. 'If you get people arguing about the length of a fucking beard, how are you going to get them to agree on anything important? I just hope to God the Sikhs and Anabaptists never get into an argument.'

'What exactly does the Middle East mean to you, Tank?' Laura asked, a hint of exasperation in her voice.

Tank thought for a while and lit the cigar he'd been twirling. 'Full employment,' he said at last. 'As long as I want a job, I've got one.'

And so the morning passed.

When Larry returned to Oak Hill Cemetery the following week he had the lowdown on his wife's new neighbour. Lydia Flores had been murdered, shot through the head while out jogging. No one had been arrested and the investigation was going nowhere. The crime appeared to have been random, purposeless – a shot in the dark.

Lydia's death had made the headlines and the story run in *The Washington News* for over three weeks. As a rule Larry would have known this, but the shooting had happened during the time he'd been writing his paper on the Desert Land Act and for those five weeks he'd neither read a newspaper nor turned on the television. He now downloaded the information from the internet, printed-off hard copies and placed them in a file.

He wondered about getting in touch with Herb Flores and proposing they meet for coffee: as their wives were now neighbours it made sense for them to know each other, too. He hated the idea of Herb sitting in his house alone – Daphne and Stanley were away at college, he'd read – and he'd suggest to Herb that he get a dog and join him and his friends in Volta Park on a Saturday morning. It would help him cope, just like Moses had helped him cope after Helen had died, and maybe the two of them could put their heads together and solve his wife's murder.

Larry ran the idea past Helen and her silence convinced him that this was the right thing to do, but only after he returned from Israel when he'd be in a position to give Herb his undivided attention. Her silence didn't help him figure out where the old armchair in the basement had come from, but it did persuade him that Wayne was quite capable of making jam in their kitchen while he was away, and a week later he and Wayne drove to Charles Town in Larry's old Volvo. It was the first day of September.

'Is the car broked?' Wayne asked, once they were on 190.

Larry told him it wasn't, that it had in fact just been serviced and that 27 mph was fast enough for anyone.

'You sure blink a lot when you drive, Professor. You know that? You're twitching like a rabbit's nose.'

Larry explained that driving made him nervous and that the driver behind – who alternated between honking his horn and flashing his lights – wasn't helping any.

'Should I stop asking questions?'

Larry thought this a good idea and suggested they catch up with each other once they reached Charles Town.

A long two hours later they crossed the Potomac at Whites Ferry, and from Leesburg followed Route 9 into downtown Charles Town. Wayne directed Larry to the corner of Mildred and Congress, the site of the Zion Episcopal Church and Graveyard, and climbed out. 'Just need to check on something, Professor,' he said.

He returned five minutes later with news that the jam making equipment was still there – just where he and Kevin had left it – and suggested that Larry go to the Mountain View Diner and buy some burgers for the drive home. 'By the time you get back I'll have everything ready, Professor. Pass me my hat and sunglasses, will you?'

Larry drove to the diner and ordered two large cheeseburgers, a portion of fries to share and a couple of cans of soda and a packet of potato chips. The air-conditioning was on high and goose bumps formed at the base of his arm hair. A man came in and asked him where the nearest gun shop was and Larry said he didn't know, that he was a first time visitor to Charles Town and only knew where the Zion Episcopal Church and Graveyard was.

Wayne was waiting by the kerb when he returned, his hat pulled down over his head as far as it would go and wearing sunglasses. He led Larry to twelve large boxes stacked behind the perimeter wall, wrapped in thick cellophane and heavily taped. 'Careful you don't drop one, Professor. Jam making equipment's easily broked.'

Larry was surprised by the weight of the boxes, as if the jars inside were already filled with jam. Wayne assured him they weren't and that the glass was heavy in its own right, made especially thick so the hot jam didn't crack it. Something else puzzled Larry: why had the apparatus been stored in a church.

'Pastor let us,' Wayne said. 'They got a storeroom they don't use and it's good and dry in there. Most of the jam me and Kevin made was sold to help pay the church's bills and so the Pastor was happy to give us a key. We'd keep it in an old tobacco tin close to my Pa's grave and that's what I checked on when we first got here.'

The drive back to Georgetown was as long and uneventful as the journey to Charles Town had been. Wayne snoozed and Larry blinked. After almost three hours, and double the time a more assured driver would have taken to travel the distance, Larry pulled into the garage space at the back of his house. He wiped the palms of his hands on his trousers and nudged Wayne awake.

'I was dreaming,' Wayne said groggily. 'Strangest dream, too.' He ran his tongue around his mouth and licked his lips. 'You got a mint, Professor?'

Larry rummaged in his trouser pocket and handed him one.

'You want to hear about it?' Wayne asked.

'Sure,' Larry said. 'It will give me time to recover from the drive.'

'Okay, then. This is what happened. There was this road I was crossing and I was taking a shortcut by crawling under a truck. I was in my good clothes, too. I'd almost made it out the other side when the truck came down on me and I got stuck. There was a man on his hands and knees close by and he asked if I wanted him to have a word with the driver and I said that I would, that I'd be very obliged if he did that. I didn't hear him talking to the driver but he must have telled him something because the truck started to rise up and I managed to squeeze out. It was then I noticed my clothes was all dirty and that the driver was standing over me and looking down. I told him not to worry about anything because it was as much my fault as it was his and that I wouldn't be bringing any lawsuit against him for his carelessness. But he said he wanted one, Professor! Said he wanted one! He said a lawsuit would be a good way of both of us making some money and asked me what my thinking on the matter was. I didn't have a chance to tell him because that's when you woke me and I won't be able to give him an answer now till tonight. I hope he don't get mad. If he leaves his truck there for another six hours he might get a traffic ticket and blame me for it.'

'It was a dream, Wayne,' Larry laughed. 'It's finished with. You'll be dreaming of something else tonight, something completely unrelated.'

Wayne looked at him. 'Not me, Professor. My dreams always follow on. They pick up right where they leave off. I'm telling you: that truck driver will be waiting for me tonight and there's no way of knowing what kind of mood he'll be in.'

Larry smiled and shook his head. Consecutive dreams indeed! Wayne had to be pulling his leg.

'Come on, young man: let's get those boxes into the house before it rains. It looks like we're in for a downpour. Where do you want to put them – the kitchen?'

'I think the basement would be a better place,' Wayne replied.

The time for Larry's departure to Israel was nearing. He'd booked his flights and reserved a room at the King David for seven nights but still had no travel guide. Apart from the university bookstore – an outlet that devoted more space to clothes than it did books – Georgetown had no bookshops and he was forced to make a special trip into Washington.

He spent an hour at Barnes & Noble browsing the shelves and reorganising them when he saw fit, and left with two books: one on Israel and one on Jerusalem. He'd hoped to find one on a subject Laura had expressed interest in and surprise her with it the next time they met, but the girl behind the counter had just looked at him strangely and told him they didn't stock books on that subject.

He then went to a nearby department store and bought three new shirts for the trip – two short-sleeved and one dress – a pair of chinos, some socks, undershorts and a white baseball cap.

Over the next few days Larry read the two guidebooks he'd bought, made notes on places he wanted to visit and formulated an itinerary. He then re-read his paper on the Desert Land Act and committed complete sections to memory. Once satisfied that his preparations for Israel were in hand he turned his attention to matters closer to home and arranged for Wayne to spend more time with Moses. Wayne now came to the house every other day, sometimes in the morning and sometimes late afternoon. He and Larry would sit for a while and then Wayne would take Moses for a walk in Montrose Park. It was on one such afternoon that Tank phoned.

'Larry! Glad I caught you. I need a favour!'

The favour, in fact, was for Tank's mother, whose blue-eyed white American Shorthair was stuck in a tree. The twelve-year-old cat had chased a squirrel up a loblolly pine that morning and five hours later was still there.

'My Mom knows I'm no good with heights, Larry, so why

the hell she called me I have no idea. It's not even as if I like Maybelline.'

'Is that your mother's name?' Larry asked.

'No, that's the name of her damned cat! Now listen up, will you? My life's miserable enough with her living as close as she does, but it's going to get a whole lot worse if anything happens to that damned cat of hers because she'll get lonely and want to visit more often. Now what I want you to do is this: I want you to drive over to Arlington and rescue the cat from the tree. You're good with heights and my mom's got a set of ladders you can use. I'd drive you myself but I'm tied up at work and it's going to be dark by the time I get off.'

'I'm happy to climb a ladder, Tank, but I wouldn't feel safe climbing around in the branches of a tree. I've never been agile and I certainly can't afford to break any bones before I go to Israel.'

'So what are *you* going to do, then?' Tank demanded.

'What am *I* going to do? I don't know what I *can* do…' And then a thought struck him. 'Hang on a minute, I have an idea. Wayne's going to be here soon and I know he can climb trees. Maybe the two of us could work together and rescue your mother's cat.'

'The weird kid! You want to take that weird kid to my mother's house? You out of your mind?'

'It's the only thing I can think of. And I wish you'd stop referring to Wayne as the weird kid. He's a nice young man and he used to make jam for his church. I think your mother would like him.'

For a moment there was silence at Tank's end of the phone and then a click. 'I'm recording the conversation now, Larry. Before I give you the go-ahead I want you to state on record that neither you nor Wayne will sue either me or my mother if something goes wrong and you get hurt. Okay?'

Larry agreed to the conditions of the favour he was about to do for Tank, and then Tank reeled off the directions to his mother's house.

'I appreciate you doing this, Larry, and for you doing me this favour I'm going to do you one. When you go to Israel next week I'll get you to the airport. I can't say fairer than that.'

Wayne arrived at the house ten minutes later and Larry explained the situation. Was he prepared to help? Wayne was: he liked climbing loblolly trees. He made it clear to Larry, though, that he was doing this as a favour for him and not Tank, who Kevin still had good reason for not liking.

They climbed into the Volvo for the second time that month and Larry headed the car to M St and then crossed the bridge into Virginia. He followed Wilson Boulevard to Buchanan Street and there took a left turn and slowed the car. 'It's the tenth house on the left,' he told Wayne, giving him its number.

'It's there, Professor!' Wayne said, pointing to a brick-based wood house. 'And there's an old woman standing on the porch.'

The driveway to the house was long and deeply pitted. Larry reduced the car's speed to three miles per hour but still hit every pothole.

'What are we supposed to call the woman, Professor?'

'Mrs Newbold,' Larry said. 'Tank said his mother was a stickler for formality.'

They climbed out of the car and Mrs Newbold came running towards them.

'Are you the men Theodore sent?' she asked.

'We are, Mrs Newbold,' Larry said. 'My name is Professor

MacCabe and this is Mr Trout. We're here to rescue your cat.'

Mrs Newbold took a closer look at Larry. 'You're the handyman who cleaned my son's gutters, aren't you?'

Larry smiled. 'I cleaned his gutters but I'm not a handyman, Mrs Newbold. I'm a specialist in late nineteenth-century American history.'

'He's an expert on the Desert Land Act, too, Mrs Newbold, and he's going to talk about it in Israel next month,' Wayne added.

Neither of these facts appeared to impress Mrs Newbold, who wordlessly led them to the garage where the ladders were stored and then to the tree where Maybelline was lodged. There she hovered, nervously wringing her hands and muttering to herself.

'I think it would be safer if you left us to it, Mrs Newbold,' Larry suggested. 'There's a chance one of us might fall and if you're standing close by we might well land on you. I wouldn't want that to happen.'

Mrs Newbold took Larry's advice and retired to the house, standing on the porch and watching from a distance.

'Ain't exactly the cheerful kind, is she?' Wayne commented. 'You think the cat run off on purpose?'

'I don't think so, Wayne. Tank gave me the impression his mother was very attached to her cat. Anyway, let's get the job done and then I'll treat you to a pizza.'

The closest branches of the loblolly were more than twenty feet up the trunk and it was necessary to extend the ladders. Larry held them while Wayne climbed the rungs and eased himself into the tree.

'Where's the cat at, Professor?' Wayne shouted down. 'I can hear her but I cain't see her.'

'She's to your right, about five, no, six branches up from where you are now.'

'I see her. What do I do when I reach her? Throw her down?'

'No, Wayne! Whatever you do don't throw her! If you can't carry her in one arm, try and get her to sit on your shoulders. Once you've got her I'll climb up the ladder and make sure you get your foot on the rung. We can't afford to have any accidents: Tank says we're not covered.'

Wayne wasn't sure what kind of reception to expect when he reached the cat and hoped she wouldn't scratch him. Maybelline, however, was as anxious to leave the tree as Wayne was to be in it, and when his head came close she climbed across it and arched herself over his right shoulder, her front paws anchored to his back and her back paws fastened to his chest. Wayne started his descent and Larry, who was now standing at the top of the ladder, guided him and told him where the branches were in relation to his feet. He took hold of Wayne's left foot when it came searching for the ladder and placed it on a rung. He then stayed close and made sure his feet connected with all the other rungs as he made his descent. When they were about six feet from the ground Maybelline jumped from Wayne's shoulder and ran towards the house and Mrs Newbold's outstretched arms.

'I'd have thought the cat might have showed some gratitude,' Wayne said. 'She never even licked me.'

They took the ladders back to the garage and knocked on the door. Mrs Newbold was dabbing tears from her eyes when she opened it, but was also smiling.

'They're tears of happiness,' she explained. 'I don't know what I'd have done if anything had happened to Maybelline.

Thank you both so very, very much! Now take off your shoes and come inside for a coffee.'

Larry slipped off his shoes and was surprised to find a large hole in one of his socks. 'Oh my,' he said and tut-tutted. He gave Wayne a hand untying a knot in one of his bootlaces and was even more surprised to find Wayne wearing only one sock when he pulled off his boots. 'I hope Mrs Newbold doesn't notice our socks,' he said. 'She might get the wrong impression of us.'

They entered the house and sat next to each other on a small couch, self-consciously hiding their feet as best they could. After a few minutes Mrs Newbold returned from the kitchen with three small cups of coffee and a plate of Maryland cookies.

'What happened to your other sock, Mr Trout? You didn't leave it in the tree, did you?'

'I think I must have forgotten to put it on this morning, Mrs Newbold. The Professor's got a hole in one of his.'

'Yes, I'm sorry about that, Mrs Newbold... anyway, how do you like Virginia? It must be very different from living in Texas.'

'It's better than living in Canada,' she said without elaborating.

Mrs Newbold had moved from San Antonio five years after the death of her husband. It was time for a change and a chance to be close to one of her four children, all of whom had long since left the city. Her decision to move to the environs of Washington was dictated less by her special love for Tank as the locations of her other three children. Her two older sons lived in Baton Rouge and Chicago and neither city appealed to her. Ideally she'd have moved closer to her daughter whose children were still young, but as her daughter was married to a Canadian and lived in Calgary, she'd decided against it. Living in Canada would be too much like travelling in coach after a lifetime of flying first class. In Washington she'd anticipated meeting a better type of person, but now, sitting opposite Larry and Wayne, she was starting to have doubts.

'I take it you don't teach any classes on a Tuesday afternoon, Professor MacCabe?'

'I don't teach any classes at all these days, Mrs Newbold. I'm retired. The only working man here is Mr Trout.'

'And what do you do, Mr Trout?'

'I deliver newspapers and collect cans,' Wayne replied.

'And he's going to be making jam soon,' Larry added with some pride.

'I am?' Wayne said looking at Larry. And then, a moment later, repeated the words with more definition: 'I am!'

Mrs Newbold thought for a moment and looked at Wayne. 'Are you the strange young man Theodore talks about: the one that hangs around the park?'

'That don't sound like me, do it, Professor? I think he must be meaning Mike... Mike's a man who believes in a man called Buddha,' he said, turning to face Mrs Newbold. 'He cain't make his mind up if he's a Christian or a Buddhist. Me, I'm a Christian. You don't need no other religions when you're born again because you get your money's worth with Christianity.'

'How do you mean?' Mrs Newbold asked.

'You get three for the price of one, Mrs Newbold. You get the Father, the Son *and* the Holy Ghost. Ain't that right, Professor?'

Conversation started to lag and Larry decided it was time

they made a move. It was clear that Mrs Newbold had decided Wayne *was* the weird kid her son talked about and he didn't want to risk the repercussions of her pressing the point, which was something she was more than likely to do if she was anything like Tank. He thanked her for the coffee and cookies and explained that he and Mr Trout had an important engagement in Georgetown.

'We're going to a pizza restaurant,' Wayne clarified.

Mrs Newbold opened the door and waited on the porch while they put on their shoes. Maybelline waited with them, but soon tired of watching Wayne thread the laces through the eyelets of his boots and wandered off into the bushes. Larry stepped in to give Wayne a hand and tied the bows in a single knot. He then shook hands with Mrs Newbold and he and Wayne climbed into the car. He reversed slowly down the drive, the wheels dropping into the potholes and then unexpectedly rising over a stone he didn't remember being there when they'd arrived.

'It's a good job that Volvos are made of sturdy stuff,' Larry said. 'You can say what you like about the Swedes, but they know how to make cars.'

'I don't want to say anything about the Swedes, Professor,' Wayne said. 'I know nothing about them.'

'It was just a figure of speech,' Larry smiled.

There was another figure of speech waiting for Larry when he returned home that evening. It had been coined by Tank and left on his answering machine.

'Why the hell couldn't you have just run over my mother?' Tank said.

It was the following Saturday and the gang were sitting at

their usual table in Volta Park. On Monday, Larry would be flying to Israel.

'I didn't do it on purpose, Tank. I've already told you that. I had no idea the cat was there.'

'Well, thanks to you and that dumb friend of yours, the cat's pushing up daisies in the backyard now – and my Mom's planning to visit me tomorrow! Hell! You're lucky I'm a man of my word or you'd be making your own way to Dulles.'

'For Heaven's sake, Tank, Larry was trying to do you a favour,' Laura said. 'It was an accident! And you didn't even like your mother's cat – you said so yourself. Now will someone please change the subject?'

Delores was happy to oblige. 'I've got details of the service for the Blessing of the Animals,' she said. She took a notebook from her purse and read them the particulars.

The service would start with Hymn 405: *All Things Bright and Beautiful* which would be followed by a Collect and a Reading from the Book of Job. There would be Prayers – one attributed to Saint Francis – and the Pastor would then bless the animals with holy water and a sprig of boxwood.

'And Donna says she's prepared to bless any stuffed animals the congregants bring along and photographs of any deceased pets or pets too big to fit into the church. She's going all out this year. I think this St Francis Day will be the best ever.'

Laura and Alice looked at each other and clasped hands. Tank chose the moment to light a cigar and Mike to hum the tune to *All Things Bright and Beautiful*.

'I wish I could be there to join you,' Larry said. 'I have a feeling it's going to be a blast.'

Larry had occasionally, but without much success, taken to using words Mike might say. Vocabulary evolved, he reasoned, and it was up to him to keep pace with the changes. He'd never felt particularly comfortable using words like *dude*, *cool* and *chick*, but *blast* he could handle. He liked the sound of it and it made him feel younger.

'Right on, Larry,' Mike said. 'I wish you could be there with us too, man. Is Wayne bringing Moses?'

'I don't think so. I mentioned the service to him, but he said that God didn't like animals going to church. He wouldn't elaborate on his thinking and I didn't push him. Maybe it's because the service is being held at the Church of Latter-Day Lutherans. He attends another church, that small one on Wisconsin just past the Hardy Middle School. I think they call it the Church of the Divine Shepherd.'

'I know the one,' Mike said. 'The minister there teaches that Gehenna – that's his name for Hell – is a hollow at the centre of the earth and that people are never physically more than twenty miles distant. I don't think Wayne's got anything against Lutherans, though. He's been hanging around the church listening to me play the organ recently and asking me how it works. One minute he's sitting there behind me, the next he's gone, and then he's right back sitting where he was. Sometimes it's difficult to fathom him.'

'I told you I saw him washing in the waterfront fountain, didn't I, and how he lived in a tree for five years?' Alice said. 'I think he's too shallow for anyone to fathom.'

'That's not a very nice thing to say, Alice. Be thankful you don't have his problems.'

'Lighten up, Laura! You know I don't mean these things – apart from not inviting him to our apartment. I mean that!'

'I'm not sure he'd come even if I invited him,' Laura said. 'He's been quite off with me the last few times I've bumped into him. You don't know anything about this, do you, Larry?'

Larry blushed and turned sheepish. 'I don't know for sure, Laura, but I think it might have something to do with you and Alice getting married.'

'How does he know that? I know I haven't told him and I'm pretty sure Alice hasn't.'

Larry shifted in his seat and looked uncomfortable. 'He heard me telling Helen,' he admitted. 'I took him with me to Willow Columbarium the other week.'

'Larry! You should have had more sense!'

Tank laughed. 'You talk to your dead wife, Larry! Jesus Christ! You're as weird as he is. No wonder the two of you get along.'

'I'm sorry, Laura.'

'Sorry doesn't always cut it,' Tank said. 'I told my mother you were sorry for killing her cat and she almost laughed in my face: "Sorry!" she said. "He said he was sorry for killing Maybelline? Theodore, he did it on purpose!"' Tank then burst out laughing.

'And I'm presuming Wayne was upset by the news,' Laura said.

'Well, he thought it was unusual for two women to marry each other and said it ran counter to God's teachings, but not much more than that. I'm sure he'll come round to the idea.'

'I've been right about him all along,' Alice chimed in. 'I knew the first time I saw him that he was strange. We'll look well if he mounts a protest outside the church on our wedding day and brings all those nuts from the Church of the Divine Shepherd with him. There might even be a riot!'

'I think we should stop giving him mints,' Delores said.

'I'll have a word with him,' Larry promised. 'I'll explain things in a way he can understand.'

'Try talking to him in shattered English, then. That's probably the only way you're going to get through to him,' Tank said. 'Hey, Mike, where are you going?'

'Nowhere,' Mike said.

'Ain't that the truth,' Tank laughed.

Mike wandered to the far end of the park to separate Uji and Sherman whose play fighting, like that of their masters, was also getting out of hand. Larry called Moses to the table where Repo and Button were sitting quietly.

'It's time Moses and I were going,' he said. 'Wayne's moving in this afternoon and I still have the house to get ready.'

Laura stood and hugged him. 'Have a safe trip, Larry, and don't forget to send a postcard.'

Alice remained seated and Delores wedged, but both wished him well. Tank said he'd see him Monday morning and Mike came over and threw his arms around him and kissed him on the cheek. 'Tell Israel to chill, man. Tell them to turn the other cheek and give the Palestinian dudes a break.'

Despite the well wishes Larry left the park feeling slightly dejected. He'd already felt badly about Maybelline's death before he'd even gone to the park, and now he'd learned that Mrs Newbold was accusing him of running her cat over on purpose. And he felt bad about letting slip to Wayne that Laura and Alice were planning on getting married and worse still that so many voices had been raised against his young friend. He couldn't sort any of the problems out before he went to Israel, but he promised himself he'd put them in order on his return, when he'd also introduce Herb Flores to the group.

At six o'clock on Monday morning Tank's horn sounded outside Larry's house. Larry was ready and waiting. He'd decided against waking Moses and Wayne at such an early hour and said his goodbyes the previous evening. He carried with him an old-fashioned wheel-less suitcase and a briefcase containing his travel documents and two copies of his paper on the Desert Land Act. He put both bags in the trunk compartment and climbed into the passenger seat. Tank greeted him with a grunt and put the car in gear.

They travelled along M St and crossed the bridge into Virginia. Instead of taking the road to Dulles International, Tank drove into Arlington and on to Wilson Boulevard, the route Larry had taken to Mrs Newbold's house.

'We're not going to visit your mother, are we?'

'Not unless you want to.'

'Where are we going then?'

'To the Rosslyn Metro Station,' Tank said. 'I said I'd *get* you to the airport. I didn't say I'd drive you there. I'll drop you at the 5A Stop and the bus will take you the rest of the way. It'll take 45 minutes and cost $3.50 – that's the senior citizen rate. If you'd have taken a taxi from your house it would have cost you $45 – and that's without a tip. I'm saving you $50 and when you get back you can put it towards a new cat for my mother. I'm damned if I'm buying her one. Who you flying with? El Al?'

'Yes. The flight's at eleven.'

'It's good you're getting there early then because they'll want to know your life story before they let you on board – probably your inside-leg measurement, too.'

Tank dropped Larry at the 5A Bus Stop at 6:30. They shook

hands and Tank told him to leave Israel as he found it. Larry promised him he would.

Six hours later Larry was sitting in a window seat sipping Diet Coke and trying to open a packet of complimentary nuts. He was sixty-seven years of age, flying to Israel to give a paper on the Desert Land Act and, for the first time in his life, about to be arrested.

9

Masada

A downside to proportional representation is that the party winning the largest number of seats – but without a majority – often has to make deals with people it doesn't really like if it wishes to assume power. The Likud had netted 30 seats in the March election and though the largest party, was 31 short of an overall majority. Negotiations proved tough, and four weeks after the election Prime Minister Netanyahu was still unable to form a government. He had the support of United Torah Judaism, Kulanu and Shas, but was still in need of another eleven votes and had only three weeks left in which to find them. Two weeks later he agreed terms with The Jewish Home, but as the 6 May deadline loomed he was still missing three votes. It was then that Netanyahu did the inconceivable and approached the Party of the Sicarii, a small grouping on the fringe of the Israeli political spectrum.

Over the years, close to 200 political parties had run in the country's elections, and more than a hundred had gained seats. Most were short-lived, here-today-and-gone-tomorrow parties, but if in their day they'd been fortunate enough to hold the balance of power in the Knesset, they were able to exert power far beyond that warranted by numerical representation. The Party of the Sicarii was one such party, a one trick pony with a one-track mind, and in the March election had won three seats – seats vital to Netanyahu if he was to form a government. With two hours remaining, and in return for their support, he agreed to the Sicarii's one and only demand: authority over the ancient fortification of Masada.

The nationalist icon rested on a remote rock plateau on the eastern edge of the Judean Desert. The bloc, though now detached from the scarp, was part of the Great Rift Valley's western wall and overlooked the Dead Sea. It was 450 metres high and had a surface area 600 by 300 metres. It was a fortress waiting to happen, and though its strategic potential had been appreciated during the Hasmonean period, it was King Herod who turned the mesa into an impregnable stronghold. On his death, and after the Province of Judea had been incorporated into the Empire, Masada became a garrison for Roman soldiers and remained so until 66 AD when, at the outbreak of the First Jewish-Roman War, the fortress was furtively taken by a group of rebels known as the Sicarii.

In that year existing religious tensions spilled over into anti-taxation protests, attacks on Roman citizens and then – after the Romans retaliated by sacking the Temple and executing 6,000 Jews – all-out war. At first things went well for the Jews and the Romans were expelled from Jerusalem and large parts of Judea. But then the war turned, and after a couple of years of toing and froing, only Jerusalem remained in rebel hands. Its defenders, however, were far from united and the city descended into a state of civil war as militants from competing factions, seemingly more interested in defeating each other than the Romans, fought for control of the city. Eventually the factions headed by the Zealots and Sicarii prevailed, and it was they who commanded Jerusalem at the time of its fall.

The Zealots and Sicarii, though often at variance, were both upholders of the Fourth Philosophy of Judaism – the previous three having been taken by the Pharisees, Sadducees and Essenes – and were intent on securing Judea for the Jews and ridding the land of Gentiles, paganism and foreign control. They looked upon themselves as the heirs of Judah Maccabee – the patriot who'd fought and defeated the forces of the Seleucid Empire almost 250 years earlier – and were prepared to use violence of any kind to achieve their goals. Their adversaries, however, were also prepared to use violence of any kind to stop them achieving their goals, and when it came to savagery, the Romans were without equal.

Jerusalem fell and the city and Second Temple were destroyed. Those Sicarii who'd survived the onslaught fled to Masada, still under their control and the last of the rebel strongholds. There they withstood the Romans for three years until in 73 AD the Tenth Legion laid siege to the mountain. Rather than twiddle their thumbs and starve the rebels into submission the Romans built a ramp against the western cliff and dragged a tower and battering ram up the slope. They punched a hole through the outer defences, set the inner defences of timber and earth on fire and the next day, once the flames had subsided, prepared for the fight of their lives. They were greeted, however, not with stones and missiles but another wall – one of silence – and beyond that wall, the corpses of 960 men, women and children.

Rather than face crucifixion or certain slavery the Sicarii had chosen to commit suicide and die in a state of freedom.

They'd drawn lots and the ten winners had been given the responsibility of despatching the losing 950. The ten winners had then drawn further lots and the victor charged with slitting the throats of the losing nine. The overall winner, who had by this time already killed 104 of his family and friends, then turned the knife on himself. It was bloodshed on a grand scale but the Roman police weren't looking for anyone else. They did, however, find two women and five children hiding in a cistern, but what happened to them is anyone's guess.

Masada sank into obscurity and remained there for thirteen centuries until rediscovered in 1838. The story of its destruction was rekindled and the flames fanned into a patriotic myth. Masada became a byword for courage, heroism and sacrifice, and a symbol of the ancient kingdom, the Diaspora and Jewish cultural identity. It came to represent the new nation's struggle for liberty, its right to exist and *Masada shall not fall again* was incorporated into the Israeli Defence Forces' oath of allegiance.

Had the myth of Masada remained undisputed, the Party of the Sicarii might never have been formed, but the story was now being challenged on all fronts and there were those in Israel unprepared to trust its legacy to others. Some critics had questioned the rationale of a Jewish state celebrating an act of mass suicide when Jewish law forbade self-immolation and considered it a serious sin. Others had cast doubt on the idea that the defenders of Masada had even committed suicide, and pointed to the fact that archaeological digs on the plateau had only ever uncovered the remains of 28 people – and most of these skeletons had been found in the company of pig bones. More damaging were the political voices that condemned the allegory for engendering a fortress mentality within the nation and encouraging its citizens to believe that the only way to deal with an enemy was to fight it to the death. For them Masada illuminated only the ruinous potential of nationalism: the Sicarii and their allies had refused to compromise during the Jewish-Roman War and by doing so had brought death and destruction to the Jewish people. The modern state of Israel had to learn from these mistakes and not compound them.

The newly-formed Party of the Sicarii ran on the platform of the Fourth Philosophy: they would secure Israel for the Jews and rid the land of Gentiles (Arabs), paganism (Islam) and foreign control (the rest of the world). Like their namesakes of the past they used violence to achieve these goals, but instead of the traditional Sicarii dagger opted for character assassination. They accused their opponents of anti-Semitism (Jew as well as Arab), of being a bunch of Uncle Toms and equated those who criticised the history and meaning of Masada with the malefactors who denied the Holocaust. Against all predictions the Party of the Sicarii won three seats in the election, and against all common sense Netanyahu invited them to join the government.

Masada and its buffer zone were owned by the State of Israel, but cooperatively managed by the Nature and Parks Authority and the Antiquities Authority. Both now reported to the Party of the Sicarii. Day-to-day administration of the site continued as normal, but changes were made to the way Masada was presented to the nation and the thousands of tourists who flocked there every year. All tour guides were now vetted and certified by the Sicarii and any straying from the given script – the Sicarii script – were banned from the site, fined and in exceptional circumstances imprisoned.

Likewise, all promotional material was rewritten and a defence of suicide-in-mitigating-circumstances added. Nowhere in the Bible was there a direct prohibition of suicide, it stated, and certainly it wasn't one of the Ten Commandments. King Saul and Samson had both committed suicide and the verses describing their deaths were written without judgement. Their suicides had been acts of martyrdom and their deaths a sanctification of God's holy name. And the deaths of those who'd defended Masada were no different, and the State had been right to accord the remains of the 28 Sicarii full military burials.

In similar vein all archaeological controversy was excised from the brochures and there was now no mention of the pig bones discovered on the mountain. The Sicarii went further and banned all scientific activity on the site. Past excavations had proved anything but helpful and only succeeded in sullying the fortress's reputation. Masada was good as it stood and could speak for itself.

The Party of the Sicarii congratulated themselves on the changes and were keen to show them to their absentee mentor, a man who had done more to rehabilitate the name of the ancient Sicarii than any other and was recognised as the world's leading authority on the Fourth Philosophy. His blessing and future writings on their accomplishments might well cement their reforms and secure the legacy of Masada for future generations. And there was also a good chance that his promotion of their achievements would bring them the necessary donations to fund future electoral activity.

They wrote to their idol care of the Baltimore Hebrew University and anxiously awaited his reply. Three weeks later they received an email: Dr Lavi Maccabee would be happy to pay them a visit.

The confusion over Larry's name started in the El Al terminal at Dulles and continued through immigration at Ben Gurion Airport. At both locations, and on several occasions, he'd been addressed as Maccabee, and his explanation that his name was pronounced MacCabe gone unnoticed. His surname was Scottish he'd told them, and roughly translated as *son of the helmeted one* and had nothing to do with hammers. Airport and immigration officials had listened to him, nodded their heads as if understanding his point, and then continued to refer to him as Mr Maccabee.

By the time Larry arrived at the check-in desk of the King David Hotel late Tuesday morning, he'd been travelling with little sleep for more than twenty-four hours and was happy to answer to any name as long as his title remained intact.

'Welcome to the King David, Mr Maccabee,' the receptionist smiled. 'Is this your first visit to Israel?'

'It is,' Larry smiled back. 'But it's Professor and not Mr Maccabee. I'm here for a conference.'

The receptionist apologised, altered the registration details and printed his key card. 'We've upgraded you to a deluxe room, Professor Maccabee. I hope your stay with us will be an enjoyable one.' She then called for a bellboy to take him to room 312.

The King David Hotel was in the Yemin Moshe neighbourhood, across the street from the YMCA and overlooking the Old City and Mount Zion. It was square-set, seven storeys high and built from pink limestone. Its outward appearance was colonial, but its public spaces were decorated with Assyrian, Hittite, Muslim and Phoenician motifs. It was the place where presidents and royalty stayed when they visited Jerusalem, and the haunt of rock stars, actors and famous hairdressers. As the world's leading authority on the Desert Land Act Larry felt completely out of place.

He napped for a couple of hours and then showered, changed into clean clothes and went down to the lobby. The day was hot and he covered his head with his new baseball cap. He turned right on King David St and followed Ha-Emek to Jaffa Gate. He'd decided to spend the afternoon wandering the streets of the Old City, finding his bearings and then returning to explore it more fully on the days that followed.

Larry was a right-turner, someone whose natural inclination in life was always to turn to the right in strange surroundings. Accordingly he set off through the Armenian Quarter, and three hours later was back at Jaffa Gate with all four Quarters under his belt and two pages of jottings in his notebook. He found a small eatery outside the walled city and stood in line to place his order. Eventually he was served and he took his coffee and piece of cake to an outdoor table at the rear of the premises and opened his journal.

He'd been surprised by how small the Old City was – by his estimation no more than a half square mile. The streets had been narrow, cobbled and irregular in pattern, dotted with small courtyards, external staircases, roof gardens and arches. He'd passed synagogues, mosques, churches and monasteries; museums, archaeological sites, bazaars and residences of differing sizes and heights. So far as Larry could determine, the Old City of Jerusalem was a jumble of pale stone buildings hedged in by walls forty feet high and eight feet thick, and the only open areas were the Temple Mount and the plaza, running the length of the Western Wall.

He pressed the remaining crumbs of cake to his finger, placed them in his mouth and took a sip of coffee. The Armenian and Jewish Quarters had been quiet that afternoon, but the Muslim and Christian Quarters had buzzed with activity, the former with everyday life and the latter with digitised tourism. He thought it sensible to mix and match his future visits to the Old City and split his time between restful and more taxing sights, the open and the claustrophobic. He'd start the next day, he decided, by spending the morning at the Western Wall and the afternoon in the Church of the Holy Sepulchre.

It was close to six when Larry made it back to the King David. He was about to enter when he was stopped at the door by a woman in dark navy uniform and asked his business. Larry was pleased to tell her. He liked it that Israelis took such an interest in people.

'I'm retired these days,' he said, 'but I used to teach late nineteenth-century American history at Georgetown University. I'm here to present a paper on the Desert Land Act to a symposium on Desert Reclamation at the Hebrew University of Jerusalem. Usually I'd have brought my wife with me but Helen died this year and she's in the Willow Columbarium at Oak Hill Cemetery and so...'

'Your business at the hotel!' the woman snapped.

'Well, I'm a guest, of course,' Larry said, taken aback by her manner. 'I'm staying in a deluxe room.'

'And your name?'

'McCabe,' Larry answered. 'Professor Larry McCabe.'

The woman scanned a list of names and started to frown. 'There is no... do you mean Maccabee?'

'Yes, that's me,' Larry said resignedly. 'Professor Maccabee.'

It appeared that getting the finer points of English pronunciation across to people whose first language was Hebrew was no less difficult than getting the finer points of grammar across to Wayne, whose first language *was* English. He decided he may as well just get used to the idea of being called Maccabee while in Israel.

Larry ate his evening meal in the Garden Restaurant and chose a table on its terrace overlooking the hotel's private gardens. He ordered hummus as an appetiser and gefilte fish for his main course. He toyed with the idea of ordering a glass of wine but decided against it and stuck to mineral water. All in all the meal was enjoyable, but probably not special enough to warrant a mention to Laura when he wrote her a postcard. He called for the check, swallowed hard when he read it and asked for the meal to be charged to his room. He left shekels on the table for the waitress and headed for the concierge's desk. It was time to make enquiries.

Larry had first read about Masada as a boy. He'd been thumbing through the magazine section of a Sunday newspaper when he'd chanced upon an article on the ruined fortress. It was the photographs that had first caught his attention, but the accompanying story had been no less remarkable and prompted him over time to read further. Although no expert, Larry had been versant with the history of Masada for more than fifty years and was excited by the prospect of actually seeing it in the flesh.

The concierge was used to arranging trips for hotel guests and knew of two tour operators specialising in excursions to Masada. He suggested that if Larry wanted to avoid the complications of the Shabbat he should visit the site on

Thursday, the day after next. Larry agreed and the concierge placed a call.

'All set, Professor Maccabee. The BeinHarim representative will meet you in the lobby at 7:30 Thursday morning.'

It was as simple as that. But then, a moment later and after Larry had left the desk, it became a lot more complicated.

A passing bellboy had caught the tail end of the conversation and overheard Larry's name mentioned. The concierge was dealing with another guest now, but details of Larry's trip were visible on the desk. The bellboy glanced at them: BeinHarim – Masada – Thursday – Maccabee – Lari – 312. He waited while the concierge finished his conversation and then asked him the vital question – the missing piece of the jigsaw taking shape in his head.

'Was that *Dr* Maccabee you were talking to earlier?' he asked.

The concierge glanced at his notes. 'Yes, I have him down as Professor but that's the same thing as Doctor in the United States – and that's where Professor Maccabee is from.'

'Dr Lavi Maccabee?' the bellboy persisted, who'd misread the concierge's misspelling of Larry.

Aware that the bellboy had problems pronouncing his R's and not wishing to draw attention to his impediment, the concierge nodded. The bellboy thanked him for the information and walked outside the hotel to a place where he could speak without being overheard. He took out his mobile phone and punched in a number: 'He's here,' he said. 'He's already arrived. He's going to Masada on Thursday.'

The next morning Larry rose late. He'd slept poorly that night – the consequence of jetlag he supposed – and left the hotel behind schedule. Rather than eat breakfast in the restaurant he returned to the cafe he'd visited the previous afternoon and again ordered coffee and a piece of cake and sat at the same outdoor table. There was nothing in Larry's life more comfortable than routine.

He left the eatery through the back entrance and retraced his steps to the Armenian Quarter, through Hurva Square and down the steps to the plaza and the Western Wall, Judaism's most sacred site. The wall had been built to retain the Second Temple but was now all that remained of the Second Temple, and hence its significance. It was sixty feet high, though only the first seven levels dated to the time of Herod: huge limestone blocks weighing anything from eight to 250 tons. (If building pyramids in Egypt hadn't been the happiest of times for the Israelis, they had at least provided them with a useful apprenticeship for constructing large monuments.)

Larry mingled with small groups of Orthodox Jews dressed in frock coats, white shirts and black felt hats: a style with proven appeal and one that had remained in vogue for three hundred years. Some wore prayer shawls and tasselled belts, and others had small tefillin boxes tied to their foreheads and arms. All had beards – some trimmed, some bushy and others in existential crisis – and Larry was reminded of the time he'd grown a beard and been mistaken for Leon Trotsky. A group of schoolboys with cropped heads and sidelocks danced in a circle, first clockwise and then anti-clockwise, their arms locked around each other's shoulders and their voices rising in praise. Larry joined in with bystanders and clapped his hands in time to their movements. Why couldn't everyone be as happy as the Israelis!

He noticed a swarm of tourists approaching from Dung

Gate – the drop-off point for day excursions to Temple Mount and the Western Wall – and decided to get ahead of them. He approached the men's prayer area with deference, taking off his baseball cap and replacing it with the paper yarmulke handed him. He'd seen the Western Wall so many times on television it was like going to a friend's house. He found a small gap between two men rocking their upper bodies and reciting psalms and squeezed into the space. He had no prayers to offer a deity but was more than happy to have a chat with Helen. He rested the palm of his hand against the wall's ancient stone, and taking a cue from his neighbours began rocking to and fro.

'You won't believe the hotel I'm staying in, Helen. It's called the King David and it's not a bit like the Days Inn. To tell the truth it's a bit grand for me and I'm nervous about going into the main restaurant. There are names of famous people engraved on the ground floor tiles, a bit like the Hollywood Walk of Fame, and they're all people who've stayed at the hotel at one time or another. People like the Dalai Lama and Billy Graham, Nelson Mandela and Hillary Clinton and a descendant of Napoleon Bonaparte who's shortened the family name to Bono. It's like a Who's Who of bigwigs and there's a good chance that my name might join them if my address to the symposium goes well and the Hebrew University of Jerusalem puts in a good word for me. I just hope they manage to spell my name right. You wouldn't believe the problems I've been having… .

'Anyway, with the exception of the woman who stands outside the hotel and asks people who they are and what their business is, everyone has been very pleasant, and the concierge was kind enough to book me an excursion to Masada. I'm going there tomorrow and I have to be in the lobby at 7:30am. I'm at the Western Wall now, which is a bit like Willow Columbarium but a lot bigger and not in as good condition. Some of the slabs are eroding, but considering they've been here for 2,000 years I suppose that's to be expected. I think the man who built the wall made the mistake of using stones from different quarries and mixing fine- with thick-grained blocks. There are crevices everywhere and people put small prayer notes into them. Look, I'll show you.' He pulled the breakfast receipt from his shirt pocket and wedged it into a crack, reminded by it of something else he needed to share with Helen. 'And you're not going to believe the prices, Helen. They charge more for a cup of coffee in Jerusalem than they do on M St! And the cake's no different. I bought a piece…'

Larry stopped midsentence, inexplicably seized by an urge to lick the wall. He cut his conversation short and immediately moved away from the stones. If he was caught putting his tongue on Judaism's most sacred site he'd be thrown out of Israel – and how would he explain that to the Hebrew University of Jerusalem and his friends back home? He had no idea what had overcome him. Had the Western Wall been made of sandstone he might have understood the craving but it wasn't, it was made from limestone, and when in life had he ever been tempted to put a pinch of lime in his mouth?

He left the plaza in a state of agitation and headed for the Church of the Holy Sepulchre, forgetting to hand back the yarmulke and covering it with his baseball cap. He walked up Chain Street to where it became David Street, turned right on Souk El-Lakhamin and then left on Souk El-Dabbagha. The approaches to the Church bustled with tourists and commerce: shops selling crosses, candles, rosary beads and statues; everything in fact but hammer-and-nail sets. Larry stopped and asked a vendor if he sold dog collars, but the man said he didn't and so he kept walking and soon arrived at his destination.

The exterior of the Church of the Holy Sepulchre was surprisingly unprepossessing, down at heel almost, and apart from the multitudes entering and exiting, easy to mistake for just another old building. Larry took off his baseball cap and yarmulke as he went into the church and waited for his eyes to accustom to the gloom. He was jostled from behind and in front, and moved to the side and stood beneath a dim lamp while he oriented himself.

The church was a maze of chapels and worship spaces administered by monks of six different denominations: Roman Catholic, Greek, Armenian, Coptic, Syriac and Ethiopian. They wore dark robes and long beards and looked like Hell's Angels. Larry knew of their reputation for brawling and gave them a wide berth, preferring to follow the advice of his guidebook than risk a punch on the nose. He turned to his right – as the book and his own proclivity suggested he do – and climbed the narrow flight of stairs to Calvary and the site of Christ's execution. Next he made his way to the Unction Stone where Christ's body had been wrapped and anointed for burial, and then to the wooden Rotunda that housed His tomb – the Lord's last known mailing address on earth.

The distance from Golgotha to the aedicule was little more than 90 feet, but pilgrims were many that day and queues long and it took Larry three hours to cover the ground. He emerged from the Church close to four o'clock and calculated that his average movement inside the shrine had been no faster than six inches per minute – slower, in fact, than a

Negev tortoise. He repaired to the cafe again and though recognised, remained unacknowledged. He ordered a small sandwich and a bottle of mineral water, careful not to spoil his appetite for dinner. His usual table was occupied and so he sat inside the restaurant and updated his journal there.

It struck him that events of great significance happened in proximity in Jerusalem, and not just inside the Church of the Holy Sepulchre. Temple Mount, for instance, was not only the location of the world's Foundation Stone, but the place where Adam had been created, where Abraham had offered his son Isaac in sacrifice and where Muhammad had ascended to Heaven on a night journey. And, as he now recalled, the location of the Last Supper was but one floor above the tomb of King David! As a tourist destination Jerusalem had it all: not only thousands of years of history and religious significance, but also convenience. The city was a miracle of twenty-first-century tourism.

Larry returned to the hotel, a fifteen-minute walk from the cafe, and was again stopped and questioned by the woman in blue uniform. He went to his room and took a short nap and then showered and went down to dinner. He returned to the Garden Restaurant, sat on the terrace and again ordered hummus as an appetiser and gefilte fish for his main course. This night, however, he drank a glass of white wine. Routine was one thing he believed, but he had no intention of falling into a rut while in Israel.

Larry was in the lobby by 7:15 the next morning, sitting in an armchair facing the door and rising expectantly every time it opened. He had a small rucksack with him containing a litre of water, a packed lunch prepared by the hotel, a tube of sunscreen, his paper yarmulke and his journal. The morning was chilly and he wore a thin windbreaker over his short-sleeved shirt.

The representative of BeinHarim walked through the door at precisely 7:29 and announced himself: 'BeinHarim for Professor Maccabee!' Larry rose from his chair and held out his hand. Amah Efros shook it and led Larry to a curtained minibus waiting on the street. There were five people in the bus, a driver and two couples, one from the Netherlands and the other from Germany. Larry exchanged early-morning smiles and chose a single seat immediately behind the driver.

The bus made three further stops and another fifteen passengers climbed on board. Amah then called roll and handed each person a name tag. The journey would take 90 minutes he told them. They'd travel through territory belonging to the Palestinian Authority, along the shores of the Dead Sea and arrive at Masada by ten. Unlike most other tour operators who travelled to Masada, BeinHarim didn't stop at the Dead Sea. The Dead Sea was for tourists Amah explained, and Masada for explorers! And like all explorers they would take the cable car to the top of the mountain and not waste time climbing the Snake Path, which in his opinion was for low-budget tourists and donkeys.

The bus headed out of Jerusalem on Route 1, stopped briefly at a checkpoint on the border between Israel and the Palestinian West Bank and then continued on Route 90 and descended into the Judean Desert, a barren land of terraces, escarpments and deep canyons. As Amah had promised the bus arrived at the eastern entrance of Masada at 10:00am. They were advised to use the toilet facilities before they ascended Masada and to wear hats and drink plenty of water while on the mountain. The ride in the cable car was fast and smooth, and five minutes after entering the gondola Larry was standing on Masada. It was a dream come true, not only for him but for the Sicarii dignitaries who were already gathered there.

Amah, whose name translated as *having the answer*, was well suited to being a tour guide. He spoke knowledgeably about the history and geography of the fortress, led his party from one site to the next and gave them time to browse and take in the views. They explored the commandant's residence, the storeroom complex, the Northern and Western Palaces, the water cisterns and bathhouse, the synagogue and the rebel dwellings, and then, as they were about to return to the cable car, a man of about Larry's age approached Amah and indicated the lines of chairs placed close to the eastern observation point. The man was Talmai Oshkeroff, leader of the Party of the Sicarii.

Amah's eyebrows rose. 'I had no idea, sir. Yes, a momentous day indeed!'

Having made this pronouncement, Amah – along with other tour leaders – guided his group towards the chairs and then went looking for Larry, who had seemingly disappeared. He found him crouched in the Byzantine monastic cave apparently tying his shoelace.

'There you are, Dr Maccabee. I must apologise for not recognising you earlier. It's not every day I have the pleasure of guiding a man of your authority.'

Larry was caught off guard, as surprised by Amah's sudden appearance as he had been by Wayne's on his first visit to the park. And the circumstances were no less similar.

Larry had sloped off to the cave after spotting a small drift of sand earlier in the day, and presumed his disappearance had gone unnoticed. He was on his second mouthful when Amah disturbed him and in no position to answer immediately. He swallowed the grit as best he could and washed it down with the last of his water, all the time wondering what Amah had meant by *a man of your authority*. He could only think that Amah was referring to his standing in the Desert Land Act community, but why would he know this?

'It's very kind of you to say so, Amah,' Larry said, 'but how did you know?'

'There are people from Jerusalem here today, Dr Maccabee, important people, and it was they who told me. They said you weren't expected until next week.'

'That's true,' Larry said, presuming that the important people from Jerusalem were the ones organising the symposium on Desert Reclamation. 'I came a few days early to do a bit of sightseeing.'

'I've been asked by Mr Oshkeroff if you would be willing to give a short presentation while you're here. There could be no better setting.'

Larry completely agreed with this sentiment. Where better place than the Judaean Wilderness to give a short presentation on the Desert Land Act?

'I'd be happy to, Amah, but it's a big subject. Is there anything specific Mr Oshkeroff would like me to talk about?'

'Yes,' Amah replied. 'He'd like you to talk about the Sicarii.'

Larry was puzzled by the reply. How did Mr Oshkeroff – whose name he still couldn't pinpoint – know that he was even capable of talking about the Sicarii? He'd never hidden his interest in Masada but neither had he broadcast it, and was about to question Amah further when he remembered the blog on the Great Revolt he'd contributed to almost nine years earlier – and then it clicked. Yes, that would be it: Mr Oshkeroff had read the blog and wanted to hear more of his thoughts on the subject and save his formal presentation on the Desert Land Act for the symposium.

'Tell Mr Oshkeroff I'd be happy to,' Larry said.

'Excellent!' Amah said. 'And after you've spoken he'd like you to join him for dinner in the main restaurant of the King David Hotel.'

'I'd be pleased to,' Larry said, buoyed by the idea of not having to walk into the restaurant alone.

Larry followed Amah to the eastern observation point where more than 200 people were gathered. Talmai Oshkeroff and his party – very similar in appearance to the men he'd mingled with at the Western Wall – were sitting on the front row and stood and applauded when he stepped on to the makeshift stage. Larry waved to them and smiled. Amah tapped the microphone and then spoke.

'It's my honour to present to you a man who needs no introduction: Dr Lavi Maccabee.'

Larry was by now used to being addressed as Maccabee and too wrapped up in the occasion to notice Amah's mispronunciation of his first name. He took off his baseball cap and revealed his paper yarmulke, there to protect his head from any rays that penetrated his hat.

'Thank you, Amah,' Larry said stepping to the microphone. 'And thank you for a splendid and informative tour today. I've dreamt of standing on Masada for fifty years and it's a privilege to be doing so at long last. I'd also like to thank Mr Oshkeroff of the Hebrew University of Jerusalem for allowing me the opportunity of speaking to you about my interest in the Sicarii.'

Talmai Oshkeroff smiled when Larry acknowledged him, completely unaware that it was Larry MacCabe and not Lavi Maccabee addressing him. He'd never met Dr Maccabee and neither had he seen his photograph. No one had. Dr Maccabee was notoriously camera shy, fearing that likenesses diminished the soul, and the only existing photograph of him had been taken on his eighteenth birthday, a gangling youth staring at the floor. On this basis there was no reason to believe that Larry wasn't the grown-up version of this man, and certainly his name tag suggested that he was. And although now no longer attached to the Hebrew University of Jerusalem, Oshkeroff, prior to his rise to political importance, had been on the janitorial staff of that institution and this was well known in Sicarii circles; it was a badge he wore with pride. Similarly, Dr Maccabee's unannounced arrival at Masada wasn't to be unexpected. Despite their willingness to book his flights and accommodation, Dr Maccabee had insisted on making his own arrangements and told them only the day he'd meet them at the Party offices. A surprise visit had always been on the cards.

'If I'd been walking alone at night in the first century,' Larry started his address, 'the last people I'd have wanted to bump into were the Sicarii. There's no telling what those rascals might have done to me. Come to think of it, if I'd been attending a rally in broad daylight I'd have probably been no better off.'

Talmai smiled at the joke. Dr Maccabee's odd and sometimes impenetrable sense of humour was well known, and Talmai waited for the expected spin that would turn the statement on its head and put the Sicarii in their true light. It proved a long wait.

Although controversy in everyday life made Larry uneasy, academic controversy never did. It had been his lifeblood for too many years, and there'd been no cause for sensitivity in his professional life. Truth was uncontrollable and unassailable and the chips had to fall where they may, irrespective of consequence. And, just as he hadn't shied from sharing the academic truth of Native Americans with Delores, neither did he now shy from sharing the truth about the Sicarii with Talmai Oshkeroff and the other members of the audience.

The Sicarii, Larry continued, had originated in Galilee and were considered an extremist splinter of the Zealots. They were named for the small dagger they carried, the sica, and their worldview was narrow, fundamental and humourless. Although some looked on them as liberators, most viewed them as sadistic thugs and terrorists of the worst kind; cowardly assassins who mingled in crowds and stabbed from behind. And their victims, unlike those of the Zealots, had tended to be Jewish rather than Roman: moderate leaders and those they accused of apostasy and collaborationism. They kidnapped for ransom, robbed the houses of the wealthy, raided Jewish villages and killed women and children.

'In short,' Larry concluded, 'the Sicarii were little better than the Taliban or ISIL. This kind of extremism…'

Talmai Oshkeroff could contain himself no longer. His agitation had grown increasingly during Larry's presentation and it was now time to bring it to a halt. He stood and shouted at Larry: 'Sorcerer! Betrayer! These are not the words of a Fourth Philosopher. They are the words of the Devil. Uncover yourself and reveal your true name, for you, sir, are *not* Dr Lavi Maccabee!'

Larry was taken aback by the vehemence of Oshkeroff's

words. Until this moment he'd thought his talk had gone rather well, especially as it had been unscripted, and he'd been expecting a round of applause from the audience and a slap on the back from Amah when he stepped from the stage. And who was this Dr Lavi Maccabee he was accused of not being?

'I think there's been a misunderstanding, Mr Oshkeroff. My name is Professor Larry MacCabe. I'm not Dr Lavi Maccabee and nor have I ever claimed to be him. It's others who say that I am.'

This was too much for Oshkeroff's ears. The man was talking like the charlatan from the New Testament: not claiming to be the Son of God but allowing others to make the claim for him. 'Take him!' he ordered his bodyguards. 'And remind this imposter that it's not the Garden of Gethsemane he's being dragged from – it's Masada!'

Larry remained in custody for twenty days.

'There's been a misunderstanding, Larry, an unfortunate misunderstanding, but one that has consequences for us all. You are here for your own good and for the stability of Israel.'

The man speaking these words was Ori Zingel, the only man in the room not wearing a military uniform. He was a government official, there to explain Larry's confinement and to apologise for his new circumstances. He introduced himself only as Ori and addressed Larry by his familiar name.

'But I've done nothing wrong, Ori,' Larry protested. 'I was asked to give a speech and I gave one. I didn't break any laws.'

'Unfortunately you did, Larry. You denied the truth of Masada as defined by the Party of the Sicarii and this, I'm afraid, is now a punishable offence. If you were an Israeli citizen you would be tried and imprisoned; that you're an American citizen complicates matters.'

'And that was going to be my next point,' Larry said. 'I can't see the government of the United States being happy about my detention. I've paid taxes my whole life and some of that money has gone to support *your* country. Does the American Embassy know I'm here?'

'No, and it's better that they don't. The matter will be resolved quietly and in a matter of twenty days. After that time you will be deported from Israel and there will be no record of your stay.'

'Twenty days! But I'm expected home on Friday. Moses will be wondering where I've got to.'

'Is Moses your friend?' Ori asked.

'Yes, he's my dog.'

'You call your dog Moses? You've named your dog after Israel's greatest Prophet?'

'Well, no, not me personally. He was already called that when he came to live with me. He used to be called Israel – after the country.'

Ori folded his arms and smiled. 'Maybe the Sicarii were right about you after all, Larry. It appears you have little regard for either our religion or our nation.'

'Oh, but I do, Ori. I have the highest regard for Israel. And I have no less respect for Judaism than I do for any other desert religion.'

'And what exactly do you mean by *desert religion*, Larry?'

'It's just a theory of mine. I don't know if you're aware of this, Ori, but I'm America's leading authority on the Desert Land Act of 1877 – one of the most momentous pieces of legislation to have ever been passed into law – and because of my research I've spent more time in desert areas than most other people. Deserts intrigue me – they always have. They have a tranquillity that emanates spirituality and I can well understand why three of the world's greatest religions were born in hot countries rather than more temperate climes. But – and I hope you won't be offended by this – I've always supposed that Judaism, Christianity and Islam came into being only because there was no good irrigation system in place at the time. As I say, it's just a theory, but doesn't it strike you as odd that the only religion to have emerged in the United States – Mormonism – is headquartered in Utah, another desert area? Which reminds me: I'm supposed to give a lecture on the Desert Land Act in Jerusalem next Wednesday. Will you be able to arrange transport?'

Ori shook his head. 'The university is no longer expecting you, Larry.'

Larry was more disappointed by this news than anything that had happened since he'd been hauled from the top of Masada the previous day. Then he'd been detained in a windowless room in the eastern complex for four hours and later transported by car to a house in Jaffa, high on a hill and overlooking the Port and the Mediterranean Sea. Here he'd been treated with courtesy and served dinner, but then locked in a well-appointed room on the third floor where he'd stayed until escorted downstairs and introduced to Ori that morning, a man who wore a dark business suit and spoke impeccable English and who was now telling him that he wouldn't be giving his presentation on the Desert Land Act after all – his sole reason for being in Israel!

Ori motioned for the other men to leave the room and

waited while the door closed behind them before continuing his conversation.

'Believe me, Larry: missing the symposium is a small price to pay. The Party of the Sicarii has been told you are in custody and will be tried on 22 October. We need them to believe this. If you are seen by them in Jerusalem, which is a distinct possibility, it will be obvious that you are not in custody and will in all probability not be brought to trial – which, of course, you won't. By then you will be home in America playing with your dog and telling him of your adventures.

'Both you and I, Larry, are the victims of proportional representation, a form of democracy that makes for strange bedfellows. We sleep in a different room from Talmai Oshkeroff, but we have to change his sheets and make him feel comfortable. He has a strange bee in his bonnet – understandable when you consider he's spent his life mopping piss and wiping shit from toilet seats – but it's a bee, unfortunately, that we have to accommodate. The government needs his support and the support of his party if we are to extend the draft to the Haredim – people who have stranger bees in their bonnets than even the Sicarii. Do you know who I mean when I refer to the Haredim?'

'Yes, they're the ultra-Orthodox Jews.'

'They are, and the government has decided that it's time for them to pull their weight. The Haredim are a financial burden on the State of Israel. They are happy to take its financial assistance but unwilling to contribute to society or even recognise the State that allows them their lifestyle of prayer and study. Currently they are exempted from military service, but on 19 October this inequality will end. And when that vote has been taken and the Sicarii have cast their votes

---

on the side of the government you will be free to leave the country.'

'But won't Mr Oshkeroff be unhappy when he learns I've returned to America?'

'He would if he thought that to be true, Larry, but Talmai will never know the truth. For his future support for the government it's important that he doesn't. Of course, we could simply blame your President – he has few friends here – but we don't want to risk escalating an internal matter into an international situation. No, Talmai must believe that you neither came from nor returned to the United States. You will be a mystery man, a manifestation that appeared and disappeared and a man without footprints. The ancient Sicarii claimed powers of clairvoyance, telepathy and levitation and I doubt their modern-day counterparts are any less susceptible to such strangeness...'

Ori returned the following day and brought Larry his belongings from the King David Hotel. He gave him books on Israel to read and suggested he pass the time by playing chess with Haim and Jaron, the two soldiers there to guard his privacy.

'It's not ideal, Larry – just a deal – so try and make the best of it.'

And so Larry did. He played chess with Haim and Jaron and lost every game. He looked out of the window and down on the Port, watched as old men cast lines and fishing boats came and went. He read about Jerusalem and made a list of all the things he'd wanted to do but now never would: walk the walls of the Old City, climb Temple Mount, explore Hezekiah's Tunnel and visit the tortoises in the Biblical Zoo. He thought of Wayne and Moses and wondered how many jars of jam Wayne had made; thought of Volta Park and Laura and the friends he met there every Saturday and hoped that the animal blessing on the Day of St Francis had gone to plan and that Repo was of old. Time, however, passed slowly...

On Wednesday, 21 October, Larry was taken from Jaffa to Ben Gurion Airport. He was sixty-seven years of age, had failed to deliver his paper on the Desert Land Act and, for the second time in his life, was about to be arrested.

'Not again, Larry,' Helen would have sighed.

10

Meanwhile, Back at the Ranch...

If Wayne Trout's life had taken a turn for the worse at birth, lumbered as he'd been with a neurological condition most others were spared, it was as nothing compared to the somersaults it suffered after Kevin became a Christian.

It was on a Sunday in the spring of 1999 when Kevin came face to face with Christ. He and Wayne had been kicking their heels that day, aimlessly wandering the streets of Charles Town in the hope of witnessing a traffic accident. They'd stopped to explore a building site on Samuel Street, and it was here that Kevin spotted a can of glue. He'd been sniffing solvents for two years, and despite its questionable legality had always assumed it to be his inalienable right – the pursuit of happiness as laid down by the Declaration of Independence.

This particular glue, however, was of industrial strength and far stronger than anything he'd previously inhaled – the equivalent of a person downing a fifth of bourbon after having only sipped beer – and his mind and body were taken by assault. Instantly he knew there was something wrong – something *definitely* wrong – and he articulated his feelings to Wayne as best he could: 'Out! Out! Out! Out!' he repeated over and again while stamping his right foot on the ground. 'Out! Out! Out! Out!'

Wayne had been around Kevin when he'd sniffed glue before, but then his friend had just acted goofy. Now he was acting something else – something *definitely* else – and he encouraged Kevin to go to the hospital.

'No, no hospitals and no doctors, man. I'll ride it out in a church. Out! Out! Out! Out!'

'But what if you don't?' Wayne asked. 'What if you get worse? What am I supposed to do then?'

'*Then* you can take me to the hospital, but don't tell them I've been sniffing glue. Tell them I've been overcome by the Holy Spirit or something. And make sure they put that on my admission slip and my parents see it. Out! Out! Out! Out!'

And then he started to scream.

Sunday evening services were about to start in the town, but Wayne was reluctant to take Kevin to his own church. His foster parents had already warned him about hanging around with the Trull boy and he didn't want them seeing Kevin in this shape. Instead – and once Kevin had stopped screaming – he took him to the Zion Episcopal Church, two streets down from the building site, and helped him into an empty back pew.

Halfway through the service something happened, something that Kevin would later describe as the Holy Spirit entering his body. The toxins tormenting his mind dissolved as suddenly as they'd appeared and an air of calm descended over him. When it came to the point in the service when the minister asked if any in the congregation would like to commit themselves to Christ, Kevin was the first to his feet.

Kevin's life changed forever that day, and by default so too did Wayne's. Rather than loaf around the neighbourhood annoying people and harming himself, Kevin became a model citizen. He took a part-time job and, apart from the money he spent having the tattoo of a skull lasered from his forearm, gave the proceeds to the church. But for Kevin this still wasn't enough. His conversion to Christianity had been recent and he pursued his calling with a zealousness that put Wayne's longer-standing and quieter faith in the shade.

'We have to do something more, Wayne. We have to get the message out to people that Christ is alive and living among us. We have to reach as many men, women and children as we can. But how? How can we do this?'

Wayne thought it over. 'We could always write something on one of them interstate bridges. Thousands of people would see it wrote there, and they'd think about what they'd see'd for the rest of their journey.'

Kevin liked the idea.

Once dark had fallen, Kevin drove Wayne to one of the bridges that spanned the I81 and parked in a quiet area. The message they'd agreed to write was CHRIST IS ALIVE. It was agreed that Kevin would write the first two words – he was an experienced graffiti artist and had already tagged his moniker to most of the public buildings in the area – and Wayne the third. It was important to Kevin that their accomplishment be a team effort and for Wayne to share in the glory. While one leaned over the parapet and wrote the letters, the other would hold him by the legs.

Kevin completed his part of the exercise and Wayne hauled him up.

'Okay, Wayne, it's up to you now. Remember what I told

you? You're writing upside down and backwards to the way you normally write, so you always have to have the mirror image in mind. Got it?'

Kevin carefully lowered Wayne over the side of the bridge, and as each letter was completed moved him to the left. It was on the last of these moves that Wayne dropped the paintbrush. There was the sound of a car braking and Wayne shouted for Kevin to haul him up.

'Let's move, Kevin! There's someone down there. We can finish up tomorrow.'

Kevin agreed. 'How far did you get?'

'One letter short,' Wayne said.

'The "E"?'

'No, the "A",' Wayne replied.

Kevin puzzled over Wayne's answer for a moment but thought nothing more about it until the following morning when news of the interstate pile-up reached the school.

Twenty-seven cars had been involved in the accident and there had been nine fatalities. The southbound carriageway was closed for seven hours that day while the damaged cars and offending graffiti were removed. Television news crews and reporters from across the country descended on the eastern panhandle and all asked the same questions: Had the Devil visited West Virginia that night? Was this small and unassuming part of the nation truly its evil centre?

The police investigation was long and exhaustive but ultimately unsuccessful. Although the offending paintbrush had been recovered, the fingerprints on it didn't match any on file, and despite the offer of a reward leading to the apprehension of those responsible, no one was arrested. The last word on the subject came from the local coroner who ruled that the deaths of the nine motorists had been caused by *dangerous writing*.

Kevin and Wayne were as distraught as anyone by the outcome of their actions, but were reluctant to hand themselves in to the police and face what to them would have been unwarranted persecution. Their intentions had been well meaning, and it had only been Wayne's execution of the task that had let them down. Unused to hanging upside down, and confused by Kevin's description of backwards writing and mirrors, Wayne had wrongly assumed that he had to write the word back to front. Consequently he'd started with the E rather than the A, and losing the paintbrush before finishing the word had unknowingly written not CHRIST IS ALIVE but CHRIST IS EVIL.

Wayne and Kevin were now bonded by a secret they could share with no one but themselves. They withdrew further into their own company and, forever fearing discovery, determined to leave Charles Town as soon after graduation as possible and seek their fortunes elsewhere. It was Kevin's idea for the two of them to join the Marines, and the Marines' idea for Wayne to remain a civilian; although they found Wayne a personable young man they judged his dyspraxia a greater danger to them than any enemy they might face. So Kevin left for boot camp alone and Wayne set off to live with his sister in Washington. They said their goodbyes at the bus depot: 'See you round, buddy boy,' Kevin said to Wayne. 'See you squared,' Wayne replied.

It would be their first time apart and their last time together.

Kevin died in Iraq. He was captured close to the city of Fallujah and killed by insurgents who tied his body to a pickup truck and hauled it to a large grassless playing field.

There they played with it, dragged it in lines and circles and then dumped it. Residents in a nearby apartment block looked down on the spectacle and cheered, applauded the truck as it drove from the field. But then, as the dust settled and the writing appeared, a strange silence washed over them.

The wheels of the truck and Kevin's swirling body had left behind what appeared to be a message in the sandy soil. At first the words were indecipherable, and it was only after someone noticed that the Arabic writing was back to front and reading from left to right instead of right to left that the meaning became clear – or, at least, almost clear. The message read either *Al Akhbar* or *Allahu Akbar*.

A local imam was called to the field and asked to make a judgement. Given the choice of interpreting the message as an advertisement for an Egyptian newspaper or a communiqué from God, the religious leader understandably chose the latter: *God is great.* Word spread through the city, throughout the country, across the world and eventually to the Glover Park neighbourhood of Washington.

By then Wayne was already unhinged, his mind plagued by the lingering spirits of the southbound carriageway dead. He heard their voices and their accusations, and had long ago surrendered to their demands for board and lodging. He'd escaped Charles Town but not the burden of guilt that had caused his flight.

The first hint of change came during his sleep, three weeks into his stay with Millie. That night, the consecutive nature of his dreams ended, and for the next month he dreamt only of cars crashing: the squeal of tyres, the blaring of horns, glass shattering and the crunch of metal. He woke in the mornings drenched in sweat and breathing heavily, the sounds of wreckage ringing in his ears and persisting into the day, sometimes intermittently and other times constant. And then, as suddenly as the visions had appeared they disappeared, and for two wonderful days he heard nothing but the sound of the television and Millie's cooing voice. It appeared that life had returned to normal, that the storm had blown itself out. But it hadn't. A force beyond his control was gathering, and on the morning of the third day he woke up to find nine people living in his head.

There was Dolph Perkins, an ex-con closing in on fifty and of no fixed address, a man who snarled and ground his teeth and transported dead bodies in the trunk of his old Mustang. He'd careered into the back of a small family SUV he'd been tailgating for five miles and been too hopped up on pills to react when the vehicle suddenly braked. 'Damn fuckers!' were the last words he'd spoken.

The SUV belonged to Scotty and Melanie Wadlington. They were in their mid-thirties, from Abilene, Texas, and had been touring Civil War battlefields with their two children, James-Fred and Josie. Melanie had already mentioned the close proximity of the Mustang, but Scotty was adamant that he had every right to drive in the fast lane at 65 mph. 'People have to learn to be patient,' he said. 'What do people have to learn?' he called out to James-Fred and Josie. 'To be patient, daddy,' the two children replied in unison. 'Oh my God!' Melanie gasped. 'Have you seen what's written on that bridge?' Scotty braked hard to crane his neck and it was then that Dolph slammed into the back of him, flipping the SUV on to the hood of a Honda Hybrid travelling in the adjacent lane.

The driver of the Honda was Booth Bailey, a local realtor

whose girlfriend, Deneice, was telling him that their relationship was going nowhere and she wanted out. 'Aw, c'mon, Deneice, don't give me the *it's not you it's me* speech. I deserve better than that!' Deneice looked at him. 'I'm not giving you that speech, Booth. I'm saying it is *you*! If you ever bothered to listen to what I say you'd know that by now. And can't you drive any faster?' In the split second of consciousness that remained after the SUV landed on the hood of their car, it was clear to both of them that their relationship would be ending sooner than either of them had anticipated.

Bob Snider was driving behind Booth and Deneice at the time, chatting to his wife on the phone. He was a ball bearing salesman out of Baltimore and was telling her about the deal of a lifetime he'd just made. Bob was old-fashioned, and, with the exception of mobile phones, suspicious of progress. He looked upon seatbelts as an infringement of his liberty and airbags as an attempt by the government to stifle opinion. Consequently, when he swerved to avoid the entanglement in front of him and crashed into a parked Cadillac, he was driving with one hand on the wheel, not wearing a seatbelt and in a car whose airbags had been disconnected.

The owner of the Cadillac was Nita Baldwin, a woman in her late eighties whose driving licence had been confiscated ten years previously. Fifteen minutes before the excitement she'd pulled over on to the hard shoulder of the interstate to take a nap and was now pouring herself a cup of hot tea from a thermos. The collision didn't kill her, but the shock of seeing Bob Snider's torn body flying through the air did.

For a while the motorists chatted amongst themselves and ignored Wayne. Scotty and Melanie talked about Abilene and its school districts, and James-Fred and Josie the Battle of Gettysburg. Booth talked about the housing market and Deneice of how difficult Booth had been of late. Bob talked about ball bearings and government conspiracies and Nita explained how to make the perfect cup of tea. Dolph ground his teeth.

And then they talked about the unfairness of death and started to argue over who'd caused the accident. Scotty blamed Dolph and Dolph blamed Scotty. Booth blamed both Dolph and Scotty, and Bob blamed Nita for having illegally stopped on the hard shoulder. Nita claimed that she was blameless and had been her whole life. Dolph said he had a good mind to stick a knife in her until Scotty pointed out that he didn't have a knife and that even if he did, what was he going to do with it – stick it into fresh air? 'Stop this! Stop this!' Melanie screamed. 'If anyone is to blame it's the person who wrote those awful words on the bridge.'

'That would be Wayne Trout, then,' Nita said. 'It's his head we're in.'

'Is that true, Wayne? Did you write those words?' Scotty demanded.

'Yes, sir,' Wayne replied, surprised to hear his name called. 'Me and my friend wrote them, but we didn't mean no offence. We meant to write something different.'

'You do realise you killed us, don't you?' Bob Snider said.

'Yes, sir, and I'm sorry about that. All I can say is that you're welcome to stay in my head as long as you like.'

'And how long is that going to be?' Deneice asked.

'I don't know, Ma'am.'

'I say we make his life as miserable as possible,' Dolph said. 'Make him die slowly and painfully.'

'We'll do no such thing!' Nita Baldwin said. 'Wayne needs

to see a doctor. The sooner he sorts himself out the sooner we can be on our way.'

And so Wayne went to see a doctor – as Millie had already suggested he do after repeatedly finding her brother talking to himself. At first, and out of loyalty to Kevin, Wayne had described only his symptoms to the doctor – the voices – but once Kevin was dead he confided the truth of their roles in the infamous I81 incident.

The doctor listened patiently and carefully, and once satisfied that the voices in Wayne's head were harmless and not inciting him to self-injury or violence towards others, prescribed drugs whose strengths and combinations he tweaked over time. Although the voices never entirely disappeared from Wayne's head they did soften, and he contented himself with eavesdropping on his lodgers' conversations rather than sharing in their company.

And then Kevin appeared, and one by one the voices disappeared until only his remained. It was a voice – on Kevin's instructions – that Wayne would never mention to the doctor on his six-monthly visits.

Kevin died in March 2004 but only materialised in Wayne's consciousness during the spring of 2014. Officially he was there to release the souls of the stranded motorists – whose lodgement, after all, was in part his responsibility – but off-the-record, and necessarily unspoken of at the time of him volunteering for the assignment, was his intention to mount a spectacular in Georgetown that would facilitate his escape from Purgatory. And to achieve this goal he needed the help of a friend he could trust – and one who knew a thing or two about explosives.

Or such was Wayne's understanding of the situation.

Kevin surfaced the day Wayne had his ears syringed. Two weeks prior to this event Wayne had been playing in the waterfront fountain – not showering, as Alice had wrongly assumed the time she'd seen him there – and become deaf in both ears after an irregular jet had entered his aural canals and expanded the wax. The noises of the outside world immediately quietened while the voices inside his head – although now magnified – had to compete with a ringing noise that was more irritating than even Dolph's high-pitched inflection. After four days of growing discomfort he made an appointment to see the doctor, and after putting drops in his ears for a further five days returned to the surgery for a nurse to wash the remaining wax from his ears with an electronic irrigator.

He was on his way back from the surgery when he heard the voice: 'You know the things I miss most about not living in your world, buddy boy?'

'Mints?' Wayne ventured, unsure if he was talking to Scotty or Booth.

'No, pepperoni pizza and ice-cream,' the voice said. 'If I had my time again I'd eat them every day of the week.'

The penny dropped as quickly – or as slowly – as the voice had enunciated the word pepperoni: *pee-peroni*. The only person to have pronounced pepperoni that way was Kevin. He'd made a joke of it: 'I'm gonna get me a slice o' that *pee-peroni* pizza.'

'Kevin! What are you doing in my head?'

'I'm here to round up the missing souls, buddy boy; send them on their way and bring some peace to your mind. And I'm hoping you'll bring some peace to my mind, too. Help me get out of Purgatory and on my way to Heaven. It's where I belong.'

Although Kevin had died in a state of grace, his level of purity had fallen far short of that required for a direct entry into Heaven. Consequently he'd been sent to Purgatory – a sort of halfway house between Heaven and Hell – and instructed to spend his time there atoning for past sins. 'No one remains here forever or goes to Hell, but they never tell you how long you're going to stay, and it's the not knowing that gets to you. There are people who arrived after me who have already gone to Heaven and this strikes me as unfair.'

Purgatory wasn't a particularly unpleasant place, Kevin said. No one was tortured or cleansed by fire as the church had led them to believe, and the worst that could be said of it was that there were too many group discussions and that the climate was a bit on the warm side. Apart from the whirring of the fans it was also quiet, and he missed the sounds of the wind and the rain and the cheeping of birds. The best days were those when the Patriarchs and Prophets of the Old Testament came to visit. Occasionally they'd give guest lectures, but most of the time they would just mingle and tell people to keep their chins up and think of the beatific vision that awaited them. 'They talk from experience, too,' Kevin said, 'because until Jesus led them to Heaven they'd been living in Limbo for hundreds of years.'

And you got to hear things, too. People like Abraham and Isaac had the ear of God and knew exactly what He was thinking – more so than any of the evangelists they'd watched on television – and they'd pass on this information. They knew what God liked and what He didn't like, and from everything Kevin had heard there was a lot more in the world that God disliked than liked. And according to several of the Minor Prophets, who were prone to gossip, there were times when God got into such a stew about things that steam came out of His ears. It was this counsel, as well as other particulars he'd gleaned during his time in Purgatory, that had prompted Kevin to volunteer his services for the *Lost Souls* assignment.

Occasionally souls went missing he told Wayne, and it could sometimes take years to track them down. 'Usually I don't bother myself with this kind of errand because they're not worth the aggravation, but when I read the names of the souls involved in this case and the date they'd gone missing and that their last known location had been the southbound carriageway of the I81, I had an idea that you might be mixed up in all this.'

Wayne's location was another reason for Kevin applying for the position. Purgatory was serviced by vents – natural fissures that cooled its environment and smoothed the heavenward journey of purified souls – and the duct reputed to be closest to the earth's surface was the one under Georgetown. 'My guess is that it's no more than twelve feet below street level,' Kevin said. 'A simple pick and shovel job.'

'And no one will mind me digging you up?' Wayne asked.

'Not if we get the spectacular right,' Kevin said. 'Nahum and Habakkuk – they're a couple of the Minor Prophets I was telling you about – think that the monitors will look the other way. They say that if God's happy with what we do – and He will be – He'll tell them to turn a blind eye and let me escape to Heaven without having to finish my sentence.'

'But you won't be in Heaven when you escape, Kevin, you'll be in Georgetown and you won't have any place to live. Rents are high here and the halfway house is full.'

'I won't be staying in Georgetown, buddy boy, I'll be going to Heaven,' Kevin laughed. 'I'm gonna get me a slice o' that *bee-atific* vision!'

Wayne was pleased to have his old friend back in his life and wasn't about to disappoint him. If Kevin wanted to be dug out of Purgatory then he'd dig him out of Purgatory, and if a spectacular was necessary for this to happen, he'd do whatever was necessary to ensure its success.

Delivering Wayne from the voices of the dead was a relatively straightforward matter for Kevin, but there were reasons for him to move slowly. It would take time to locate the whereabouts of the duct in Georgetown, and to identify its position he needed to remain inside Wayne's head; if it was empty of voices he would have a hard time justifying his continued presence. He was also having difficulty resolving the type of spectacular that would both draw God's attention and prompt His blessing, and he needed time to think this through.

Wayne, too, was in no rush for the voices to disappear and was happy to go along with Kevin's agenda. Apart from Dolph, whose profanity and threats occasionally disconcerted him, he looked upon the deceased travellers as friends. There were occasions when the Wadlingtons were a bit too good to be true and their children a tad on the precocious side, but Nita was kind and grandmotherly, and her advice on making a good cup of tea had been spot on the mark. Bob Snider was an oddball but interesting, and Wayne had been particularly intrigued by his theory that John F Kennedy had been assassinated by the two keepers from the National Zoo. He took most interest, though, in Booth's relationship with Deneice. He'd never had a girlfriend and didn't realise that love could be so complicated. He was hoping they'd reconcile and get married before Kevin sent them on their way, but in this he was to be disappointed. Booth Bailey and Deneice were the first to leave. There was no happy ending.

They were quickly followed by Nita Baldwin and a few months later by the Wadlingtons and Bob Snider. The only voice remaining belonged to Dolph Perkins and Kevin was having a hard time tracking him down. Dolph was now on the move, changing location every two days and planting booby traps, determined to stay in Wayne's head and delay his descent to Hell for as long as possible. Three weeks before Larry left for Israel, however – and at a time when both the location of the duct and the nature of the spectacular had been defined – Dolph's luck ran out and he too was evicted. 'Fuck you, Trout!' were the last words he spoke to Wayne.

Now only Kevin's voice remained, louder and clearer than ever now that Wayne had stopped taking his medication.

The position of the duct had been pinpointed by Kevin three months earlier. He'd had a feeling its location would be found somewhere in the East Village, and his hunch proved right the day Larry led Wayne down to his basement. Not only did his voice become stronger here, it also started to echo, and this was the tell-tale sign he'd been waiting for. 'This is it, buddy boy! This is where you have to dig!'

It seemed too good to be true, too good for the Divine not to have intervened for Wayne to have been asked to house-sit Moses while Larry was in Israel. Everything was falling into place and Kevin believed his redemption to be at hand. And in the weeks that followed – and again with Larry's unwitting help – it became clear to Kevin that God wanted him to destroy the Church of Latter-Day Lutherans, a church that seemingly catered to everything but His Word and served as a nesting place for all He abhorred – drugs, homosexuality, animal worship and polluted Christianity.

Kevin knew these things from Wayne, and Wayne had learned them from Larry – an emeritus professor prone to gossip. It was him who'd told Wayne that the church organist was a cokehead and that the substitute organist a man who blended Christianity with Buddhism; him who'd divulged that Dolores was a curator of heathenism and planning to be buried in a pet cemetery; and him who'd let slip that the Pastor, a divorced woman, was about to marry Laura and Alice in a house of God. And it was also Larry who'd told Wayne that the Pastor was preparing to admit animals into the church on the Feast Day of St Francis – a saint who Kevin knew to be on the outs with God – and anoint them with holy water. Of all the abominations, it was this that clinched the argument for laying waste the church.

Based on everything he'd learned from his time in Purgatory, Kevin explained his logic to Wayne as best he could. God, he told him, had made *man* in His image – not fish, birds or animals because God didn't look anything like a fish or a bird or an animal. And He resented the fact that false gods had, and still were being worshipped through their medium – baboons, bulls, cats, cows, crocodiles, dogs, elephants, goats, ibises, leopards, snakes, tigers… the list went on.

God had given man dominion over *every living thing that moved upon the earth* for a reason, and not so man could deify them. Animals were there to be eaten, to have clothes made from them, to be beasts of burden and for the purposes of medical experimentation. And – and this was something that had been forgotten over time – they were also there to be sacrificed. Animal sacrifice had always been an essential part of God's special relationship with man, and as a show of respect He'd expected cows, goats, rams, lambs, oxen, pigeons and turtledoves to be offered to Him on a regular basis. In the good old days this had happened, and God still had fond memories of the occasion when Solomon sacrificed 22,000 oxen and 122,000 sheep on His behalf.

The world, however, had turned on its head and God held one animal more than any other responsible for this change – the dog! God's Janus word had turned the tables and replaced Him as man's best friend. Not only had dogs been raised to the status of humans, they'd been put on pedestals and adorned like the Golden Calf of old, fancy bangles placed around their necks and designer clothes on their backs. Dogs, He believed, were being deified, and no one was more to blame for this aberrant state of affairs than Italian Francis, the saint who should have stuck to making pizzas and using meat for his toppings instead of pestering Him with all his weird ideas. The guy just couldn't get it through his thick skull that Heaven didn't accept the souls of dead animals because animals didn't have souls. When an animal died it died and that was the end of the story. Boo-hoo! And a sure-fire way for a person *not* to be admitted to Heaven was for that person to leave his money and chattels to a dog charity rather than one that alleviated human suffering. Dogs, God believed, needed to be taught a lesson and be put back in their place.

'So let me get this straight,' Wayne said. 'You want me to blow up the Church of Latter-Day Lutherans on the Feast Day of St Francis and then start digging you out of Purgatory?'

'You got it, buddy boy,' Kevin replied. 'But it's a favour you'll be doing God and not just me. God wants you to do this.'

'But what if people get killed? Won't God get mad like He did when we wrote those words on the bridge?'

'God's not mad at either of us for that,' Kevin reassured him. 'I'm in Purgatory because of my earlier life and not because of what we wrote on the bridge. He knows our intentions were good, and it was just a coincidence that you got those motorists stuck in your head. And we need a few casualties, Wayne. It's the only way we can get God's message to hit home.'

'But I ain't got no explosives. How am I gonna blow up a church with no explosives?'

It was then Kevin reminded him of their cache in Charles Town.

If the panhandle of West Virginia hadn't been awash with explosives during the time Kevin and Wayne had lived there, it had certainly been well lubricated. Mostly it was black powder – bought over-the-counter and used for reloading bullets and shooting anvils – but under-the-counter, and if a person knew the right (or wrong) people, it was also possible to buy sticks of dynamite stolen from the mines of Logan County and, very occasionally, C4. There was also an active patriot movement in the area, a hodgepodge of militiamen, preppers and survivalists stockpiling explosives for the day they would have to defend themselves against a government in the process of building concentration camps – and this thinking even before the election of a black president! It was a simple matter of supply and demand, the economic law that had made America great. If there was demand for a commodity, there would always be a supply.

Kevin's interest in black powder stemmed from his

fascination with anvil shooting. He'd seen anvils weighing 90 lbs shot 200 feet into the air – the idea being that the launched anvil would return to the ground as close to the base anvil as possible – and was determined to replicate this feat without having to enter a controlled competition. Although a man of ideas Kevin was short on technical know-how, and for this he relied on Wayne – the same way he depended on him during school science practicals.

Oddly at such times, and for reasons the educational psychologist could never explain, Wayne's dyspraxia stilled and the messages from his brain travelled to his fingertips uninterrupted. It also helped in these situations that Wayne's understanding of science and technology was a lot more intuitive than his grasp of the English language, and once Kevin had sourced the necessary anvils he quickly worked out the mechanics of shooting them into the air. First he placed one of the anvils upside-down on a piece of flat metal and filled its hollowed base with black powder. Next he tamped down the powder and sealed it with paper and then did the same with the second anvil – the one that would be shot into the air – and placed it on top of the first anvil the right way up. He then stood at a safe distance and allowed Kevin the honour of lighting the fuse. Boom! Lift off!

After a time Kevin tired of shooting anvils and decided they should try something more adventurous and shoot a car into the air. The only downside to this idea was the amount of black powder it would take to fill two cars, and though Kevin's allowance was generous – sufficient to buy 8 lbs of powder a month – it would have taken him years to amass the necessary quantity. It was then he came up with the idea of stealing it from others, and the logical starting point was

Howie Pillsbury – or at least the strange people that Howie Pillsbury associated with.

Wayne had confided in Kevin that Howie was as unhappy with the government as he was with him as a stepson, and that some weekends he would go camping with people who shared his grievances. Kevin had little doubt that the people Howie met were the patriots his father had talked about, and though unsympathetic to their cause, he was appreciative of the fact that if anybody in the area had the amount of powder necessary to launch a car 200 feet into the air it would be them. When Wayne later told him that his stepfather would be heading out of town that weekend, Kevin decided to follow him, and believing it would be easier to remain unnoticed if Wayne wasn't with him, he went alone. He tailed Howie to two small cabins in a remote area of Preston County, and returned there with Wayne the following weekend behind the wheel of his father's pickup truck.

Once they were sure the cabins were deserted, and worried that the doors might be booby trapped, Kevin took a glass cutter from his pocket and removed a window from each of the cabins. The first cabin was a disappointment, beds and chairs only, but the second cabin proved an Aladdin's Cave of illegality: 500 lbs of black powder (20 cases), 50 sticks of dynamite sealed in plastic bags and packed in wax-coated cardboard, and 5 lbs of wrapped white C4, the Cadillac of explosives. They loaded the pickup truck and drove back to Charles Town – carefully.

The problem now was where to store the explosives. After some thought Kevin decided to hide them in his grandmother's garage, which was empty now she'd stopped driving. He then set Wayne the task of learning how to handle plastic explosive which, in the days before the internet was closely monitored, wasn't an unduly problematic matter. A month later they'd driven to a deserted stone quarry near Cranesville and detonated two sticks of dynamite, a small amount of C4 and a homemade pipe bomb. 'You done good, buddy boy,' Kevin said. 'It's like you're a born bomber!'

The weekend that followed was the weekend Kevin became a Christian and his interest in explosions ended. The problem of where to store the explosives, however, remained. They couldn't stay in his grandmother's garage forever, and if she died and the house was offered for sale, how would he explain the contents of the boxes? The problem was resolved in the short-term once Kevin was accepted as a trusted member of the Zion Episcopal Church and he and Wayne recognised as its official jam makers. He was given the key to a disused dry cellar to store his equipment, and it was here they secreted the explosives. It was a temporary state of affairs that lasted fourteen years, and one that was only finally decided after Larry unknowingly transported them to Georgetown – from one cellar to another.

Apart from a shovel and a gardening fork, Larry had little in the way of tools, and the day he left for Israel Wayne went shopping for a sledgehammer and pickaxe. He also made other purchases with the money Larry had set aside for emergencies and placed them on the basement floor in alphabetical order: a quantity of 9 volt batteries, three disposable cell phones, a set of Christmas tree lights (a source of tungsten), five sacks of fertiliser, several fuses and a reel of fuse wire, a utility knife, 50 boxes of matches, three cartons of extra strong mints, a bag of 3 1/4 inch nails, a pair of pincers, a large tub of Plasticine, a small screwdriver, a roll of black electrical tape, a head torch and a pack of black plastic trash bags.

It took Wayne most of the day and several trips to gather these materials, and it was close to five by the time he arrived at the halfway house. His repeat prescription was due that day, and although he hadn't taken his medications in over a month he'd been told by Kevin that it was important to give the house director the impression that he had and, more importantly, that he would be continuing to do so while staying at Larry's house. It was, in fact, the only stipulation the house director had made to Larry when he'd visited the house to ask permission for Wayne to house-sit while he was in Israel.

A year earlier it would have been doubtful the director would have given such consent, but the doctor's most recent report had indicated that the voices in Wayne's head had stilled; unaware of Kevin's residency, the doctor had also reduced the dosages of some of the medicines and taken another off the list. It appeared to the director that progress was being made and that Wayne's reintroduction to mainstream society was on the horizon. A taste of independent living might well be a good thing for the young man.

The speed of his decision was also motivated by an impatience to get Larry out of the house as quickly as possible. He was already aware that the building they were standing in was a Wardman row house – he didn't need to be told this – and neither did he have any interest in knowing that the builder's first name had been Harry or that he'd been born in England in a city called Bradford or that his parents had been textile workers or that he'd emigrated to the United States at the age of seventeen and worked in a department store or that he'd apprenticed himself to a carpenter in Philadelphia and later moved to Washington and learned how to build staircases and then homes and apartments and hotels or that he'd become fabulously wealthy and then lost all his money in the stock market crash of 1929 or that he'd died of cancer at the age of sixty-four and been buried in Rock Creek Cemetery which was often confused with Oak Hill Cemetery where some woman called Helen was interred who he also had no interest in hearing about.

When Wayne returned from the halfway house he flushed the pills down the toilet. Kevin had never liked him taking the medication and had often complained that the drugs impeded their communication and how some days it was like wading through paste to get his attention. And once Dolph had been evicted and there was no longer a reason for him to be in Wayne's head and the only place they could now commune was Larry's basement where the signal was often intermittent, Kevin had instructed Wayne to stop taking his meds. The success of their mission, he said, depended on them being able to communicate! As usual, Wayne had gone along with his reasoning, if indeed it had been Kevin doing the reasoning.

The only part of Kevin's plan that Wayne ever questioned was the need to sacrifice Moses. What harm had Moses ever done anyone? Personally he'd always liked the Basset Hound and was pretty sure that Larry wouldn't be too overjoyed to return home and find he didn't have a dog to take to the park anymore. But on this point Kevin was adamant. Moses' death, he'd told him, was the only way to send the signal that God wanted them to send, and he knew this for a fact because Moses the Prophet – who, incidentally, wasn't particularly thrilled to have a dog named after him – had told him so personally, and no man was closer to God than Moses the Prophet! Besides, Kevin added, he'd also heard that there was a good chance that Moses might make it to Heaven if he blew up in God's service and be the first animal to ever sit at His feet, which to his way of thinking was a much nicer place to lounge around than Larry's house. They should look on the bright side and think of the positives, he advised.

'Well, if you say so, Kevin,' Wayne said.

'I do say so,' Kevin replied, 'but it's also God and Moses saying this. They told me straight, Wayne. They said: "Kevin, go make us an omelette, will you, son?" And the only way you can make God an omelette is by breaking eggs. You have to look upon Moses as one of the eggs God wants cracked.'

And so Wayne put his misgivings aside and set to work.

He mixed the black powder with the fertiliser and match heads, added a sprinkle of nails and poured the amalgam into 'socks' made from plastic trash bags and sized to drop easily into the tin pipes of an organ. The Church of Latter-Day Lutherans had two organs, a Moller and a Richard Howell. The Moller was the original organ, set at the front of the church in view of the congregation. Although no longer in use it was too much a part of the church's architectural fittings to be removed, and its replacement, the Richard Howell organ, had been placed at the rear.

It was the Moller organ, however, that had attracted Wayne's attention the times he'd visited the church. Its facade pipes (21 in number) were dummy pipes, there simply for show and according to Mike easy to lift out. He'd made a note of their widths and approximated their lengths while Mike had his back turned practising his pieces for the Sunday service, and then, at a later time, gone on to explore the church's basement.

There he'd discovered, and wedged open, a small window at the base of the bell tower, large enough for a person to climb through and hidden from the street by clumps of overgrown bushes. It was this window he used to access the church in the week leading up to the Feast Day of St Francis.

Wayne would leave the house at midnight carrying the thickly-taped socks of explosive in an old holdall he'd found in Larry's bedroom. He would drop the bag through the window of the church and ease himself through after it and, if lucky, land on the old hassocks he'd placed on the floor below. He would then strap the torch to his head and make his way to the Moller organ, take down one of its tin pipes and fill it with explosive socks. He would then seal the pipe with Plasticine and return it – usually with difficulty considering its increased weight – to its original position. Some nights he would make two trips to the church and other nights three; some nights he would graze or bruise himself climbing through the window and other nights be injury free; and some nights he would drop and dent a pipe and other nights not. Life, as usual for Wayne, was very much a hit-and-miss affair.

On the Friday night before the service he attached the electronic firing systems to the pipes and connected them to a cell phone. He then sat down on a pew, took a last look at the organ and considered his achievement. 'You done good, Wayne Trout,' he told himself. He then returned to the house and put the finishing touches to Moses' suicide vest.

Wayne slept little that week and ate even less. He sucked mints the whole time, watched religious television and focused on the job at hand, which wasn't always easy with Kevin interrupting him all the time. And when he wasn't building bombs or listening to Kevin he was taking Moses for long walks and preparing special meals for him. He wanted Moses' last week on earth to be a good one, one crammed with memories he could take to Heaven and share with God. He also wanted to be able to tell Larry that Moses had died a happy dog – the same time in all probability he'd be telling him it would be no big deal to get his basement back to how it had been before he'd connected it to Purgatory.

The day of the animal blessing arrived and Wayne dressed Moses in the vest of Larry's only suit. The waistcoat had sticks of dynamite taped to it, a cell phone in one of its pockets and a small piece of C4 in another. Wayne covered it with a pillowcase fashioned with holes for Moses' legs and tail and decorated with a red painted cross. He then put Moses on his leash and set off for the church.

The service was scheduled to start at eleven and Wayne made sure to arrive at the church no earlier than 11:15. He could hear the sound of the organ and people singing as he climbed the steps and entered the foyer. The door to the main body of the church was to the left, and before opening it he took Moses' head in both hands and kissed him on the nose. 'See you in Heaven, ol' buddy,' he whispered. He then released him from his leash and eased him through the door. The last he saw of Moses was his wagging tail.

Wayne exited the church and hurried to the corner of Wisconsin and Q St. There, and at a safe distance from the church, he took out the third of the three cell phones he'd bought and dialled the first of two numbers stored in its memory. There was a loud but distant boom and Wayne punched in the second of the two numbers. Another boom!

It was time to go dig up Kevin.

'You done good, buddy boy, real good,' Kevin said after

Wayne returned to the basement. 'There's folks down here with smiles on their faces big as bananas. Was the tank guy there?'

'I don't rightly know, Kevin, but Larry said he would be. Said he had a crush on the Pastor woman and wanted to show off his dog to her.'

The news heartened Kevin. He begrudged all tank commanders and blamed them for his untimely death: if the tanks had got to Fallujah on time – and when they were supposed to – he would still be alive today and not stuck below the basement of Larry's house. If not divine retribution, then Tank's presence in the church would hopefully be his.

Wayne took hold of the sledgehammer and brought it down on the concrete floor. The blow was skewed and the head skidded to the side without doing damage.

'You ought to get some shuteye and fix yourself a meal,' Kevin advised. 'You'll need to get your strength back before you start on the floor. And do me a favour, will you? Stop sucking those damned mints! I can smell your breath down here.'

Wayne didn't argue. He was on the home stretch now and from what Kevin had told him the digging would be easy once he'd smashed his way through the concrete. He stretched out on the narrow camp bed and was soon fast asleep. He slept for fourteen hours.

Two things happened before the police broke into the house on Wednesday afternoon. About 9:30 on Monday morning there was a loud banging on the door, and 48 hours later another explosion.

11

The St Francis Day Massacre

Larry was sentenced to 99 years' imprisonment, which would, with time off for good behaviour and advances in medical science, make him eligible for parole in 2066, shortly before he turned 119. It wasn't as bad as it sounded, his lawyer, Osmo McNulty, assured him, and he'd be surprised by how quickly time passed when life went on hold. And on the plus side he'd never have to buy groceries again or pay any more utility bills. Think of the savings he'd make. The way Osmo described things, it was as if he'd just scored Larry the deal of the century.

Throughout his trial Larry was depicted as an eminence grise, a Svengali of evil intent who had manipulated a vulnerable young man into doing his bidding. Wayne had planted the bombs and killed Dr Young, but he'd done so only at Larry's request. It was Larry who was responsible for the destruction of the church, the deaths of four people and seventeen pets – and the deathbed testimony of his accomplice confirmed this: 'Kevin told me to do it,' Wayne had told the FBI.

And there was only one Kevin the FBI had identified in their inquiries.

An explosion in any city would have sent the FBI scurrying, but this one had them running a four-minute mile. Georgetown wasn't a neighbourhood of Joe Lunchbuckets and plain Janes; it was the home of foreign embassies, important government officials, legislators, the rich and the powerful. An attack on Georgetown was an assault on the vital organs of the nation. But who would want to blow up a church on the Feast Day of St Francis? And why the Church of Latter-Day Lutherans?

Explosions were usually the handiwork of terrorists and if not, then the act of disaffected loners. When no group either known or unknown had claimed responsibility within the first forty-eight hours, and preliminary examination of the bomb fragments had shown them to be amateurish and with no discernible signature, it was decided that the perpetrator was probably of the latter grouping. Having come to this conclusion, however, the FBI was no nearer to identifying that person.

From eyewitness accounts, the Bureau pieced together the following picture.

About fifteen minutes after the service had started, and towards the end of the singing of *All Things Bright and Beautiful*, a dog dressed in the garb of a mediaeval crusader had walked into the church. The dog had disappeared under a rear pew for about two minutes and then padded down the aisle towards the Pastor, who had just lifted a small tortoise from a white plastic bucket and was trying to find its head. The dog, whose breed and owner had yet to be confirmed, was seemingly recognised by Laura Parker – a witness injured in the explosion and currently without memory – who called attention to the thick vest underneath its heraldic surcoat. On hearing the word vest, a man identified as Theodore Newbold had leapt from his seat and gathered the dog in his arms. He'd been moving towards the exit when the dog exploded. There then followed more explosions when eighteen of the Moller's twenty-one organ pipes rocketed into the air. Although three people had been killed and the church badly damaged, the potential for greater destruction was forestalled by the crude nature of the bombs and the sparse number of nails in their construction.

A breakthrough in the investigation came on the Wednesday morning when a witness came forward and identified Wayne – though not by name – as the man seen leaving the church and crossing Wisconsin shortly before the explosions. He described him as a neighbourhood character, a challenged man who delivered free sheets and usually pulled a cart. 'I didn't get my copy of the *Current* last week and I wanted to ask him why. Usually he likes to chat but that day he rushed straight past me.'

The FBI visited the halfway house and learned that Wayne was house-sitting a dog on Dent St. What kind of dog? A Basset Hound, the director thought. (A Basset Hound had been mentioned by one eyewitness, but others had suggested the dog was more likely a Dachshund, a Beagle, a Springer Spaniel or Bloodhound.) The agents drove to the house on Dent St with no real expectations. They parked on the street opposite and were about to knock on the door when there was an explosion. Immediately their spirits lifted.

A bomb disposal unit arrived within minutes, but a good hour passed before the door was broken down. They entered the premises to find dust and smoke rising from the stairs leading to the basement and through a six-foot hole in the lounge floor, and the body of a man lying on the kitchen floor with his head resting on a cushion. All other rooms on the first and second floors were empty, but under a pile of rubble in the basement they found another man, unconscious but still breathing. In the same cellar they found quantities of black powder, fertiliser, an opened bag of nails and ten sticks of dynamite.

In the days that followed, the FBI put the pieces of another picture together. Wayne Trout, a local paperboy, had used the basement of the house on Dent St to assemble a dog's suicide vest and the bombs placed in the organ pipes of the Church of Latter-Day Lutherans. He'd then, for an unknown reason, tried to blow a hole in the floor of the cellar and unintentionally brought down the ceiling. The house belonged to Laurence MacCabe and the body of the man lying on the floor was that of his neighbour Dr Eustace Young, who had either been lured to the house or gone there of his own accord.

Wayne regained consciousness in the hospital but died soon afterwards. He had breath enough only to answer three of the FBI's questions. Why did you blow up the Church of Latter-Day Lutherans, Wayne? Why did you kill Dr Eustace Young, Wayne? To both questions Wayne had answered that Kevin had told him to do it. And who is Kevin, Wayne? Kevin's my best friend, sir, Wayne had replied before inconveniently dying.

The more complete picture would have been this. The floor of Larry's basement wasn't a simple pick and shovel job as Kevin had thought. It was eight inches thick and made of reinforced concrete, and only a man with a pneumatic drill would have been able to break through it. A pickaxe and sledgehammer barely scratched its surface and only served to disturb Dr Young's sleep. The next morning he'd banged on the door and, unaware that Larry had gone to Israel, was surprised to be greeted by a strange-looking man with a sledgehammer in his hand and a torch strapped to his head. He'd brushed past him and started shouting for Larry.

'MacCabe, you damn fool, where the hell are you? How's a man supposed to sleep at night with you making all this goddamn noise? I've a good mind to call the police!'

'What's the man want?' Kevin called.

'He wants to call the police, Kevin. He says we're making too much noise.'

'Then tap him on the head and tell him to mind his own business!' Kevin said.

A tap on the head with a sledgehammer would have been difficult for any person to gauge, never mind one suffering from dyspraxia, and Wayne's gentle tap simply caved in Dr Young's skull. Within seconds the retired plastic surgeon was singing duets with Frank Sinatra.

'Aw shoot!' Wayne exclaimed. 'I've gone an' done it this time, Kevin. I think I've killed him.'

'Serves the man right,' Kevin said. 'He's got no business sticking his nose into matters that don't concern him. You might want to think about speeding things up, though. People might come looking for him.'

After two more days of fruitless hammering Wayne decided to use the dynamite…

As it was his house where the bombs had been assembled Larry was a person of interest from the start, and the more the FBI learned about him the more convinced they became that he was the Kevin behind the St Francis Day Massacre. They found their first clue in the hallway restroom of Dr Young's house. On its wall was a framed letter from Larry: *Dear Dr Young: One day, I hope someone puts you down. Yours sincerely, Larry K MacCabe (Professor).* It was the note he'd pushed through Dr Young's letter box on the day Loop had been euthanised.

It wasn't so much the threat to Dr Young as Larry's middle initial that caught their attention – K. It was an initial that turned up on Larry's bank statements, on invoices, on correspondence of an official nature and on a restraining order preventing him from delivering any further shopping trolleys to Madeleine Albright. And then they found his birth certificate and the mystery was solved. The K stood for Kevin. Larry's middle name was Kevin! And despite Larry's later protestations that it was a name he neither used nor was called by, and that the Kevin Wayne had referred to was, in all probability, his childhood friend killed in Iraq and that Laura Parker could confirm this, his words fell on deaf ears – especially as Laura now had no idea who Kevin was. She also had no memory of ever having met Larry, and this proved a problem for his defence.

Laura had emerged from the church with a nail in her head, and it had taken the doctors a full day to recognise this. Apart from a small cut on the forehead treated in the emergency room, it appeared that she'd survived the explosions unscathed. The next day, however, she'd started to feel nauseous and her speech became slurred, and when she returned to the hospital for a scan it emerged that she had a 3 1/4 inch nail lodged in her brain.

'You're joking!' Laura said. 'I don't even remember being hit by a nail.'

'I never joke about 3 1/4 inch nails stuck in a person's brain,' the neurosurgeon replied. He was a man without humour and tactless. Life and death were his next-door neighbours and he'd yet to decide which of them he preferred. He then went on to explain that she wouldn't have felt the nail because there were no pain-sensitive nerves in the brain.

The surgery lasted for two hours and the neurosurgeon replaced a part of her skull with a titanium mesh. 'You were lucky, Ms Parker,' he later told her. 'The nail came within millimetres of destroying your motor function. You're going to make a full recovery.'

'A recovery from what?' Laura asked.

'From the extraction of the nail in your skull.'

'What nail?'

'Get some rest, Ms Parker.'

He left the room and walked down the corridor muttering: 'Shitshitshitshitshit!'

While Laura's motor functions had been spared, the surgery had inadvertently wiped the events of the previous year from her memory. She was experiencing what was called retrograde amnesia. Her memory would return, the neurosurgeon told her, but without timetable. It might take six months or it might take a year.

'Where's Alice?' Laura thought to ask on one of his visits. 'I'd have thought she'd have come by to see me.'

'Alice is in Junction City,' the neurosurgeon replied.

'At her parents' house?'

'Only if she was cremated.'

Alice had been one of the Massacre's three fatalities. Her

claims to being a marked person had been borne out that Sunday and her usual close encounters with death this time intimate. The cat with nine lives was now without life, buried in a cemetery close to the centre of the United States.

'Try not to think about it,' the neurosurgeon advised Laura.

'But, but what about Repo?' Laura asked between sobs. 'Who's looking after Repo?'

'I wouldn't worry too much about Repo,' the neurosurgeon said. 'He's dead, too.'

Laura wailed and the neurosurgeon told her not to touch the titanium mesh in her head.

In telling Laura that Repo was dead, the neurosurgeon had been wrong. Repo was in fact in better health than he'd been for some time, living with Mike and now free from canine dementia. It was difficult to determine if it had been the vet's pills that had won the day for Repo or the explosions that had shaken him back to his senses, but for Laura – when she regained her memory – it would always be the intervention of St Francis of Assisi, the kindliest saint of all.

While rummaging through the papers in Larry's house the FBI had also found a file of documents pertaining to the murder of Lydia Flores. It had never been one of their cases but it now suited them. Who but the person who shot Lydia Flores would keep a file on the crime? Larry's explanation that he'd gathered the information solely for the benefit of his wife who was a neighbour of hers in the Willow Columbarium again cut no ice, especially when Larry could provide no alibi for his movements on the day of her murder. It also appeared that he had motive for killing her as her husband, Herb Flores, was the biggest local importer of the brand of vodka favoured by

Helen that had apparently hastened her death. It was an eye for an eye, a tooth for a tooth, a wife for a wife.

The FBI had come across a treasure trove of the empty vodka bottles while searching Larry's backyard for the remains of Rutherford and Grover, the MacCabes' twin sons who had mysteriously disappeared shortly after they'd graduated from college: neither had filed a tax return or taken out a credit card, married, crossed the border or registered to vote. It appeared the two men no longer existed, and Larry's matter-of-fact musings that he too had often wondered where they'd got to, struck them as cold.

They started to think that Larry might be a psychopath, a view encouraged by the testimony of a young girl who worked at Barnes & Noble and with enough metal in her face to set off the shop's security alarms whenever she entered or exited the store. She volunteered that Larry had once come into the shop and asked for a book on Washington psychopaths. 'I remember him because he was real strange and creepy-looking; the kinda guy who leaves you feeling like you've pissed your pants.' Larry, of course, had refuted this and told the FBI that the girl was mistaken. What he'd asked for was a book on Washington *cycle paths* because his friend Laura – who still had no idea that she was his friend – had once shown interest in the subject.

Further background checks cemented the FBI's belief that Larry was the man they were looking for. They started by interviewing his neighbours, most of whom either claimed not to have known him or known him only well enough to avoid. Only Mr Cotton, the neighbour Larry had once tried to befriend, was more forthcoming. He told the FBI that Larry had once made light of his wife's death and likened her to a pigeon, and that he'd seen him and a younger man unloading a large number of cardboard boxes from his Volvo shortly before the church exploded. He was no expert on explosives he said, but if he had to put money on it he'd wager that they came in cardboard boxes. Larry never tried to hide the fact that he and Wayne had returned from West Virginia that afternoon, but insisted that the cardboard boxes had contained Wayne's jam making equipment. When the FBI visited Zion Episcopal Church they found not only the jam making equipment Larry had supposedly brought to Georgetown (one large pan and thirty jam jars), but also traces of black powder.

Next they interviewed the faculty and staff of the university's History Department. They learned from them that Larry was a loner, a man without friends and again a person others chose to avoid. Scott Clayton, the man now teaching The Emergence of Modern America, described Larry as a nutcase and recalled the day he'd visited his office unannounced and tried to make him change his syllabus. 'It was unpleasant,' he said. 'There was malevolence to the man and he made veiled threats. I wish now that I'd punched the sonofabitch.' Clive's testimony was even more damning. He described how Larry would interfere with his janitorial duties and tell him he was using the wrong cleaning products and how his mop technique was faulty. 'He walked around as if he owned the place,' Clive said, 'and there were times when I'd lock myself in the closet and be afraid to come out.' Bill Parish, the Head of Department, who probably knew Larry better than most, told them he was an acquired taste and that, for Larry, was about as good as it got.

When Osmo McNulty got wind of Professor Parish's statement he asked him to be a character witness for Larry, and when he refused, sent him a subpoena. (Larry had been hoping that Clive would also be a character witness and was surprised when McNulty told him that Clive had already signed up for the prosecution.)

It was unusual for a character witness to be deemed hostile and McNulty trod carefully.

'You're looking very dapper, Professor Parish,' he smiled.

Professor Parish nodded his thanks.

'Tell me, Professor Parish: is your appearance today voluntary?'

Professor Parish said that it wasn't.

'So, what you're telling the court, Professor Parish, is that someone else told you to wear that suit?'

Professor Parish's brow furrowed. He said that he failed to understand what his clothes had to do with anything and wondered if Mr McNulty had misunderstood his answer. McNulty reminded the judge that Professor Parish was a hostile witness and requested that he direct him to answer the question. The judge, who also didn't understand what Professor Parish's clothes had to do with anything – but interested in McNulty's line of questioning – told Professor Parish to answer the question.

'No one told me to wear this suit, Mr McNulty. I chose to wear it myself.'

'And is this your best suit?'

'One of them, yes,' Professor Parish replied.

McNulty then turned to the jury and asked his next question while facing them. 'So you decided to wear one of your best suits today when you were called as a character witness for Professor MacCabe?'

Parish made no answer and McNulty reminded him that

the question required a yes or no answer. Parish shrugged and said yes. McNulty then turned to the jury and repeated that Professor Bob Parish, Head of the History Department at Georgetown University, had decided of his own free will to wear one of his best suits to court that day to give evidence on behalf of his ex-colleague Professor MacCabe. It was probably then he should have sat down and excused the witness, but he persisted.

'When you were questioned by the FBI, Professor Parish, you told them that Professor MacCabe was an acquired taste and a person it took time to know. Is this correct?'

Professor Parish said that he had indeed said this.

'And after you spent time getting to know Professor MacCabe and acquired his taste so to speak, what was your opinion of him?'

Professor Parish shuffled in his seat for a moment and then answered. 'I didn't like him,' he said.

McNulty tut-tutted, as if disappointed with Parish as a human being and excused him from the stand. He then turned to the jury and reminded them that Professor Parish had worn one of his best suits to court that morning...

For a man described as a loner and a person best avoided, it came as a surprise to the FBI when they learned that Larry met with a group of people in Volta Park on Saturday mornings. Although the testimony of his supposed friends was less damning than that of his neighbours and former work colleagues, it was also equivocal, and that two of these friends were now dead was another reason for the FBI to be suspicious. Mike Ergle, the substitute organist at the church and local waterfall tuner, claimed to have liked Larry on first meeting but been troubled by some of the things he'd later said. 'I mean for one, the cat didn't see anything wrong in killing Pekingese dogs and said he was sympathetic to the communists in China for wanting to do this. His comment was cold, man, as if it was okay to detach yourself from murder.' And then he recalled Larry's parting words the Saturday before he supposedly left for Israel. 'We'd been rapping about the animal service at the church and the dude said he was sorry he was missing it. But then he said something else, something that didn't register at the time. He said he had a feeling it was going to be *a blast*. Larry was no hipster, man, and he didn't carry words like that in his bag. It was out of character for him to speak like that and I'm wondering now if he'd meant it literally.'

Delores Bobo spoke both for herself and Alice when she talked to the FBI. 'Alice always thought there was something odd about him,' she said, 'and she could never understand why Laura had brought him into our group. She felt he was trying to put her down and turn Laura against her. I thought she was over-reacting at the time, but after the night of the Wabanaki Exhibition I realised she'd had him pinned all along. I'll never forget what he said about the Indians that night or the callous way he said it. He got up and made a speech and told everyone that there was nothing wrong with weak people being destroyed, that it was inevitable and we shouldn't waste tears on Native Americans who'd had it coming to them anyway. I thought then there was a cruel side to him. In my heart of hearts I don't believe that Larry has anything to do with the bombs, but if he did, it wouldn't surprise me. And if that proves to be the case then I'll never forgive him. Never! How could I when I'd know it was him who killed Button, even though it was me that fell on her?'

Delores told the FBI that Laura had met Larry at the retirement home, and as Laura could neither confirm nor deny this, they decided to interview the staff. Unaware that Larry was the supplier of the DVDs that brought contentment to the centre, they remembered him only as the man who'd brought unease whenever he'd visited. 'The residents complained about him,' a senior member of the administrative team told them, 'and one of them thought he was an emissary of the Devil. We had to ban him from the premises.'

Just as Alice's voice was silent after the Feast Day of St Francis, so too was Tank's. By taking it upon himself to remove Moses from the church and risking his life to save others, Tank Newbold had died a hero. His was an act of bravery, of selflessness and duty borne of military service, wrote *The Washington News* – and all of this was probably true. It was, however, primarily an act of infatuation that caused his death. When Laura had mentioned the vest, and Tank seen Moses approaching Pastor Millsap – the as yet unrequited love of his life – he was motivated not by a desire to save a congregation he barely knew, but by the vision of him and Donna lying in bed together.

Tank's death was yet another blow to Larry's defence. Had he been alive he could have corroborated Larry's choice of the King David Hotel and confirmed his departure to Israel, or at least as far as Rosslyn Metro Station. And he would have stilled the voice of his mother who, in his absence, continued to claim that Larry and Wayne had run over her cat on purpose.

Mrs Newbold had naturally been upset by the news of her son's death, but not just because he was dead. Tank's death meant that she'd relocated to Washington for nothing and would now have to think about moving to either Baton Rouge or Chicago. Bereavement was one thing, being inconvenienced another, and by the time the FBI called at her house she was in no mood for sweet talk. That the Bureau had Larry MacCabe in their sights suited her fine.

'I thought he was a gardener the first time I met him,' she said. 'He was at my son's house cleaning the gutters and Theodore said that he'd thrown a dead squirrel at him. Mr MacCabe tried to laugh it off but I could tell that Theodore hadn't found it funny, and he made a point of telling Mr MacCabe that he was an acquaintance and not the friend he was claiming to be.

'He was the last person I expected Theodore to send to my house. And he didn't come by himself, either. He came with Mr Trout, a young man my son had already warned me about. They looked like a couple of runaways from a homeless shelter. I kept my distance when they were rescuing Maybelline, but once she was safe – and because I'm a Christian lady – I invited them into my house for a cup of coffee. Mr Trout was only wearing one sock and Mr MacCabe had a large hole in one of his. When I noticed this I started to get nervous. It was like having Frank and Jesse James sitting in my living room, and I was more than relieved when they got up to leave. And then...' Mrs Newbold's throat caught and she waited for her composure to return. 'And then they ran over Maybelline! And they did it on purpose and laughed about it. I'll never forget the looks on their faces, especially that Trout boy's!'

While one team of agents delved into Larry's background, another put Wayne's into the juicer. Charles Town: *educational psychologist* and *Social Services*. Washington: *psychiatrist* and *Social Services*. It appeared that the Trout boy – as Mrs Newbold referred to him – had struggled in life, but in death hit the Big Time. Had this been his intent on the Day of St Francis? His psychiatrist said no, and that if the FBI thought this, they should make an appointment to see him on a weekly basis.

'There's no question in my mind that Wayne was acting for another,' Dr Respess told them. 'Wayne was *happy* being a Nobody. He neither sought nor wanted the Big Time. He was a man of faith and believed that God wished him to live in the shadows.'

'If he was a man of faith, as you say he was,' the agent leading the interview asked, 'why do you think he blew up a church?'

'I have no idea,' Dr Respess replied.

'You mentioned earlier that Wayne heard voices, and that this was the reason he came to see you. Is it possible that one of these voices might have urged him to blow up the church?'

'I doubt it,' Dr Respess said. 'The voices Wayne heard were benign and had started to quieten. Six months from now it's possible he would have been free of them.'

'Did he ever mention anyone by the name of Kevin?'

'In the early years, yes. Kevin was a friend of his, the one who suggested they write the message on the bridge. He was killed in Iraq from what I understand.'

'And he's never mentioned him since?'

'No.'

'Did he ever mention another person to you?'

'He mentioned several, but the one he talked about most was an elderly man he'd met in the park. A retired professor, I think.'

'And what did he say about this person?'

'He liked him. He said the man wanted to take him under his wing and mould him.'

'Mould him how?'

'I'm not sure. He did say once that the man was trying to make him do things he didn't want to do, but he wasn't forthcoming on this point.' (Larry's explanation that he'd only been trying to improve Wayne's grammar again failed to make an impression on the FBI.)

'You said you were certain in your own mind that Wayne would have been acting for another. Why do you think this?'

'Because Wayne wasn't a thinker. He was born to be a sidekick, someone else's lieutenant. He was following his friend Kevin's instructions when he painted the words on the bridge, and he'll have been following another person's instructions when he planted the bombs. But this person would have been a friend, someone he trusted.'

And so, before the FBI had even met Larry, they'd come to a decision. Professor Laurence K MacCabe was a psychopath, a loner who had difficulty forming relationships and a man indifferent to the suffering of animals (Pekingese dogs, squirrels and cats) and humans (Native Americans and Mr Cotton's wife). He was a person others chose to avoid and described variously as cold and detached, callous, cruel, malevolent and threatening and as either a member of the Jesse James Gang or an emissary of the Devil. Professor Laurence K MacCabe (aka Kevin) was the mastermind behind the bombing of the Church of Latter-Day Lutherans and responsible for the deaths of Joyce Flake (the owner of the tortoise), Alice Manzoni, Theodore Newbold, Dr Eustace Young and Wayne Trout, his unwitting accomplice. He was also the prime suspect in the death of Lydia Flores and the disappearance of Rutherford and Grover MacCabe.

All that stood between them and a conviction was if Professor MacCabe had an alibi and, naturally enough, Larry didn't – or at least not one he could substantiate.

Larry returned to Washington in the company of two diplomatic attachés, an agent of Mossad and a dentist. He was dressed in the garb of a Hassidic rabbi and had a long grey beard and answered to the name of Lochesh Penzag. The five of them had the first-class to themselves but one was required to sit with Larry. They drew lots and the Mossad agent's straw was the shortest. He sat down in the seat next to Larry and remained there for the next fifteen hours.

'*Where there is no guidance, a nation falls, but in an abundance of counsellors there is safety,*' Larry said to the agent once his belt was clipped. 'That's your motto,' he smiled. 'I don't know if you know this, but the original motto of Mossad was something else, something along the lines of...'

An hour before the plane landed, and to the relief of the agent, the dentist injected Larry's gums with novocaine. Although Larry had promised to remain silent while passing through immigration, the Israelis doubted his aptitude for wordlessness and were unprepared to take chances. When in his days of detention had he ever kept his mouth shut? Consequently it was an attaché who spoke for him when they entered the diplomatic channel, explaining to the official on duty that Rabbi Penzag spoke no English, was in Washington to perform a necessary ritual at the embassy and would be returning to Israel in two days. The official stamped their passports and wished them a pleasant stay.

(Two days later Rabbi Penzag did return to Israel – this time as the guise for an Israeli citizen suspected of industrial espionage.)

Once in the safety of the El Al terminal Larry's beard was carefully removed and he was told to take a shower. The clothes in his suitcase were washed in American water and detergent, and all traces of Israeli soil removed from his shoes. 'If I didn't know better I'd think we were in New Zealand,' Larry joked, who was now sitting in an armchair and wearing a bathrobe. 'I don't know if you know this about New Zealand but it has very strict biosecurity procedures...'

No one could understand a word Larry was saying and the agent from Mossad asked how long it would be before the novocaine wore off and they could take him to the city. Considering the dosage he'd pumped into Larry's gums the dentist estimated about another three hours. The agent looked at his watch and then punched the wall with his fist.

Larry was dropped at Dupont Circle and took a taxi to Georgetown. Normally he would have taken the bus but he was tired and wanted to get home. He was looking forward to seeing Moses again and hoped that his extended absence hadn't caused Wayne too many problems. He told the driver to drop him at Dumbarton Oaks, and from there he walked the short distance to Dent St. It was good to be home he thought, and he breathed the air of Georgetown deep into his lungs. It was less good to be home when he saw the yellow crime scene tape criss-crossing his boarded front door, and worse still when two men stepped out of a car and told him he was under arrest.

The news dumbfounded Larry: Moses dead! Wayne dead! Tank dead! Alice dead! Dr Young dead! A woman he'd never heard of dead! The Church of Latter-Day Lutherans destroyed and his house on Dent St badly damaged! His head filled with thick warm smoke and the insides of his body crumbled. He didn't speak, was unable to speak, and his stillness was mistaken for indifference. When Helen had died his old world had been destroyed and now his new world was destroyed: Moses, Volta Park, and his friendships with Wayne, Tank and Alice. It was too difficult to take in and so he just sat there blinking and said nothing. And then a man who identified himself as an agent from the FBI asked him why he'd killed his friends and blown up the church and he'd started to laugh and found he couldn't stop.

The agent nodded at the mirror on the wall and the people behind the mirror nodded back. Done Deal!

Larry spent the following three weeks being shuttled between the City Jail and the FBI's field offices on 4th St, but once the Grand Jury gave the go-ahead for charges to be brought against him he was sent to a correctional facility in Alexandria to await trial. The evidence against him was circumstantial and hearsay, but the Assistant US Attorney in charge of the prosecution was confident of a conviction, especially as Larry could give no satisfactory explanation as to his movements immediately before, during and after the bombing of the church. 'But I keep telling you,' Larry repeated over and again, 'I was in Israel!'

The problem for Larry was that the government of Israel said that he wasn't, and claimed to know this for a fact because they ran the country. There was no record of him ever entering or leaving the country in October, and certainly no American citizen had been placed under arrest and held in Jaffa that month. What kind of country did America think

Israel was? The next thing they'd be accusing them of was having nuclear weapons!

The FBI was apologetic and asked for forbearance while they investigated a claim they too found ridiculous. They didn't have any axes to grind with the Israeli government they said, but for the sake of justice – which was still a big deal in their country – would it be all right if they approached the Hebrew University of Jerusalem, El Al and the King David Hotel to tie up a few loose ends? Go ahead. Knock yourselves out, the Israeli government told them.

The King David Hotel, although privately owned, was in many ways a government hotel and born to please. No one by the name of Laurence MacCabe had stayed at the hotel in October or eaten in its Garden Restaurant or booked a trip to Masada at the concierge desk they told the FBI.

Similarly El Al, the nation's flag carrier, was also happy to confirm that Larry had never travelled with them, and apologised for the erroneous information passed to the Transportation Security Administration that indicated he had. It was forwarded by an inexperienced member of staff and the mistake subsequently corrected. Laurence MacCabe *had* been booked to fly to Israel on the day he stated but in the event had been a no-show. And certainly no Laurence MacCabe had ever flown back to the United States with El Al.

The Hebrew University of Jerusalem verified that Larry hadn't attended the Symposium on Desert Reclamation, and told the FBI that Professor MacCabe had phoned his apologies the previous week from what proved to be a payphone in downtown Washington.

'Check his clothes if you don't believe us,' an attaché at the embassy said. 'If you find any traces of Israeli washing powder, water or soil on them, I'll eat my kippah!'

The Israeli ducks were in a row and Larry's alibi blown out of the water.

If capital punishment hadn't been forbidden by law in the District of Columbia, Larry would have been as good as dead, and the only man standing between him and a lengthy prison sentence was a personal injury lawyer called Osmo McNulty.

'That course you taught on The Emergence of Modern America really changed my life, Professor MacCabe,' Osmo told him.

Larry was flattered by the comment and wanted to know why.

'It made me realise I was studying the wrong subject,' Osmo said. 'I changed fields at the end of that semester and I've never looked back. If it wasn't for you I'd have never been an attorney.'

Osmo had bumped into Larry at the City Jail while visiting a client suspected of staging traffic accidents. He'd offered his services pro bono in the hope that such a high-profile case would boost his career. If Wayne Trout hadn't been interested in the Big Time, Osmo McNulty was. At the time Larry had thanked him for his thoughtfulness but told him he didn't need a lawyer and that the misunderstanding that had brought him to jail would soon be cleared up. When it became clear that it wouldn't, Larry asked Osmo to represent him. Who better than an alumnus of Georgetown University to speak on his behalf?

Before Osmo got to work on Larry's defence he asked him a couple of questions. Had he ever been involved in a traffic accident in the last three years that hadn't been his fault, and had he ever suffered from whiplash? Larry said that he hadn't.

Osmo asked if he was sure about this and Larry said that he was. Osmo then asked Larry if he knew of anyone who had, and when Larry said that he didn't, Osmo again asked him if he was sure.

Osmo told Larry that the prosecution's case was circumstantially damning and he was glad he wasn't sitting in his place and wearing his shoes. They were, however, short on motive. Apart from their assertion that Larry, if not a psychopath, was a thoroughly disagreeable person who took his own unhappiness out on the world by making the lives of others as miserable as possible, it appeared they had little. The problem for Larry was that no one was stepping forward to refute this picture, and his best witnesses were either dead or suffering from amnesia. It was looking to Osmo that he'd have to rely heavily on his own dimples if he was going to win over the jury. 'Everyone likes a man with dimples,' he told Larry.

'I could understand them bringing these charges against you if you were black, Larry, (they were on first name terms by now), because that's how the system works. But you're not black, you're white, and so they're trying to portray you as a white man with a black heart. And I doubt they'd have brought these charges if so many animals hadn't been slaughtered at the church. People are more sensitive to pets being killed than they are to people being murdered. They get desensitised to human suffering because it happens all the time, especially in Washington. With pets it's different. Pets are innocents, no bad bones in their bodies and no bad thoughts in their heads. You wouldn't believe the number of stuffed animals left outside the church after the bombing or how few were the bouquets for the three dead people. I think this is an angle we could explore.'

J. PAUL HENDERSON

In thinking this, Osmo might have had a point. Four days into the trial a note was passed to the judge and proceedings interrupted. 'I've just been handed the good news that Steady Eddie is alive and well,' the judge smiled. The courtroom had then burst into applause. (Steady Eddie was the tortoise taken to the church by Joyce Flake. Miraculously, considering how close he'd been to the bombs, the tortoise had survived the explosions and been spotted walking down Wisconsin by a motorist.)

It was difficult for Osmo to make headway against the prosecution's case and his questioning of witnesses – intended to damage their credibility – was often oblique, seemingly without purpose and continually being interrupted by objections and sustentions. He asked Clive if he held a grudge against Professor MacCabe because his client knew more about mops and cleaning products than he did, even though it was his job to know more about mops and cleaning products than Professor MacCabe. He wondered aloud if Professor Clayton's purpose in shaving his head was to make it look like a football, and suggested to Mr Cotton that his wife had been pigeon-toed and that only his client had noticed this and that Mr Cotton now felt badly that he hadn't and was taking his guilt out on Professor MacCabe. When Mike came to the stand wearing a hemp jacket with the sleeves cut off at the shoulder, Osmo asked him if he'd smoked the sleeves and, if so, how often did he smoke his clothes? After Mrs Newbold had given evidence he implied that she appeared more upset by the death of her cat than she did her son, and when it became clear in his cross-examination of Delores that she was unhappy with her weight, he asked her why she hadn't done something about it and blown up a church for instance.

From what he'd gathered from the prosecution this was what unhappy people did.

When Larry took the stand it became apparent that Osmo McNulty wasn't the best of attorneys to defend him and that he was his own worst enemy. It would have gone better if they'd spent more time rehearsing and twenty-four people hadn't walked into Osmo's office claiming to have suffered whiplash after the bus they'd been travelling in had been rear-ended by a Chevrolet Sonic. The only advice he'd been able to give Larry before he took the stand was to keep his answers short.

The idea was for Larry to appear to the jury as an average Joe and not the sinister person the prosecution depicted. Osmo instructed him to face the jury when he answered the questions and look them in the eyes. Larry did, but his incessant blinking made them uncomfortable, and after several of the jurors started blinking, the foreman asked the judge to direct Larry not to look at them.

'How did you meet Wayne, Professor MacCabe?' Osmo asked.

'I was running away from a wasp and he fell out of a tree,' Larry answered.

When Osmo asked him to elaborate Larry turned on the taps, and for the rest of his evidence forgot they were running. 'Well for breakfast, I usually alternate between cereal and toast but that morning I'd decided to eat pancakes...'

Larry's answers became ever longer, more convoluted and overly detailed, and the only things that stuck in the jury's mind were that he occasionally ate sand, often discussed things with his deceased wife and had been bitten by seven different dogs. Twenty minutes into Larry describing his trip to Israel, and at the point where he'd just emerged from the Church of the Holy Sepulchre, Osmo noticed that the jury was yawning and decided to cut Larry's testimony short.

'So what you're telling the jury, Professor MacCabe, is that you were in Israel until the time you left?'

'Yes,' Larry replied.

'The defence rests, your Honour,' Osmo said.

It took the jury less than a day to decide Larry's guilt, but only in relation to the church bombings and Dr Young's death. The judge directed them to find all other charges against him not proven: in the case of Lydia Flores no gun had been found, and in the case of his sons, no bodies.

Even before the jury sat down to consider the evidence, a majority of them had already decided Larry was guilty. For a start he *looked* guilty – that weird forehead and his incessant blinking – and who but a guilty man would talk so endlessly? And did he really expect them to take his word against the word of two governments and have them believe he'd been duped by a simpleton? Did he take them for simpletons, too? And as the jurors deliberated over plates of sandwiches and a choice of either coffee or soft drinks, the pieces of jigsaw fell into place and his guilt became clear to all.

Professor MacCabe, they determined, had accepted an invitation to speak at the Hebrew University of Jerusalem only as a cloak to blow up the Church of Latter-Day Lutherans. He'd gone out of his way to tell people he was going to Israel and even bought an airline ticket, but in the event had remained in Washington and only left his house after Dr Young had been killed. Where he'd gone to after that was unknown, but one thing was clear: he hadn't gone to Israel.

The answer as to why he'd chosen to blow up the church

was also clear: Professor MacCabe was a no-good! He was a cold man, embittered and without feeling, and out of deep dissatisfaction for his own life had manipulated another hapless man into planting bombs that would kill both humans and animals. He might have held no specific grievance against those killed in the church – or even the Church of Latter-Day Lutherans itself for that matter – but he'd used the gathering, and the friendship of a weak-minded flathead, to wreak 'representative' havoc on a society that had shunned him and the dogs that had bitten him.

Case closed! Lock the fucker up!

Osmo and Larry stood as the judge pronounced sentence.

'Don Lokey's agreed to take the case,' Laura said. 'He's going to appeal the decision.'

It wasn't quite the news Larry had been hoping for.

Laura's memory had returned nine months after the operation borrowed it. Immediately she'd known that Larry was no murderer and that only an outbreak of war in the Middle East would have stopped him from going to Israel to deliver a paper on the Desert Land Act. And she'd also known who Kevin was! And in the intervening period it had also become evident that Larry had played no part in either the murder of Lydia Flores or the disappearance of his sons. She'd gone directly to the US Attorney's Office and told them there'd been a terrible miscarriage of justice and that Larry MacCabe was an innocent man.

Justice and innocence in the US Attorney's Office, however, were abstracts and without currency. The vogue was for conviction rates and never admitting a mistake, moving on to the next case and climbing the ladder. The St Francis Day

Massacre had made the headlines, bolstered the reputation of the department, and on the back of Larry's conviction the prosecuting Assistant US Attorney was now running for political office. It didn't matter that Herb Flores was currently under indictment for arranging the death of his wife or that Grover MacCabe had turned up in an Alaskan hospital with an arm missing, because Larry had never been found guilty of those crimes. Maybe the FBI had been overly hasty in connecting him to Lydia's shooting and the disappearance of his sons, but on the matter of the St Francis Day Massacre, they held firm. The evidence pointed to Professor MacCabe, and they would need more than the word of a middle-aged woman recovering from a brain injury to convince them otherwise. Unless Laura could bring them actual proof that Larry was innocent – and more than the name of a dead person – the case would remain closed.

It was then she'd gone to Don Lokey, an attorney with a high profile in the city and whose mother was a resident at the care home.

'Don can't believe you were convicted on such circumstantial evidence,' Laura said, 'and the mere fact that Osmo McNulty was defending you is grounds for appeal. And I can testify to the fact that Wayne talked to Kevin on a regular basis even if his psychiatrist claims that he didn't. It's clear now that Wayne was a lot more disturbed than either of us thought.'

'It's good of you to think of me, Laura,' Larry said, 'but, well... um... would you mind if you didn't? The truth is I'm happy here. I like being in prison.'

Laura stared at him, wondered for a moment if she'd misheard him and asked him to repeat his words. Larry did and she felt like slapping him. She told him to pull himself together and stop being a bufflehead and that she had no intention of abandoning him to a life in prison. Like it or not, he would just have to get used to the idea of being a free man again. It was going to happen!

'Well, if that's what you want,' Larry said with an air of resignation. 'But there's no rush, is there? I mean, you could take your time, couldn't you?'

Laura left for Georgetown and Larry went back to his cell, neither of them smiling and both despairing.

Larry had been sent to a Federal Correctional Institution in Virginia, 25 miles south-east of Richmond. Apart from Laura the only regular visitor he had was Osmo, who kept dropping by to see if he'd had an accident that wasn't his fault. He'd settled in well at the prison, and his reputation as the mastermind behind the St Francis Day Massacre had held him in good stead with the other inmates, who all made a point of addressing him as professor. It was the first time he'd enjoyed such status. There were people on tap in the prison every day of the week and every week of the year – 1800 not counting the guards. He'd made friends here, lots of friends, and there was always someone to talk to. He taught literacy classes, wrote and read letters for prisoners who couldn't and helped with their appeals and official paperwork. When in life had people ever needed him more? And he'd also been put in charge of the prison library and allowed to keep a pet mouse called Joshua (named after Moses' lieutenant) in his cell. The only thing he missed about not being on the outside was visiting Helen at Willow Columbarium.

He'd tried explaining this to Laura, but Laura had told him he'd been watching too many old prison movies and it was time he got a grip on himself. But what did he have to return to? His house was uninhabitable, he didn't have a dog and, apart from Laura, whose time was committed to the care home, no friends. Wayne and Tank were both dead and it had been difficult during the trial to learn how Alice had thought of him and to hear the doubts of Mike and Delores. It would be difficult going back to Volta Park and taking up where they'd left off. No, he was better off staying where he was. As long as he was in prison he'd never be lonely again.

That night Larry lay in his bunk thinking, something he always did before going to sleep. Usually he would remember his years at the university and his days in Volta Park, the Desert Land Act and Moses. He would think of his wife and his three-armed twins, of Laura and Tank and the people he'd met in the park. And he would think of Wayne and every night wonder if he'd failed him in some unknown way. He would never understand the young man's reasons for planting the bombs and sending Moses to his death, but he remembered and missed him as a friend. If only he'd focused more on his grammar...

Tonight he wasn't thinking of the past or dead people, but of life, and how awful his would be if he was ever released from prison. 'Oh dear,' he sighed repeatedly. 'Oh dear.'

'Hey, Larry! Pssst! Larry!'

He leaned over the edge of the bunk. 'Did you say something, Bill?'

Bill was his cellmate, a forty-year-old man serving a twenty-five year sentence for armed robbery. He made no reply and continued to snore.

Larry returned to his thoughts.

'Pssst, Larry! I can help you!'

Larry propped his elbows on the pillow and looked around the room. 'Who is this?' he asked.

'It's Kevin,' the voice whispered, 'Wayne's friend. There's a vent...'

About Us

In addition to No Exit Press, Oldcastle Books has a number
of other imprints, including Kamera Books, Creative Essentials,
Pulp! The Classics, Pocket Essentials and High Stakes Publishing
> oldcastlebooks.co.uk

For more information about Crime Books > crimetime.co.uk

Check out the kamera film salon for independent, arthouse and
world cinema > kamera.co.uk

For more information, media enquiries and review copies please
contact marketing@oldcastlebooks.com